Season
of
Crimson
Blossoms

D0057478

A CIP catalogue record for this book is available from the British Library.

ISBN 978-1-911115-00-7
eISBN 978-1-911115-01-4

Book design by Allan Castillo Rivas.
Printed and bound in Great Britain by Bell & Bain Ltd, Glasgow.
Distributed in the UK by Central Books Ltd.

Stay up to date with the latest books, special offers and exclusive content with our monthly newsletter.
Sign up on our website:
www.cassavarepublic.biz

To download a Hausa glossary to accompany this title, please visit our website:
www.cassavarepublic.biz

Season
of
Crimson
Blossoms

Abubakar Adam
Ibrahim

For Beloved Jos,
tainted eternally by the gore of our innocence
and memories of the innocents slain

PART ONE

The Second Birth of Hajiya Binta Zubairu
(1956 - 2011, and beyond)

1

No matter how far up a stone is thrown,
it will certainly fall back to earth

Hajiya Binta Zubairu was finally born at fifty-five when a dark-lipped rogue with short, spiky hair, like a field of minuscule anthills, scaled her fence and landed, boots and all, in the puddle that was her heart. She had woken up that morning assailed by the pungent smell of roaches and sensed that something inauspicious was about to happen. It was the same feeling she had had that day, long ago, when her father had stormed in to announce that she was going to be married off to a stranger. Or the day that stranger, Zubairu, her husband for many years, had been so brazenly consumed by communal ire when he was set upon by a mob of intoxicated zealots. Or the day her first son, Yaro, who had the docile face and demure disposition of her mother, was shot dead by the police. Or even the day Hureira, her intemperate daughter, had returned, crying that she had been divorced by her good-for-nothing husband.

So Binta woke up and, provoked by the obnoxious smell, engaged in the task of sweeping and scrubbing. She fetched a torch from the nightstand and flashed the light into every corner and crevice. But deep down she knew the hunt, as all others before it, would end in futility.

It must have been the noise of her shifting the wardrobe that drew her niece Fa'iza, who, dressed in her white and purple school uniform, lips coated in grey lipstick, came and leaned on the doorjamb of Binta's bedroom with the distracted air typical of teenagers.

'Hajiya, what are you looking for?'

Binta, now busy rifling through the contents of her bedside drawer, straightened with difficulty. She pressed her hands into the base of her aching back and shrugged. 'Cockroaches. I can smell them.'

Fa'iza made a face. 'You won't find any.'

Binta looked at the girl's face and her eyes widened. 'What kind of school allows girls to wear make-up as if they are going to a disco?'

Fa'iza had turned and started walking away when Binta called her back.

'Come, wipe off that silly lipstick. It makes you look ill. And your uniform is too tight around the hips. You should be ashamed wearing it so tight.'

'Ashamed? But Hajiya, this is the fashion now. You are so old school, *wallahi*, you don't know anything about fashion anymore.' Fa'iza pouted and wiped her lips with a handkerchief.

'You better put on the bigger hijab to cover yourself up or else you aren't leaving this house.'

Fa'iza grumbled and, as if standing in a pool of fire ants, stamped her feet in turns.

'The way you girls go strutting about all over the place these days, the angels up in heaven will have a busy day cursing. Looking at you, who would think you are just fifteen, going about tempting people like that. Fear Allah, you insolent child!'

Fa'iza went off to her room and Binta, determined to ensure compliance, came out to the living room to await her.

Little Ummi was sitting on the couch stuffing herself with bread and tea.

'*Ina kwana*, Hajiya?' She smiled up at Binta.

Binta moved to her and brushed away the crumbs that had collected on the girl's uniform. 'And how is my favourite grandchild this morning?'

'Fine, Hajiya. Do you know what Fa'iza did when she woke up this morning?' Ummi smacked her lips in a way that always made her grandmother think she was too smart for an eight-year-old.

'No, what did she do?'

Ummi sidled up to Binta and whispered into her ear. Binta missed most of it but smiled nonetheless. Ummi sat back down and beamed.

Fa'iza emerged from her room pouting, her slender frame covered in the hijab whose fringes danced about her knees, her books swept into the crook of her arm. She pulled Ummi by the arm, barely leaving the child time to pick up her bag.

'Won't you have breakfast first?' Binta put her hands on her hips and regarded the girls.

'Later.' Fa'iza was already stamping out with Ummi in tow.

Binta shouted her goodbyes. And because the stench of roaches had faded from her mind, she wondered what she had been up to before the interruption.

She went back to her room and sat on the lush blue tasselled prayer rug. And just as she had been doing since she received the news two weeks ago that her childhood friend and namesake Bintalo had keeled over and died of heart failure, she spent time counting her prayer beads and sending off solemn petitions for friends and kin lost. She prayed for a full life and asked God to receive her with open arms when her time came. However, in the midst of this communion with divinity, the meddlesome Shaytan prodded her with reminders about Kandiya's unfinished dress lying on her sewing machine. Binta had promised to complete it later in the day. She also had to go to the madrasa, where women were taught matters of faith.

After a quick shower, Binta rushed down her breakfast. Then she retrieved her reading glasses from the nightstand where she had placed them the night before, atop the English translation of Az Zahabi's *The Major Sins*.

She oiled and cleaned the sewing machine stationed in the alcove where the dining table, if she had had one, would have been. Picking up Kandiya's wax print blotched with nondescript floral designs, Binta pedalled away. The task strained her muscles. And her backache grew worse as she was fixing one of the sleeves.

It was almost time for the madrasa anyway, so Binta put on her hijab, hoisted her shoulder bag, locked up the house and left.

———

Ustaz Nura, the bearded teacher, had called in sick and the women were left to their own devices that day. They agreed to make good use of the time by revising previous lessons, but disagreed on whether to start with Hadith, Tarikh or Fiqh. Binta sat through the deliberations, her books piled before her, watching the women over the rim of her reading glasses. After a lengthy and discordant debate, garnished with thinly coated sarcasm, the women left in groups. Binta found herself tagging along with a number of aged women. They chatted about the symptoms of impending senility, the inanities of their grandchildren and how much better things had been in their youth. Until each one made the turn to her own house.

Binta pushed open her gate. She crossed the austere yard where, after dawn, little finches, itinerant pigeons and other birds hopped, pecking the grains and crumbs she occasionally cast for them. On reaching the front door, she discovered, much to her surprise, that it was ajar.

'Subhanallahi!' It then occurred to Binta that Fa'iza might have returned early from school. So, driven by a mild irritation over her niece's escalating eccentricity, she pushed open the door and went in.

A strong arm clasped her from behind, pressing firmly across her mouth. 'Understand, if you scream, I'll cut you, wallahi.' It was a grating male voice. Even though whispered, it almost made her heart, devastated already by the ravages of age and the many tragedies she had endured in her life, burst. The point of a dagger pressed lightly into her throat. She discerned the pungent smell of marijuana coming off her assailant. And with that offending smell came gusts of memories eddying in little swirls around her mind. She struggled and moaned in fright.

'Money, gold.' His grip around her tightened. When she nodded, his left arm tightened around her chest while his knife, clasped in his right hand, dug into her flesh, drawing a little pool of blood.

He allowed her to catch her breath. And because she could not see her decoder and DVD player in their places on the stand, she assumed they were already in the khaki-coloured duffel bag on the coffee table. Obviously he wanted things he could take away with ease.

'Please, I'm old, *saurayi*.' She knew from his voice and strong arms that he was a young man. 'I only want to make peace with my God before my time. Please, don't kill me.'

'Money, handset, gold.' His voice rattled her ear, her heart.

She made to move but he held her tighter. His arm crushed her breasts. She realised, even in the muted terror of the moment, that this was the closest she had been to any man since her husband's death ten years before.

'*Subhanallahi! Subhanallahi!*' She hoped her muttered appeal to God's purity would cleanse her mind. Beneath her breath, she damned the accursed Shaytan who persistently sowed such impious thoughts in the hearts of men.

'Handset!'

She indicated her bag under the folds of her hijab and he allowed her reach for it.

But, having learnt to be suspicious, her assailant speculated that she might be trying something. Like the woman who had sprayed perfume into his eyes in his early days. So he grabbed Binta's hijab and tried to pull it over her head. She resisted. In the brief and unorthodox tussle that followed, her reading glasses fell from the bag and were crushed underfoot.

'I'll cut you, I swear.'

And she knew he meant it. She allowed him to pull off the hijab and seize her bag, the contents of which he emptied onto the floor. He rummaged through the pockets and found a small roll of money. He picked up her handset from amongst the books in the bag and shoved both, money and device, into his pocket.

He straightened. 'Gold.'

She took the opportunity to look at him for the first time. He was in his mid-twenties, his lips were dark, and his short, kinky hair was like a field of little anthills. He rushed at Binta and held her, positioning himself behind her once again.

Holding her, his dagger at the ready, he guided her to the bedroom. His breath on her neck and the heat from his body made her knees weak. She almost buckled several times. He clasped her firmly so that they tottered like an unwieldy four-legged beast. The friction of her rear against his jeans made his crotch bulge and push hard against her.

In the bedroom, he released her so she could function unencumbered. She leaned over the trunk by the side of her bed to fetch the jewellery, presenting her full backside to him. When she turned, holding a casket of her valuables, he saw that she was not that old. Perhaps a little heavy around the hips, a little heavy at the bosom. Not too mamarish. And when he caught sight of the gold tooth in her gaping mouth, his countenance dimmed further.

She watched him come towards her. '*Haba*! My son, I am old enough to be your mother. Please.'

When he stopped, Binta could not discern the expression on his face.

'You don't know a thing about my mother.'

She was perplexed when he put away his knife under his shirt and held up his hands. She held her breath as he fetched a handkerchief from the pocket of his jeans.

'You are bleeding.' He reached out and dabbed at her neck, at the spot his dagger had dug into. He looked at the cut and dabbed some more. 'It's not deep, you understand?'

Her bosom rose and fell just an inch from his chest. Her breath staggered as he looked into her eyes.

'I will leave now, ok?' He stepped back from her. 'I didn't mean for this to happen. I just . . . just . . .' He turned and walked out of the bedroom.

He took her things and left, having sown in her the seed of awakening that would eventually sprout into a corpse flower, the stench of which would resonate far beyond her imagining.

———

The mystery of the missing appliances and Binta's smashed reading glasses would baffle her daughter Hadiza. Quite unaware of the robbery the previous day, Hadiza had arrived from Kano to pay her mother a visit.

Ummi had jumped on her aunt, who had been trying to set down her bag in the corner of the living room. 'Aunty Hadiza, thieves came to our house yesterday.'

'*Inna lillahi wa inna ilaihi raji'un!*' Hadiza shrugged off the girl and straightened. She turned to her mother who smiled wanly and waved her hands before her face. 'Hajiya, what happened?'

'What happened?' Fa'iza had just emerged from her room. 'What happened was that we went out to school and they came and broke the lock and took away the DVD, the decoder and . . . I don't know, stuff.'

Binta scowled at the girls. 'Is that any way to welcome a traveller, you? These girls!'

And so with measured excitement and subtle evasion, Hadiza had been received into her mother's house.

But later that day Hadiza sat on the edge of Binta's bed flipping through Az Zahabi's *The Major Sins,* astounded by the chance discovery of a well of knowledge in the Sahara. She nodded every now and then and made clucking noises at the back of her throat.

'I had no idea there were so many mortal sins, Mother.'

When she got no response, she looked up from the book.

Hajiya Binta was still seated on her prayer rug beside the bed, where she had said her Maghrib prayers minutes before. Her lemon-yellow hijab covered her entire body, its hem gathered away from the Qur'an lying next to her foot. She had fetched it earlier to recite after the prayers but Hadiza had invited herself in for a chat. And because her head was turned to the flaxen wall, her daughter could not see her face.

Hadiza turned back to the book and continued browsing through, plucking nuggets planted by the long dead sheikh in a field of papyrus. When she satisfied herself with the limitations of her ignorance, which was far greater than she had assumed, she closed the book and sighed. The intricate oriental design on the spine appealed to her and she ran her fingers over it. She shook her head and wondered what it would feel like to write a book someone would read and marvel at centuries later. Carefully, she put it down on the nightstand. In the process she knocked off her mother's reading glasses, but caught them as they fell.

'Mother, how come your glasses are broken?'

Binta shifted beneath the cover of her hijab but said nothing.

'Hajiya!'

'Mhm.'

'I've been talking since I came in and you haven't said a thing.'

'Don't mind me. My thoughts were elsewhere. What were you saying?'

'Your glasses, what happened to them?'

'They broke.'

'Yeah? How come?'

'I ran into a wall.'

Hadiza gaped. 'How could you run into a wall, Hajiya?'

'It was dark.'

'Oh.' Since she arrived with her little suitcase in tow, greeted more warmly by the mid-morning sun than her mother's distracted smiles, Hadiza had been dismayed by Binta's inattentiveness. She felt guilty for not having seen Hajiya Binta for seven months. Since her mother relocated to the fringes of Abuja. Now she wondered if her trip was going to end in disappointment.

At twenty-seven, Hadiza, Binta's youngest child, was already taking care of a husband and three children; boys who would not stop trashing the living room and shredding their exercise books. For her, any disorder was an excuse to rearrange the interior. So she was always moving the furniture around and planting and uprooting hedges and flowers in every available space in her courtyard. Often, her husband, Salisu, who wore spectacles and spoke with effeminate gestures, would return home to discover that the settee or table had been moved. He had tired of complaining and would simply sit down wherever was convenient.

The last time Binta had seen her, Hadiza, having been seriously vexed by the ban on the wearing of face veils in France, news of which she had ardently monitored, had just acquired the habit of wearing a niqab. Her hands and feet had been tucked away in black gloves and socks. This time though, she came with several jilbabs with sequins down the front and short hijabs that had intricate lace fringes and which stopped at her bosom.

Binta sighed. And Hadiza sighed too. She put down the glasses and turned again to look at her mother, whose face was still turned away. 'Hajiya, this has nothing to do with the break-in, does it?'

When Binta smiled, the smile disturbed Hadiza more than it reassured her.

'Of course not.'

'What happened exactly?'

'I ran into a wall.'

'No, I meant with the break-in?'

'Oh, nothing. Just the small *'yan iska* who break in to get something for dope.'

'I see. So what exactly did they take?'

But Binta was looking at the wall again.

Hadiza leaned forward and observed the lost look in her mother's eyes, how she seemed to be looking through the walls at some mystery in the nascent night.

When Binta sensed Hadiza prying into her face, she turned her back to her. 'Do you think of him sometimes?'

'Who? Father?'

'Your brother.'

'Munkaila?'

Binta was silent awhile. 'The other one.'

Hadiza's eyes widened. 'Yaro?'

'Sometimes I wonder what he would have become had he lived.' And then Binta allowed silence to swallow her thoughts.

In the silence, Hadiza's bafflement increased. Were they actually talking about Yaro? It was the first time since his death, fifteen years ago, that she had heard her mother make any reference to him. It had seemed to her, when she thought about him, that they had buried not only his corpse but also his name that was not a name. And memories of him as well. She shifted closer to her mother. 'Are you all right, Hajiya?'

But then Fa'iza breezed in. 'Aunty Hadiza—'

'Don't call me that. How many times will I tell you to call me Khadija? That is the proper name. Say Aunty Kha-di-ja.'

'Aunty Khadija? But everyone else calls you Hadiza, and you know, you are not really my aunt, technically.'

'*Lallai*, this girl, you have no respect. Is Hadiza not a corrupt version of Khadija? And don't forget, I'm not your mate, whether I'm your aunt or not. Technically.'

'Ok, Aunty Khadija.' Fa'iza sat down on the bed, sweeping her dress under her and posing proficiently with her hands on her lap like a queen holding court, a pose she had adopted from Kannywood home videos, which, along with *soyayya* novellas, occupied the bulk of her leisure time. She would not admit, not to Hajiya Binta especially, that they had become an obsession. A refuge from the shadows in her head.

Fa'iza had been living with her aunt since her mother, Asabe – Binta's younger sister – had returned to the village, having lost her husband and only son in the incessant turbulence in Jos. She had been embarrassed, when her mother decided to remarry, by the choice of a stepfather. This sentiment was inspired by her loyalty to her late father's memory, by the fact that he was gone forever and would have no further need of his wife.

Whatever she found worthy of scorn in the man who now paraded himself as her mother's husband – his buck teeth and always-dirty feet, and the fact that he was, in the manner of country folks, less refined than her father had been – was born out of these sentiments. Fa'iza would not even visit. How could she possibly live in the village?

But beyond the distraction she craved from the romantic life portrayed in the films and literature of Kano, which was an escape from the haunting memories of Jos, living in the village would make her less appealing to men in the class of Ali Nuhu. Manifestations of her teen infatuation with the film star were evident everywhere in her room in the form of stickers stuck in the corners of her mirror, on her varnished wardrobe, her cream-coloured walls, the door panel and windowpanes and on the covers of her notebooks. Even on the easel she had used for her fine arts practicals, which was now tucked away behind the wardrobe.

Whatever would Ali Nuhu do with a village girl?

Living on the fringes of Abuja, in the sprawling suburb of Mararaba, was not the same as living in the heart of the city. But at least, here, she could nurture her ornate dreams. So she would paint her face, stick up her posters, watch Kannywood films and read *soyayya* novellas in which handsome men in sedans fell in love with beautiful girls with moon-like eyes and aquiline noses. Women not unlike her cousin Hadiza.

'I like your henna decoration.' Fa'iza held Hadiza's hands and marvelled at the intricate designs so pronounced on her delicate skin. She looked up and saw Hadiza smiling. 'When I start writing *soyayya* novels, I'll put your face on the cover.'

Hadiza laughed. 'Stupid girl, my jealous husband will kill you and burn all your novels. Who reads those things anyway?'

'That's all she reads, this girl.'

They both turned to look at Binta, who had spoken.

But Binta was looking straight ahead. 'She reads them from morning till night, if she's not watching films on Africa Magic. I was wondering where she gets them from until I realised the Short Ones supply them.'

'*Kai*, Hajiya!' Fa'iza protested.

'What Short Ones?'

'Some short girls she has made her friends. They live nearby.'

'Sounds like you don't like them, Hajiya.'

'Those girls, they are too smart for their own good. I wish Fa'iza would stop associating with them.'

Hadiza frowned. 'Fa'iza! Behave yourself and keep away from bad friends, *mara kunyar yarinya.*'

Fa'iza puckered her lips and turned her face away.

'Anyway, now the decoder is gone, she won't get to watch all those useless channels.' Hadiza adjusted her scarf.

'Useless channels? *Haba*, Aunty Khadija. Anyway, Alhaji Munkaila will replace what was taken, *insha Allah.*'

'Was that what he told you?' Binta's voice sounded burdened by the weight of unrelated memory.

'Me? No.' Fa'iza was flippant. 'Well, he brought these ones. *Insha Allah,* he will replace them.'

Hadiza turned to her mother. 'Well, has the break-in been reported to the police?'

'The police?' Binta chuckled. 'It has been reported to Allah.'

'Since when has Allah become a policeman, Hajiya?'

'He will dispense justice in His own fashion. Even on the police who go about shooting innocent people. Allah will judge them.'

Hadiza flinched at the virulence in Binta's voice. It must have something to do with this sudden mention of Yaro, this exhumation of disregarded memories. 'Well, I still think a formal report should have been made. You never know.'

Binta conveniently observed that the muezzin had called for Isha prayers. 'Go look for your sister, Fa'iza. I'm sure she's playing next door.'

'Me?' Fa'iza shot up, without waiting for an answer, as if she had been sitting on a spring. She threw her veil over her shoulders and walked out, leaving a whiff of thick perfume in her wake. Hadiza savoured it for a while and then waved her hand, with a dismissive carelessness, in front of her face as if to dispel the scent. Her eyes wandered around the room and lingered on the mournful curtains, the heap of unwashed clothes in the corner and the litter on the floor.

Hajiya, I think I'll help you move your bed and re-arrange the room.'

Swiftly, Binta picked up the Qur'an before her and handed it to Hadiza. She rose and recited the Iqama for her prayer.

Hadiza sighed, replaced the Qur'an on the nightstand, on top of *The Major Sins*. She gathered her gown about her and left the room.

———

Hadiza, plagued by pre-slumber agitations, turned over on the mattress. 'What's wrong with Hajiya?'

For a while only little Ummi's soft snores filled the room. Then Fa'iza, who was lying across the room on the mattress she was sharing with Ummi, looked up from the book she had been reading by the flashlight of her phone and sighed. 'Hajiya? I don't know.' She buried her face in the pages once more.

Hadiza turned again. 'How long has she been like this?'

'How long? I don't know, since yesterday, I guess.'

Hadiza sighed. 'She seems evasive about this break-in, I don't understand it. And I don't understand why she is talking about Yaro all of a sudden. She has never talked about him before.'

'Yaro? Your late brother?'

Hadiza nodded, put her fingers on her forehead and scratched. 'Her explanation about her broken glasses was just implausible. What happened really?'

'What happened?' Fa'iza sighed and put her book down on the rug by the mattress. The cover showed the face of a beautiful woman with large eyes, and *Biyayar Aure* written in bold across the top. The flashlight from her phone, which she placed on top of the book, expanded and chased the darkness into the corners. Having turned onto her back, she pulled the sheet over her bosom. 'What happened was that I just came back home from school and saw the front door open and the decoder and DVD player were gone and Hajiya's glasses were lying on the floor, broken. I took them to her room and met her sitting on the bed like this . . .' Fa'iza paused and stiffened to demonstrate. 'I asked her what had happened and she sighed like this . . . hmmm . . . and said a thief broke in.'

When Hadiza said nothing for a long time, Fa'iza rolled onto her side and lay quietly. Little Ummi, too far gone in her sleep, made little noises and farted. They both looked at her. Fa'iza made a face.

Hadiza, too, turned over on her mattress. A house without a man would look like easy pickings for fence-jumping miscreants of the sort that had broken in. Or was it possible that her mother was just lonely? How had she endured a decade without a man?

'What about the man who is courting her?'

'That man?' Fa'iza scoffed. 'That dirty old man, Mallam Haruna. He has two wives already, *wallahi*.'

'Hajiya, too, is old, you know. Does she like him?'

'Like him? *Haba*! How could she like him?'

Hadiza said nothing for a while. When Fa'iza started snoring softly, Hadiza called her name and asked her to switch off the light on her phone.

'Me? No, I don't want to sleep in the dark.' Fa'iza mumbled and was soon snoring again.

Hadiza listened to the noises of the night. A cricket in a crevice somewhere struck up a solo. A cat, out in the dark, startled Hadiza with its meowing, which sounded like the cries of a human newborn. It kept on for a while and then there was silence. The hush was suddenly ripped by the racket two cats made fighting in the moonlight. Finally, staggered quietness ensued, punctuated by Fa'iza's mild snores, which in time grew into agitated moaning. 'No . . . No!' Fa'iza thrashed about, arguing with the shadows in her dreams, and kicked off the sheet. Hadiza, horrified, sat up, torn between bolting and waking the girl. Fa'iza now started whimpering like a beaten dog. Eventually, she curled up into a foetal position. Soon enough, she was almost quiet, her mild wheezing strumming the night like tender fingers on a guitar.

2

A butterfly thinks itself a bird because it can fly

The first time Binta was woken by the ominous smell of roaches was in the harmattan of 1973. She was sixteen or seventeen. She could never be sure of her age because her mother, who had never attended school, kept dates by association, as did most people in Kibiya. Binta gathered, from conversations that did not involve her, that she was born the year the British Queen visited Nigeria.

She had woken up before sunrise that morning, all those years ago, and lit the hurricane lamp. She shook the mattress, drawing protests from her sleeping younger sister, Asabe, who grumbled. Binta picked up the lamp and searched the small confines of the hut, lifting the mats, probing the calabashes and the single *kwalla* containing their clothing. She found the crumbling moult of a spider in the first, and the remains of a long-horned beetle in the other. She gave up after prodding the major crevices on the wall with a broomstick and finding nothing of interest.

She went out, performed her ablutions and said the Subhi prayer. Then, as she had been doing for years, she joined her taciturn mother in the faint light of the awakening sun. Together they worked in silence sifting pap with a translucent piece of cloth. Her mother, who was Fulani, slim and dignified but bulging in the middle, hardly said a word to her. Binta was her first daughter and, as was customary, she rarely acknowledged or called her by her name lest she be deemed immodest. But each time Binta sneaked a look into her mother's eyes, she glimpsed, before it was blinked away, a clandestine love she wished she could grasp and savour. She would have given anything to hear the sound of her name on her mother's lips. Anything.

When the sun was up, she balanced the tray of kamu on her head and went out, her yellow veil tied around her swaying waist, hawking the kamu around the neighbourhood. As soon as she had sold out, she hurried home, washed, ate a breakfast of kunun tsamiya and kosai and hurried off to school, her school bag – a cut out sack with a shoulder strap attached – swinging as she went.

She walked by Balaraba's house and met her friend waiting at the entrance. Together, they moved on to Hajjo's and then Saliha's. Saliha had not yet returned from hawking bean cakes so they moved on to Bintalo's.

School was no more than a couple of raffia mats spread out under the ancient tamarind, on which a black board leaned. Mallam Na'abba, the schoolteacher, had often told Binta that she was smart. That she could, if her father consented, continue schooling and perhaps some day become a health inspector. Each time he said that, she would smile and chew on her forefinger, turning her face away from him. It was a far-off dream. She knew that much then. But Mallam Na'abba was passionate about its possibility. It was he who convinced her reluctant father to let her pursue her education for a while longer. That she could benefit the whole of Kibiya with her knowledge. Her father, skeptical as always, had agreed, but carried ridges on his forehead for days afterwards.

After school, the girls went home and met plump Saliha loitering under the moringa tree at the entrance to their house. When she was not hawking, Saliha had inexplicable bouts of headache, backache and a variety of fevers that conspired to keep her away from school most of the time. Her afflictions healed as soon as the prospects of attending class had been eroded. Since she did not seem to be suffering from any of those infirmities at that particular moment, the girls decided to play *gada* under the barren date tree.

They ran to the field laughing, piling their school bags at the foot of the tree. Because Bintalo was belligerent enough for the entire coterie, they started with her. They formed a semicircle and Bintalo leaned back into their waiting arms. They caught her each time and threw her on to her feet, singing and clapping. Saliha was next and then Binta, who felt the little buds on her chest jiggle each time they threw her, singing:

Karuwa to saci gyale
Ca ca mu cancare
Ta boye a hammata
Ca ca mu cancare
Ta ce kar mu bayyana
Ca ca mu cancare
Mu kuma 'yan bayyana ne
Ca ca mu cancare

Mallam Dauda, who had been standing at the edge of the field, stroking his greying beard and watching the little jiggles on Binta's chest, asked why they were behaving like tarts. Did they not have things to do at home?

The girls picked up their bags and went home, wondering what business it was of his that they were singing about a prostitute who hid a stolen veil under her arm and were jiggling their little buds. They agreed to meet later that night under the leaning papaya tree to play *tashe* in the moonlight.

Mallam Dauda went on to have a talk with Binta's father, Mallam Sani Mai Garma.

Her father returned from the farm that evening with the ridges on his forehead more pronounced than ever, and his limp, caused by his polio-sucked leg, even more obvious. Binta rose from washing the dishes to relieve him of the hoe slung over his shoulder. He brushed her aside and called her mother indoors.

Binta heard him thundering about how big his daughter had grown under his roof and how men now watched her jiggling her melons in public places, and how it was time for her to start a family of her own. He stormed out, kicking his food out of the way. Binta ran into the hut to weep at her mother's feet. The woman turned her face away to the wall, her hand poised uncertainly over her abdomen.

Two days later, Binta was married off to Zubairu, Mallam Dauda's son, who was away working with the railway in Jos.

———

This time, it was the sound of movement in the living room that woke her. She heard wood squeaking on the tiles like some oppressed animal and wondered what was happening. Then she heard Hadiza issuing directives to Fa'iza, who kept echoing each question.

'Fa'iza, hold that end.'

'Me? This end?'

'Move it this way.'

'This way?'

'*Haba*! Fa'iza, for God's sake, what are you doing?'

'What am I doing? But, Aunty Hadiza, I was only doing what you asked.'

Hajiya Binta, who had gone back to sleep after her early morning prayers, listened to the noises from the living room. She imagined she could feel the weight of her liver, imagined that it felt a little heavier. As she lay in bed, she listened to an unfamiliar birdsong floating in through her window. It was sonorous and confident and if she had not felt weighed down by her body, she would have gone to the window to see the bird.

The sound filled her heart with tranquility and she closed her eyes to savour the sensation. Images of her late husband, Zubairu, the stranger she had spent most of her life with, flitted into her mind. Every time she thought of him, he seemed to be smiling, something he had not been famed for doing so often. Memories of his touch were shrouded in a decade of cobwebs. What she recalled, albeit vaguely, was the sensation of his hands pressing down on her shoulders, his lower lip clamped down by his teeth to suppress his grunts as his body hunched over hers. She remembered how he used to chew his fingers before he told a lie, and how he always slapped his pocket twice before pulling off his kaftan. These memories were vivid. A strong arm around her, crushing her bosom. A strong body behind her. A bulging crotch pressed hard against her rear. Warm, desperate breathing on the back of her neck. A face, young, crowned with spiky hair. Binta realised then that her thighs had been pressed together, that she was moist, down there. Just a hint of it.

'*Subhanalla!*' She shook her head and saw the images dissipate like a reflection on disturbed water. Sitting up, she reached for the Qur'an Hadiza had placed on the nightstand the previous evening. She found that her cracked reading glasses were useless so she put them down. Undeterred, she flipped open the Qur'an and tried to read. The elegant curlicues of the Arabic letters blended into an indiscernible pattern before her eyes. Binta sighed, kissed the Qur'an, replaced it on the nightstand and went out to inspect the commotion in the living room.

Hadiza and Fa'iza were contemplating where best to place the framed painting of a waterfall ornamented with red blossoms that had been on the adjacent wall. Fa'iza held up the frame, while Hadiza, having made up her mind, hammered a nail into the tan-coloured wall.

Ummi stood beside Hadiza with a cardboard box of nails in her hand and a hopeful look in her eyes. 'Aunty Hadiza, will you bring back our decoder?'

Hadiza, biting down her lower lip, continued to hammer in the nail. Ummi repeated her question and, when nobody said anything, she shook the box of nails. 'It's Saturday. I want to watch Cartoon Network.'

Binta stood by the door and observed the transformation of her living room. She thought of it as a minor calamity of sorts. Chairs had been rearranged, the TV stand had been snuggled into a corner and the cornflower-blue vase that had been by its side was now atop the TV. The sewing machine had been moved up against the wall in the dining alcove.

Her greeting, when it eventually came, was mumbled. '*Sannun ku da aiki.*'

They turned to her.

Hadiza contemplated her mother with a scrutiny that bothered the older woman. 'Hajiya, *lafiya ko?*'

'Yes, I'm fine. Why?'

'You just look . . . strange, that's all. Anyway, I didn't want to wake you. But now that you are awake, I'm going to rearrange your bedroom as soon as I'm through here.'

'No!' Binta had not meant to snap. What on earth was wrong with her? She took a deep breath and added in a much softer tone, 'No rearrangements, please. Just cleaning will do, thank you.'

Realising she was being grouchy, Binta sighed. The images she had woken up with had excited and vexed her more than she would admit. And to think that this moistening of her long-abandoned womanhood had apparently been provoked by someone who reminded her of Yaro was an added irritation.

Hadiza stood, hammer in hand. Ummi picked up a crooked nail from the box and stuck it in her mouth.

Binta made an impatient gesture with her hand. 'Fa'iza, get me some water. I need to bathe.'

'Me? Hot water?'

'Yes, you, God damn it!'

The nail in Ummi's mouth fell on the tiles and clicked-clicked several times, rattling the sudden silence. Binta turned and went back to her bedroom.

Before Hadiza and the girls could recover from the eruption of Binta's temper, there was a sound at the gate, succeeded by urgent footsteps crossing the yard. A woman salaamed at the front door and admitted herself.

Fa'iza beamed. 'Good morning, Kandiya.'

'Where's Hajiya?' The woman's puffy cheeks quivered. The edge of the khaki green hijab encircling her face was damp with perspiration. It formed a jagged-edged halo around her pudgy face.

Hadiza considered her with interest. 'Is there a problem?'

Kandiya ranted about how Hajiya had promised to have her dress ready four days before and how nothing had been done about it. She breezed across the room and picked up the dress on the sewing machine. She held up an unattached sleeve between the thumb and forefinger of her other hand.

'My dress has remained in this state for four days and I've paid her in full. I'm supposed to be at a wedding right now wearing it. And because she couldn't fulfil her promise, she has been avoiding me.' She observed the dress with considerable disdain and hissed.

'*Iskanci*.' She let the dress, and the unattached sleeve, fall to the ground. Then she stomped out, brushing Fa'iza aside as she went.

When Hadiza went to ask her mother about Kandiya's dress, she met her huddled on the edge of the bed, her hijab gathered around her, her eyes, before she turned them away to the wall, dark and unfocused.

———

By the time her son Munkaila arrived, Binta's mood had improved. She sat in the alcove oiling the Butterfly sewing machine and asked why he had not brought her grandchildren with him.

'I left them playing with their mother.' Munkaila, sitting on the couch, hunched forward and jangled his car keys around his finger.

Hadiza, sitting next to him, looked at the keys, at his chubby finger, and saw how it almost filled the key ring. The folds of flesh around his neck and his pot belly, which he patted intermittently, baffled her – things she could not explain as she could his dark skin. That had come from his father's genes. She could also explain his shortness but not the receding hairline that made him look older than his thirty-four years.

'I don't understand how these rascals can break into people's houses and make off with things.' Munkaila jangled his keys again.

Binta oiled the shuttle and slipped it into place. She lowered the presser foot and it landed with a thunk. Putting down her feet on the treadle, she felt the machine run. Smoothly. From the huge carton beside her, which had once held a TV set, she picked a piece of cloth, slipped it under the feed dogs, and threaded the needle. She leaned forward to observe the stitches as her foot worked the treadle. But because she wasn't wearing her glasses, she had to lean further in so that her forehead brushed the machine. She adjusted the tension control and the stitch length and pedalled away until the stitches were no longer oily. She removed the cloth and picked up Kandiya's unfinished dress.

'Hajiya, why don't you use your glasses? Or don't you like them?' Munkaila tapped his foot on the floor.

'Oh, my glasses were broken during . . . when I ran into a wall.'

'How come?'

'It was dark. But I am fine. No need to worry.'

'I suppose I have to get you another pair then. But you should be more careful, Hajiya, please.'

'I will be,' she smiled.

The TV was on but only Ummi seemed mildly interested in it. Soon enough, she drew out a square of bubble wrap, which had been discovered during the rearrangements, and started busting the bubbles.

'Alhaji, should we go out for a bit?' Hadiza stood up.

'Ok.' Munkaila rose and together they went out into the yard, where he stood observing the house.

It appeared to Hadiza that the smirk on his face had become part of his comportment; he seemed so comfortable wearing it. She adjusted her headscarf. 'Hajiya is straining her eyes too much, I guess. I was wondering if she could maybe stop this sewing business altogether. I don't like the way women come here and insult her over unfinished dresses.'

Munkaila sighed. 'She's just doing that to keep busy. I take care of her.' He jingled his keys some more and as if Hadiza did not know the details already, Munkaila recounted how he had rented the house for his mother and relocated her from Jos when he reached the conclusion that the riots and killings would not end; how he had installed satellite TV and paid the monthly subscription so she would be comfortable in old age. 'What else would she do with her time?'

While he talked, Hadiza wondered if she was the only one who remembered him as the scrawny undergraduate he had once been, with just one pair of jeans and a couple of spandex shirts to last him an entire semester. Those days at Ahmadu Bello University had been tough for him. When Munkaila graduated at twenty-five, with a degree in Economics, and could not find a job, he interned at Harka Bureau de Change. There, he made money buying and selling foreign currencies. He got lucky when he won the trust of some politicians in government who decided to run their foreign currency business through him.

'Well, she could maybe go back to teaching. There are primary schools around here she could work with. Maybe even part time. She always enjoyed teaching.'

Munkaila's palm moved up and down his midsection for a while. The image Hadiza's words conjured in his mind contradicted the one he had of his mother living out her days in contented grace. In the fashion of a queen mother.

'Look, I don't want her being subjected to all sorts of . . . indignities. She should be comfortable now. She shouldn't suffer all her life.'

'Hajiya is not that old, you know.'

'I know, I know. But still—' He shrugged.

'I was thinking she could perhaps remarry.'

'Remarry?! *Haba*! Hadiza, remarry?'

'Sure, why not? Her age mates are remarrying all the time.'

Munkaila cocked his head to one side as if to consider the proposition. The prospect had no appeal for him whatsoever.

Hadiza read the expression crystallising on his face as that of a man who had by chance tasted bitterleaf. 'Listen, I am a woman and I know how important it is to have a man around. Hajiya is lonely. She is open to the idea. She had mentioned before that there was a man here trying to court her.'

'Ah-ah! Here?' His mouth dropped in horror. The thought of his mother with another man, other than his father, was shocking enough. He had never imagined anything so horrendous.

'Don't worry, I won't be leaving until tomorrow so I will find time to talk to her about it. Whatever she says, I'll let you know.'

Munkaila sighed and jiggled his keys some more. He looked down at his shoes and stamped his right foot. Then he looked up at her. 'Your husband is taking good care of you. Who would have thought you are a mother of three already?'

'Thank you.' Hadiza bowed with the grace of a practised thespian. And they both laughed. 'But all this smooth talking won't stop me from reminding you that you need to sponsor me to hajj.'

'In time, Hadiza, in time. My plan was for Hajiya to go first and *Alhamdulillah,* she went only last year. As for you and that crazy sister of yours, I'm afraid you will have to wait because of the house I'm building. It's taking all my money, *wallahi.*' He went on about how he so desperately wanted to live in his own house and stop paying the exorbitant Abuja rent. About how he wanted Hajiya to move into the quarters he was building for her,

how Hadiza needed to see the place to appreciate how much he
was spending. And then he invited her to spend some time at his
house, since his wife and two daughters had been asking after
her. He stopped when Hadiza sighed.

'What is it?'

'She mentioned Yaro.'

'She did?' Munkaila's face, dark already, darkened further.
Unmindful of his sparkling white kaftan, he leaned back against
the wall and held his chin in his hand.

In the grave silence that followed, Hadiza looked around and
imagined what colours some hedges and flowers would add to
the austere yard that stretched before her eyes like a patch of
wasteland, like the last decade of her mother's life.

———

The next day, Hadiza threw aside the sheets and rose. She
looked at the wall clock and saw that it was already a quarter to
eight. Because of her two boys, Kabir and Ishaq, who had to be
readied for school, and the little one, Zubair, named after her
father, who insisted on having breakfast alongside his brothers,
she was unaccustomed to sleeping late into the morning.

From across the room, Fa'iza's mild snores reached her. Hadiza
saw that the girl had kicked away her sheet and her legs were
thrown carelessly apart, one resting on little Ummi, who was too
busy sleeping to notice.

She got up from the mattress and looked at her face in the mirror
that had Ali Nuhu's face stuck at each corner. She observed the
oily sheen of sleep on her face so she used her palms to wipe it
off and went out to the kitchen. There, she searched the drawers
and cabinets and came up with a pack of noodles. Uninterested,
she put it back where she found it. She should ask her mother
what they could have for breakfast.

In Binta's room, she found the clothes that her mother had
slept in strewn on the bed. Her mother was having her bath, so
she sat on the bed and waited.

When Binta emerged, she smiled at Hadiza and enquired how well she had slept. Hadiza assured her that her night had been pleasant enough.

'Is that an injury on your neck, Hajiya?'

Binta felt the spot where the rogue's dagger had punctured her skin. It was no more than a scratch that had hardened into a little black scab, which was peeling off of its own accord. 'Just a scratch. Have you spoken to your sister?' Binta sat on the stool before the vanity table and looked at the healing wound in the mirror. In one swift movement, she peeled off the scab and examined the fresh skin.

'No, not since I arrived. Should I call her?'

'Perhaps not. Hureira is so much trouble, you should just let her be.' Binta applied lotion to her body. 'Her husband called me the other day to complain about her tyranny. I promised to talk to her but she wouldn't take my calls.'

'Hureira *kenan*!' Hadiza chuckled. 'She should have been a man with that temper and rebelliousness.'

'*Lallai kam*! She would have been worse than your father was, may Allah rest his soul.'

'*Kai*! Hajiya.'

'Well, you know it's true.'

Hadiza said nothing and after a while she stood up. 'Well, I was wondering what you wanted for breakfast so we could send Fa'iza to the shops.'

'How about masa?' Binta smiled as she powdered her face. 'Tabawa makes the best masa in these parts. Fa'iza knows her place.'

'Ok. Masa it is.'

When Hadiza got back to Fa'iza's room, the girl was already up, wiping sleep from her eyes with a cotton ball dipped in facial cleanser. Hadiza gave her instructions and some money from her purse while she went to the kitchen to heat a pot of water.

Fa'iza took time powdering her face and drawing lines around her lips with an eye pencil. When she was done, she pulled a hijab over her head, fetched a food flask from the kitchen and went out.

'Hajiya! Hajiya! Aunty Hadiza! Come and see.' There was more elation than fear in Fa'iza's voice.

The two women rushed to investigate the excitement, Binta's hijab flapping like the wings of a desperate bird. On the threshold was the missing decoder, sitting on the DVD player. And on top of them all was a transparent plastic bag containing a mobile phone and some jewellery.

'Our decoder is back!' Little Ummi, eyes puffy with sleep, had snuck into the space between her grandmother and her aunt.

'But this is not Hajiya's handset,' Fa'iza observed.

3

*The egret has always been white, long before
the soap-maker's mother was born*

The whir of the electric motor filled the house. The power had just come back on and, knowing very well the vagaries of the power company, Binta sought to make the best of it. She had no more than some minor mending to do – having finally discharged her duty to Kandiya – and this she finished in no time.

She then went about dusting the TV, the DVD player and the decoder that Hadiza had put back on the stand before she had left for Munkaila's place the day before. While dusting the small pile of books shelved on the little cupboard in the corner, her eyes fell on Hemingway's *The Old Man and the Sea*. But Binta picked out a Danielle Steel novel instead and tossed it on the couch. With the little chores completed, and Fa'iza and Ummi at school, she sat down and started reading. The print was large so she could manage without her glasses. Her reading was interrupted by a knock on the door. Had she been so engrossed she did not hear the gate disturbed? She rose and opened the door.

Her assailant from the other day, looking less fierce, was standing at her door. 'Hajiya, please, I'm not here to hurt you.' His spiky hair was covered by a black beanie so that only his sleek sideburns showed.

She threw her weight behind the door and was about to shut it when she noticed the way he fidgeted with his hands before him, the rings on his fingers gleaming in the morning sun.

'I'll scream.' But her strained voice was no more than a low growl above the wild rhythm of her heartbeat.

'Please, don't.' He stepped back and held up his hands in a gesture of surrender.

'What do you want?'

'You understand, I don't want to hurt you. I just want to—'

In the fraction of a second their eyes locked, he reminded her of the countless new students who had stood before her during her teaching years, shifting from one foot to the other, desperate to run to the toilet but not certain how to go about asking permission.

'I don't want to rob you, you understand?' When he saw she was looking into his eyes, he looked away. He took another step backward and was now at the edge of the veranda.

Binta pushed the door a little further.

'I brought back your things: the decoder, DVD player, your gold—'

'What was left of it.'

'Yes, yes. I had already sold the others . . . but I'll get them back, you understand? I'll get them back. And your phone too.'

When she said nothing, he went on: 'You understand? The person who bought your phone has travelled. But I will get it back. That's why I brought another one, in the meantime.'

'I don't want it. Just leave me alone.'

She saw him standing awkwardly, not sure what to do with his hands. Her eyes grew soft because he reminded her then, more than ever, of Yaro, who had first tainted her perceptions with the smell of marijuana all those years before.

'You understand? I want to apologise for what happened.' He rubbed his hands. 'I am sorry. I will bring back the phone . . . and the other jewellery too.' He turned and left.

When she closed the door, she discosvered that her face was wet with tears – testament to the confusing sentiments that besieged her heart.

———

The assailant walked past the little police post to the next building, an uncompleted structure whose nondescript entrance was screened with roofing sheets. Someone who had stumbled into some money had thought it wise to build a multi-storey shopping complex. He obtained a piece of land big enough for several shops but had only managed to build the ground floor before the money dried up. The moss-covered bricks had seen many rains.

San Siro, as the place became known, was special. In the feigned ignorance of the neighbouring police post, its fame blossomed. In the evenings, it teemed with young men whose motorcycles would crowd the entrance and take up most of the street. The riders, and many others besides, would be inside enjoying thick joints and lively arguments about life seen through cannabis fumes. They debated football and ganja-inspired philosophies plucked gingerly from the precipice of inebriation. Dealers, too, came for the serrated leaves. At San Siro, the weed was supreme. On the side, some of the boys dealt other things – codeine, solution, tramol and other assorted mixures, but for the rogue with spiky hair, weed was *the* thing.

Walking past the young men lifting weights in what would have been the front of the building but was now effectively a compound, he slid a key into the last shop and turned it. He hissed, replaced the key with another and was rewarded with a click. He had had to change the lock after the rather unusual events of the previous week. Their next-door neighbours, the police, under the charge of the new commanding officer, had raided San Siro and bashed in all the doors. And under the guise of police work, they had carted away sacks of premium and dirty weed, which later turned up with some other dealers elsewhere. Such an occurrence, commonplace as it was elsewhere, was as astonishing as it was unprecedented at San Siro.

He went in and slumped on the mattress that was pushed against the wall, beneath the huge poster of the entire AC Milan squad, whose grounds the place was named after. Because the rogue with spiky hair, lord of this San Siro, was a fan.

'Reza, what's up?' Babawo, his friend and right-hand man, stood shirtless by the door, his knotted muscles glistening with sweat.

His friends called him Reza, a corruption of razor, a title he earned after weed had given him the courage to cut his half-brother on the arm with a blade he had been carrying for months under his shirt. That was eleven years earlier, when he was just fourteen. 'Give me a stick, Gattuso.' Reza pulled off his shirt, dumped it on the mattress beside him and collected the proffered cigarette. Babawo drew back and waited while Reza smoked. Because he was short and stocky and kept a beard, they called him Gattuso, after the rugged Italian footballer. He had been living at San Siro since he was seventeen and had never, in the eight eventful years that had passed, talked about going back home. Home was a distant memory for him, a flickering image of him smoking hemp in the bathroom and his father coming at him with a belt. He remembered wrestling down the old man and running out. When the news caught up with him that his father had broken his hip in that encounter, it was easy for him to decide not to return, since his mother had died when he was two. He drifted for a couple of months until he arrived at San Siro and met Reza.

'You understand, Gattuso, there is a reason for everything.' Reza leaned back against the wall.

Gattuso assumed Reza was in the mood to dispense his peculiar philosophy, which often came on the wings of cannabis-scented meditation. So he leaned back on the doorjamb, scanning the room for something to keep his hands busy.

'What happened?' Gattuso slapped his feet together. He reached into his pocket and pulled out a roll of hemp. He put it back and folded his arms across his chest.

Reza took his time puffing on the cigarette. Then he shook his head. 'I robbed this woman who reminded me of my mother. She had this gold tooth, you know, just like my mother, you understand.'

Babawo's eyes popped. It was the first time he had heard Reza mention his mother. He patted his pockets with accustomed agitation, and finally settled on cracking his knuckles.

'Just go now. I want to sleep.' Reza seemed tired of speaking. He picked up his shirt and dusted the mattress with it. Then he sat waiting for Gattuso to leave.

But Gattuso sat on the worn blue rug instead and yawned. 'I think I will catch some sleep too.'

'Go to your room!'

Gattuso sighed and rose. He slapped his pockets for no particular reason, and went out humming.

———

Hassan 'Reza' Babale was ten the first time he saw his mother. His father, sitting next to him in the car, turned to him every other minute, patting his head, asking if he was tired. He plucked the boy's cheeks and turned his head this way and that, inspecting the hollows on his face with his one good eye, as he often did with the cows he traded in. Each time, a shadow would crawl across his face and he would urge the boy to eat more of the biscuit he was holding.

The boy had been in class when his teacher, with his usual animated gesticulations, announced that his father was waiting for him. That he could take his bag along and he wished him a safe journey. When he came out, his father was standing in the sun, beaming.

'Come, we are going to see your mother.' He took his arm and led him away.

They went home and his father made him take a bath and put on his finest clothes: the pale blue embroided kaftan from the last Eid. Then they got into a car heading to Lafia, to see a mother he had only heard whispers of.

The boy brushed away crumbs from his mouth with his sleeve and raised his innocent eyes to his father's face. 'Will she be staying with us now?'

'You want her to stay, don't you?' His father leaned forward, using his handkerchief to clean the child's face, his damaged eye looming closer. The boy could almost imagine how the highwaymen had struck him with a club all those years before and how his father had desperately clung to his bag of money. 'Tell her that; that you want her to stay and look after you, mhm?'

The fat driver yawned and threw a piece of kola in his mouth. He slotted a tape in the cassette player. Musa Dan Kwairo's voice poured out from the device. They listened to the renowned praise singer lauding another royalty in some far-fetched place, a distant kingdom closer to that mystical shelter where the sun set.

The boy shifted on the seat. 'Why did she leave, Abba?'

His father sighed and leaned into the backrest. 'You will not understand.'

'But Bulama said that his mother said—'

'Shush. Never mind what your brother says about your mother. She is *your* mother.'

But he was tormented by the taunts of his half-siblings. Even Talatu, one of his two stepmothers, had said his mother was a 'Kano to Jeddah'. There had been muted talks about her questionable liaison with dubious Arabs.

His father, Babale Mairago, had long been buying cattle from the Fulanis in the North and selling to the Igbos in the South-east. He had lost his left eye on one such trip when he and his friend Buba Mohammed ran into bandits on the highway. Regardless, his good eye remained fixed on Buba's spirited seventeen-year-old daughter, Maimuna. And when she was forced to marry him, a stormy affair that lasted less than two years, she dumped their six-month-old son and caught a flight to Jeddah, for purposes other than hajj.

When Babale received news of Maimuna's deportation from Jeddah, he decided to take his son to see her and help tame the wild flames she was infamous for.

The boy saw her; saw her supple skin, her almond eyes and long lashes, saw the diagonal scarification on her left cheek. She rode on a zephyr of musk towards him. When she patted his head and ran her hands down the sides of his face, his little heart did a cartwheel.

'You have grown so big.' Her voice caressed his ear like the evening breeze sweeping through a grass field. 'You are in what class now?'

'Primary six.'

She smiled and enchanted him with her gold tooth so that he stood lamely, waiting, hoping for her to smile again.

'Do you know who I am?'

He nodded.

She contemplated him for a while as one would a feeble kitten, then pulled one of the silver rings from her fingers. This she clasped into his palm, pressing his fingers close around it. The elegance with which she performed the gesture mesmerised the boy.

She turned and was walking away, past his father, whose good eye had been on her the whole time, when the man reached out and held her sleeve.

'Maimuna.' His voice was husky, desperate even. His lower lip trembled but no other words came out.

She eyed him. 'Get your filthy hands off me, dirty old man.' She hissed and wrenched her sleeve free.

The boy ran after her and caught hold of her jilbab by the door. 'Mother.' He was uncertain, scared. 'Take me with you?'

She looked down at him, a hint of sadness in her eyes. She bent down and gently, very gently, loosened his grip on her dress. Her fleeing footsteps echoed in his memory amidst the swirl of musk, the gleam of gold in her teeth and her beautiful face shimmering like an image under water.

——

'Reza.' A boy burst into the room while Reza was tossing on the mattress, his face buried in the pillow, absorbing the smell of his own sweat.

'What?'

The teenager, who heard only a mumble, waited for Reza to look up.

'Sani, what is it?'

'You said to tell you if Ibro came back. I just saw him heading to the teashop.'

From the compound, excited voices streamed into the room. The concrete-weighted dumbbells the young men were lifting thudded on the ground, signifying someone's capitulation, an occurrence always greeted with great euphoria.

Sani stood rubbing his palms together.

Reza grumbled some more. 'You can go now. I'll see you later.'

Sani shrugged and left.

Reza looked at his face in the fragment of a mirror he kept by his mattress and wiped the dampness from his brow and chin. He put on his shirt and strolled out of the door. In the compound, Babawo was lying on a bench, lifting weights, his muscles rippling. A group of five surrounded him, goading and cheering. Reza walked past them and out onto the market road.

'Do you want me to come with you?' Sani had broken away from the crowd and was looking hopefully at Reza.

Reza regarded him and saw why the boy's mother's incessant lamentations were often inspired by his waif-like frame. These doleful monologues were a great irritation to Sani especially when he had to endure them as he helped her with her business of making and selling kosai by the roadside. It was not something he enjoyed doing, this business of tending to open flames and frying bean cakes that he thought was best suited to girls. But his upkeep depended on it. Having his mother point out how thin his arms were to strangers coming to buy kosai did not endear him to the task either. It seemed she had conveniently forgotten that Sani's late father had been pint-sized as well.

When he was not fending off his mates, who taunted him for doing sissy chores, one could see in his eyes the wistful look of a boy who wanted to be someone else, somewhere else. But he had been trapped by the death of his young father years before, and a mother determined to live for her son. She wanted him to become a doctor or an engineer someday. He wanted to hang out with Reza and make the occasional quick buck.

Reza patted him on the shoulders. 'No, I should be back soon.' He noted the disappointment in Sani's eyes and sighed. 'There are things I want you to do for me later.'

In the gathering dusk, Reza walked past the bleak police post. The new commanding officer, Dauda Baleri, sat on the bench by the entrance, caressing his moustache and looking up and down the road. Reza turned his face the other way and walked on. He walked past Sani's mother stoking the flame in the hearth before her as she prepared for the evening sales. He walked past the mosque where men were gathering, performing ablutions and awaiting the muezzin's call for Maghrib prayers. He turned into a tapered alley and took several shortcuts that brought him to the tarred street. After a short stroll, he was soon in front of Mahmood's teashop.

Looking through the large glassless window, he saw the men seated around the table crammed with loaves of bread and huge tins of beverages and milk. When he saw Ibro among them, lifting a steaming mug to his lips, Reza went in.

Some of the men mumbled greetings. Others looked down into the mugs before them or at the open flames on which Mahmood's mammoth teapot was boiling.

'Mahmood, give me a mug.' Reza sat down next to Ibro.

Mahmood was deftly flipping hot tea from one cup to another. He shoved the mug to a waiting customer and started scooping powdered milk into another. Mahmood had been at this spot, doing this, for as long as Reza could remember. 'Tea or Bournvita?'

'Tea, Mahmood. Tea.'

Reza watched him fetch hot water, pre-boiled with ginger-spiced tea, into his mug from the great teapot hissing on a tripod. Then he turned to look at Ibro, hunched forward over the table, shoving bread in his mouth, his dim bleary eyes staring straight ahead.

'Reza.' Ibro, still unsmiling, put down his mug on the old, scratched-up table and stretched out a grease-stained palm to him. Reza slapped it. Ibro's hand, much bigger than his, felt hard from all the years spent taking apart generators and putting them back together.

Reza's smile was a brief flash. 'Back from your trip already?'

'Yes.'

'So how are your folks?'

'Oh, they're all right.'

Mahmood placed a hot mug before Reza and handed him a thick slice of bread.

Ibro put down his mug. 'Well, I'm done. Will be heading home now.'

'Why don't you stay a little, mhm?'

Ibro made to rise but Reza put his palm firmly on his thigh. 'Stay, mhm? I'll pay for your tea, you understand?'

Ibro sat still, his eyes turned from one corner of the shop to the other, his hands tucked between his knees. When Reza was done, he paid their bills and together they went out into the falling dusk. They stood side by side, Ibro taller, darker, in the evening breeze, watching the midges caught in the yellow glare of passing vehicles.

'What about the phone I sold to you?' Reza patted Ibro on the back.

'It's working fine.'

'Do you have it here?'

Ibro frowned down at Reza, his large nostrils flaring. Reza, unfazed, stretched out a hand and Ibro grudgingly reached into his pocket and handed over the phone. Reza examined it. He shook it as if to weigh it and satisfied, switched it off, removed the battery and the SIM card, which he handed back to Ibro.

'I'll give you back your money. I just need the phone, you understand?' Reza put the phone back together and shoved it in his pocket.

'But I'm using it.'

'I know, I know.' Reza looked up at the star-speckled sky and back at Ibro's grumpy face. 'Ok, don't worry. I'll get you another one. See me tomorrow'

He shoved his hands in his pockets and headed into the night, leaving a bewildered Ibro watching his silhouette, cast with lavish abundance on the street by the lights of passing cars.

———

He scaled her fence, as he had done twice already, at a quarter past eleven because he knew that if she had not gone to the madrasa, she would be alone. Having gone round to the front, he peeked from behind the wall and saw her watering the beds of petunia that had not been there the last time he had taken the liberty to invite himself in. He watched her scooping water from a yellow bowl and sprinkling it on the plants. She put down the bowl and straightened up, one hand on her back, the water dripping from the fingers of the other. She turned and their eyes met. He came out from behind the wall and she threw an arm across her breasts.

'Good morning.' His voice faltered, but he bowed briefly and held up his hands in front of him.

She placed a hand over her thumping heart.

'I, uh, I just brought back your phone, you understand. As promised.' He reached into his pocket, his other hand still held up, and pulled out the device. He held it up for her and she considered it for a while. She nodded. He moved forward, extending the phone to her.

'Sorry about . . . everything.' He watched her run her thumb over the phone as if to reassert her ownership, marking her possession like an animal would with its scent. 'I don't usually do this, you know, going into peoples' houses . . . you understand. None of my guys will ever bother you again, *insha Allah.*'

She looked up at him and, because she was thinking of Yaro, there was a watery glint in her eyes. 'Thank you.'

He nodded and turned to leave.

'Wait.'

He turned to face her.

'Your name? You didn't tell me.'

'Reza. They call me Reza.'

'Reza?' She rolled the word on her tongue like one savouring the taste of a new meal. 'You must have a real one?'

He had had a real name, once. His lisping teacher with narrow shoulders used to call it every morning when he took attendance. 'Hassan Babale.' The name sounded like an echo from his memory. 'But everyone calls me Reza now.'

'Hassan. I will remember that.'

He nodded, mumbled something and made to leave again. She was fidgeting. Then she ran her fingers over her temple.

'Would you like to . . . have some water or something. I mean, I'm all alone, here . . . for now.' She was looking down at the damp bed of petunias Hadiza had so lovingly planted to add colour to the yard that hosted little birds at sunrise. That was the precise moment, Binta would reflect later, that the petals of her life, like a bud that had endured half a century of nights, began to unfurl.

4

Don't bother looking at where you fell,
but where you slipped

She first felt the unmistakable pangs of labour on 13th February, 1976. It was a memorable day for reasons quite unrelated to her circumstance. Her siesta had been truncated by contractions that took the form of giant fire ants gnawing at her innards. When the pain eased, she lay on the bed and listened to the voices of children playing in the courtyard. They laughed in more languages than she had ever imagined existed. She spoke Pidgin with her Yoruba neighbour, Mama Bola, who only knew a couple of offensive terms in Hausa. They were five, the women. Each with her husband; each speaking a different tongue. In that big house, mid-morning reveries were often interrupted by excited children who horsed around barefooted in the courtyard.

But that morning it was Zubairu who slipped in, shoulders slouched, his dark face long. She sat up, the springs of the Vono bed squeaking in protest at her movement.

'They've killed him! They've killed him!' Zubairu reached for the radio in the corner.

'Who?' Her hand was poised protectively over her belly.

'Murtala, they've killed the Head of State.' He was fiddling with the knob while static poured out from the radio. When he eventually tuned into a station, martial music blared over the static. Zubairu sat on the plastic carpet, legs spread apart, as if he had been personally bereaved. As if General Murtala Mohammed had been his blood brother. He removed his cap and slapped it on the floor. Beads of sweat dotted his head, scraped clean by the *wanzami's* blade.

'*Inna lillahi wa inna ilaihi raji'un*! Murtala? When? How?'

'They shot him dead.'

They sat like ancient statues in a forgotten shrine while the Panasonic radio belched martial music. The news spread outside, casting a sullen mist that stretched across the country from the fringes of the Sahara to the shores of the Atlantic, and swallowed the noise in the compound. Children were called away to their rooms by anxious parents.

'Zubairu! Zubairu!' Their neighbour Nnamdi's huge frame darkened the curtain fluttering in the open door. When Zubairu came out, he saw Nnamdi standing, head bowed, hands folded on his abdomen. He had closed his fabric shop at the market, as had other traders, as soon as the news broke.

'*Chei, e be like say na true say Murtala don die o!*'

Zubairu leaned on the doorpost and looked down at a spot between his feet.

'*But na Murtala o. Murtala! That man no fit die like that.*' Nnamdi, too, had heard legends of General Murtala Mohammed's invincibility during the civil war. He had been in Aba, having fled the North, when Murtala's Second Division was devastating rebel lines in the Mid-west. From the stories he heard, Murtala walked through rains of bullets and swam across rivers of blood, emerging unscathed.

'*Na so I hear um.*' Zubairu's pidgin, which he had picked up working at the railway corporation, was heavily accented.

'*Chei!*' Nnamdi shook as if rousing himself from an impossible dream. '*So, wetin go happen now?*'

Zubairu shrugged. He sighed because no one knew exactly what was happening, or what was going to happen thereafter.

Joseph Dindam strutted in at that moment. He too, like Nnamdi, towered over Zubairu. He was infamous for his drunken singing, which infuriated the neighbours, and for the racket he made beating up his wife and children, often well after midnight.

He had been a policeman until a few months before when he suddenly stopped putting on his uniform. And the drunken brawls became a nightly occurrence.

'*Fellow Nigerians, we are all together!*' Those were the words the coup plotters had used to close their speech after the assassination. And Joseph Dindam delivered them with aplomb and a triumphant guffaw. '*General Murtala Ramat Mohammed is gone!*'

'*Cheiiii!*' Nnamdi shivered.

'*Very good!*' Joseph laughed again.

Zubairu eyed him.

'*You dey look me? No be good thing? No be him dismiss me from police, say I no competent. If to say I see am, I for shoot am to pieces myself.*'

Zubairu reached up and struck him on the jaw. It happened so fast that Joseph was momentarily stunned. The brawl that ensued, loud and shocking since it involved grown men behaving like enraged dogs, was, however, short-lived. While Zubairu was striving to break Joseph Dindam's jaw, at the cost of a bruised lip, Binta's waters broke of their own accord. Startled by this, she hollered. Her wails reached the men and put an end to their scuffle. The other women came out, led by Mama Bola and Joseph's battered and scrawny wife, Mama Bulus. It was they who, hours later, received Binta's first son, covered in slime and shrieking like a furious imp.

Few people were surprised when, a week later, Zubairu named the boy Murtala. But because of *kunya*, the socially prescribed modesty his mother had to live with, she called him 'Boy' instead. And that was how Murtala Zubairu, born on the day a general died, came to be known as Yaro.

———

Binta finally made up her mind to be more adventurous after their second son, Munkaila, was born. They had been married three years then and that was enough for her regardless of what Dijen Tsamiya, the marriage counsellor of Kibiya, had told her on the day of her wedding.

'When he's done, always put your legs up so his seed will run into your womb.'

Binta, shocked, had looked at the woman's rheumy eyes and shrunken jaw. She had wondered how many other young brides of Kibiya Dije had so pragmatically dispensed this knowledge to on their wedding eves.

When Dije smiled, her toothless mouth was like a cavern leading into her antiquated interior. No one, it seemed, remembered what Dijen Tsamiya's married life had been like. Her husband had died many years ago and the last of her three children had passed on a decade before.

Dije had slapped her playfully, her frail hand like a cow whisk on Binta's shoulder. 'See how you look into my eyeballs. Don't look your husband in the eyes like that, especially when you are doing it. Don't look at him down there. And don't let him look at you there, either, if you don't want to have impious offspring.' She removed a piece of kola from the knotted end of her wrapper, threw it in her mouth and proceeded to crush it with her gums. Binta watched her jaw move from side to side as she knotted back her wrapper with trembling hands. 'And don't go throwing yourself at him. You wouldn't want him thinking you are a wanton little devil now, would you?'

Binta had shaken her head, resisting the urge to cry. The prospect of being intimate with any man, particularly one she hardly knew, was far from comforting.

'And don't forget what I told you about searching the pockets, mhm. The loose change could amount to something if you are thrifty, *kin ji ko?* You could buy your mother something decent.'

When Binta gaped at her, Dijen Tsamiya clucked at the back of her throat. 'Young people, they think they know everything.'

Three years, in her estimation, had surely earned her a licence to be licentious, with her own husband of all people. But then on the night she made up her mind, Zubairu returned home with a torn kaftan and another bruised lip. She was sifting garin tuwo in the courtyard when he had breezed in, anger radiating from his flaring nostrils. He sat down on the raffia mat in the corner of the room and turned on the radio. Binta went in after him and sat by his side.

'What's wrong?' She wiped her hands on her wrapper, the white of the cornflour rubbing off on her Ankara fabric.

He shook his fist at her. When she leaned away, his fist came down on the mat with a thud that almost woke the little boy wrapped in a fluffy shawl on the bed. When the boy stopped wriggling and resumed his slumber, Zubairu sighed.

'I lost my job.'

'*Inna lillahi wa inna ilaihi raji un!*' Binta slapped her palms alternately. '*Maigida*, how come?'

'I beat up my boss.' The words tumbled out as if racing with each other. 'He called me a goat and I hit him and broke his nose.'

'But *Maigida*, you could have—'

'I could have done what?! What?! Don't you tell me what I could have done, you don't know the first thing about this so just shut your mouth, you hear me! *Wawiya kawai!*'

Munkaila started wailing, kicking away the shawl with his tiny feet. Binta crossed the room and sat on the bed. She picked him up and shoved a nipple in his mouth. The boy turned his head this way and that, screaming. She put him on her shoulders and burped him. Then she positioned him and again tried to breastfeed him. He turned his head away but would not stop screaming.

'What the hell are you doing? Do you want to kill him?!'

She wiped away the tears that streamed from her eyes and hoisted the boy onto her shoulder. His screams filled her ears. Zubairu hovered for a while and then stormed out of the room. Moments later, he stormed back in, his furious presence startling her. He went to his clothes hanging on a rack and changed his kaftan before heading out again.

Two nights later, when he was tossing and turning on the bed next to her, she knew he would nudge her with his knee and she would have to throw her legs open. He would lift her wrapper, spit into her crotch and mount her. His calloused fingers would dig into the mounds on her chest and he would bite his lower lip to prevent any moan escaping. She would count slowly under her breath, her eyes closed, of course. And somewhere between sixty and seventy – always between sixty and seventy – he would grunt, empty himself and roll off her until he was ready to go again. Zubairu was a practical man and fancied their intimacy as an exercise in conjugal frugality. It was something to be dispensed with promptly, without silly ceremonies.

She wanted it to be different. She had always wanted it to be different. And so when he nudged her that night, instead of rolling on to her back and throwing her legs apart, she rolled into him and reached for his groin. He instinctively moaned when she caressed his hardness and they both feared their first son, lying on a mattress across the room, would stir.

'What the hell are you doing?' The words, half-barked, half-whispered, struck her like a blow. He pinned her down and, without further rituals, lifted her wrapper. She turned her face to the wall and started counting. The tears slipped down the side of her closed eyes before she got to twenty.

5

*One who eats an old man should not complain
when he vomits grey hair*

Hadiza returned from her overnight stay at Munkaila's to find Binta's place suffused in the aromatic incense her mother had lit in the corners of the house. It was some time before she realised that there was a muted ambience that the incense complemented. But aside from Binta's inexplicable coyness, something more befitting of Fa'iza than a woman well into her fifth decade, there was no sense of anything dramatic having happened.

Hadiza had returned with residual excitement from having seen Munkaila's two daughters and presented her mother with the new glasses Munkaila had bought for her. She had met Binta lighting another stick of incense and tucking it into a corner where one had just burned out.

Binta bashfully accepted the proffered glasses in their exquisite casing and put them down by her side. When she said thank you, her voice had sounded off-key.

'Aren't you going to look at them?'

'Oh. I will, later.'

Hadiza looked at her mother. Binta, sensing the probe, turned and flashed a smile at her daughter. She opened the case and put on the glasses. Just as suddenly she took them off and replaced them in the case.

'They are nice.' Binta glanced at her bathroom door. 'I must take a bath now.'

'You look so fresh I would have thought you had bathed. And your perfume is strong, Hajiya. How can you stand all that perfume and all this incense? One could choke on it all.'

Binta smiled and walked towards the bathroom.

Registering her mother's discomfort, Hadiza excused herself and went in search of Fa'iza, who she found in her room, lying prone on the mattress. Fa'iza, smiling to herself, was lost in the novella she was reading.

'*Ke*! Put that rubbish book away.'

'Rubbish book?'

'Why is Hajiya acting funny?'

'Hajiya? I don't know, *wallahi*. I just returned from school and met her like this.'

Hadiza leaned against the doorjamb. 'I shall go back and ask her as soon as she is done bathing.'

'Bathing? This should be like the third time she has had a bath in the last few hours.'

That was when Hadiza knew for certain that there must be something her mother was trying to enshroud in folds of fragrance, or wash away in her numerous baths.

She went out to the bed of petunias she had planted two days before to enliven her mother's yard. There were dry patches emerging so she watered the plants rather generously and sat by them, imagining what they would look like when they grew.

Binta emerged from the house to find her daughter meditating by the damp flower bed. She did not want Hadiza to catch a whiff of the objectionable smell of fornication she was certain she exuded. From a distance, she asked if Hadiza was all right. But when Hadiza turned to her, Binta averted her eyes.

'Are you still leaving tomorrow?'

'Yes.'

'Stay a few more days.'

Hadiza chuckled. There had been little conviction in her mother's voice. 'My husband called earlier to remind me I had agreed to return home tomorrow. The kids are missing me, I'm sure.'

'Yes. The kids.'

'He told me Kabir had a cut on his hand. I should go see how he is faring.'

Binta envied her this liberty she enjoyed, this luxury of calling her first child by its name and holding it and treating it like one's beloved. Such affection she, Binta, had never experienced from her mother, nor dispensed to her late son Yaro.

'Don't you ever feel . . . strange calling him like that? By his name? Your first son?'

Hadiza turned to her mother and laughed. '*Lallai kam,* Hajiya, this is the twenty-first century. I shall not subject myself and my children to the shackles of the old ways like you did.'

Her eyes misty and her heart heavy, Binta leaned on the pillar and turned her eyes to a bulbul hopping on the fence. Her daughter's response both pleased and saddened her. There were things she wished she had done differently. Such as showing Yaro some affection, protecting him as every mother should do her child. And here she was, fifteen years after his death, seeking him in the eyes of the miscreant who had scaled her fence. That felon she had shielded because she saw the shadow of Yaro in his eyes. The son she had loved, but to whom she had been forbidden to show love.

She had not meant for it to happen, the heady events of that afternoon. At least not exactly the way they had. It all seemed like a blur now. She remembered him looking at the fading scar on her neck and saying how sorry he was. The little spark of concupiscence deep within her had burst into a flame. She had seen its reflection in his eyes, the fire, blazing until he could no longer subdue it. Her heart had been racing. And when he had ventured to fondle her breasts, she had moaned and tried feebly to move away. He had put his arms around her, and she had found his lips.

Shame had come much later, after they were done and lay side by side trying to catch their breath. She got up and pulled down her dress. When he had come to leave, he had halted before her as she stood by the door, eyes averted. Uncertainly, they had stood like that, until he parted the curtains and went out. And when she sensed him gone, because she did not hear his footfalls, she had exhaled. She knew then that her search for Yaro in the eyes of a stranger had unshackled her long-suppressed desires and left the objectionable stench of fornication clinging to her.

'Mother, you have not said anything.'

Binta sighed. 'You girls are so lucky.'

'Really?'

'In my time, such things as a woman calling her first child by its name were frowned at. Some women didn't even acknowledge their second or third child.'

'This is not your time as such, Hajiya.'

'Well, make the best of it.' And this Binta said with such sincerity that Hadiza turned to look at her. But Binta had her face nestled against the side of the pillar, staring at the fence where the bird had been.

The evening breeze ferried a sweet fragrance to Hadiza. She savoured it for a while before deciding it had been applied rather too lavishly. 'Your perfume smells nice, Hajiya.'

Binta was silent for a while. 'Thank you.'

'You have suddenly grown fond of perfumes and incense.'

'Hmm. I have always been fond of perfumes and incense.'

'Yes. But you have been burning incense non-stop since I returned.' She stopped short of mentioning the three baths.

Binta's silence stretched almost into disregard. Finally, she drew her hijab tightly around her. 'You should talk to your sister Hureira. I fear she might end up ruining her second marriage just as she did with the first one.'

Their talk strayed from Binta's sudden infatuation with sweet-smelling things to Hureira's startling eccentricities. Until the gathering dusk ushered them in to make plans for dinner.

6

A snake can shed its skin, but it will still remain a serpent

When Reza slipped his hand under her wrapper, he discovered, much to his surprise, that the clump of ancient hair he had encountered the first time was gone. She was amused by his startled expression and offered only the faintest resistance when he undid the wrapper and looked at her. She allowed him to sit her on the cushioned stool before the dressing table. When he knelt before her, she turned her face away and pressed her thighs together. But once he prised them apart, gently, and took his tongue to her, she held his head of minuscule anthills and quaked. And because they were alone in the house, because she had always wanted to, because she could not stop herself, she moaned. With his tongue, he unlocked something deep within her. She soared with tears streaming down her face.

When they were lying on the bed, still unable to look each other in the eye, Binta, her back to him already, moved further away. 'I am not a *'yar iska.'*

Reza frowned. 'Well, I never said you were. I think very highly of you, you understand?'

'I don't want you making assumptions about me because of what happened. I am a decent, respectable woman, you know. I have never been with any man other than my husband, God rest his soul.'

'I understand that, trust me. I would never think of you in such a light.' He sat up and swung his legs over the edge of the bed. 'I don't understand how this thing happened.'

She sighed. 'Since the last time you came and . . . I have been thinking people could look at me and see fornication written across my forehead. Or perceive its smell on me.'

He chuckled. 'You smell nice. And there is nothing written on your forehead.'

'No, you don't understand. You may be used to such things. I am not. The first few days, I was overcome by guilt and shame. I couldn't attend classes at the madrasa for fear people would know what had happened. And when you didn't come back I thought you despised me for what had happened, what I let happen. And then a week passed and I thought oh, well perhaps I wasn't even good enough for him. What could he possibly do with a hag like me?'

'No, no, you are not a hag, stop saying that.' He reached across the bed and put an arm around her. 'And I don't despise you. I thought you despised me for taking advantage of you and I had no idea what to expect if I came back. I didn't plan for any of this to happen, you understand.'

'No one must ever know about this.'

'They won't hear it from me. I promise.'

She sighed. 'So, why do they call you Reza anyway?'

He scoffed and moved away from her, turning his back to her. 'It was a long time ago. I was young then.'

She turned and looked at his tight muscles and saw how well chiselled his body was, reminding her how young he was, and how old she had become. She drew the sheets over her bosom.

'I have many brothers, from the same father, you understand.' He cleared his throat, as if to cough away the dust the years had cast on these unvisited memories. For a while he was silent.

'They always made fun of me, because my . . . because my . . . because I was different, you understand.'

She reached out and stroked his back, tracing the scythe-shaped scars.

'They always said bad things about . . . you know, they were always saying bad things, you understand. So one day, when we finished from school, Bulama came to say things to me. He is older than me and he was always picking fights because . . . he was always fighting me because I allowed him to. But I had had some grass then, my first time, and I was feeling . . . you know, bold, you understand. So I gave him a good beating. He picked up a stone but I cut him with a blade, made a huge gash on his arm. His mother Talatu said that my father had given birth to an accursed razor. She started calling me Reza to mock me. But I didn't mind.'

'So that was how.'

When he turned and smiled, she saw how ruggedly handsome he was. They looked into each other's faces, their eyes saying the things their hearts were thinking, things they would not voice.

Binta looked away first, thinking how insane it was that she had just slept with someone who reminded her of her first son, who was probably younger than Yaro had been when he died. She covered her face with her palms. 'How far did you go, with school I mean?'

He sighed. 'I was expelled in my final year in secondary school.'

'Why?'

'I broke a teacher's nose.' He shook his head. 'He wanted to flog me on the assembly ground because they found me dealing weed to some students.'

'So, what stopped you from going back and finishing up somewhere else?'

'Too much metal in my head, too many knife fights, too much weed, too much . . . stupidity.' He tapped his temple with his finger. 'Ten years is a long time. There's too much smog in my head now, you understand.'

When her silence, so profound, resonated with him, he glanced over his shoulder and found her with her palms over her face.

'Are you all right?'

She could not tell him that some of her tears were for him. But that most of them, the ones gilded with reminiscence, were for Yaro. So she sniffled and wiped her face with the bed sheet. 'You could always go back.' Her voice was thick with remorse. 'I went back. You could do it too. You are a man; it would be easier for you.'

'You?'

'I was taken out of school to marry a man I barely knew, Allah rest his soul. After I'd had my first two sons, I told him there was an adult education class in the neighbourhood and I wanted to join. He was reluctant at first, but I persuaded him. I studied while raising my children. I had my daughter Hureira, who is married now in Jos, and Zainab, who died at birth, and then I had Hadiza. All whilst studying for my teacher's certificate. I was a primary school teacher for about twenty years in Jos. I had to quit when my son relocated me here.'

He looked at her with renewed admiration. 'A gaishe ki, Hajiya.' He tapped his right fist in his left palm, offering her the salutation of the 'yan daba thugs.

Binta threw back her head and laughed.

He watched her laughing, and wondered what his mother's laughter would sound like, or if she ever laughed like this. When the sheet she was holding against her bosom slipped, exposing the mounds of her breasts, he wondered why he was sexually attracted to a woman who was older than his mother.

But whatever magic was manifesting between them at that moment was disrupted by his phone. The little device chimed and the choice of his ring tone, a rather bawdy pop song, caused him to hurriedly reach for the phone and press the receive button.

'Afternoon, sir.' He got off the bed and moved away from Binta.

She reached for a book on the bedside drawer and her hand fell on Az Zahabi's The Major Sins. She withdrew her fingers, tainted by the fluids of her indiscretions, and instead put on her dress, pretending not to be listening to him muttering into the phone.

'Sir, what about these people? The new man is giving me trouble, sir. All right, sir, all right, sir.' He shoved the phone in his pocket and started looking for his shirt. 'I've got to go. My boss just called.'

She opened her mouth to speak but was interrupted by noises from the gate. She knew it would be little Ummi, who always used all her might to open the side door of the gate, pushing it until it rebounded off the fence. She knew that Fa'iza would be right behind her. Binta scrambled across the bed and furtively peered through the window. Ummi entered, dragging her backpack on the ground, the front of her uniform dusty. Fa'iza strolled in behind her, swinging her hips for the benefit of a drooling audience of imaginary admirers.

'Quick, my granddaughter is back.'

Reza found his shirt and threw it over his shoulders.

'Hurry, out the back.' She pulled her hijab over her head and stumbled towards the door.

'My shoes are at the front.' His alarm was conveyed not only in his voice but also in the expression on his face.

'No time.' Binta led him out through the living room to the kitchen. She opened the back door, shoved him out and closed the door. Through the keyhole, she spied him deftly scaling the fence and disappearing into the narrow alley behind. Fa'iza was salaaming at the front door. Binta sighed, patted down her hijab and re-entered the living room in time to see the two girls entering. There were dried tear-tracks on Ummi's face.

'There is a pair of men's shoes outside.' Fa'iza ushered in a stream of sunlight as she held up the curtains.

Keeping as far away from Fa'iza as she could manage, Binta hurried across to her room, locked the door, lit two sticks of incense and watched the alluring smoke curling up to the ceiling. But the unmistakable miasma of sin still prevailed. So she lit two more sticks and then headed to the bathroom to wash away her indiscretions.

———

The sun was a russet glow on the western horizon as Reza returned to San Siro. The noise and the pungent smell of weed greeted him from beyond the makeshift fence of roofing sheets that formed a curtain between San Siro and the thriving market that surrounded it. Reza stood by the entrance and looked at the dozen or so young men crowded into the small confines, some lifting weights, others smoking weed in the corner. On the veranda, by the four shops that had been converted to rooms, young girls sat, ogling the men, gossiping, giggling while pretending to be minding the cheap noodles swimming in palm oil or the sun-beaten, almost-expired alale and the danwake they were vending. Farther away, near the crude toilet hemmed in by the fence and the pile of yellow jerrycans that some of the boys used for their black market trade in petrol, Reza saw a boy fondling one of the foodsellers, who was laughing like a hyena.

Apart from the residents – the five or six people who had called San Siro home for years – there were many others who came for weed, or the other intoxicants sold on the sly.

'Aha, Reza is here. Ask him.'

Babawo Gattuso jumped up from the worn jerrycan on which he had been sitting and was instantly at Reza's side. 'Reza, how many times has Milan won the Champions League? How many times?'

All eyes turned to Reza.

'Seven.'

A raucous uproar greeted his statement. Some of the boys beat on empty jerrycans and whooped derisively.

'I told you, I told you, you ass!' Gattuso's voice rose above the noise. 'You don't know anything and you want to argue. When did you even start watching football, *dan iska?*'

'You are the ass, you idiot!' Joe shouted. He was a lanky fellow who wore a flat cap drawn low over one eye. When he first came to San Siro he had said that he was a student somewhere but he was drunk so often that no one was certain which school he was supposed to be attending, or even where he came from. He assimilated into San Siro until he became a fixture, like the mould on the walls.

Reza looked around him at the excited young men shouting, at those in the corners smoking pot and sniffing glue, at the boy in the corridor pawing at the breasts of one of the vagrant hawkers. 'What's the argument about exactly?'

A melee rose up in response. Reza tried to make sense of it but could not. He soon lost interest and tried to slip through the crowd of eager faces.

'Man U for life!' Dogo, one of the residents, shouted impulsively. His real name was Musa Danlami and he had been living at San Siro since his mother, tired of his thievery, cursed him and sent him out to the street. He had the knack for turning up at meal times, or just when his mother had put away some money for his siblings' school fees, only to disappear with the money afterwards. It was said that he got his sense of timing from his father, an itinerant labourer, who turned up every other year to get his wife pregnant and disappear again 'in pursuit of wealth'.

Joe looked at him and hissed. 'You know, Dogo, you are a goat, I swear to God.'

'Man U for life, *dan uban mutum*! Useless drunk. You stink of beer and your words smell like shit, bastard dog!'

Joe would have hit him but was restrained by Dan Asabe, the carpenter.

'You romancing me or what, faggot? Get your hands off me, *dan daudu*!'

Dan Asabe let go and retreated to a corner. There had been whispers about his sexual preferences. His liaison with Obinna, who owned a provisions shop down the lane, had fuelled these. Obinna had, on occasions, been accused of luring young boys with money. And when he got close to Dan Asabe – who had been caught several times spying on the other boys in the bathroom, and had never had Rita, who everyone else had had, or even been seen with a girl – everyone made assumptions. Every time allegations were thrown at him, Dan Asabe would sneak away and try to make himself unobtrusive.

Reza held Gattuso by the arm and led him to his room. 'Gattuso, I have told you to keep this place in order. You know this new policeman has not been sorted out yet.'

'Guys just came, you know.' Gattuso tugged at a yellow plastic band on his wrist.

'How much have you made?'

'We sold everything. That guy, Johnny from the university, came and bought a lot.'

'No credit, I hope.'

Gattuso reached into his pocket and put a thick roll of money in Reza's outstretched hand.

'Saved some for us? We need to charge up a little, you understand.' Reza, with serious commitment, set about straightening out the notes, one after the other.

Gattuso, looking at his friend's face, got the impression that Reza derived some pleasure from the task. 'Sure, trust me.' He waited for Reza to count and tuck the money away in his pocket.

'The new policeman said he wanted to see you. He said he would be waiting.'

'What on earth for?'

'Don't know. Corporal Bako has been here twice now. This man wants to prove stubborn, *wallahi*, he is playing with fire.'

'Don't worry about him, Gattuso. I have spoken to the boss about him, you understand. I'm sure that's why he is looking for me.'

'You spoke to the boss?' This time, Gattuso scratched his glistening beard. His experiment with black dye on his browning, malnourished hair left it shiny and matted, jet black against his dark skin.

'Yes. He wants us to prepare some guys. We are going for some rally.'

'Elections are drawing near then?'

'Yes, very soon. So get the boys ready, I have arranged for a bus to come for us tomorrow morning, you understand?'

Gattuso nodded, cracking his knuckles in his palm.

'Is this all the money there is?'

'*Wallahi*, that's the whole of it.'

'All right. Let me go see this idiot policeman.'

'I'll come with you.'

'No, don't bother. There's nothing, no problem.' Reza started heading out of the room.

'How much for the new shoes?'

Reza looked down at his shoes and shrugged. 'Not expensive.'

'What happened to the old ones?'

'Lost them.' Reza hurried away before Gattuso could rattle his comfort with another intrusive query he would not be inclined to answer.

———

Assistant Superintendent of Police Dauda Baleri was sitting behind the scratched-up table in his little office when Reza walked in, grinding his teeth. From the way the policeman was crooning into the phone, Reza knew there had to be a woman on the other end. When Baleri looked up and saw him, he frowned and said he would call back in a few minutes.

The office smelt of fresh paint and Reza looked around to see the light glinting off the wall. There was something about police stations that he could never get used to, perhaps some intangible markers of illegality filed away in the dank air.

'New OC, new paint.' Reza sounded unimpressed. To him and the boys, whoever was in charge, regardless of rank, was the 'Officer Commanding'.

'Reza?'

'OC?'

A small storm gathered on Baleri's brow. He did not like this weed merchant who had just interrupted his talk with Christy, whom he had been trying to persuade to marry him. She had refused his advances first because he had remained jobless five years after graduating from the university. Then, when out of desperation he had applied to the police and had been taken on as an Assistant Superintendent, she was reluctant to marry a policeman. Baleri was getting desperate. And now he had to put up with this weed dealer, who was trying to make his first post uncomfortable. He watched the thug pull out a chair and sit down opposite him. Baleri's frown deepened.

'You, you want trouble, eh?'

'No trouble, officer. You wanted to see me?'

'Yes, yes. You are making trouble for me and I don't like it.'

'Me? Making trouble? How?'

Baleri thumped the table between them, attracting one of the officers sitting outside on the bench. 'Problem, sir?'

The ASP shook his head and waved the constable away.

'See, my DPO has been calling me, saying his boss has been calling him about this nonsense San Siro business. You want to make trouble for me, eh?'

'You understand, OC, I don't know where you came from, but before you, there have been OCs here and we never had problems, you understand. But you, you just came, raided my place, confiscated my goods, harassed my boys, took my money, locked me out—'

'Yeah, yeah, yeah. I know, I know.' Baleri tapped a biro on the table, pounding out the rhythm of his frustration. He looked up at the calendar on the wall for some time – three weeks into his new post and he had to negotiate with an insufferable weed dealer over the right to do his job. He turned again to Reza. 'Ok, from now on, no more trouble. You do your business but don't disturb the neighbourhood, don't disturb my men and don't disturb me. Every Friday evening, four o'clock on the dot, bring the small something for protection and you and your boys can go smoke yourself to hell. No fighting, no shouting.'

Reza shook his head and Baleri gaped.

'You understand, OC? You took my money and my goods. I know your men sold my stuff to those boys at the junction. You took my things and sold them and you ask me to pay for protection. The others never took my stuff, that's why I paid them. But not you, you understand? Not you.'

Baleri leaned forward, astonished by Reza's audacity. 'You want to spend the night in the cell? I will shoot you now and nothing will happen.' But the impotence of his own words rang louder than his voice.

'What sort of night has the bat not seen?' Reza delivered his words flippantly. 'You want me to pay for protection? Bring back my money and my goods, you understand. We can't be doing something while you are doing something too. It won't work that way.'

Baleri snapped the pen in his hand. 'Ok, don't pay up and see!'

Reza shrugged. 'OC, we've been in this business for long. Long before you even joined the police, you understand. We know people and you know it. What I say is only fair but if you think you can harass me, fine. *Allah ya taimake ka.*' He pushed back the chair and was rewarded with the irritating screech of wood on concrete. He rose and looked down at the fuming officer before walking out, thankful to escape the nauseating smell he always associated with police stations. He paid no heed to the five uniformed men sitting outside, even when they made furtive gestures to draw his attention.

7

Evil enters like a splinter and spreads like an oak tree

When Hajiya Binta peeked through her window to see who had disturbed her gate, she saw the Short Ones letting themselves in and laughing as if they were walking into their own house. Kareema and Abida swayed their hips, just as Fa'iza was now in the habit of doing. Binta, peering through the curtains, wondered why the girls felt the compulsion to torment themselves in such a fashion, even when there were no ogling men to tease. She scoffed, pouting and clucking at the back of her throat, drew the curtains and lay down to rest her eyes, tired from watching the needle jumping all morning as she worked on her machine. Moments later, she heard them salaaming at the door.

Fa'iza emerged from her room smiling.

'Kareema. Abida.'

The Short Ones smiled. They were in the same class as Fa'iza but were considerably smaller since Fa'iza had, of late, been sprouting like a reed. Kareema and Abida – born of the same father to different mothers – carried on like twins, dressing in matching outfits of different colours, Kareema persistently in the darker shades. They conducted themselves with the air of evolving women who knew, with a certainty bordering on arrogance, that they were beautiful. And they did not really care what the world thought of their height. Or what their mothers thought about their closeness.

Kareema was born first – by three days. But her mother, Aisha, was actually the second wife. Alhaji Babangida, their father, had married Zainab first. After a year without being blessed with a child, he married Aisha. The co-wives took the competition to heart and were soon racing each other to see who would first have a baby, seducing their husband each night and wearing him thin after his day's exertion at work, until he started faking trips and spending nights in hotels by himself, recuperating from too much sex. After Kareema was born a girl, Zainab desperately willed the child in her womb to magically transform into a boy.

After the birth of Abida, there was a race to see who would deliver the first son. Zainab won at the third attempt. That race was succeeded by the competition to deliver the most children, a contest that resulted in the two having thirteen between them. As the children grew, the mothers limited their interactions to flashes of hostile glares, while Kareema and Abida would be out on the veranda playing with stuffed dolls, much to their mothers' dismay. When the girls turned eight, and had refused to inherit their mothers' caustic quarrels, as their younger siblings had, Aisha did something dramatic. In a misguided attempt to disabuse Zainab of an unfounded claim of potent witchery, Aisha smacked her with a broom. A huge fight broke out. Neighbours, attracted by the ruckus, rushed in to break up the fight and were baffled to find the indifferent girls before Aisha's dressing table, painting their faces with the radiant colours of girlish dreams.

'What are you doing, Amin?' Abida caressed the lace fringes of her short hijab.

The Short Ones always called Fa'iza by her surname, which had originally been Aminu before Fa'iza decided to streamline it. Fa'iza Amin sounded slicker. Of course, she wished she could be more avant-garde without desecrating her family name. And the hallowed memory of her beloved father.

'Me? I was trying to get some sleep until I heard your voices. Let's go to my room.'

'What about Hajiya?' Kareema flipped her scarf over her shoulder.

'Hajiya? She's inside.'

Announcing their intentions to greet Hajiya Binta, the girls started making their way to her room.

'Ah, ah, Kareema, Abida.' Binta, who had no intention of letting them into the room where her indiscretions had manifested, filled the doorway in her saffron-coloured hijab.

The girls knelt to greet her and answered in the affirmative when asked about their mothers' wellbeing. But all through the exchange, Binta's eyes were on the *soyayya* novellas rolled up in Abida's hand.

'Don't you girls tire of reading these books? What value do they add to your lives anyway?'

'I asked them to bring them, Hajiya.' Fa'iza, quite conversant with Binta's mistrust of the Short Ones and their corrupting influence, stood behind her friends.

'They are the only things Fa'iza reads and now she even dreams of writing them someday.' Binta's eyes danced over the tops of the girls' bowed heads. 'And she had wanted to be a doctor, you know.'

When the girls said nothing, Binta asked after little Ummi and seemed satisfied when she was told that the girl had gone to the neighbour's house to play. Kareema and Abida rose and stiffly walked off to Fa'iza's room, carefully placing one foot directly in front of the other and resolutely keeping their hips from swaying.

'Let me see them.' Fa'iza shut the door and hurried over to the girls standing in the middle of the room.

Abida was amused by the desperate look in Fa'iza's eyes as she held out the books to her. Fa'iza shuffled through the titles: *So ko Kiyayya? Me Ne Ne Aibi Na?* and *Bilkisu Mai Gadon Zinari*. Fa'iza's shoulders slouched and she pouted. 'I've read all these, apart from the part two of *Mai Gadon Zinari*.'

'Oh, well, you are in luck.' Kareema sat down on the mattress. 'That woman who rented the second part has just brought it back. I will send one of my sisters with it later.'

From their bedrooms, the sisters ran a lucrative lending library of *soyayya* novellas, stacks of which they had accumulated over the last two years, renting a book out for the price of a box of matches per day. But with Fa'iza, they were generous and let her borrow whatever titles she wanted for free.

'Have you finished the others you borrowed?' Abida took her place on the mattress beside her sister.

Reluctantly, Fa'iza handed over the books and sat on the floor opposite the Short Ones. 'The others? Finished three. Will finish the rest soon. Don't you have anything else by Anty Balki Funtua?'

'Oh, sure.'

'Sure, she's good.' Kareema nodded. 'But sometimes she can be – a bit far-fetched.'

'Sure, what with the glass floors and all.' Abida agreed.

'I like her stories anyway.' Fa'iza smiled. 'Get me some of her latest.'

'Sure thing.'

'Sure, why not? But you have to give these ones back. Other people have been lining up for them.'

'Sure, and we need the money, you know. My aunt in Kano will be sending new books and we need to pay up.'

'*Kwarai, kwarai.*' Kareema was looking at her henna-dyed fingernails.

Fa'iza kept shifting her eyes from one sister to the other to keep up with their sure-sure. She wondered why two people would want to be so similar. Yet she admired them for it, as she envied them their army of siblings and their living parents. The thought made her lonely.

'What?' Abida looked into Fa'iza'a face.

'Oh, nothing.'

'She's missing her boyfriend,' Kareema laughed.

Fa'iza gaped. 'Of course not.'

'Sure.'

'Yeah, sure. She still doesn't have a boyfriend.'

'Sure she does.'

'Sure. Bala Mahmud.'

Bala Mahmud was the adorable boy in her class who always seemed desperate to help Fa'iza with her assignments and was eager to lend her his notes if she fell behind with schoolwork.

Fa'iza shrank at the suggestion. She had never thought of him in that light, really. Thoughts of Ali Nuhu had not left room in her heart for the likes of the boy who could barely express himself when in her presence. Not that he was much of a talker to begin with. 'Bala Mahmud? He's just a nice boy.'

'Sure. As if we are kids.' Kareema smirked and waved her hand dismissively.

'Sure.'

'He's not my boyfriend.'

'Sure, all right.'

'She's in love with Ali Nuhu,' Abida laughed. Kareema joined her and the sisters high-fived. Fa'iza laughed shyly and denied her infatuation with the actor.

'Sure. That's why his face is all over your room.'

'My room? Well—'

'Well, what?'

Fa'iza smiled coyly.

'*It's cool, I think he's cute.*' Abida, as she sometimes did, switched to English.

'*He's not.*' Kareema sounded unnecessarily belligerent.

Fa'iza's eyes popped. It was the first time, in the eventful seven months she had known the sisters, that she had heard the Short Ones disagree on anything. Overwhelmed by this insignificant bit of history, she opened her mouth to speak but could not say anything.

Abida spoke instead. '*What's wrong with him?*'

'*Blubbery lips.*'

'*His lips are fine.*' Fa'iza was shocked by her own voice. By its high-pitched ring of desperation, which she hoped would shut Kareema up.

'Sure they are.' Abida smiled and the undressed sincerity of it pleased Fa'iza.

'And he's arrogant too.' Kareema was not quite done with her offensive.

'Arrogant? He's not.'

'Sure he is.'

'Sure he's not!'

The sisters had a stare-down that, in reality, lasted all of three seconds. But in Fa'iza's baffled mind, it must have lasted an entire hour. Kareema rolled away from her sister, picked up one of the novellas they had brought and started flipping through the pages.

Abida got up and went to look in the mirror hanging on the wall, the one embellished with stickers of Ali Nuhu's face. Fa'iza picked up the book she had been reading before the Short Ones arrived and took up from where she had left off.

Abida patted down her nose with her palms and, satisfied with her looks, sought something else to engage her attention. Her eyes fell on a notebook at the other end of Fa'iza's mattress. She would not have thought much of it but for the words scribbled on the cover: *Fa'iza Amin's Secret Book.* She went and sat down on the mattress, her back turned to the other girls. She picked up the book and opened it. There were sketches of figures wielding clubs standing over a person on the ground. The felled figure was a little more elaborate, with a distinct beard.

She turned over the page and started reading what Fa'iza had written each time she had been hounded out of her tenuous sleep by the roaring shadows that prowled her dreams, and which were now manifesting in her wakefulness as well.

When the silence in the room grew uncomfortable, Fa'iza looked up and saw Abida hunched over on the far end of the mattress.

'Abida, please.'

Abida looked up at Fa'iza's troubled face and closed the book. She tucked it under the mattress. They looked into each others' eyes – Fa'iza seeing the glint of understanding in Abida's and Abida, moved, in no small measure by the glimpse of Fa'iza's secret struggles with something she could not name, saw her friend in a new light. It was a significant interlude in which trust and understanding were forged and Fa'iza felt closer to anyone than she had in years.

Kareema scrutinised her dyed nails once more and frowned 'I need a razor.'

Fa'iza rose and searched in her make-up basket. She offered the sheathed blade to Kareema and went back to her book.

Abida lay back on the mattress, scowling at the ceiling. 'So, you want to write?'

'Me? Maybe.' Fa'iza was still embarrassed that Abida had actually read the repository of her most private fears and terror-laden dreams.

'Why?'

'Why? I don't know.'

Abida looked at her sister expertly cutting her nails, collecting bits of henna-dyed fingernails into a little pile on the handkerchief spread out before her. She turned to Fa'iza and asked: 'What are you going to write about then?'

Fa'iza sighed. 'Me? Maybe I want to write about other things and other places and other people, about love and people being happy and not—' she was staring past the cream-coloured walls and the meadows beyond into a distant space illuminated only by the light of her imagination. 'I want to write about beautiful things.'

Kareema smiled with a hint of mischief. 'Speaking about beautiful things, I know a cute boy.'

'Who?' Abida sounded eager.

'Reza.' Kareema's smile took on roguish proportions.

'Reza?'

'Sure, he's cute.'

'*Oh! Shit!*' Kareema exclaimed.

When the girls looked at her, she was holding up a cut index finger, watching the blood trickle down it with a small smile on her face. Fa'iza's eyes widened and curiously her lips started trembling. And then her entire body, as if determined not to be outdone, caught on. Her little hurt-kitten whimpers terrified the Short Ones, who involuntarily drew together.

'What happened to her?' Kareema's voice quavered.

'I don't know.'

When little beads of perspiration started sprouting on Fa'iza's forehead and above her upper lip, Abida reached out to touch her. Fa'iza screamed like a vexed djinn in the profundity of night.

———

Jos: November 28ᵗʰ, 2008

Her father knocked softly on the door of the room she shared with her ten-year-old sister, Amina. 'Mommy, wake up, dear. Time for prayers.'

He also knocked on her brother's door and walked out into the predawn light to the mosque from which Manshawi's emotive recitation of *Sura An Nisa* from the Glorious Qur'an reached her.

Fa'iza had been close to her father, Mu'azu Aminu. Sometimes she thought it was because of the long wait he and her mother had endured before their first son, Jamilu, came, as she had been told, one dawn when the rain washed the silent hills clean. That was what her mother Asabe always said when trying to appease Jamilu – which was quite often. Everyone knew Jamilu was Asabe's favourite. Fa'iza was not quite sure about the rain because her mother herself was not sure about a lot of things. But it made sense when one considered that Jamilu had washed away the doubts about her fertility that had lingered for all of twelve years.

Two years later, Fa'iza was born and placed in her father's tender hands.

He looked at her, at her button nose and beady eyes, and his own eyes welled up with tears. 'She has my mother's eyes.'

So she was named after his mother, who had died after years of waiting in vain to welcome her grandchildren. When Fa'iza was still a child, her father would hoist her onto his shoulders and walk round the neighbourhood, introducing her as his mother to everyone they met. When she got older, she would sit on the *dakali* at the front of the house, looking in the direction of the setting sun. Her father, framed by the light of dusk, would hurry home from the Jos Main Market after he had closed his babyware shop. On the occasions he travelled to Lagos to stock up, she would sit with the stuffed doll he had bought her and look longingly into the evening light. Then she would go inside to her mother, always busy cooking, while her younger sister Amina would be strapped to her mother's back, shrieking like an enraged wild thing.

Even when she was thirteen, her father still offered her choice pieces of meat from his soup while Jamilu fumed. And then they would sit and talk about school and his business while her mother, sitting in the corner, told Amina stories about the clever spider and the dubious tortoise.

So that November morning, she knew she wanted to be by his side when the news reached them. He had returned from the dawn prayers and was hoping to catch the results of the previous day's council elections on the BBC Hausa Service. He had just turned on his shortwave radio when a neighbour, Umaru Sanda, barged in.

'What are you still doing here when the whole town has gone gaga?'

But because not even Umaru Sanda's dimwit wife paid much attention to Umaru Sanda, her father hadn't taken any notice. How could there be another riot when so many policemen had been deployed for the elections? But the sounds of gunshots drawing ever closer vindicated Sanda, who had since left to evacuate his family. Because they had lived through riots in 2001, 2002 and 2004 they knew their neighbourhood would not be safe. Their likes were far outnumbered. So Mua'zu started packing up valuables and Jamilu tried to roll the mattress off the bed. Amina clung to her mother's wrapper, both were crying.

Gunshots thundered close by. Then the banshee screams of Umaru Sanda's wife leapt at them from across the fence and shredded, with decided finality, any hope they had of the unfolding nightmare ending before it fully manifested.

'Where is he?! Where is he?!' There was a heavy bang on the door.

Amidst so much screaming and so many enraged voices, no one could be certain what was happening.

Mu'azu snapped out of his stupor first. 'The bathroom, quick!'

It was the sound of desperation in her father's voice that struck Fa'iza. And when she tried to look into his eyes for some reassurance, he turned his face away. They crammed into the bathroom, all five of them, and locked the door. In the small space, they waited, like the cows Fa'iza had seen packed into open trucks at the Yan Awaki market on their way to the slaughterhouse. The smell of overnight piss, still waiting to be flushed in the toilet bowl, swelled. But above it, the raw stench of fear made Fa'iza's head turn. She wanted to bend down but bumped into Jamilu.

'Watch it.' It was a whisper.

'Shush!' Even in that whispered word, there was anxiety in her father's voice.

Amina began whimpering and would have started wailing but for Asabe, who hugged her tightly, hushing her and suppressing her own cries.

'Keep her quiet.' Now there was anger in Mu'azu's voice.

Asabe held the girl and clasped a hand over her mouth. Then she herself started whimpering, her steady drone filling the silence.

Jamilu wriggled his way to the top of the toilet bowl and squatted, resting his weight on his legs. Fa'iza heaved and wriggled into the little space her brother had vacated.

When they heard the front door being bashed in, Asabe's stomach rumbled like a disgruntled volcano. 'I want to use the toilet.'

Jamilu's foot slipped and he hurtled into his father's back. They crashed into the door. The commotion outside blanketed the noise and they waited, holding their breath.

'*Ayatul Qursiy*,' Mu'azu ordered. Fa'iza mechanically started reciting the verse from memory.

'In the toilet?!' Jamilu was incredulous.

'In your hearts.'

But they froze as they heard the doors being broken down and furniture overturned; the crash of the TV and the splintering of glass. Some maniac hacked at the wall with a machete, the angry sound of metal on concrete and his hate-filled scream jarring Fa'iza's nerves. The warm smell of shit bloated and filled the room. Fa'iza turned to her mother and saw her mouth moving mindlessly, her face, in the dim light, glistening with tears and sweat.

Fa'iza felt a hand searching for hers and knew it was her father. He squeezed it and quickly let go. But she still sensed the trembling.

When they broke down the bathroom door, her father went first, hands raised above his head. Fa'iza felt a warm liquid run down her thighs and pool around her feet.

'Spare my children, please.' Mu'azu knelt down before the armed mob that had invaded the house.

'Kill him! Kill him! What are you waiting for?!' It was a woman.

Fa'iza knew then that she would never forget the voice of that woman. She would never forget the hate in it. She perceived the contagious nature of hate that makes one want to murder people they have never interacted with. Or people with whom they have eaten from the same bowl, mourned alongside and shared laughter, people with whom they have nurtured the verdant canopy of a friendship that was on occasions closer to kinship. But that woman's voice, in one sweep, ripped that canopy, letting the pieces fall, heavily, like shredded foliage around their feet.

Fa'iza stepped forward and saw the face of Jacob James, her maths teacher, who always dressed smartly – his shirt ironed and tucked in with a neatly knotted tie. The students made fun of his sturdy brogues because they had never seen him wear any other shoes. He always smiled at their jokes. But, that morning, he was not smiling. His face, made fierce by war paint, glistened with sweat and odium as he raised his machete and brought it down. Bright, red blood, warm and sticky, splashed across Fa'iza's face and dotted, in a fine spray, the shell-pink nightdress that her father had bought her.

———

She dreamt in sepia. Like rust-tainted water running over the snapshots of her memories, submerging her dreams in a stream of reddish-brown. But when the blood spurted and flowed, it would always be in astonishing red. That night, the sounds too echoed in her head – the dull thump of metal chopping into flesh. Cracking femurs. Splitting skulls. The first agonised screams. The moans and grunts. And the thunderous silence of disbelief that followed. She woke up panting and was further startled by little Ummi's frightened eyes peering into hers.

'You were screaming in your sleep.'

Fa'iza sat up and was shocked to find her dress, drenched with cold sweat, clinging to her skin. She got up and changed and then sat on her mattress, hugging herself. Ummi sat looking into her face.

'I am scared, Aunty Fa'iza.'

Fa'iza looked at her and patted her head. 'So am I.' She got up and held Ummi's hand. 'Come.'

With her other hand, she picked up the novella she had been reading before she fell asleep. She looked at the lovelorn face of the girl on the cover and wished she could disappear into the pages and be woven into the words. Into the sentences, into the story, where there would only be love. And sweet, whispered conversations wrapped in the veils of adoration. And marriages. And fragrant happy endings. No blood or chopped flesh or dreams in painfully toned shades.

Holding hands, they went to Hajiya Binta's room. Ummi knocked on the door. 'Hajiya, we are scared.'

Fa'iza tentatively opened the door. Binta sat up in bed and rubbed the sleep out of her eyes. She looked from her niece to her granddaughter, her gaze resting briefly on the book in Fa'iza's hand. She shook her head, made a clicking sound from the back of her throat and gestured for them to join her on the bed.

When they were tucked in beside her, Binta asked the girls to say a prayer to ward off the bad dreams and the officious Shaytan who implanted such terror in their hearts. Not long after, Ummi's steady breathing complemented the screech of the crickets serenading the night. But from the way Fa'iza lay, one hand tucked under her face, which was turned away from her aunt, the other hand resting on the book she had laid before her, Binta knew the girl was far from sleep.

'They will pass, these nightmares.' She squeezed Fa'iza's shoulder. 'They will pass.'

Fa'iza wiped the tears on her face and nodded. 'Do you still think about it?'

For a while, Binta pondered how cruelly fate had united her with this girl who was still grappling with the meaning of life. How they had both lost the men in their lives, almost a decade apart, to the conflagrations of faith and ethnicity, to Jos. Fa'iza had been a toddler when Zubairu left home and never returned, when it had first started on September 7th, 2001. She still thought about it, about how they said Zubairu's corpse was butchered and burnt in the street. She thought about it, all the time. 'Not any more, child. Life is too short to dwell on things that have already happened.'

Fa'iza nodded. 'But you still think about him, don't you?'

Binta sighed. 'I do. All the time.'

Fa'iza patted the book under her. 'You must have loved him a lot.'

'Love?' The word felt strangely heavy on Binta's tongue. 'I don't know, really. But when you have lived with someone all your life it doesn't matter whether you love him or not.'

'How can you live with someone you don't love?'

'In my day, we lived by what our parents taught us. We obeyed what they said. Now, things are different. Little girls like you are talking about love. And what good has that done to the world?'

Speechless, Fa'iza lay still and listened to Ummi's steady breathing, as the chirping crickets inscribed their own stories on the desolate night.

8

An elephant's tusks are never too heavy for it to carry

There was a shadow hanging over San Siro. Inside, in one of the rooms the boys shared, the stream of ganja fumes reached up to the bare rafters, where some of the youths had taken to stowing their personal effects: snakeskin amulets procured from shifty marabouts promising protection from the evil eye; bundles of medicinal bark reputed to cure ninety-nine ailments acquired from itinerant medicine vendors who cavorted with live crocodiles and displayed photos of people with disease-ravaged genitalia; and sometimes stashes of cash wrapped in plastic bags.

Dan Asabe lay on Babawo Gattuso's dingy mattress, staring up at a package squeezed into the thighs of the rafters. He seemed unmindful of the horrified faces looking down at him. When Reza pushed his way through the half dozen bodies and examined the huge machete gash on Dan Asabe's head, he saw that the blood had soaked up the black powder that Dogo the resident herbalist had administered to stem the bleeding.

'This thing is poisoning his blood.' Sani Scholar was squatting over Dan Asabe's prone figure with a bowl of warm, salted water and a piece of cloth. He still fancied himself the doctor he might someday become, should he ever go back to school.

'Don't you lay a hand on him.' Dogo was sitting against the wall with angry eyes, puffing on a joint. 'Don't waste my medicine, you hear?'

The damp cloth in Sani's hand hung between the bowl and Dan Asabe's battered head. 'Your herbs will give him an infection.'

'What the hell do you know, boy? I said leave him alone.' Dogo stood up and slapped the dust off the seat of his trousers. 'That is the problem with this place. Nobody listens. When Dogo says take this for *tauri*, take this for protection, people say Dogo is high. Now see what has happened.'

'Dogo, don't start now.' Gattuso glared at him.

'Why not? Before we left for this rally business, I said take this, take this. Reza said no, that nobody would attack us. Now see.' Dogo had offered, for a fee, of course, some charms and amulets for protection against all sorts of weapons. He had extensively investigated the potency of amulets procured from various mallams, often using himself as the guinea pig. He had dedicated himself to the pursuit of *tauri,* which would make his skin impenetrable to metal, a useful asset considering the occupational hazards of their existence. The procedure was never clear-cut as Dogo was prone to experiment with mysterious herbs and decoctions of questionable origin and intent, but his dedication to these pursuits had earned him a reputation as the resident herbalist of San Siro, and he was often consulted when there were stomach upsets, fevers or headaches to be remedied.

Dogo's standing, however, suffered when he had been forced to admit that he had indeed been swindled while trying to obtain an amulet that would enable him vanish in times of trouble. He had stolen from his mother and some of the boys at San Siro and gone on a burgling spree in the neighbourhood. When he had amassed enough money, he went to the travelling mallam and collected the talisman reputed to contain, among other things, the eye of a leopard. For a week he followed the instructions diligently. He refused to come into contact with water or eat anything that had been subjected to the torment of fire; he slept wedged between the wall and some bricks, for the charm demanded he slept only on his back. And he stayed away from babies, whose pee or puke had the power to render the talisman ineffective. After the prescribed seven days of preparations, he put on the amulet and discovered that he did not disappear. And when, in a fit of rage, he shredded the talisman, he discovered it contained nothing but the folded pages of old newspapers.

'Okay, Dogo, cut the crap. We gave as good as we got.' Reza leaned against the wall, his voice quietly authoritative.

'Sure.' Gattuso punched his palm with his fist. There was a timbre of pride in his voice. 'Kai! I must have slashed off that boy's arm—'

Dan Asabe coughed and Sani tried to make him comfortable by prodding the grimy pillow beneath his head. 'I think we should take him to the hospital.'

Dogo took a long last drag on his roll and cocked his head to one side. 'Can I get my balance now?'

Reza eyed him. 'Wait, like everyone else. You saw how the rally was disrupted before the boss settled us.'

'What do you mean? No balance? *Kan huran ubunnan*! With this broken head and the entire day in the sun, no balance? And I had to travel with my head hanging out of the bus like a travelling chicken, almost grazing my face against the flyover—'

'Dogo, that's enough now.' Gattuso cracked his knuckles.

'It won't work, Gattuso, you hear me? It won't work. I need my money now!'

'Come and take it then.' The challenge in Reza's voice was unmistakable. He looked Dogo in the eye. The tall youth looked away and started rolling another joint, grumbling under his breath.

'No one has got his balance yet.' Reza's voice took in the entire room. 'I am going to see the boss now about that. Wait until I return.'

As he stepped out into the compound and stood studying the battered bus parked out at the front, Gattuso caught up with him.

'Reza, we need to get Dan Asabe to the hospital.' Gattuso rolled his head. 'This thing doesn't look good.'

Reza thought for a while and hissed. 'Have you not lived through worse?'

'A lot worse.'

Reza examined the huge spiderweb crack made on the windshield of the bus by a rock missile. 'Next time, don't bring this *dan daudu* to any rally. He doesn't have the stomach for it.' He took a final look at the battered vehicle and walked away, the light of the evening sun in his eyes.

———

Reza reached the huge fenced house in Maitama, where peacocks walked the lush lawns. He was ushered into the anteroom where several other people, mostly elderly men, were waiting. A large flat-screen TV showed Barcelona in battle with Osasuna. He leaned against the wall and watched.

'The senator is in a meeting, you have to wait.' A man grinned toothily at Reza as if he had known him all his life. Reza smiled back.

'You know, elections are drawing close, he will be busy seeing all these people.' The man continued to smile as if imploring Reza to say something.

Reza said nothing.

'This is politics!' The man's voice made the seven heads in the room turn to him, glaring. When he said nothing more, the men turned back to the screen. The man drew close to Reza. 'Tough rally this afternoon.'

This time Reza deigned to look at him. The man adjusted his zanna cap, which had seen better days. The red and the blue and the yellow yarn embroided into it had washed out and there were strands of thread coming undone.

'Yes,' Reza nodded.

'All these people trying to cause trouble for the senator's candidate will be put to shame *insha Allahu!*' The man adjusted his old cap again. 'Did you know they tried to disrupt the rally? If not for Allah's favour, I tell you *wallahi*—'

The account the man gave of the rally, embellished with choice onomatopoeic expressions for effect, could have been plucked straight from a blockbuster. Reza, despite being a principal actor in the whole melodramatic episode, did not remember it that way. He did not even exist in the man's account. One of the other waiting men, probably as irritated by the man's incessant chatter as Reza was, said it was time for prayers and rose. The others followed him out to the mosque.

'Shall we go to the mosque then?' The man with the old cap stood uncertainly.

'You go ahead. I will be along shortly.' Reza slid onto a leather seat one of the men had vacated and threw one leg across the other. He turned his face to the screen but out of the corner of his eye he could see the man hovering by the door before he eventually went out.

When the men returned, Reza did not give up the seat and the man who had been sitting on it before stood deliberately over him until he noticed the scowl on Reza's face. He moved away and perched on the armrest of another seat occupied by his friend.

Men emerged from the adjacent room periodically and, each time, a young man in a shirt and tie would poke his head round the door and scan the faces. He would then point at one of the waiting men and usher him in.

By the time the match on the TV ended, Reza had given up trying to suppress his yawns. They came at regular intervals, and each time he felt more exhausted and leaned further back into the seat. He thought of Hajiya Binta and her long gone clumps of ancient pubic hair, and her gold tooth. It was then he allowed himself to think about the woman who had ridden towards him on a scented breeze, whose gold tooth still gleamed in the dimness of reminiscence.

———

He had been seventeen in 2003 when he next saw his mother. He was playing football with the other boys on the plot down the lane when she came. Because the field was small with a huge rocky outcrop in one corner, they played 'monkey post', with four boys on each side trying to sneak the ball through a pair of stones placed three feet apart at both ends of the field. Reza's team was playing skin, their bare torsos glistening in the dimming sun.

She must have been standing there for a while, behind the rock where the other boys sat waiting their turns, because when Reza looked up to pass the ball, he saw her. It was the radiance of her

flowing, silky white jilbab with sequins down the front, like little
mirrors catching the sun, which first arrested his attention. And
then he saw her face, and the pride beaming from it. He made
the pass and stood indecisively.

She was smiling when he finally walked towards her, stopping
by the rock to collect his shirt. The boys watched, and as soon as
he walked past them, the whispers began.

She was as beautiful as she had been seven years before but
the years had added crow's feet around her eyes when she smiled.
The fingers of musk wafted in his direction, drawing him to her.
He resisted and stared down at his dusty feet.

'You play well.'

He looked up and saw she was smiling and then looked down
again at his feet, grinding his teeth.

'My father used to do that a lot. Grinding his teeth like that
when he was angry. You are not happy to see me, are you?'

'What do you want?'

There was an irreverence in his tone that made her flinch.
He wished his anger had reached out and smacked her in the
face, because he could not do that himself. He wanted her to
understand that he wasn't the meek boy she had seen back in '96.
He had grown past the age of becoming and Reza had swallowed
whole the puny Hassan Babale who had clung to her jilbab all
those years before.

She sighed and adjusted the headscarf that framed her face.
'It's been a while.'

'Were you deported again?'

She held her breath for a moment. 'No, I wasn't. I came back
to see you.'

He looked up at her and their eyes met.

'I went to the house and they told me I could find you here.'
She glanced about her at the boys in the field. 'Look, let's leave
this place.'

He turned back and saw that the boys were gazing at them.
They must have figured out who she was by then, the great whore
of Arabia who had birthed him and abandoned him to scorn. He
walked with her up the lane, away from the football field to the
mango grove some distance away. They stopped, as if by unspoken

agreement, under a tree. He kicked away a fruit that birds had half-eaten and left to rot at the foot of the trunk.

'So, you've finished school?'

He scoffed.

'What happened?'

The concern on her face seemed genuine to him. He turned his head this way and that. 'I was expelled.'

She sighed. 'What for?'

'I was caught selling weed to some students and I broke a teacher's jaw.'

'*Ya Salam*! Why on earth did you do that?'

'Because I wanted to, you understand.' This time he held her eyes until she looked away and hugged herself, as if a cold gust had rattled her soul.

'Hassan, my son . . .'

'Don't call me that.'

She swallowed hard. 'Hassan. You have every right to be angry, I know. Whatever happened between your father and me was not your fault and it was wrong of me to make you suffer for it. But I am still your mother and . . .'

He dug his fingers into the bark of the tree and peeled off a chunk, exposing a colony of ants to the mild glare of the sun. The dazed creatures ran about chaotically while he broke the bark into tiny bits that fell to his feet. 'I have to go now. You go back to wherever you came from, *kin ji?*'

'Wait . . . please.'

Beneath the desperation in her voice, he felt an emptiness that might have hounded her across the desert and brought her running to him. But the anger he had lived with since the day she unclasped his little fingers from her jilbab devoured any sympathy he could have felt for her.

He glowered at her mouth, which was moving, trying to form words. She wanted to say something important. He could see that in her tear-filled eyes. But he was not interested. Not any more. 'If I had known you were coming I would have brought your stupid ring along.'

As he hurried away, he heard her calling his name. The voice reached out and yanked at his heart. He sprinted, as far away as he could get from the haunting hollowness in her voice and the whirl of musk that had lingered for so long in the recesses of his mind.

———

The young man beckoned at Reza from the door, before noticing that his eyes were closed. 'The senator will see you now.'

Reza opened his eyes, looked at his watch and then at the young man. Why would anyone be wearing a tie at a quarter to midnight? He rose and followed the smartly-dressed man into the senator's study. The old man was sitting on an exquisite leather settee positioned before a floor-to-ceiling bookshelf. He was peering at a file on his lap through the glasses on the bridge of his nose.

Reza knelt and greeted the man. The senator held up a hand and the two younger men waited. Reza scanned the books' spines and spotted titles on politics, philosophy and civil engineering. On the wall, there was a painting of the Eiffel Tower, from a period when men donned top hats and carried walking sticks and the women on their arms wore long extravagant dresses and dramatic hats. On the other wall, there was an exquisite painting of a semi-nude girl. He was haunted, not by her jauntily poised breasts but by her eyes, and the innocence they exuded.

Senator Buba Maikudi, who was a professor of civil engineering and owned Bulwark Construction, a company that had enjoyed favourable contracts under several governments, patted his stomach beneath his white *babban riga* and adjusted his glasses. He shifted his slight frame on the leather seat and rubbed his nose before putting away the file.

'Reza.' He looked over the rim of his glasses at his guest, as if just realising he was not alone.

Reza greeted him afresh, more reverently, but the man leaned forward and extended a hand. His grasp felt weak and Reza wondered, for an insane second, what it would be like to crush the hand of this powerful man. He was small, and he was getting old too, old enough to put wrinkles on his face, grey in his eyebrows and a quaver in his voice. He was sixty-nine. But his beardless face was still boyish and his eyes, above the rims of his glasses, were lively even this late in the night. Reza wished he could grow old in money like this man. He pushed away the image in his mind of his ageing one-eyed father.

'Ah, Reza,' the senator's voice perked up. 'Busy day at the rally, *ko?*'

'Yes, Alhaji.' Reza settled down on the rug.

'But how come you allowed the situation to get out of hand like that?'

'Alhaji, they came at us. They just wanted to disrupt the rally—'

'Yes, that was their objective. *Yan iska kawai!* I know who is behind this and we will be dealing with them soon, don't worry.'

'Anytime you give the word, Alhaji.'

The senator leaned forward as if to confide a secret. 'You see,' he whispered, 'politics is a tricky business. And you have to play your cards well. You know, this rally, ehm? I organised it to know exactly who is with me and who is against me. What do you think I would do with a House of Reps seat? You know I'm bigger than that.'

Reza nodded.

The senator leaned back and cleared his throat. 'I have been a senator twice and a minister three times. I am almost seventy; I am too old for this. That is why I said let that young man go to the House, because he is reasonable, is that not so?'

'Indeed he is.' Reza had never seen the man, Audi Balarabe, before the rally. He had heard that the man was a cousin of the senator.

'Come, Moses,' the senator beckoned the young man who had retreated to a corner of the room and stood against the wall, arms folded. 'You know Audi. Is he not a reasonable young man?'

'He is, sir.'

'You see.' There was triumph in the senator's voice. 'The problem with this country is that we don't want to make way for the younger ones to come in. That is the problem. Especially in our party. That is why you had these miscreants coming to disrupt our rally. But we will deal with them. *Shegu!* Is it not me they want to challenge?'

'How do we deal with them, Alhaji?'

'Reza, Reza.' His laughter belied his size. 'That is why I like you. You are always ready for action. But don't worry. When the time comes, *ko*?' He patted his pockets and looked around. 'Moses, ask Musa to get me some tea. You will have some tea, Reza, won't you?'

'Oh, no, Alhaji—'

'No? You are not married yet, are you?'

'Not yet, Alhaji.'

'So, why not stay to have some tea? It will be good for you, *ka ji ko*?'

Moses went to fetch Musa. Alhaji Maikudi stood up, stretched, and walked round the room.

Reza worried that the man showed no intention of retiring for the night. And the boys were waiting at San Siro.

'Alhaji, there's something.'

'Oh, yes. Yes.' He returned to his place on the settee. 'What is it?'

'The little . . . something for the boys. Because of the skirmish, we weren't sorted out—'

'Oh, yes. But I thought, ah, I thought I asked . . . well, never mind.' He reached beyond the armrest and pulled up a briefcase. He snapped it open and pulled out a wad of notes.

'One of the boys was badly injured, Alhaji. We need to take him to the hospital.'

The senator looked at him over the rim of his glasses and added one more bundle. 'You know, Reza, you don't come to me unless you are having troubles.'

'You are always too busy, Alhaji.'

'But we've been together for how many years now? All the politics, is it not to help you, our people? I am already rich, you know, and I am old. This entire struggle is for people like you, *ko ba haka ba ne*? We are just unfortunate to have terrible leaders in this country. But you don't even call to say, senator, *sannu da aiki*, except when you have troubles.'

'I call, Alhaji, but your people won't put me through.'

'My people? Sometimes you speak and I don't understand what you are saying, *wallahi*. Are you not one of my people? Or are you no longer with me?'

'*Haba* Alhaji, of course, I am.'

'Good. Good.' He handed over the wad of bills to Reza, who shoved them into his pockets. 'And how is your policeman? I hope he's not troubling you anymore.'

'Not so much. He just raided our place and took our stuff and sold it to other boys.'

'You see the injustice we are fighting?' The senator threw open his palms as if to receive an affirmation. 'That is why we must never give up.'

'Exactly, Alhaji. The man is new in the force.'

The senator snapped shut the briefcase and placed it back by the settee. 'They are just recruiting illiterates in the force, and yet there are qualified people out there looking for something to do. When you called me that time, I called up his boss immediately and said his boys should stop harassing my boys. If he disturbs you again, let me know. *Aikin banza da wofi*! You see now what I am talking about? They don't want the masses to eat, eh?'

Musa, a young man in his early twenties, came in with the tea and set the tray on the footstool by the settee. Moses was standing by the door waiting. He closed the door after Musa stepped out.

'Yes, Moses, give Reza my direct line. He is one of my good boys.'

'Yes, sir.' Moses whipped out a card from his pocket and handed it to Reza.

'If you call this number, Moses will take the call. Moses is my P.A. He is always with me.'

Reza thanked the senator, sat down for tea, wondering why anyone would want it at midnight, and listened to him talk as if the night was just beginning. When he eventually left for San Siro, it was a quarter to one in the morning, long after the dogs had tired of howling.

9

*A bird that flies from the ground onto an anthill doesn't know
that it is still on the ground*

The sewing machine whirred and chased the silence into the
corners of the living room. Binta squeezed some more oil under
the presser foot. She rummaged through the cardboard box next
to the machine and found a bundle of cloth.

'Are you going to sew that today?' Fa'iza gestured at the cloth
with the remote in her hand. She was sitting on one of the seats
with little Ummi perched on the armrest beside her, her eyes on
the TV.

Binta looked at the girl over the top of her glasses. 'What does
it look like I'm doing?'

The two women sitting across on the sofa looked at each other
– Kandiya in her dampened hijab and Mallama Umma with her
shrivelled face and sunken eyes that had witnessed sixty rains
and sixty-one harmattans.

Kandiya cleared her throat. 'Mallama Umma, perhaps we
should leave now.'

Mallama Umma looked down at her hands, the wrinkled fingers
blackened by henna. It was something she did whenever she was
confronted by a challenge such as this. In her six decades, she
had dealt with all sorts of children – nieces and nephews and
grandchildren – not wanting to go to school. To her, the challenge

posed by Hajiya Binta's case was not entirely peculiar. She shifted forward on the seat. 'Hajiya Binta, we have been waiting to see you and you just came in and went to your sewing machine as if we were not here.'

Binta looked up at the women, and then turned to her niece. 'Fa'iza, go to the kitchen and prepare the kasko.'

'Me? But Hajiya, I want to watch this—'

'Fa'iza, go now and prepare the kasko before Munkaila and his family arrive.'

Grumbling, Fa'iza got up and left. Little Ummi curled up on the chair, taking over the space Fa'iza had just vacated, and picked up the remote that Fa'iza had dumped on the seat.

'And you, what are you waiting for? Is there any age mate of yours here?'

'But Hajiya—' Ummi's protest trailed off into a grumble in the wake of Binta's fiery glare. She left, rocking from side to side like a swaying palm tree in irreverent winds.

For a while after the children had left, the whir of the sewing machine filled the room.

'Hajiya Binta,' Mallama Umma seized the opportunity as soon as Binta slowed down, 'we have been worried about your not coming to the madrasa.'

'Mallama Umma.' Binta's brow furrowed as she examined the stitches she had just made. '*Wallahi*, I respect you, but your coming to my house with Kandiya is a bad idea.'

'Mhm!' Kandiya gathered the folds of her hijab around her bulk. 'Mallama Umma, I will be leaving now.'

Umma put a hand on Kandiya's thigh. 'You women should stop behaving like children, *haba*.'

'This is the woman who came and insulted me in front of my granddaughter and now she comes here pretending she cares about me. *Munafurci kawai!*'

'It is not hypocrisy,' Umma spoke quickly before Kandiya could snap out of her shock. 'Whatever was said then was out of anger. Or have you forgotten how the Prophet, peace be upon him, admonished against anger, saying *laa taghdab*.'

'Leave the Prophet out of this, Mallama Umma. Leave him out of it.'

Umma smiled. 'You know you can't leave the Prophet, peace be upon him, out of anything, Hajiya Binta. We all live by his teachings and he admonishes us not to hold grudges against one another.'

Binta pressed down the foot control and the women had to wait yet again.

When the machine stopped, Umma cleared her throat. 'Ustaz Nura and the students, too, have been wondering if you've been ill, but your neighbours assured us of your good health. So we thought we should come and find out why you haven't been to the madrasa for some time now.'

Just then, the power went off and Binta hissed. She detached the foot motor and slipped on the pedal cord.

'I haven't been feeling too well, actually. Nothing serious, just *ciwon tsatsaye*.' Binta put her foot on the treadle.

'You see, we are growing old already – healthy today, ill tomorrow, which is why we must prepare ourselves for our encounter with Allah, the Merciful. A moment lost can't be regained and we never know when death will come knocking. Every step you take to the madrasa is like walking on the wings of angels and Allah will reward you. You know this, Hajiya Binta, and yet you allow yourself to lag behind.'

Binta sighed. Thoughts of her sins weighed on her. There she was, at fifty-five, cavorting with a hemp dealer who was younger than her youngest child. Faith reached out a hand and squeezed her tear glands and she leaned closer to the machine, pretending to thread the needle so the women wouldn't see her tears.

'Are you all right, Hajiya?' There was a note of concern in Umma's voice.

'I'm fine, Mallama Umma, thank you.' Binta raised her head and worked the treadle with some desperation, hoping to mask her tremulous state of mind. Her voice had almost betrayed her. She tried to focus on guiding the material into the feed dogs but the machine was running too fast, clattering as it ran, and the material zipped through her fingers.

There was a sudden racket as she lost control. The needle ran across her fingers, sending jabs of pain through her nerves.

'*Inna lillahi wa inna illaihi raji'un!*' Binta grimaced.

The women jumped to their feet and Fa'iza came running in from the kitchen. She froze when she saw the blood. Binta wrapped her wounded fingers in a piece of cloth and turned away from her niece. When the stabbing burned its way to her brain, she fell to her knees. The women were torn between attending to the agonised woman on the floor and the dazed teenager, with sweat on her upper lip, trembling like the last leaf of a baobab caught in the chilly gust of harmattan.

———

Munkaila arrived with his wife and children while Binta was still in the kitchen making masa and filling the corners of the house with the aroma of taushe sauce. She abandoned the kasko and, mindful of her plastered fingers, hoisted her youngest grandchild, Khalida, into the air. The eighteen-month-old baby squealed and buried her face in Binta's shoulder. Zahra, who had just turned four, put her arms around Binta's legs and pressed her little body against her. Sadiya, their mother, stood smiling proudly. When eventually she stooped to greet her mother-in-law, Binta looked with disapproval at Sadiya's translucent powder-blue veil, with its gleaming sequins, hanging from her shoulders and looping over her chest. And the silky hair peeking from beneath Sadiya's scarf. Sadiya noticed and adjusted the *gyale*.

Binta had had reservations about Sadiya when Munkaila had first brought her to Jos back in 2005. She thought the woman looked too delicate; her hair too lustrous, fingers and waist too slender, hips too narrow, nose too tapered to take in enough air, with eyes so wide they readily betrayed her frailty. Her beauty was such that when she stood next to Munkaila, with his dark, pudgy face and blunt nose, she made him look like the Beast. Binta had concluded that if her son had not made some money, Sadiya might not have married him – her rich father certainly would not have allowed it.

They all settled on the plush rug in the middle of the living room. Fa'iza knelt by the food flasks and proceeded to serve out masa on the plates, which she passed on to Binta who doused it with miyan taushe and topped it with choice pieces of meat.

Munkaila observed Binta's swollen fingers when she reached out for another plate. 'That looks bad, Hajiya.'

'Ah, it's nothing,' Binta smiled.

As if that was her cue, Sadiya reached out and took the plate in Binta's hands and picked up the serving spoon. 'Don't worry, Hajiya, I'll take care of this.'

Binta watched Sadiya's wrist deftly flicking as she ladled sauce on the plates. She disapproved of the way Sadiya soused the masa with too much sauce. Rich, spoilt children had no idea how these things were done.

'Come and fetch your plates, kids.' There was a tinkle in Sadiya's voice as she beamed at the children.

The little ones had been sitting cross-legged on the floor, watching Tom chasing Jerry on the screen. Ummi, delighted to have someone to boss around for a change, commanded Zahra to fetch her plate. Fa'iza carried hers and was heading to her room when Munkaila's voice made her stop.

'Fa'iza, are you sure you are all right? You've been acting funny, you know.'

Fa'iza smiled with none of her teeth showing, and proceeded to her room.

'What's wrong with that girl?' Munkaila directed the question at no one. Little Ummi sidled up to her uncle and whispered in his ear. He listened with a furrow on his brow. 'Why? What happened?'

Ummi leaned in further and whispered some more, her eyes gleaming.

'Get away from there, *'yar gulma kawai.*' Binta's voice had a mocking tone. The laughter of the adults rang up to the ceiling. Ummi made a face and went back to her place.

Sadiya shook her head, sipped some water and carefully set down the glass in the middle of the intricate pattern on the rug. 'Hajiya, you will teach me how to make masa this good, *wallahi.*'

Binta laughed drearily. 'To make good masa, you need an open flame and you can't stand the heat.'

'I can't, Hajiya? *Haba!*'

'You don't even know how to stoke firewood. The smoke will chase you all the way out of the house – all these gas- and electric-cooker girls who can't put their breath into embers.'

Munkaila, mouth full, directed impatient gestures at his mother, then his wife. They waited for him to swallow. 'I've been telling her how much richer food cooked on firewood tastes.'

'Oh, trust me, you won't want your wife smelling of all that *makamashi*; all that burnt rubber and whatnot.'

'People have stopped using firewood like that.' Munkaila motioned meaningfully. 'It's not healthy for the environment. That's why I had to get you the gas cooker.'

Binta nodded. 'I am fortunate, I know. But my neighbour here, Mama Efe, she sent her daughter to buy kerosene at the filling station the other day and after spending half the day in the queue, the girl was knocked down by a bike on her way back.'

'I hear the queues are back at the stations,' Sadiya addressed her mother-in-law.

Binta's eyes popped. 'Back? They never left.'

'And we produce oil in this country, *saboda Allah fa!*'

'Bad leadership, that's all.' Munkaila's smirk grew more profound. 'Bad leadership *kawai.*'

'And I hear they are already asking this president to contest.' Binta paused and took a sip from her glass. 'Do you think he will?'

'He's not supposed to because of this zoning agreement they have in the party, but he is in power now, I'm sure he will find a way around it.'

'If only Yar'adua had not died—' Sadiya reached out and wiped the sauce running down her chin.

'*Wallahi fa,*' Binta agreed.

Munkaila swallowed the food in his mouth noisily. 'Are they any different? Their interests are all the same, I think. They are all in it for what they can get.'

'I'm sure Northern leaders won't allow it.' Binta emphasized this by waving her spoon before her face. 'Oh no, they won't.'

'Hajiya *ke nan.*' Munkaila's tone was condescending. 'Northern leaders, Southern leaders, what good have they done the country?'

Binta had her mouth full and couldn't say anything. Just then, the power, which had come back on a while before, went off again and the children, in accustomed fashion, moaned in despair. Binta motioned to her grandchildren to come over for more helpings and she fished in the sauce for chunky bits of meat, which she judiciously placed on their plates.

———

The little Chinese-made generator with its blue tank sputtered and roared to life. Fa'iza pulled down the changeover lever and the power came on. The children yelped in delight and ran back to the room.

Munkaila had brought the machine in the boot of his car. He had removed it from its pack and set it up in the shed – a little affair of roofing sheets nailed together to keep such devices from the elements. The landlord had built the shed and, because she had had no other use for it before now, Binta had used it as a sort of purgatory for her broken furniture and fitments. It was some distance away from the house so the rattling noise wouldn't be unbearable, like Mama Efe's, which kept Binta awake until it was turned off late in the night.

Munkaila straightened and slapped the dust from his palms. Binta had been standing over him, showering him with prayers of prosperity, good health, and loving children to take care of him in his twilight years. His 'Ameen' was accompanied by a deep-throated, luxuriant laugh; the sort that Binta had never got used to hearing since he became rich.

'Hajiya, we need to talk.' He looked around, as if assessing the appropriateness of having a proper conversation in these surroundings.

'Really?' She was slightly disturbed by the grave expression on his face, by the tone of his voice.

He led her away from the rattle of the machine to the foot of the wall. He twirled his car key around his finger and allowed a moment of silence to grow between them. 'I am worried about Hureira. She has been calling to complain about her husband.'

'Oh, *la ilaha ilallahu*! This girl and her troubles!' Binta slapped her palms together before holding her chin between her thumb and forefinger in a posture of deep concern. 'You know, she called me two days ago and said they were quarrelling again and I asked her to maintain her home.'

'Well, obviously she isn't listening because she called last night and said she was going to slit his throat.'

'That girl has a leper's temper, *wallahi*, just like your father, God forgive him.'

'*Haba*, Hajiya!'

'Well, it's the truth and you know it. All this for what, mhm? See what this girl wants to do to herself; divorced already and now trying to end another marriage. If Hureira terminates this marriage, she will have me to answer to, *wallahi*.'

'What I think needs to be done now is for you and Hadiza to travel to Jos and talk to Hureira and her husband. I have spoken to Hadiza already—'

'Can't she even see how Hadiza is living peacefully with her husband?'

'It's all right, Hajiya. Just call her and talk sense into her. If it becomes necessary then you might have to go and reason with her in person.'

He watched her fold her arms across her chest, the way she used to after she had argued with his father. She had always captivated him, folding her arms like that and quivering with rage – an anger that would thrash around inside and then expire in a sullen sigh.

He considered the grey patterns on his white snakeskin half-shoe and sighed. 'Hajiya, there is something else.'

'What?'

'It's not about Hureira. It's about you.'

'Me?' She felt her heart lurch.

If he had glanced up at her face then, he would have seen the look in her eyes and the furrow on her brow that distinctly spelt guilt in bold letters. 'A man came to see me.'

She still held her breath.

'Mallam Haruna, he said his name was, the man who has been coming to see you.'

Finally, she breathed out.

'Are you all right, Hajiya?'

'Yes, I'm fine.'

He looked at her, but the letters on her forehead had already dissipated, leaving only a half-hearted frown. 'You know him, don't you?'

She grunted.

'Well, he said he's serious about marrying you and he came to ask for your hand. I spoke to Hadiza about it and she seems to think it's a good idea that you remarry. But I don't know what you think.'

She grunted again.

'Hajiya, you need to say something.'

'Did I say I want to remarry?'

'But Hajiya, ten years is a long time.'

She snorted. 'Look at this boy. What do you know about life to talk to me about marriage?'

'*Haba*, Hajiya, it's not my idea, you know. Hadiza seems to think you need a man around and I don't know how you relate with this Mallam Haruna.'

'That will be enough.' Her frown deepened.

He did not miss the note of finality in her voice. They stood awkwardly, their silence filled by the roar of the new generator.

'Ummi tells me Fa'iza had a fit earlier today. What was that about?'

'Blood.' Binta adjusted her headscarf. 'Fa'iza has issues with blood, and meat too.'

———

He came that night, Mallam Haruna, in a starched kaftan with a transistor radio pressed to his ear, and a cap that caught the light of the bare yellow bulb on the wall. He had a long history with radios running back some forty-two years. He was sixteen when his father had died in 1969 and bequeathed his son his prized possession – a black Silver radio with dual bands, a type they don't make anymore. He had listened to the world unfold around him, an endless river of tales streaming into his ears. He listened when the civil war ended in '70, listened when Murtala toppled General Gowon in '76, listened when Murtala himself was assassinated months later, listened when General Obasanjo handed over to Shagari in '79 and listened when Obasanjo returned in '99. Neither of his two wives had been a closer companion than the string of radios he had had over the years – and he had told them that in no uncertain terms. He was an honestly blunt man, Mallam Haruna.

Fa'iza went out and spread a mat on the veranda for the guest. Mallam Haruna thanked her and sat down. Because he was enraptured listening to the BBC in Hausa, he did not notice how long Binta took to come out. When she did, it was the fragrance of her perfume that first caught his attention. She stood for a while looking at a gecko primed to seize a blowfly under the glow of the bulb. Mallam Haruna sat looking at her, covered as she was by her enormous hijab whose hem fell to the ground around her feet.

The gecko moved, astonishing her with its speed. She barely glimpsed the fly's wings disappearing into the reptile's mouth. She moved away from the wall and sat as far away from her guest as the mat would allow.

'Ina wuni?'

He answered her greeting, wanting her to look at his cleanly-shaven face. He had had the *wanzam* shave off the grey hair sticking out of his ears and nostrils. He was glad for the light; it meant that his efforts wouldn't go unnoticed.

But her head was turned the other way, looking now at a cat sitting on the fence, staring at her with iridescent eyes.

'You got a new generator.'

Binta had known him long enough to know that he had a way of making questions come out like statements. 'Yes. My son bought it for me.'

'Oh, Alhaji Munkaila. He came.'

'As if you didn't know.' She was still looking at the cat, its white-tipped tail held up by its side like a defiant flag.

'Wait.' Mallam Haruna pressed the radio closer to his ear. They were interviewing the former minister of petroleum Alhaji Shettima Monguno. He was appealing to everybody to support President Jonathan, explaining how people were mistaken about the agreement the ruling party had of zoning the presidency to the North for another four years, and how voting in Jonathan, a Southerner, would be the same as voting in a Northerner because he was merely filling in the gap that President Yar'adua, a Northerner, left when he died in office.

'These people are amazing!' Mallam Haruna exclaimed.

Binta leaned further away from him still, resting her shoulder against a pillar. She hissed, long and hard. 'I hate radios, *wallahi*.'

'What! You hate radios! You don't want to know what state the world is in.'

'What state? Is it not always the same; bomb here, bomb there, murders here and there and hunger and war elsewhere?'

'You are being so pessimistic. Good things happen too, you know.'

'Switch it off.'

'What!'

'The radio. Switch it off.'

'*Haba* Binta—'

'Switch it off or I leave.'

He looked at her and switched off the radio with a heavy sigh. The generator continued to hum from a distance. The cat stood, arched its back, and took long, elegant strides on the fence. Then it settled down again to chaperone the cheerless couple sitting in the humid night, beneath the harsh light of the naked bulb.

'What did you tell the person you went to see?'

'Who? Munkaila?'

She said nothing.

'I told him I want to marry you.'

'And you think he can compel me to marry?'

'Hajiya Binta, you speak like a child, *wallahi*. We are building a relationship—'

'Look, we will talk about this some other time. I can't stay out in the night like this.'

'Why?'

She stood up. 'Because the cat has been looking at me.'

'Cat? What cat?'

She pointed. He saw the animal now, eyes gleaming with the intensity of jewels. He shooed it away but the cat sat unmoving, staring back. He picked up one of his shoes and feigned to hurl it. The cat only stared. When it finally stood up, Binta did not wait to see what it would do. She ran into the house, the folds of her hijab flapping like a curtain in the wind.

10

*The search for a black goat should
start way before nightfall*

Binta patted the bundle of Dutch wax on her lap. For a while she allowed herself the luxury of losing her thoughts in the intricate yellow-tinted horseshoe patterns scattered on the blue background of the fabric. She raised it to her face and buried her nose in it, filling her nostrils with the smell of new cloth.

'It's beautiful. But I can't accept it.' Her voice sounded muffled from behind the material.

Reza raised his head from the pillow and looked at her. 'What?'

'I can't accept it.' She placed the cloth on her lap once more. She wished she had said no from the beginning, when he first presented the gift. But she had been full of desire then. Now the footprint of that desire had been calligraphed into the bed on which they lay. And inside, she felt the tender incandescence that she now knew came from sin.

'You don't like it?'

'No, no. I do. It's so lovely. I just feel it's wrong to—'

'I bought it for you, you understand? For you.'

His caramel eyes, with their imploring look, sucked her in and teleported her back to that day, so long ago now, when she first looked into her son's little brown eyes and swooned in the cascades of maternal adoration. It disturbed her, this constant reminder of her son when she looked at Reza. But Reza was not Yaro. He was her lover. She sighed. It was the first time she had thought of him using that specific term – lover.

'You understand, I just want you to have it.' He was sitting up on the bed now.

She shifted her eyes from his and found herself gazing at his modestly built chest. She turned away when she saw that he was looking at her looking at him.

'All right, Hassan. Just this once. But I don't want you bringing me presents.'

'I bought it, you understand. I bought it. I didn't steal it.'

'Oh, no, I never said anything like that. I just meant you must have your mother who needs—'

'I don't have a mother.'

Their eyes locked – hers startled, his defiant. She got out of the bed and started dressing, picking up her clothes from the floor: her brassiere at the foot of the bed, her panties half-hidden under it and her wrapper close to the door. She looked around for her scarf.

He found it under his body, where his sweat had dampened it.

She accepted the scarf from him and tied it around her head. 'It's all right if you don't want to talk about your mother.' She sat down on the edge of the bed. 'I understand.'

Reza nodded and reached out for her hand. It was warm. 'Your hands are soft.'

Binta smiled and looked down at his fingers intertwined with hers. She closed her eyes and savoured the strength in his hand. Then he got up abruptly and started looking around for his own clothes.

'I don't want what happened the other time to happen again, you understand.'

'Oh, I always lock the gate now.'

He went to the mirror and patted the little anthills on his head. He tilted his face for some different perspective and, satisfied with his looks, turned back to her. The smile on her face pleased him and when she indicated the space next to her, he came and sat down.

'There's something on your mind, isn't there?'

He pulled out a wad of notes from his pocket and held it out uncertainly. 'I want you to keep this for me.'

'Hassan.'

'It's just for a while, you understand. I just need somewhere safe to keep my money.'

'It's not safe here. It's not safe keeping money at home.'

'It's not safe at San Siro either. This useless policeman is bugging me. I'm not sure what he's planning next. So I need to keep some money somewhere, in case.'

'You should open a bank account.'

'Really?'

'Yes. You should think about it. You can save some money and go back to school.'

'School?'

'Yes, Hassan. Don't you want to?'

'It's strange the way you say my name. Nobody calls me by my name anymore.' He was grinning. Then he remembered the last time she had called his name all those years before, his mother, with a gleam of gold in her teeth. He turned his face away from Binta.

'It's all right if you don't want me to.'

He shook his head. 'You understand—' he stopped to clear his throat, 'you, you are different. I respect you.'

When he thrust the money at her, she took it. She sat there on the bed, feeling her insides dissolving.

———

She opened the lowest drawer on her dressing table and found the leather-bound photo album. Tenderly, she brushed away the film of dust and pressed the album to her bosom. The dust of memory stirred and she could almost smell the times gone by. She could, she imagined, taste the briny tears and visualise the smiles, the cryptic winks and the little fragments of daily life that had coalesced into treasured memories.

She sat on the bed and flipped through the album. Halfway through the laminated pages, she found the picture. The four of them, her children, in 1987, lined up against a pocked wall, staring into the lens as if startled by their own existence. The photographer, a Yoruba woman, had strolled from house to house; a troubadour of images, scribbling memories with the ink of light.

Hadiza, at four, stood fingering her cheap beaded necklace, an Eid present from her father, the thumb of her other hand stuck in her mouth. Hureira stood next to Munkaila in garish make-up; startling red lipstick and three dots of eye pencil on her forehead, while Munkaila hunched forward, staring into the lens as if daring it. And, over his shoulder, her Yaro standing as if stealing into the shot, eyes wide and asking questions of life, arms hanging uncertainly by his sides.

She ran her thumb over his face, a reflection of her mother's, that demure Fulani woman of Kibiya. That day, after the picture had been taken, he came to ask her for Cafenol pills. She had turned her back on him. 'Why on earth are you standing there asking me questions? Go pick them up from the drawer.'

When he downed the pills, he sat down by the door staring into space, looking as if he wanted to be somewhere else, someplace where the warmth could seep into his heart. Across the compound, Hureira and Hadiza sat playing house with their plastic doll.

When she emerged from the bathroom, Binta saw the blank look in his eyes. She knew she had felt that way too, longingly wanting the Fulani woman to touch her, to call her name, to display even a hint of affection. He was the one she wanted to make hers, to claim for herself, for the memories she wished she had had with her own mother. She wanted to touch her son, to feel his temperature, to whisper his name and tell him it would be all right. She wanted to. But she could not. So she loomed over him. 'What are you doing sitting there?'

He said nothing, preferring instead to slink away and sit on the *dakali* and stare out at the street. He was there when the other boys spotted a girl in tight black trousers heading up the street. Her hair – permed in the Michael Jackson *Thriller* style – streamed behind her as she swung her hips ostentatiously. Then the chants started.

'*Biri da wando!*' the boys sang, running after her. Some ran ahead and pulled down their trousers and wiggled their little backsides before the embarrassed girl. The racket drew more boys from their houses and playfields and Yaro, too, was sucked in. Women in purdah came out and stood by the front door, trying to call back their sons, but their voices were drowned in the maelstrom.

Then the pelting started.

Missiles of damp mud struck the girl on her offending trousers, the imprint of dirt standing out starkly against the black of the nylon. She started crying, cowering and shielding her head from the missiles. The racket went up several decibels. Some women ran out and tried to dissuade the boys, but they were too many. In the excitement, they did not see Zubairu, who was not much taller than the biggest boys, until he reached out and grabbed his son. Like flustered bees, the boys scattered, dodging into neighbouring houses and running down slime-covered alleys.

Zubairu led Yaro by the arm back to the house. He stormed past Binta, who was busy washing the mortar in the compound. She turned it over and allowed the water to trickle out before wiping it clean with a piece of cloth. She poured in some damp guinea corn from the basin beside her and when she heard the flogging start, she began pounding. The harder the boy cried out, the harder Binta pounded, her pestle thumping heavily. Munkaila and Hureira abandoned their play to stand by the door, listening to the wails of their elder brother. Hadiza tugged at her mother's wrapper, imploring her to intervene. But Binta would not stop pounding.

It was her neighbour Mama Ngozi who rushed into Binta's room to rescue the boy. She led him to her room. But in the brief interval between fluttering curtains, Binta saw the raw welts on Yaro's back and legs. She saw the blood dribbling down from them. She turned her head away and kept pounding, oblivious to the tears streaming down her face. Finally, she put down the pestle. 'Hadiza, come let me see what is in your eyes.'

She knelt before her daughter and peered into the baffled little face. She drew the girl to her and held her tightly against her chest.

———

Zubairu sat on the sofa fiddling with the knob of his radio. Across the room, legs stretched out before them on the plastic carpet, sat Hadiza and Hureira. Their eyes were on Krtek, the wide-eyed silent mole going about his business on the 14-inch black and white screen in the corner. The volume was turned down because Zubairu was listening to the Voice of America Hausa service.

Zubairu hissed. 'This country is going to shits, I tell you.'

Binta, sitting on the prayer rug, whispered petitions to God into her upraised palms and patted her face. She leaned against the wall and counted her tasbih once more.

'Imagine!' Zubairu was grumbling again, 'Selling us off to the IMF! SAP this, SAP that! What nonsense structural adjustment? The kind of accursed leaders we have in this country—'

He went on ranting about SAP, about General Babangida and his proposed new constitution and illusory transition to civil rule. He went on about the bad roads, the cost of fertilizer, the unyielding taps and the wells that dried up once the rains ceased. He talked, but no one else said anything.

Patting his pockets, he heard the crackle of a plastic wrapper. He reached into his pocket. 'Yauwa, Hadiza, come have a sweet.'

Hadiza looked from her mother to her sister and then down at her hands tucked between her thighs.

'Come, come. Buttermint, eh?'

When he saw that she would not go to him, Zubairu got up and tapped her on the shoulder. She trembled at his touch. He considered her for a while and then unceremoniously dropped the Buttermint on her lap. He announced that he was going out and used a rag by the door to dust his shoes. The flapping curtain confirmed his departure.

That night, Binta lay beside Zubairu, irritated by his snores. Beneath his wheezing, she heard the wind whistling outside and, in the distance, a lonesome dog barking. She climbed out of the bed, crossed the room and opened the adjoining door to the living room where her children slept. The girls were on one mattress in the corner, their chests heaving. On the far side of the room, Munkaila was sprawled on another mattress. Beside him, Yaro lay on his stomach, shivering. Even in the faint light of the hurricane lamp, the welts on his back glistened from the soothing balm Mama Ngozi had massaged into them. Binta knelt beside him and felt his temperature. She was startled when he opened his eyes and looked at her, by the questions his eyes held.

She got up and fetched a cup of water and a foil of Cafenol and made him sit up and swallow the pills. When he was done, she took the cup from him and put it away. Then she did something she had never done before.

'Murtala,' she whispered and put an arm around his tensed shoulders, drawing his quivering body to hers. 'My son.' She felt his stiffness thawing, until he leaned on her body and they both wept quietly. She hoped that someday, unlike her, he would remember that his mother had once called him by his given name.

The next time she dared to call him by his name, years later, he was lying dead in her arms, his blood drenching the ground.

———

Little Ummi rushed in and whispered something to Fa'iza. Fa'iza shut the novella she was reading and hurried out of the room with Ummi following. When she burst into Binta's room, they found browning pictures on the bed, an open album beside the pile and Binta poised with a photo in her hand. Fa'iza cautiously peered over Binta's shoulder. She saw the picture she was holding. Even with Binta's thumb on the young man's face, Fa'iza knew it was her cousin Yaro.

'Hajiya, are you crying?'

Binta wiped away the tears from her eyes and sniffled. 'I'm fine.'

Fa'iza sat down and put her arms around her aunt's shoulders. Binta shrugged her off and, holding her hand to her face, hurried to the bathroom.

11

A hyena cannot smell its own stench

After growing wings through indiscretion, Hajiya Binta, contrary to her expectation, did not transform into an eagle, but an owl that thrived in the darkness in which she and Reza communed. Yet, during the day, she was caged by her fears, wrapped in the perceived miasma of her sin.

On the day she decided to venture to the market, she doused herself in perfume, took a deep breath and headed out of the gate. Each time she walked past anyone, she looked down and held her breath. She would look over her shoulder to see if they were looking at her. Relieved, she would walk on.

She ran into Mallama Umma returning from the market clutching a plastic bag to her bosom with some spinach peeking out the top. The older woman stopped right in front of her. 'Hajiya Binta.'

'Mallama Umma, *kin wuni lafiya?*'

'*Lafiya lau*. Where are you going?'

'Oh, the market. I need to get some things.'

'I thought Fa'iza did all your shopping.'

'I don't want her having trouble at the market. I need to get meat from the butcher and Fa'iza can't stand that.'

'Oh, too bad really. Perhaps you should take her to Ustaz Nura for prayers.'

'You think that would help?' Binta was mindful of Umma standing inches away from her.

'Well, you have to try. It seems she's getting worse.'

'I will do something about it. But I have to go now.' She hurried past.

'Hajiya Binta, hold on a bit.'

She stopped and held her breath.

'When are we going to see you at the madrasa?'

'Oh, certainly one of these days, *insha Allah*.'

'I hope so.'

There was a stream of people coming from the direction of the market and Binta walked towards them feeling as if everything was coming her way. She skipped round the muddy middle of the road where the barrage of motorcycles had trudged rainwater into the dirt, forming a slushy pool. She joined a crowd in front of the grocery shed run by the Igbo couple. The little bird-like woman was inside taking orders for ugwu, spinach and curry leaves. Her husband was outside, gutting fish and slicing them into plastic bags for customers. When the woman saw Binta she beamed. 'Hajiya, long time O. What do you want?'

Binta bought fresh tomatoes and crayfish and moved on. At Balarabe's shed, the glittering trinkets caught her eyes and Binta procured some cheap earrings for little Ummi. While she was buying beverages from Salisu's shop, she realised how much she had missed the vibrancy and chattiness of the market. The colours; the green of the vegetables and the red of cayenne and tomatoes, the yellow and blue of plastic merchandise showcased outside shops, the smell of decaying vegetables cast into the middle of the dirt road, of smoked fish on wire mesh by the roadside, of drying ginger and tamarind at Mallam Audu's spice shop where she bought garlic powder.

She thought of Fa'iza as she watched the butcher cut pieces of meat on his table with a scimitar-like knife. He packed the pieces into a transparent plastic bag, knotted it and handed it over to her. She put it in her bag and went to Nura Jangali's grain shop for some measures of guinea corn.

When Jangali bent over and was measuring out the grains, Laure, the petite whore from Magajiya's brothel on Bappa Avenue, stormed in and pounced on him. Binta was surprised by the abruptness of the attack, and the ferocity of the little woman. Jangali overcame his initial shock and grappled with Laure's hand. Binta stepped in and pulled the angry tart off the man.

'Who is holding me like this? Allow me deal with this man *dan ubanshi*!' But when Laure turned and saw Binta's matronly face, she allowed herself to be restrained. Laure went on to issue warnings to Jangali, whose daughter had apparently been in a fight with hers.

When she was done, Laure disengaged herself from Binta and breezed through the crowd that had gathered, blocking half the road.

Binta picked up her measures of grain and headed home, transformed by the thought that she had held one of the famed whores of Bappa Avenue in her arms and the only smell she could perceive on her was that of cheap cocoa butter cream.

————

Reza now had to call each time he was coming so she could leave the madrasa at break time to find him sitting on the rear fence waiting. Sometimes they didn't make love; they just sat on the bed and talked – about opening a bank account for him, about his going back to school, about sin and forgiveness and prayers, and God's infinite mercy. Once, after she had told him she had never watched porn, he had come with a DVD of blonde women desperately slurping over manhoods as if sucking the milk of life. Disgusted, and aroused, Binta ran to the bathroom to spit and Reza ran after her laughing. As she leaned over the toilet seat, he raised her wrapper and took her from behind. Her cheery laughter rivalled the noises from the video in the living room and was barely masked by the generator, whose metallic drone reached them through the little window high up on the bathroom wall.

On another day, he came with lacklustre eyes and sat on the floor. He prepared a joint, licked the ends and lit it with a lighter from his pocket.

'What are you doing?' Binta sat up on the bed, alarmed.

'Understand,' he gestured with his hands as he puffed, 'sometimes, life fucks us all.'

'You can't smoke that thing here.'

'You want to have some?'

'Hell, no! Put it out. Now!'

'Someday, I will die.' He looked dreamily into the distance. 'And then they will say, oh the bastard is dead. And the boys at San Siro, they will sit down gloomily, roll up and light up and say, Oh! Reza, the motherfucker, he did this and he said that, you understand.'

'What are you talking about?' She was suddenly frightened.

He looked at her through the fog of odorous smoke rising to the ceiling like the tenuous fingers of time. 'And you, maybe you will say, Oh, Reza? I used to know him, the dickhead. But you will be too embarrassed to mourn me, you understand, because I live in the shadows of your life.'

'What are you talking about? Why are you talking like this?'

He smiled stupidly and waved the joint before his face, the smoke drawing dissipating patterns in the air. 'My poor old father, you understand, he will say, Oh, that boy has always been trouble but he's my son, and tears will come out of his good eye. And that *woman* in Jeddah, she will be too busy being fucked by some Arab she won't even notice. *The whore!*'

Binta shivered, rattled by the anger in his voice.

He wiped away a tear and puffed on his joint, lay down on his back and watched the smoke coil up to the ceiling. 'And God? He will have his angels question me. They will say, you, wretched son of Babale the one-eyed old man, you mugged this person and you did in this one, and slashed off that idiot's hands and of course, dishonoured so and so person's daughter and sold ganja to this other great dickhead, who went and raped his sister and broke open his father's head with a machete.' He paused. 'Have you ever thought about it, Hajiya? Of Judgement Day?'

She sighed. 'May God forgive us all.'

'You know what I fear most?' He paused and looked at her. 'The moment I will be asked what good thing I have ever done in my life and I can't think of any.' He jabbed the air with his joint, as if putting an invisible full stop in nothingness.

'There must be something. Please, stop talking about death.'

She reached out and he, disenchanted by the joint, allowed her to take it from his hand. She convinced him to perform his ablutions and say his Salat. He went through the motions with the impatience of one desperate to get on with other things, his forehead barely touching the tassels of her prayer rug.

He came one night, long after most well-meaning folks had gone to bed, and knocked faintly on her windowpane. She was frightened until she made out his whispered voice. Slithering across the bed, she parted the curtain.

'What are you doing here? Are you crazy?' She, too, spoke in hushed tones.

'No, just wanted to see you.'

'It's two in the morning, what are you doing out so late?'

He grinned and held up a roll of papers and a paintbrush. 'Just out with some of the boys sticking up posters.'

'In the middle of the night?'

'It's the best time. No one to say, hey, don't put that on my house, you understand.'

'Whose posters?'

He put down the roll under his arm and held one out for her. In the dim light, she made out the face of the president with his fedora.

'*Allah ya isa!*'

Reza laughed. 'Hey, I don't like him either but that's what my boss paid me to stick up, you understand.'

'Well, go now before the children hear you.'

He smiled, picked up his things and headed to the back of the house where he scaled the fence and went about his business in the dark, in the night.

The next morning, on her way to the flea market to buy thread for her sewing machine, Binta saw the posters pasted on trees and power poles and on the façades of houses lining the streets. On any space that was within reach. But most of the posters, having provoked the ire of house owners and those not particularly well disposed towards the president, had been ripped off, leaving only traces of where they had been. She couldn't help feeling sorry that Reza's overnight work had been ruined.

When he came that morning, she ran a hot bath for him to wash off the glue under his fingers and the leftover sleep in his jaded eyes. And, because he still would not open a bank account, each time he came his money continued to swell at the bottom of her suitcase, beneath the folds of her camphor-scented cloths.

———

At night, sometimes, she would sit down on the veranda and submit herself to the advances of Mallam Haruna, who had the noble intention of having her compete for his heart with his radio. He would dutifully switch off the transistor radio each time she came out and shook her hijab, liberating the scent of jasmine.

She would listen to him recount and analyse the news, how the politicians were depleting the federal accounts to run their campaigns, how the former vice president and the accidental president were slinging huge gobs of mud at each other. Mostly she just listened but once in a while she chipped in.

'They won't let Buhari win.' She was candid. 'They know he will deal with all of them, the corrupt bastards!'

'Sure he will,' Mallam Haruna beamed. 'The General is a no-nonsense man, that's why all these powerful men are ganging up against him.'

'But we the people are behind him and we are going to make sure he wins.' Binta was enthusiastic.

Mallam Haruna laughed. 'Don't delude yourself, Hajiya, we all know how elections are held here. You vote, they announce whomever they want to announce as winners. You can go jump in the well if you don't like it. Nobody gives a damn really.'

'Oh, that was before. Now there's an honest man at the electoral commission. He will make sure elections are free and fair.'

'What can one man do against a corrupt system?'

'Oh, you will see.'

But before he could say anything, the gate was pushed open and a woman came in lugging luggage. As her silhouette approached, Binta held her breath and tried to make out the figure.

Eventually, the silhouette became her daughter, Hureira. '*Ina wuni*, Hajiya?'

Binta looked at her daughter's puffy eyes and turned her face away to the cat with its white-tipped tail and gleaming eyes chaperoning them from the fence.

12

A snake will always beget something long

For the third consecutive morning, Binta woke to the aroma of omelettes and the strong smell of café au lait. Hureira, having inherited her father's affinity for coffee, amongst other things, had scoured the shops the first morning after her arrival. When she came back with three tins of Nescafé, a bottle of shampoo and a pack of sanitary pads, Binta knew that her daughter's matrimonial strike would linger.

Hureira, desperate to apply herself, had scrubbed the kitchen units and made the floor tiles glisten. Binta returned from the madrasa the first day and was astounded by the sparkling whiteness of her bathroom fittings. When she ran her finger over the cistern, it actually squeaked. She was uncomfortable with Hureira cleaning up after her, in her room, where evidence of her fornication might be found. So she took to locking her bedroom door each time she went out.

Amidst the clatter of utensils in the kitchen and the protest of potatoes or some unfortunate eggs being fried, Hureira's voice would startle the habitual peace of breakfast time. 'Ummi, eat up. You mustn't be late for school.'

Ummi would look up at this mother she had not seen for half the months on the calendar, marvelling at the sheen of the honey and egg-white face mask she was wearing.

Fa'iza would look up from her breakfast or from the handheld mirror into which she was pouting. 'Late? We are not going to be late, Aunty Hureira, *haba!*'

Hureira would look at her daughter. 'Ummi, you are spilling crumbs on your uniform, for God's sake!'

Ummi, stunned by the aggression in her mother's voice, would brush away the crumbs and lift the mug to her mouth, looking over the rim at her mother now busy flipping an omelette in the pan.

After the children had gone off to school, Hureira would lie on the couch with slices of cucumber over her eyes, allowing her face to benefit from the wonders of whatever concoctions she had applied. She would say, 'Hajiya, *a dawo lafiya*,' when Binta breezed past on her way out to the madrasa. The older woman would only grunt and shut the door behind her.

After three days, they still had not had *the* talk.

Until Reza called Binta's phone. She was at the madrasa, just after Ustaz Nura had left with his *Fathul Majid*, from which he had just read, under his arm. Mariya, one of the students, heaved up the bag from under her desk and placed it on the table. She proceeded to draw out baby wares, assorted flip-flops, printed *Ankara* wax cloths, heady incense from the Orient and exotic underwear from the Occident. Mariya had a piece from all corners of the world in her bag.

The women crowded around her. They fingered the fabrics, sniffed the incense and tried out the printed material against their complexions.

'I am dark; I think this will go with my skin tone.'

'Don't you have a bigger size for this, Mariya?'

'This bra won't fit my boobs, don't you have a bigger one?'

And in the middle, Mariya sat, handing out goods. 'This will suit you just fine.' Her voice was coated with the sweetness of a practised merchant.

Binta feigned interest in a pair of slippers whilst she cast sidelong glances at the booster pills and vaginal creams and ointments Mariya had displayed on the table. Women with husbands contemplated these, unscrewing the lids and sniffing the contents.

'Try this, you can thank me tomorrow.' Kandiya picked up a small jar and handed it to another woman.

Binta's phone rang. She dropped the slippers and rummaged through her bag. She found the phone and looked around at the women. They, too, were looking at her as she said hello into the phone and hurried out of the class.

'Hi.' She stood under the zogale tree outside.

'You're still at the madrasa?' Reza's voice sounded hazy.

'Yes. Did you go to the house?'

'No. You asked me to wait until you called first. It has been two days since.'

'I know,' she whispered into the phone as some women from the madrasa walked past. 'She's still here.'

'When is she leaving?'

'I don't know. She is waiting for her husband to come and do *biko*.'

'Oh, runaway wife.'

'Unfortunately. Do you want to see me?'

'Yes.'

She cradled the phone closer to her ear and sighed. 'Don't worry. It's just for a couple of days, I'm sure.'

'OK.'

'Have you been taking care of yourself?'

'Yes.'

'And your prayers? Have you been praying?'

'Yes.'

'Try not to neglect your prayers.'

There was some hesitation. 'I will try.'

'I will see you soon then.'

'OK.'

She hesitated. There was also a long pause at the other end. When the call had ended, she was not certain who pressed the button first.

——

Binta emerged from the bedroom with a plastic basket of hairdressing paraphernalia. 'Come braid my hair.'

Hureira, who was lying on the couch flicking through an old magazine, sat up, collected the basket and placed it by her legs.

Binta sat on the rug between Hureira's thighs and took off her scarf. Hureira opened the jar of hair oil in the basket and massaged blobs of it into her mother's thick, dense hair. She took a yellow plastic comb from the basket and proceeded to untangle Binta's hair.

'You are going grey, Hajiya.'

'I know.'

They fell silent as Hureira picked up the *misilla* from the basket and expertly ran the metal tip along Binta's scalp, drawing intricate patterns in her mother's hair. She dipped a finger in oil and briskly ran it along the swathe the *misilla* had made before she started weaving curving cornrows.

'*Wayyo*! Not so hard, Hureira, you are not fighting with my hair.'

'I'm sorry.' Hureira's grip on the hair slackened. 'You are angry with me, Hajiya.'

'No.'

'You haven't said anything to me since I came. Do you want me to leave?'

'What mother would want her daughter to be a serial divorcée?'

'I'm not a divorcée, Hajiya. *Haba*!'

'What are you then? First marriage annulled, second one on the rocks.' Binta felt a tug on her hair. 'Don't yank off my hair, you.'

Hureira's first marriage had come loose after twenty months. The unravelling had started with one of those insignificant tiffs that characterise marriages. She had found Cyprian Ekwensi's *The Passport of Mallam Ilia* amongst her husband's things. The novel was a gift from a former girlfriend with the provocative inscription 'With all my love'. Even though it had predated their wedding by two years, she had set the book ablaze and inadvertently burnt down her marriage. After that, the arguments had become more intense, more frequent, fuelled perhaps by her husband's inability to hold down a steady job, which had been Binta's major objection to the marriage in the first instance.

Hureira patted her mother's hair and gingerly grabbed a handful. 'The least you could do is to ask me what happened. But no, you just made assumptions.'

'Only a fool asks why a man and his wife are quarrelling.' Binta's voice, at that point, was quiet, deep and confident. 'I did not marry you off a child. I trained you well before you went and chose that good-for-nothing for a husband. You messed that up, as expected. Now Allah, in His infinite grace, has given you another opportunity and you are messing that up as well.'

Hureira picked up the comb and yanked. Binta felt her hair being tugged from the roots and winced. She could imagine the scowl on Hureira's face, how she must be biting her lower lip, as her father Zubairu used to do.

'It's not my fault, Hajiya.'

Binta said nothing as Hureira parted her hair, applied oil and yanked again as she began to weave another cornrow.

'You don't expect me to sit down and allow him to trample over me. I'm not that kind of woman.'

Hureira kept parting and combing, yanking and weaving. And Binta endured. She flinched each time her daughter put down the comb to reach for her hair. She did not want to give Hureira the satisfaction of knowing that she was hurting her. Finally, she cleared her throat.

'They say a patient man cooks a rock and drinks its broth. Your quarrel is with your husband, not with my hair.'

'I'm not quarrelling with your hair.'

'But you are quarrelling with your husband.'

Hureira said nothing.

'You chose him from among your suitors, this husband of yours, as you chose the one before him.' Binta massaged her forehead to ease the pain at her hairline. 'I did not choose your father. We didn't even have a courtship. Yes, we had our differences but we still lived together until he died. We raised four children, your father and I, and we never talked about love.'

'That was then.'

'And what has changed? Husbands and wives still quarrel and make up, why can't you? You compromise a little and you make peace. Stooping to a dwarf is not a shortcoming.'

Hureira finished the last row and put the comb and *misilla* back in the basket. She screwed the lid on the jar of hair oil and put it back in with the other things.

Binta trawled through the basket until she found the handheld mirror. She twisted her neck this way and that so she could examine Hureira's handiwork. She nodded, barely. 'It's a bit taut.'

Hureira kicked away the basket, almost spilling the contents, and moved her legs away from her mother.

'I pray your daughter doesn't inherit this leper's temper as you did from that father of yours.'

Snatching up her magazine, Hureira rose and as she stomped to Fa'iza's room, her mother called.

'Go and make peace with your husband and don't be living here in shame, *mara kunya kawai.*'

The sound of the door slamming marked Hureira's depature. But the shadow of her rage lingered in the living room like dark clouds in timid skies.

———

Hureira woke up the next morning with hangover rage. She banged the utensils while making breakfast. No one came to find out what the racket was about. She ate standing over the worktop and, having quelled the unrest in her stomach, retired to her room. Her honey and albumen masked face and cucumber-shaded eyes faced the ceiling in an icy glare as she lay down on the mattress.

Fa'iza crouched at one end of the other mattress, scribbling into her Secret Book. At the other end, Ummi sat looking from her mother to Fa'iza. Eventually she got up and left the room.

When Fa'iza's hand started to tremble, she slammed the book shut and huddled against the wall. Her eyes jumped around, bouncing off the ceiling, to the mirror on the wall embellished with stickers of Ali Nuhu, to the ceiling fan languidly slicing the light. Then, she started whimpering.

Hureira carefully raised the cucumber from her eyes to see what was happening. She hissed, got up and walked out of the room. In the living room, she turned on the TV and flicked through the channels.

In her room, Binta sat on the bed reading Priscilla Cogan's *Compass of the Heart*. Every now and then she looked up to see Ummi dressing up her stuffed doll, winding a piece of cloth around its head, laying it down or burping it. Binta would smile and return to the book.

When the noise of the TV from the living room reached Ummi, she picked up her doll and ran out. She stood and watched Hureira scowling at the TV and flipping channels.

'Mommy, can we watch the cartoons?'

Hureira flicked back to the cartoon channel and flung the remote onto one of the seats. She watched Ummi sit down on the floor, not too far from her, her eyes trained on the TV. She saw her daughter's dainty smile, the dimples on her cheeks, the excitement gleaming in her eyes. When Ummi chortled, Hureira felt her anger defrosting.

She remembered the first time she looked at this child of hers, wrapped in a fluffy shawl in the hospital, and understood what the joy of being a mother really meant. Even though Ummi looked like her father, a man Hureira now loathed, she felt the glow spreading inside, filling her up.

The screen went blank. Mother and daughter instinctively looked up at the light bulbs that were now dead. Yet another power cut.

Ummi whined. Hureira sighed and got up. She opened the door and went out to the generator shed. She saw the blackened side of the shed where the generator exhaust had been blasting since it was installed there. She saw the expanding blotch of machine oil that had trickled from the generator. But the machine wasn't there. She looked behind the shed and then at the gate that was still latched shut. Then she looked around at the fence.

'What do you mean the generator is gone?' Binta rushed out of the room after Hureira had reported her find.

Hureira followed at some distance. 'We need to call the police.'

Binta looked into the shed and behind it and satisfied herself that the machine was in fact gone. The only person she could think of calling was Reza. 'Bring me my phone, Fa'iza.'

It was Ummi who found the footprint; evidence that a large-footed miscreant had scaled Binta's fence, yet again.

13

*One whose mother is by the stove will not lack
soup in his bowl*

At San Siro, Reza sat on a bench with a wad of notes in his hands.
The young men presented themselves before him one at a time
and he handed out a thousand naira note to each of them. He
yawned, wearied by all the shouting and exuberant antics he had
put on at the rally, as had most of the boys. He wiped away the
dust in his eyes and continued to hand out the notes.

But soon the boys, whose scant sense of propriety had been
melted by the punitive sun and were now animated by the prospect
of getting paid, began to push and shove. Their outbursts and
cursing rivalled the noise coming from the flea market by the
corner. Reza stood up on the bench and held the notes high
above his head. 'You will keep quiet now and behave yourselves,
or I'm not paying.'

One of the rented boys pumped his fist with revolutionary gusto.
'No way, man! No way! After all this wahala! *Allah ya sauwake!*'

Reza glared at him. 'You said something?'

The thug looked into Reza's daring eyes, shook his head and
withdrew into the crowd.

'You understand, I don't like this nonsense. That's why I never
handle this myself. If Gattuso were here, you would be dealing

with him because I don't like idiots shouting at me because of a little money. Everybody who was at the rally will get paid.'

The chaos dampened by Reza's temper, payment went on without a hitch. Having dispensed the task, Reza retreated to his room. He flopped on the mattress, looking indolently at the giant poster of the AC Milan squad. Eighteen months on the wall – masking the emptiness of the room – had taken some of the gloss off the poster. He turned away from it and faced the door, just as Sani Scholar and Joe came in.

Sani held up the curtain. 'The bus drivers are here to see you.'

Reza rose and walked past the duo. The two bus drivers were standing by the door, arms hanging by their sides. One was Yoruba and the other Kanuri, but Reza thought they looked alike; the same worn faces, the same sweat-stained jumpers and the same strained eyes. Occupational siblings.

The Kanuri man cleared his throat and spat on the floor. 'We came for the balance.'

Reza reached into his jeans and counted out some notes. He handed it to him and counted some more for the Yoruba man.

The first man collected the notes and then said in his thickly accented Hausa, 'Ah, brother Reza, you didn't add the something for the flat tyre.'

'What flat tyre?'

'We had a flat tyre on the way back.'

'So, how is that my fault?'

'It's your people I was carrying and you know we carried more than the recommended.'

'Lasisi, it's like you don't want me doing business with you.' Reza was growing irritated.

'Ah, no. It's not like that.'

The Kanuri man again cleared his throat, but this time, he didn't spit. '*Maigida* Reza, you and Lasisi have been together long. This is a small matter.'

Reza whipped out a two hundred naira note and handed it to the man. Lasisi took it and said his thanks. Reza could not help noticing the identical shuffle of their worn slippers on the concrete as they headed back to their buses, back to the sun-beaten blacktop where they fetched their bread, where someday, their bones would be scraped off and their stories would be forgotten, trampled into the road, like countless others, by the whizzing wheels of time. He shook his head and headed back to the room.

Joe and Sani followed him. They stood by the door. Joe's face bore the weightiness of one about to broach a heavy subject.

'What about the guys?' Joe stepped forward.

Reza slumped on the mattress and said nothing.

Sani shifted on his feet. 'They have spent the night in a cell, they must have learnt their lesson.'

'Is the cell your father's house?'

The two men looked at each other, stunned by the anger in Reza's voice. But the confused expression on each of their faces, despite the circumstances, amused them. Joe started laughing. Sani, too, joined him. They fell to their knees and laughed long and hard until they broke the tension and Reza, tickled by their hysterics, smiled.

'You understand, I told everyone that this policeman is looking for ways to make trouble for us but Gattuso and Dogo, stupid as they are, went and started a fight.'

Joe stopped laughing. 'It has already happened, Reza. *Ka yi hakuri mana.*'

'If they wanted to fight they could have taken it elsewhere, not here in San Siro, you understand. Making all that noise and drawing the police here like that.' Reza shook his head. 'How could they be so stupid?'

Sani sat down and stretched his legs on the floor. 'It will not happen again, *insha Allah.*'

Reza made a face showing the extent of his disgust. 'You don't understand. I don't like going to the police for anything. Anything! Now if I go to bail them, this OC will think he is doing me a favour.'

Joe bowed his head. 'It will not happen again.'

Reza sighed and rose. He walked out of the door and headed for the gate.

Outside the police post, ASP Dauda Baleri sat on a bench, flanked by some of his men. He was tending to the irritations of the shaving bumps that plagued his neck and sullied his mood. He saw Reza approaching, looked the other way and caressed his jaw, scratching and grimacing. When Reza stood before them and offered a greeting, Baleri grunted in reply.

'OC, I came to see you.'

Baleri took his time rising and Reza followed him into his austere office. The smell of fresh paint that had filled the air when Reza last visited had been replaced by the smell of mosquito coil and stinking shoes. From outside, the stale stench of urine from the corner where the officers peed wafted in with the occasional breeze.

'I am here to bail my boys.'

Baleri sat back in his chair and picked up his pen. He twirled it in his fingers with the satisfied air of one savouring a victory sure to come. 'So they are your boys?'

'Yes.'

'I see.' Baleri swivelled on his chair. 'I see.'

The cheap clock on the wall marked time with the apathy of a wearied device. Reza turned to look at it. It had the photo of a stern-looking policeman in it as the clock face, with 'Congratulations' boldly written across it. The other writings were too small for him to read from where he sat. He turned back to Baleri.

'You see, these boys were disturbing the public peace, using dangerous weapons and causing grievous bodily harm,' Baleri began. 'We are going to take them to court.'

'To court?'

'Yes.'

'Well then.' Reza rose. 'In that case, there is nothing to talk about, you understand.' He caught the alarm that flickered in Baleri's eyes. The officer must have found the thought of losing the extra he would make from the transaction disturbing. It would be the weekend soon enough, a period during which every decent crook knew that the average policeman would be desperate to make some quick cash. Reza turned and made for the door, certain that Baleri would not let him leave just like that.

The officer's stuttering voice reached him as he got to the door. 'But – we don't have to go that far if—'

'How much?' Reza turned. He saw the battered pride flash in the policeman's eyes. But it was gone in an instant, consumed by the brazenness of avarice and desperation.

Baleri named his price and watched as Reza counted out five one thousand naira notes and put them on the table. He picked up the money and shoved it in his breast pocket. He gestured to the seat Reza had just vacated and cleared his throat.

Reza sat down.

'You see,' Baleri opened his hands imploringly, 'this is a small matter. If you had been paying the protection fee, none of this would have happened. When your boys started fighting and trying to kill each other, we would have gone and settled the matter there. No need for all this, eh.'

Reza tapped the soles of his shoes on the cement floor.

'You see,' Baleri went on, 'we all know how these things work. You scratch my back, I scratch yours, like that, eh, but you, you are proving stubborn.'

'You understand, OC, last time we talked about this, I told you I have no problem with you people. But you took my stuff and sold it to the boys at the junction, and you took my money and harassed my boys. There was no respect in that. *Ko kadan.*'

'Ok, ok. That has happened. Now we can move on.'

'If you bring back my stuff and the money you took, you understand. But for now, release my boys. When you bring my things, we can talk business, *ka gane ko?*'

Baleri nodded and bit down on his lower lip. He called in one of his officers and ordered him to release the San Siro boys.

Reza waited outside while Gattuso and Dogo, bleary-eyed, collected their items and strolled out of the cell. They were heralded by the smell of frustration, tinted with the odour of clothes dampened by overnight piss. His anger towards them had been quelled when he realised that trouble was inevitable – all that ganja coupled with muscly hotheads, there were bound to be some sparks and some confrontations.

He slapped the palms of the three policemen sitting on the bench outside and shared a joke with them. When they were cackling, he reached into his pocket for a thousand naira note.

'For soft drinks.' He made a magnanimous gesture that included them all.

One of the officers grabbed the bill out of Reza's hand and tucked it into his breast pocket. Then he looked furtively at the door of Baleri's office.

'Reza, Reza,' the officers hailed and slapped his hand.

Gattuso walked out of the police office, bristling with rage. 'You let me spend the night in the cell.'

Reza started walking away. 'And I will do worse next time.'

But Dogo, gifted with the sobriety only a night in the cell could confer on someone of his disposition, nodded reverently. 'Thanks, Reza.'

'Next time you guys want to fight, take it elsewhere. San Siro is not a fucking battlefield.'

Reza's phone chimed, this time a more subdued tone than the bawdy one that had shamed him at Binta's, and he reached into his pocket. He looked at the screen and glanced up at Dogo and Gattuso. Dogo had bent over and was dusting off his jeans, but Gattuso looked at him as he cracked his knuckles. Reza turned away and put the phone to his ear. He walked away from them as he talked.

When Reza shoved the phone back in his pocket and returned, Gattuso noticed that he was grinding his teeth.

But it was Dogo who spoke first. 'What's wrong?'

'Some mamafucker hit the house I asked to be left alone.'

'Which house?' Gattuso cracked his knuckles.

'Hajiya Binta's.'

'The one with the green gate?'

'Yes, God damn it!'

'What did they take?'

'They took her generator.'

'*Lallai kam!*' Gattuso clicked at the back of his throat and crashed a clenched fist into his palm.

'Find the generator and find out the *dan shegiya* who did it. Bring me the mamafucker, you understand. Ask Ibro the generator repairman. Let him tell us what he knows, who has sold a generator, who bought one. Anything, you understand. I want that little prick now. Now, God damn it!'

———

They found the prick by evening – only he was not little. Marufu was the large-limbed fellow who fancied himself a footballer. Every morning and evening he would wear his studded boots and bare his red shin guards as he jogged ostentatiously to the football field. Once in a while he came to San Siro for a fix or to trade off pilfered items, such as condoms he had stolen from a pharmacy. Having met a football agent who claimed he could arrange a trial for him with Belgium giants Club Brugge or Anderlecht, Marufu saw an opportunity. But it would cost more than Mama Marufu's milling machine and his father's security man salary could afford. So Marufu, driven by desperation, took to scaling fences. When he tried to sell his loot to Elvis the barber, word got round to San Siro.

Reza, standing in the dimming light of day, took one last drag from the joint in his hand and passed it on to Gattuso. He, too, took a long drag and passed it on. Finally, when it got to Dogo, he smoked the last of it, crushed it under his shoe, and threw dust over it with the blade of his machete. Joe took a swig from his bottle of schnapps, screwed on the top and shoved it into his back pocket. Reza led the way. They went past Mama Marufu's milling machine standing in the gathering dusk and dust at the front of the tenement compound. They passed by Baba Alade the thrift collector's room, which he shared with his two wives, past the identical twins' room and past Mama Marufu's and the chicken coop in the corner. They kicked in the last door on the left, where Marufu, just back from his evening training session, was eating and watching a replay of the Champions League final.

Reza saw the consternation on Marufu's face give way to terror when he recognised him. He saw the generator partially hidden by Marufu's bed and smiled. He approached Marufu, certain that there wouldn't be any interruptions with Dogo, Joe and Gattuso standing guard just outside.

Marufu's resistance was feeble. He got a blow in, on Reza's jaw, but Reza hit him with precision. The assault was swift and the damage was done way before Mama Marufu came out screaming like a deranged woman, startling the drowsy sun and the indifferent chickens that had just settled down in the roost.

14

What has horns must not be hidden in a sack

'Ah! Do they have to sing about everything?' Ummi lamented from her place on the floor as she watched the actors on TV singing and dancing in the Hindi style that Hausa film-makers had also adopted.

'This is so lame, *wallahi*.' Kareema curled up on the couch next to her sister. Abida was in sky-blue lace, Kareema in royal blue.

Fa'iza, baffled, looked at the Short Ones. 'Lame? This film?'

It was Abida who, equally disgusted, tackled Fa'iza. '*Kwarai kuwa*. How can you come home and find your wife in bed with some idiot and just stand there singing like a moron?'

'It's prayer time.' Binta, who was sitting across the room from Hureira, delivered her observation in a solemn tone that suggested she wanted the crowd to disperse.

'*Wai*! Prayer time? Come, let's go pray.' Fa'iza rose. She realised that she wasn't enthralled by the movie after all, since Ali Nuhu was not in it. She waited for the Short Ones to rise and together they headed for her room, swinging their hips as they went.

Abida hissed. 'I would rather be reading my novels than watching this crap.'

'Sure, sure.'

Hureira watched them disappear into the room and close the door behind them. She turned to her mother with a questioning look.

Binta nodded, as if assenting to Hureira's unarticulated assertions. 'Those are the kind of friends Fa'iza keeps.'

'*Lallai kam!*' Hureira nodded and made clucking noises.

Binta, too, rose to say her prayers, and because it was that time of the month for her, Hureira, nursing a mild grouchiness, was left with her daughter, watching the tedious film crawl to a climax.

In Fa'iza's room, the girls took turns saying their Maghrib prayers. While Abida sat on the rug supplicating, Fa'iza sat on the mattress flipping the pages of the new cache of novellas the Short Ones had brought hidden under the folds of their hijabs. Kareema stood before the mirror patting her face. When Abida was done, Fa'iza took her place on the prayer rug and performed her Salat. And then it was Kareema's turn. After saying Salaam, she sat on the rug supplicating endlessly.

Fa'iza tired of waiting for her to finish. '*Wai!* A long prayer like this? What were you praying for so earnestly?'

'Things.'

'Boys?' Abida asked.

Kareema smiled. 'Maybe. What woman doesn't pray for a good husband?'

'Sure, sure.'

Fa'iza was excited. 'Who is he?'

Abida smiled, batting her eyes like a repository of secret things. 'She has many.'

'Sure, and so do you.' There was pride in Kareema's understated smile, and in her voice as well. Then she turned to Fa'iza. 'How many do you have, Amin?'

Abida giggled. 'She's still drooling over Bala Mahmud.'

'Me? Bala Mahmud? Of course not.'

'And do you know who Kareema has been drooling over?'

'Kareema? Who?'

'Should I tell, Kareema?'

Kareema smiled and shrugged. She rolled on the mattress.

'Reza,' Abida whispered.

'Reza? The San Siro guy?'

'Sure, sure.'

'Isn't he soooo handsome?' Kareema's eyes lit up with the incandescence of dreams.

'Handsome? But he's—'

'Sure, I know, I know. But it's not like I want to marry him or anything, you know. Just tripping, the way you go on about Ali Nuhu.'

'Me?'

'Sure.'

'I saw him the other day, Reza, you know.' Kareema stirred the conversation back to herself. 'He looked at me and you could tell there was something.'

'Something?'

'Sure. A connection, you know. A spark.'

Ummi came in with a dish of couscous, which she placed in the middle of the room and left. She returned with a jug of water and cups and then ran back to the living room. The girls sat around the plate, folded their legs and ate in silence. But each time Fa'iza looked up, her eyes met Abida's.

'What?'

Abida shrugged. 'Are you all right?'

'Me? Yes.'

Cutlery clinked. More couscous disappeared from the plate. Then Kareema looked up from the food. 'Amin, how soon can you finish these books?'

'Me? Well, it's Saturday. You could have them back by Monday, at school.'

'Sure. Great. Then I will give you one in English.'

'In English?'

'Sure. Mills and Boon.'

'All right.' But when Fa'iza looked up, she saw that Abida was looking into her eyes, yet again. And it occurred to her that Abida's eyes shone with empathy, not pity, an assuring gleam of understanding like a beacon meant only for her. And she knew that it was because of what Abida had seen in her Secret Book. Fa'iza looked down at the vanishing mound of couscous.

But Abida too had seen how Fa'iza looked at her. She, too, felt what Kareema had, only moments before, referred to as a spark, a connection. 'Do you still dream?'

Fa'iza nodded.

Kareema looked from her sister to Fa'iza. 'Dream? About what?'

'Nothing.' Abida sipped some water. 'Just dreams.'

The glare in Kareema's eyes was accusatory but it faded as noise from the gate reached them. Apparently, someone was intent on barging in. Fa'iza was startled, her eyes widened. The girls ran out of the room and found Hureira standing by the front door, peering into the courtyard.

Binta emerged from her room. 'Who's there?'

'Some men.'

'It's Reza.' Abida, having joined Hureira by the door, and familiar with Reza's physique, was able to make him out in the dim light.

Kareema pushed her way through, desperate to catch a glimpse of the man who, with increasing regularity, had featured in her fantasies. The women came out and gathered by the front door, their apprehension lost in a maelstrom of curiosity.

Reza and his cohorts, clearly excited, as evidenced by their boisterous demeanour, approached and set down the generator, not too far from where the women were huddled. The San Siro boys stooped in greeting. Binta answered, her pleasure concealed behind the faint smile that made only the corners of her lips tweak. She kept her eyes on the generator, away from Reza's face, as Dogo proceeded to recount how they recovered the machine. Gattuso and Joe fetched a rag from the clothes line and wiped the machine clean. Kareema inched closer to the boys, closer to Reza.

Finally, Binta, unable to contain her excitement, clapped her hands together. 'Thank God for His mercies. May Allah bless you all, *samari*.'

Hureira peered over her mother's shoulder. 'Is it still working?'

Reza stepped forward and unscrewed the lid of the tank, shook the device with some gusto and was rewarded with the sound of the fuel splashing against the sides of the tank. Binta saw the blood on his knuckle and shivered. She wanted to reach out and take his hand.

Reza worked briskly, unmindful of the blood. He tilted the generator so that the little fuel left in it would run into the carburettor. He set it down again and screwed the lid back on. He balanced himself, legs slightly apart, and pulled the starter. The machine sputtered and quietened. He pulled again, and again, and finally, the engine coughed and roared.

'*Allahu Akbar!*' little Ummi exclaimed.

Fa'iza had missed being traumatised by the blood on Reza's hand, for she was looking at his shoes. She was certain, even in the dim light, that they were the same ones she had seen at the front door the other day; the ones that had disappeared as mysteriously as they had appeared.

15

A wise bird is best ensnared by the throat

Abida stood looking at the kosai browning in the boiling oil. Sani Scholar's mother, Jummalo, was sitting before the open flame, adding salt into the bean paste and stirring it with a ladle. She beat the ladle on her open palm and held it up to her face. Her tongue flicked out to have a taste. Satisfied, she nodded. 'Some customers want it a bit more salty.'

Abida smiled into Jummalo's tired eyes and wondered if she could help. She pushed the damp firewood further into the heart of the flame with her foot. A furious column of white smoke rose into the mild morning air and drove back the children waiting for the kosai to be ready, their money clenched in their little fists. They stepped back, waving away the cloud.

Kareema did not budge. She remained by the flame, disregarding the smoke wafting in her direction.

'The firewood is not dry enough.' Jummalo stuffed bits of plastic into the flame. 'Kareema, get away from the smoke.'

Kareema was impassive. 'What good woman can't withstand smoke?'

'Sure, sure,' Abida's voice was cheery.

Kareema had woken in a sullen mist that morning and Abida, when she was going out to get kosai for breakfast, had dragged her out of the house to help her get over her dour mood. Kareema hadn't responded to her attempts to start a conversation. Abida knew it was something that would quickly pass. It always did.

She reached for the stripped twig Jummalo used to flip the frying balls, but Kareema beat her to it. So she stood back and watched her sister flip the balls deftly as if she had been doing it all her life.

Jummalo too seemed impressed by Kareema's dexterity. 'Maybe I should hire you to help me, Kareema. You do it so well, *wallahi*.'

Kareema's expression remained bland. 'I am a woman.'

Abida turned her face away from the white smoke and sighted Hajiya Binta down the lane in her hijab, hovering about the entrance of San Siro. She watched Binta look around furtively and, even from that distance, Abida could almost see the worry on the older woman's face. Finally, she saw Binta put her phone to her ear.

Kareema had sensed that her sister was enthralled by something. She looked up and saw Binta and she, too, became curious. When Jummalo noticed that the flipping had stopped halfway, she also turned to see what the girls were looking at. She collected the twig from Kareema and continued flipping, casting occasional glances at Hajiya Binta in the process.

Down the lane, in his room, Reza put on his shirt and wiped his face. He reached for the broken mirror and peered into it. Then he hurried out to the waiting woman at the entrance. She appeared distressed and afraid, constantly looking over her shoulder.

Binta looked at his face that bore the evidence of sleep – swarthiness and bleary eyes. 'You were sleeping.'

'Is everything all right?'

'Yes.' She nodded. 'Yes, yes. Everything's fine.'

'Are you sure? You look worried.'

'Let me see your hands.'

He was taken aback by the urgency in her voice and dumbly held out his hands, palms facing the morning sky. She drew a circle in the air with her finger and he turned the hands over, his face betraying his curiosity.

'I thought you were hurt, from last night.'

'Me? I'm fine.'

'There was blood on your hand.'

He turned his hands over and looked at them, screwing his face up thoughtfully.

'You were in a fight, weren't you?'

'No, not a fight.'

'You were. I saw the blood.'

'Oh, just taught him a lesson, you understand.'

'You didn't—' she couldn't finish.

But he saw the word in her eyes and smiled. 'No, no. He just won't be troubling anyone for a while.'

'I don't want you getting into fights, Hassan.'

'Ok.'

'You are sure you are not hurt?'

'I'm all right, *wallahi*.'

'Ok, I just wanted to check on you, and to say thank you.'

When he looked into her eyes she bowed her head. She did not want him to see that she had agonised over him all night. 'I've got to go now. I told them I was going to buy bread from the store.'

'I want to see you.'

She looked around, at the muddy gutter slinking past in the middle of the dirt road, at the strips of plastic bags sticking out of the damp earth, at the sodden mud about her feet. She sighed. 'So do I.'

'When?'

'I don't know.'

He sighed.

'You haven't prayed this morning, have you?'

He looked down this time.

'Please, go now. Say your prayers.'

He nodded. She turned and started walking away, chased by her desire to hold him in her trembling arms.

Further up the lane, Abida glanced at Kareema and they turned to look at Jummalo, who had been watching over her shoulder. Kareema retrieved the twig and continued the business of flipping kosai in the pan with dedicated solemnity. The white smoke, as if terrified of the sullen mist about her, drifted away up into the vast heavens.

———

Reza was shocked when he saw his withered father stretched out on the bed. He knelt down and held the old man's hand. It felt weak, not like the hand of one who had grappled with bulls most of his life. He could not believe that in the twelve months since he had last seen his father, the old man could have been reduced to this decrepit amalgam of skin and protruding bones.

He had been on the prayer rug that morning, offering supplications to Allah, when the call came. His sick father was calling for him so he had a quick shower and made the hour and a half journey to Akwanga, this place where he was born.

The lanes had seemed narrower than he remembered. The buildings, too, seemed smaller. His father's house appeared like a giant concrete coop with large patches of flaking paint. He had stooped slightly to get through the door. And with little patience, he had tolerated his father's wives, Talatu and Lubabatu, as they feted him, offering food and drinks. He had looked at them, at their faces and the shifty eyes that betrayed their deviousness, and moved on to his father's room.

He sat holding the old man's withered hand, waiting for him to wake up from his drugged sleep. Those hands had hoisted him into the air every morning and pressed him into an embrace. Now he watched the narrow chest rising and falling, drawing in breaths in staggered wheezes.

Reza leaned back in the chair and was staring ahead into the space before his eyes when Lubabatu came in with a covered dish and placed it by the bed.

'How is he?'

Reza mumbled. He rubbed his eyes. 'What did the doctors say?'

'Dr. Linus said—'

'What Dr. Linus?'

'You know Dr. Linus, the one at the pharmacy.'

'He is not a doctor, he just sells drugs!'

Luba blinked rapidly and shifted on her foot. 'Well . . . well, he said your father has chronic malaria.'

'He doesn't know crap about anything! He sells paracetamol and ampiclox and stuff. He doesn't know crap about anything!'

Her eyelids fluttered again.

'God! Don't tell me you haven't taken him to a hospital.'

When he saw her eyelids fluttering yet again, he rose and walked out of the room. He went to the back of the house and lit a cigarette.

He had been seriously ill once, long before he became Reza. His thirteen-year-old body, ravaged by typhoid and malaria while his father had been away grappling with bulls, lay for days on a tattered old mattress, wasting, wishing for death.

In a delirious blur, he had seen his stepmothers shoving drugs into his mouth, pushing plates of food at him. He had closed his eyes and refused to open them until he was certain he was in heaven. But when, after an eternity, he felt himself levitating, he opened his eyes and saw his father's one good eye, filled with love and concern, looking down at him.

'Hold on, son, don't die on me.'

The next time he opened his eyes was in a hospital, with his exhausted father sleeping in a chair next to him.

The old man woke up with a smile and held the boy's hand. 'Welcome back, Hassan.'

'Father, I thought I was going to die,' his voice was weak.

His father squeezed his hand. 'No, no. I won't let that happen. You are going to grow up and be someone special. You will make me proud in my old age, my son.'

His father had kissed him on the cheek that day.

Reza took one last drag on the cigarette and crushed it underfoot. Then he went in search of a cab to take his father to the general hospital.

———

Flanked by his mother and sister, Munkaila put his hands behind his back and went round the house, scrutinizing the fence in the manner of a politician inspecting a government project. Fa'iza and Ummi stood by the door watching him stamp his immaculate leather half-shoe every now and then.

The smirk on his face deepened and he shook his head. 'We will have to put razor-wire on this fence.'

Fa'iza watched Binta look back over her shoulder at the fence and then down at her foot. Munkaila reached into his pocket and pulled out his phone. He punched the buttons and put it to his ear.

The labourers came a little later. They perused the fence, then retreated to a corner to confer with Munkaila. He counted out some money, handed it over to them and they hurried out of the house.

Each time the men came to work, Binta would retreat to the bedroom and lie on the bed with a book. On her bedside table, the novels and self-help books she had read continued to pile up on top of Az Zahabi's *The Major Sins*. Hemingway was a favourite she returned to often. The struggle of the old man against the fish had taken on a new meaning in her mind because she could relate to him, to his battle against the ravages of impending senescence. She was him. In her heart, there was a part that would fight to stretch those golden years.

'Hajiya, they are putting on the wires!' Ummi shouted out once afternoon, her voice loud enough to wake her mother Hureira, who had taken to sleeping most of the day. Ummi held up the curtains, her eyes wide with excitement.

'Get away from here!' Binta hissed and turned her face to the wall.

Mallam Haruna came that night and sat down with his radio on the veranda. Binta took her time coming out. This time she did not flap her hijab to herald her arrival but just sat down. When she did not complain about the radio, Haruna left it on, pressed to his ear. He was so involved in the news that he didn't notice that she did not even greet him. She rested her shoulder against the column and waited.

'*Allah ya kyauta.*' He sighed and switched off the radio. 'There is so much nonsense going on in this country, I tell you.'

She said nothing.

Up on the fence, the cat was walking majestically through the wire loops as if they didn't exist. It was the first time Binta had seen the completed work, this reinforced fence that imprisoned her scented dreams. The cat sat down, meowed once and began its chaperoning duties.

'Can you believe what is happening in this country, Hajiya!'
Again, there was the inflection in his voice, towards the end of
the sentence, which made his question come out like a statement.

She said nothing.

'Imagine these people, running around on motorcycles and
gunning down local chiefs. These Boko Haram people, you must
have heard about them!'

She said nothing still.

When he tired of waiting for her response, he cleared his throat.
'And the governor in Borno State wants to ban okadas, so these
people won't be running around shooting down people like that.
And you know, they told us they had suppressed these people,
they had wiped them out, now see what is happening.'

Binta grunted.

After a while Mallam Haruna caressed his beard. 'Love is a
wonderful thing, you know.'

This time, she looked at him, her curiosity hooded by the
shades of night.

'Yes, yes, it is. Imagine what the world would be like without
love. It would be terrible, you know. Terrible! People hating people,
people killing people. Total chaos, I tell you, *wallahi.*'

'Isn't that what's happening now?' There was a sonority in her
voice that came from not wanting to use it, a reluctance to speak.

'What!' Again, it didn't sound like a question. But Binta was,
by now, used to his way of speaking.

'Are people not killing people now? These people riding bikes
and shooting people, what else are they doing?'

'Oh, but you know, that is a bit different. See me and you now.
Is it not because of love that we are sitting, here! Love, I tell you,
wallahi kuwa.'

She looked at him, saw the stubble and the shadows the dim
light cast on his face. She wondered what she was doing sitting
in the night beside an old man who already had two wives and a
radio. 'You are too old to be talking about love.'

'Me! Old! By Allah, wait until our wedding night, then you will
see how virile I am.' He winked at her and guffawed.

'What the hell do you take me for?'

'Hmmm!'

'What kind of woman do you think I am that you will come here talking to me like that!'

'Ah ah, Binta, I only—'

'*Iskanci kawai!*' She let out a long drawn out hiss that startled the cat on the fence. When she rose, she shook her hijab and gathered it about her as she headed into the house, leaving him alone with the alarmed animal, scratching at his grey stubble.

———

In the silence of morning, Hureira slunk to the kitchen and made coffee and tea. She didn't disturb the morning by making omelettes or potato chips. She arranged the cups and slices of bread on a tray and carried it quietly back to the room. She sat down with Fa'iza and Ummi, their legs crossed in front of them, and they ate in silence, their cups barely clinking on the saucers.

'Mommy, can I—' Ummi started saying but Hureira shushed her. The girl tried again but Hureira's sharp look silenced her. Ummi looked from her mother to Fa'iza and couldn't understand. Hureira gestured with her hands. Ummi pointed at the jar of sugar. Hureira frowned and shook her head.

They heard Binta stomping out of her room. They froze – Fa'iza with her cup halfway to her mouth and Hureira with eyes wandering wildly. Ummi sat looking from her mother to Fa'iza. They heard Binta barge into the kitchen; they heard her banging utensils and hissing. They heard her come out. They held their breath and imagined her standing by the door, contemplating whether to intrude on their silent breakfast. Finally, they heard her footfall slapping the tiles as she walked back to her room.

The girls crept about preparing for school. When they were done, on their way out, they saw Binta sitting on the couch in the living room and froze. She looked at them and turned away.

'*Ina kwana*, Hajiya?' Fa'iza greeted.

'Hajiya, good morning.' Ummi curtseyed.

Binta grunted.

Fa'iza held Ummi's hand and together they crept out of the room, gently closing the door behind them. It was Hureira who had to remain imprisoned in the bedroom, away from Binta's strop. Until the phone call came in the early afternoon.

Binta showered, dabbed her face with powder and applied a dash of lipstick. She put on her fitted blouse and stood before the mirror, shored up her breasts and adjusted her bra. She put her purse and a make-up kit in her handbag and threw a hijab over her head. But heading out, she caught her reflection in the mirror and paused. She looked again.

She removed the hijab and pulled a jilbab from the wardrobe and put it on over her blouse. She took a *gyale* and wound it around her head and torso. Then she picked her bag and locked the bedroom door.

Outside, she walked as far away as she could from the house and hailed a motorcycle taxi. The okada man pulled up, revving his engine.

'Do you know Shagali Hotel?'

When he nodded, she climbed on the pillion with as much grace as her wrapper would allow and the okada man zoomed off.

16

A hippo can be made invisible in dark water

Holding the sheet about her chest, she looked around the tiny hotel room, at the ornate shell-shaped lampshades, at the ceiling fan that whirred indolently as if burdened by the weight of witnessed improprieties, at the little TV where a D'Banj music video was playing. She watched the sultry women dancing on the screen and marvelled at the audacity of their shamelessness.

When Reza emerged from the bathroom, she looked at the scars on his torso before turning her face away. He seemed leaner and there were shadows on his face, in his eyes.

He smiled at her. 'You want to shower?'

She looked in the direction of the bathroom and then back at him. 'So, how many times have you done this? Bringing women to a hotel room, I mean?'

He shrugged. When he said never, she knew he had just told her his first lie.

She felt a little whirl deep down in her heart and she knew if she could have seen the wind that stirred, it would have been yellow. She was too old to rage over another woman. After all, she did not want to think of herself as one of his girlfriends. She shouldn't. She shook her head. 'This is my first time in a hotel room.'

His smile was small but almost empathic. 'It's very private here. Everybody minds his business, you understand.' He came and sat next to her. 'Are you not hungry?'

She reached out for the wrap of suya he had bought. He had arrived at the hotel ahead of her and booked the room. But when she came, her hunger – their hunger – had been of a different sort. She had barely waited for him to close the door when she covered his lips with hers, pushing him against the panel.

Overcoming his initial surprise, he had responded with fervour, his hands reaching down to lift her dress over her head. Their tongues intertwined, their bodies entangled, their hands feeling each other's bodies – as if to be sure that in the period of their forced abstinence they hadn't changed. They moved to the bed and, because she wanted to, fought for it even, he let her sit astride him and ride him, her moans reaching up to the ceiling.

She put a piece of spiced meat in her mouth so she would not blurt out how she had never wanted any man so badly. She savoured the meat; a bit hard, but tasty. 'How is your father?'

Reza nodded, suddenly sombre. 'They think it's his kidney. They have to do some tests.'

'I'm sorry to hear that. Is he very old?'

Reza looked up at the ceiling. 'Seventy-two, seventy-five. I'm not sure.'

'You care for him, don't you?'

It wasn't a question anyone had ever asked him. He considered it for a while. 'My father, he used to travel to Potiskum, sometimes even to Sokoto to buy cattle and then travel to the east to sell them to the Igbos. He was the only one who ever cared about me, you understand.'

He was almost choking now so she put her arms around him and held him to her, whispering into his ear that his father would be all right.

They lay down again on the bed, listening to each other's breathing. When next she opened her eyes, it was almost four in the afternoon. She nudged Reza and he woke up, wiping his eyes.

She sat up on the bed. 'I've got to go now. It's late.'

'Must you?'

'Of course, don't be silly.'

She reached for her bag, fished in it, brought out a receipt and handed it to him. With her hands on her lap, she watched his face.

'WAEC registration? For me?'

She nodded and smiled.

'*Kutuma!*' He frowned at the paper, his expression transforming from amazement to delight, and then to one of profound thought.

'I think it's important you go back to school, Hassan.'

His head was still bent at the receipt. 'Wow! And you paid for me?'

'I know if I asked you to pay you would dally, so I took the liberty.' She reached again into her bag and fetched a brown envelope. 'Now all you need to do is fill the forms, attend some classes and write the exams.' She extended the envelope to him.

'Yes, yes.' He folded the receipt neatly and put it in his jeans pocket. He covered his face with his hand and sighed.

'You are not happy about this, are you?'

'No, no. I am, I am. It's just that, you understand, I just have to think about this.'

She nodded. 'I know. Think about it.'

They were silent for a while.

She wanted to say something to thaw the awkwardness. 'The fence has barbed wire now.' And she told him how Munkaila had brought the workmen to install the wire after the generator theft.

'So, I will have to find another way in next time,' he laughed.

Binta, too, laughed. Then she got out of the bed. 'I hope they have hot water here, I need to shower now.'

———

Jos: August, 1995

She first heard rumours that Yaro was hanging out with the boys at the junction; the boys who ran the black market selling petrol to motorists by the roadside. She heard that they were making good money because there was a shortage of petrol at the filling stations.

She raised the issue with Zubairu several times but he had only grunted. He was preoccupied with the new suya spot he was struggling to keep afloat. The first, which he had started back in

'82, was destroyed in '85 by the government task force that seemed determined to demolish anything it did not like the sight of. For years he went to the *majalisa*, where jobless men sat and argued all day, drank fura da nono in the afternoon and returned home at night with dark faces and limp pockets.

It was Binta's paltry salary as a schoolteacher that kept them afloat in those days until Zubairu started another suya spot. It prospered for several years until he got into a fight with a police sergeant. The officer wanted Zubairu to buy a 'licence to operate' from him, except there was no receipt for the transaction, and the fees were renewable each time the officer got broke. The negotiations ended in a fist fight, with Zubairu knocking out two of the sergeant's teeth.

The police confiscated his goods and locked him up. It took a week and some significant payments to get Zubairu released. He then tried his hand at several trades: selling used clothes; running a motorcycle taxi (that ended when he crashed the bike and was left with a limp for months) and a failed trade in onions procured from farmers in the villages. In the end, he went back to his suya business and had just got another spot up and running at Angwan Rukuba Junction. He was struggling and Binta's salary had not been paid in eight months. Teachers had been on strike the last six.

Finally, she decided to do it, to have this talk with the son she had been brought up not to acknowledge. She had meant to talk to Yaro that day because she had heard the rumours of the rolls of ganja under the black marketeers' tables, she had heard how they leered at and harassed passing girls.

But it was Munkaila who came at dinner time, smiling broadly, a bulging plastic bag dangling from his hand.

Binta looked up from the lesson notes she had been updating for whenever schools resumed. There were talks going on between union leaders and the government. But there had been talks before. Binta was not certain that this round of talks would be any different from the previous ones.

'Where is that coming from?'

Munkaila's smile broadened as he reached into his pocket, pulled out a wad of notes and held them before her eyes. 'My GCE registration fees.' He beamed.

'What! Registration fees! Your father must have come into some money.' She raised her hands heavenwards with a smile in her eyes.

'Not Father. Yaro.'

Her hands dropped. 'What do you mean Yaro?'

'He gave me the money and the things in the bag. And he gave me this for you.' He pulled out a smaller wad from his other pocket.

She looked at the money and thought of Hadiza's worn shoes and Hureira's aching tooth. 'Put it on the table.' She knew that she would hate herself for saying that.

She started to perceive the smell of ganja lingering about Yaro each time he returned. He came back very late and left early, after he had come to say good morning to her, always squatting down, supporting himself with his fingers on the floor. Each time she would grunt and look the other way. Sometimes he lingered, as if waiting for her to say something or wanting to tell her something. Because she never looked in his eyes, she would never know. And each time he rose and left, she would feel her heart clench three times – always three times.

But the money kept coming, and the shopping bags too. And Zubairu's shame no longer loomed as large because this time, it wasn't from his wife's purse they fed. It was from his son's, his *first* son.

But one dawn in December when the harmattan rattled the windowpanes, Binta had come out to perform her ablutions for Subhi prayers when she noticed the smell. For some time she stood still, her nostrils filtering the cold air. She allowed her nose to lead her towards Yaro's door. She stood, her heart racing. What she had always feared was true. The smell of ganja slipped out from the chinks of *his* door. She rapped on the door and felt the panel rattle under her fist. She pounded until he opened.

The men, their co-tenants, had already left for the mosque so only the women in the compound were left to peek through their curtains. She slapped him and he bowed his head.

'Under my roof, Yaro? Is this what you want to teach your brother, you useless boy? Men are at the mosque praying while you are here smoking your useless life away, under *my* roof!'

He looked her in the eye, briefly. She slapped him again. And then rage gave her hands a life of their own. They moved frenziedly, left and right. Left and right. He retreated from her into the narrow room, until he tripped and fell backwards onto the mattress. She stopped, looking down at him. He was panting, as she was, his eyes were angry, and hurt. When he looked away, it was the hurt that she remembered more, it was the hurt that endured in her mind.

That was the last night Yaro spent under her roof. It was also the last time she saw him alive. He packed his things in a small bag and left. Munkaila reported that he had moved in with one of his friends from the junction.

That was where the police found him. They had been looking for Yaro's host on suspicion of robbery. They broke down the door and opened fire.

When his friends brought home his bloodied corpse, Binta held him in her arms and called him by his given name. Her wailing voice dazed the soaring birds and pierced the underbelly of the heavens.

17

*An old woman is always uneasy when dry bones are
mentioned in a proverb*

There was something appealing about the bunch of strawberries
topping the fruit bowl; something about the shape and the redness
and the yellow speckles on the skin. Reza wondered what they
would taste like, these exotic fruits, arranged exquisitely, the green
tufts facing the ceiling. He watched as Senator Buba Maikudi's
hand hovered over the bowl and settled on one. He watched him
chew, observed the expression on his face and wondered what
sensations his taste buds must be experiencing.

'You didn't bring me a birthday present, Reza.' The senator took
another bite. 'I just turned seventy, you know.'

He was reclining on the plush rug, supporting his elbow with
an ornate leather cushion, an impressive ensemble of snacks and
the fruit bowl arranged before him. Beside the strawberries, there
were apples, apricots, avocados and grapes. On a side plate, there
was steamed groundnut.

Reza swallowed. 'Senator, I didn't know.'

'See all the cards I have recieved,' the senator gestured
expansively at the array of assorted cards. Some were small and
dainty. One was as big as a small child.

Reza nodded in admiration.

The senator sat up and reached for one. He picked up his thin-framed glasses on the rug beside him and put them on. *'Your life has been a blessing,'* he read in English and paused to clear his throat, *'and that is why I pray God multiply your years. Happy birthday, Grandpa.'*

Not knowing what to say, Reza nodded again.

'That was from my granddaughter,' the senator's voice resonated with pride. 'She's just five you know, very smart girl.'

'Yes, she seems smart.'

The senator scanned the display before him with obvious satisfaction and chose an apple. He reclined again, the fruit hovering before his face. 'You know, it is because of these small ones, eh, these little children, that we work so hard to make sure their future is not mortgaged by incompetent idiots who want to rule this country by whatever means.' The crunch came and a huge chunk of the apple disappeared.

'Exactly, sir.'

The senator gestured at the fruit and nodded to Reza to make his choice. He pushed the bowl towards the young man and nodded again, watching as Reza eyed the strawberries.

'You know, you people are just killing yourselves with all these useless chemicals you consume.' The senator waved the apple before his face. 'Our fathers lived on fruit and see how long they lived. My father, may Allah rest his soul, as far back as 1937, used to walk from Azare to Kano carrying all these goods on his head. He was a big trader, you know. He bought the best zanna caps from Maiduguri and sold them in Kano, travelled to Zaria and bought the best embroideries and sold them in Kano and Maiduguri. It made him pretty rich, *wallahi.*'

'He trekked from Azare to Kano?' Reza marvelled.

'Oh, yes, he did. And he lived well into a ripe old age, my father. You know, he ran into some bandits once. He was walking with heaps of money tied around his waist when he noticed someone trailing him. He pretended he had stepped on a thorn and managed to get a good look at the bandits, how they were positioning behind him—'

Musa the tea man came in with an exotic tea set. Reza admired the dainty porcelain cup with intricate powder-blue floral designs;

and the teapot in the centre, which was giving off a steady stream of steam through the spout. Musa placed the tray on the rug before the senator.

'*Sannu, Musa. Nagode ko,*' the senator greeted.

Musa nodded shyly. As he stood up to leave, the senator's son came in. He was young – younger than Reza, and slimmer too. He sat on the rug next to his father and it was easy for Reza to see how much they looked alike. He didn't even acknowledge Reza, so the outsider sat quietly, pretending not to be listening, wondering how the senator's father had fared against the bandits back in '37.

'Dad, about the trip?'

'Ah, Hamza, this trip again?'

'But, Dad, we've talked about this.'

'Hamza, this trip is not important now, is it?'

'I am going with my friends. Dad, please.'

'Well, I am not paying for it.'

'Oh, Dad, come on. Do you want me to be stranded?'

'I thought you were going back to school next month, so why must you start globetrotting like that?'

'*Haba*! Dad, I'm so bored and besides, I've never been to Madrid before. I want to learn Spanish.'

'I thought the trip would last a week.'

'Yes.'

'And how are you going to learn Spanish in a week?'

'At least I will pick up the interest and see places and you know—'

'Oh, all right, all right. You can go.'

'Thanks, Dad. But I will need some pocket money.'

'Hamza, see all this your pestering—'

'And I will need you to help talk to your people about the visa.'

The senator put a grape in his mouth and gestured uncertainly. 'Later, Hamza, you can see I have a guest.'

The young man looked at Reza and nodded vaguely, abandoning the gesture halfway through. He started tapping the buttons of his Blackberry. Reza looked at Hamza's delicate fingers, and couldn't imagine them ever curling around a hoe, even to clear the backyard garden.

Still tapping his phone, Hamza huddled closer to his father and spoke in low tones. Reza could still overhear them. And when he picked an apple and bit into it, it made such a crunch that father and son looked up at him.

As Reza watched the senator pour tea for himself, sipping and smiling as he listened to his son whisper, he couldn't help thinking of his own father languishing on the narrow hospital bed, one on which someone else had probably recently died. And as Hamza was leaving, Reza saw the little smile that lingered on the senator's lips and the gleam of pride in his eyes.

'Hamza *kenan,*' the senator laughed. When the boy closed the door behind him, the old man turned to Reza and motioned for him to have tea.

With a 'thank you', Reza declined. He still could not get his head round the idea of having tea for the fun of it – tea without bread! 'Is he studying, your son?'

'Yes. He just finished his first degree. I want him to go for his master's immediately. He wants to go to Madrid, to learn Spanish, in one week, can you imagine that?' The senator shook his head. 'He is just like my father, Hamza, always wanting to see new places.'

'He's schooling in Madrid?'

'Oh, no. He did his degree in London. Do you know Madrid, Reza?'

'Oh, I just know Real Madrid.'

'Yes, the football team, right?'

'Yes.'

The senator sipped tea. Reza ate more of the apple. But he had heard them mentioning UCLA. He didn't want to ask what that was.

'UCLA.' He nodded in admiration.

'Yes, for his master's.'

'Is that in London?'

The senator laughed. 'The US, Reza, UCLA is in America.'

Reza smiled. 'I am thinking of going back to school myself.'

The senator nodded and raised his teacup to Reza. He seemed in a hurry to say something, but because his mouth was full, he took his time. Then he sipped more tea. 'Very, good, Reza, very good.' He set the cup gently on the saucer and reclined again, his eyes shifting from side to side.

'I just thought I should re-write my GCE and see how it goes, you understand.'

The senator nodded. 'Good idea. So, you were in school before?'

Reza chuckled. 'I was.'

'You see, Reza, that is what we are fighting for. Imagine someone as intelligent as you; you can't go to school because of one thing or the other, mhm? This is the injustice we are fighting. That is why I am still struggling at my age so that people like you can have a brighter future.'

'Exactly, sir.'

'How is your business doing?'

'We thank God.'

'And the policeman? He is not troubling you anymore, is he?'

'No, sir.'

The senator cleared his throat and sat up. He sipped his tea and seemed surprised there wasn't much of it left in the little cup. He put the cup down on the saucer and poured more from the teapot. 'You see, my cousin Bello, he spent seven years in the university because of all these useless strikes and now three years since he graduated, he still hasn't found a job.'

Reza's eyes broadened a fraction.

'And this man came here the other day, he said his younger brother has been looking for a job for five years and still hasn't found one. Five years, in this country!'

'My brother too,' Reza began, wondering why he was talking about Bulama, his useless half-brother. 'He has a diploma now. He couldn't find a job either.'

'You see!' The senator poured milk into the cup and watched the spiralling white storm imploding from below, bleaching the tea, subtly dominating it. 'Too many people these days going to all sorts of schools and there are no jobs for them to do. When they are frustrated, they take guns and rob somebody.'

Reza looked at the fruit bowl, at the apple green and the red of the strawberries and their yellow speckles, at the night shades of the grapes and the mellow yellow of the cashew.

'So your brother went to school?'

Reza nodded.

'And you and him, who is better off now?'

Reza thought of his father in the hospital and how powerless his brother had been even to buy the needed drugs. He didn't want to say that Bulama had married and that, on his meagre teacher's salary, they barely managed through to the end of the month, from what he had heard. He didn't want to say how pleased he was that he seemed to be faring better than his father's son.

'You see!' There was a note of triumph in the senator's voice. 'You are doing better than he who spent all those years in school, all that money gone, all that time wasted, for what? That is why I think young people like you who are entrepreneurs, who have business acumen, should not waste your lives chasing illusions. That was why when I heard that policeman was messing with your business, I had to intervene. You've heard of Bill Gates, haven't you?'

Reza nodded.

'See, he is one of the richest men in the world and did he not drop out of school? The problem with us is that everything becomes a fad. Because Mr A goes to school, everyone else wants to go to school, so we lose the farmers, lose the businessmen, lose all sorts of people who will all rush to school and when they come out, there is nothing for them to do.'

Reza contemplated the fruit once more.

'See this boy Hamza, do you think if he had any business sense like you I would be wasting my money sending him to school? I would rather give him capital to start a business.'

The senator stirred the tea and took a sip, then he reclined on the ornate cushion and picked up the card his granddaughter had sent him. He read it again and smiled, as if at a private joke.

Hamza opened the door to announce that some 'honourables' had been waiting for the senator. The old man said he would see them when he was done with his guest. Reza now wondered why the senator had summoned him, why he had been talking to him about everything apart from what he had called him for.

'Reza, you said your old man was ill. How is he now?'

'*Alhamdulillah*, he is better.'

'Has he been discharged?'

'Not yet.'

'Take care of your old man, Reza, pray that you part in peace. That is very important.'

Reza nodded.

'You know, your *aljannah* is under your parents' feet. If they are not happy with you, they stomp on it, if they are, they raise their feet for you to gain access to paradise. Take good care of your old man, *ka ji ko?*'

The senator reached for his bag and fetched some money. He handed the notes to Reza and urged him once more to take care of his father. Reza thanked him and made to leave.

'Reza, *zauna mana.*' The senator motioned for him to take his seat once more. 'Do you know why I called you?'

'No, Senator.'

'You see, when you are doing something important, you need strong men around you, *ko ba haka ba?*'

Reza agreed.

'Reza, you are a strong man. I am going to ask you to do something, something very serious, very important.'

'Anything, Senator.'

'*Yauwa!* That is why I like you. You don't waste time when it is expedient to act. You don't waste time asking questions. I want you to—' he leaned forward and seemed to have frozen, his index finger held up before his face, 'I want you to be ready. I will ask Moses, you know Moses, my PA? He will contact you and brief you on what to do. Whatever he tells you, just do it, *ka ji ko?*'

Reza nodded again.

'It is a very sensitive matter and I want you to handle it with care.'

'No problem, Senator.'

'All right, you may go now so I can see the honourables. Just be ready, ok?'

Reza thanked him and shoved the money into his pocket. On his way out, he saw the 'honourables' waiting in the anteroom. The three men looked important and smelt of expensive cologne. One of them had a face that was always on TV. He was probably a minister or something of the sort but Reza, not one to waste time watching the news, couldn't really be sure.

18

*It takes more than a bucket of dye to change
the colour of the sea*

Mallam Haruna sat surrounded by a battalion of zanna caps fitted on wooden *kwari*, the special handmade dummies he used to give the caps their size and shape. The caps, washed and set out to dry, and turned inside out so only their blue interior showed, occupied all of the shop, save a small path leading out to the narrow side street, traversed by traders and customers heading home from the market.

Up on the shelves, populated by rows of colourful caps stacked atop each other, glistening in transparent waterproof wraps, was Mallam Haruna's trusted radio, from which the afternoon news blared. But the man himself was focused on the piles of caps beside him, picking them one after the other and fitting them on the dummies. There was a secret to his success as a cap washerman – the skill of *wankin glass,* of making caps gleam as if they were bottles in the sun. It was in the myrrh and its application; in smoothly beating it into the threads. In the careful application of a weighted, hot charcoal iron. He learnt the technique from a friend who had learnt the secret in the desert fringes of Maiduguri.

People from the capital trooped to Mallam Haruna's shop, tucked away in the corner of the Mararaba market, keen to have him make their caps emit the aura of prosperity. And with the referral from a member of the House of Representatives, word spread to the red and green chambers of Mallam Haruna, the man who made caps glimmer.

While his three apprentices did the actual washing and, under the master's supervision, applied myrrh, Mallam Haruna was left with the task of fitting the caps into the right *kwari* for a perfect fit. It was a gift, being able to look at someone's head, even from a distance, and tell exactly which *kwari* would fit his cap. At night, if he did not carry his radio and go in pursuit of other things, he would lock himself in the shop and apply the finishing touches. By morning, the boys would come and find rows of gleaming caps neatly stacked on the shelves.

In the afternoons, usually after Zuhr prayers when the boys were doing the grunt work, Mallam Haruna would carry his radio and head out of the market to see his friend, Mallam Balarabe, who sold earrings, necklaces, wristwatches and other such trinkets beside La Crème.

Mallam Balarabe had a good spot, right on the kerb of the fast food joint where men trying to impress their dates were easily cajoled into buying ornaments for twice the normal price. Sometimes, guests at Shagali Hotel across the street also came to look at Mallam Balarabe's merchandise.

That afternoon, Mallam Haruna turned the corner and saw Balarabe sitting under his sun-beaten parasol, no longer the eye-catching red it used to be. With his radio pressed to his ear, he walked up to his friend and salaamed.

'Mallam Haruna, *barka da zuwa*,' Balarabe greeted, making space for Haruna on the bench.

Haruna contemplated the parasol and sat down. 'Your parasol is dead. Get another one.'

Balarabe was already listening to the Deutsche Welle Hausa service on the portable radio beside his wares, but because Mallam Haruna's was clearer, Balarabe switched off his own set. 'I will, *insha Allah*.'

'Nothing much on the radio today.'

'Not much, mostly a repeat of the morning broadcast.'

'Yes.'

'You see how these politicians are messing up.' Balarabe caressed his greying beard. He removed his cap and placed it on the bench.

They had first met in Mallam Haruna's shop three years before when Balarabe had had his cap shrunken by another *maiwanki* and was referred to Mallam Haruna. Mallam Haruna took on the cap, only because of a certain reverence he felt for Balarabe. He had the luxury of choosing whose cap he serviced and especially resented cleaning up other people's mess. When he was done, Mallam Balarabe had been impressed by the finished work, by the way the colourful threads had brightened and how the cap had been perfectly shaped to fit his head. Balarabe had told Mallam Haruna that he had had plans to buy a new cap for his third wedding a couple of weeks away, but would instead reserve that one for the occasion.

Mallam Haruna had been awed. 'Third wife! *Masha Allah!*'

And that had marked the beginning of their friendship, forged on the plurality of wives.

Now, Mallam Haruna grunted. 'This idea of using corps members to conduct elections, I'm not so sure about it.'

'*Atoh!*' Balarabe exclaimed. 'This man, Jega, we thought he was coming in to do something reasonable. See how they are mismanaging the voter registration already.'

'Power! Power! Power is a treacherous thing, I tell you. Once you join these men in their affairs, no matter how pious you are, they will find a way to corrupt you. That is why I say Buhari should just let them carry on with their politics and save himself the trouble.'

'And if everyone stays away, who do you think will come and fix the system?'

'Only God will rescue us from these greedy people, *wallahi*.'

'God! And why should God come to rescue us when we are not willing to raise a finger to help ourselves?' Mallam Balarabe posed expectantly; as if ready with another salvo should Mallam Haruna say the wrong thing.

But Mallam Haruna wasn't listening. His eyes were trained on the entrance of Shagali Hotel, where a motorcycle taxi had just set down a woman. Even though she wasn't wearing a hijab, as he had grown accustomed to seeing her, he could tell who she was from afar. He could imagine the smell of lavender wafting from her as she fished in her purse and handed the okada man his fare.

'*Subhanallahi!*' Mallam Haruna exclaimed as Binta adjusted the veil over her shoulder and hurried into the hotel.

'What?' Balarabe looked from his friend's face to the hotel entrance where Binta had already walked out of view.

'Oh, nothing. Nothing.' Mallam Haruna clutched his beard and shook his head. '*Lallai kam!*'

———

Reza opened the door and watched Binta walk straight past him to the bed. When she took off her veil and dumped it beside her, his smile froze.

'Are you all right, Hajiya?'

Her eyes flitted over him and she looked away. 'I'm fine.'

He locked the door and walked to her. He sat down beside her and tentatively put an arm around her shoulders.

'I brought the money.' She reached into her bag, fetched some notes and handed them over to him. 'You see why I keep asking you to open an account? You could have gone to an ATM and withdrawn money without me even knowing.'

'No problem, I trust you.' He received the money and put it away.

'How is your father now?'

'He is getting better, they say. I need to go back and see. They said I need to get some money for further tests, you understand.' Then he added a '*Thank you,*' in English.

She thumped him on the chest lightly. 'No need to thank me, it's your money, isn't it?'

'Thank you for keeping it and bringing it when I need it.' He brushed his lips to her ear. 'Thank you for being my bank, where I deposit my money, and other things.'

She looked at the mischievous light in his eyes and smiled. She shoved him away and he fell on his back on the bed and laughed up to the ceiling.

She, too, laughed. 'God, what have I done? I have corrupted this small boy.'

'I wonder who is corrupting who?' He pulled her down beside him. They lay on the bed, looking up at the ceiling fan turning, slicing the air like an indolent scythe. He would never understand the sexual attraction he felt for her. Sometimes his intimacy with Binta bothered him, not least because occasionally he ended up thinking about his mother when he thought of Binta, or the other way round. It made him uncomfortable at times. It was making him uncomfortable now until Binta sighed. He raised himself on his elbow to look at her.

'What is wrong with you today? You seem distant.'

She sat up on the bed and he, too, sat up.

'I have been thinking, you know, about my late husband.'

'Oh, I see.'

'I just woke up this morning and thoughts of him kept looping in my mind.'

'What have you been thinking about him?'

She shook her head and chuckled sadly. 'You know, I have spent more of my life with him than with anyone else. I was sixteen or seventeen when I married him.'

'Were you in love?'

'Love?' Again she found herself reflecting on the word and what it meant, and found herself wandering in nothingness. 'Oh, no. I hardly even knew him before our wedding. He used to work at the railway back in Jos then. He would come to Kibiya once in a while and we always said that Mallam Dauda's son, who worked at the railway, is back. I never thought I would end up spending most of my life with him.' She wiped a tear from her eye and held her face in her hand.

Reza rose and walked to the window. He pulled apart the curtains and unimpressed by the view, drew them back together. He turned and regarded her. Then he moved the chair from across the room and sat facing her. 'May Allah have mercy on his soul.'

Binta looked up at him and smiled. 'Ameen. Thank you.'

'When did he die? I mean you never told me anything about him.'

She sighed. 'He died in 2001. September 7th, 2001. You know, that morning, I woke up to the smell of roaches and I knew something was not right. I always awake to the smell of roaches when something major is going to happen.' Binta paused and drew her legs closer to her body. 'But you know, he was in a good mood that morning. He had his bath and came to the room. He made a joke about how enormous my panties had become.' She chuckled again. Then she reached up and wiped the tears in her eyes.

'You don't have to talk about it, you understand—'

'It's ok. I haven't talked about it since it happened, you know.' She sniffled. 'So, he came in and made jokes about the size of my butt and other things, you know. And then he sat down and listened to the radio. He talked about things he normally didn't talk about, made small jokes and things. Then he went out to his suya spot.

'Later in the day, they said oh, they've started fighting in town, Muslims and Christians. And I was like, oh *maganan banza*! Such a thing had never happened in Jos, how can people start fighting just like that? But then it was true, it was the first of many riots. They found his corpse two days later at the Central Mosque among hundreds of others. You know, they collected all the corpses and took them there. He was butchered and his corpse was . . . torched.'

Reza put his hands to his face.

'They said the boys who did it, they knew him. They bought suya from him every night; they called him by his name, as he called them by theirs. And they chopped up his corpse, there on the street, and pissed on it before they torched it.'

When she broke down and wept, Reza crossed over and put his arm around her. He sighed again. 'May Allah rest his soul.'

'The last thing I said to him that day when he was going out was, don't come back with that grilled meat smell on you.'

Reza had never had a woman weep in his arms. He had no idea what was expected of him so he just held her and allowed her cry.

When Binta had finished crying, she went to the bathroom and washed her face. She returned and tried to smile.

He knew he was supposed to say something comforting, but he could not find the right words. So he said what came to his mind. 'You want to watch some TV?'

She smiled again, sat down next to him and leaned her head on his shoulder. 'I am so sorry.'

They watched a Nollywood movie they couldn't make head or tail of. When she got tired, she adjusted her scarf. 'I suppose

I should go home now. Sorry, I have ruined the day with all this talking.'

'Don't go, please.' He held her arms. 'When is your daughter leaving?'

'I really have no idea.'

'Shouldn't you send her away, back to her husband?'

She sighed. 'I have no idea what to do with Hureira.'

'This hotel business is expensive, you understand. I can't see you every day, anytime I like.'

'I know, Hassan. I will figure something out, I promise.' She smiled up at him. 'So, have you decided on going back to school?'

He cleared his throat and moved away from her. 'Not yet. There are things, you understand, things.'

'What things?'

'You know, things. Just things that need taking care of.'

She sighed and looked down at her hands now tucked between her thighs. He looked at her and stood up. He walked to the window, parted the curtains and looked out at the lawn where a sprinkler was turning around and raining down on the lush grass.

'I thought this was important. That was why I had you registered.'

'I know, I know.' He turned to face her. 'You understand, what purpose is there in going to school if not to make money?'

'It is to get an education.'

'And what use is an education without money?'

'Money isn't everything, you know.'

'You understand, all these people going to school, it's because they want to become big men someday. Look at Bulama with his useless diploma; he can't even feed his wife.'

'Who's Bulama?'

'He is my father's son, you understand. He spent all those years in school and got this diploma in something, I don't know what, and now he can't even do anything about our sick father. I am the one doing everything. Me! You understand, me, the one who didn't finish secondary school, me, me!'

She looked down at her henna-dyed hands, at the reddish-brown nails. When she looked up, she saw that Mr Ibu was busy making a fool of himself on the screen, but he did not interest

her. She looked at the lampshades now, at the intricate designs
on them and she bit her lower lip.

'I suppose I should be leaving now.' But she didn't move.

Reza turned back to the window. There was a squat gardener in
the distance, dressed only in a vest, pruning the hedges. Reza was
enraptured by the man's shears, how deftly he used them, how he
sent bits of twigs and leaves cascading in his wake. He imagined
snapping those giant scissors at someone's throat, imagined the
splash the blood would make, and shook his head.

Behind him, Binta shifted on the bed. 'Why must you compare
yourself to your brother?'

He said nothing for a while. 'Have you seen how many graduates
there are running around with their silly ties and stupid file holders
looking for jobs? People are just wasting their time when they could
have been doing something else with their lives, you understand.'

She looked at him, as if he were a stranger in Reza's body. 'My
children went to school. Munkaila, he went to school too, and if
not for his education, I don't know what would have become of us.'

'I'm not your son, you understand.'

Binta's eyes widened and she shrank into herself, suddenly
seeming smaller on the bed.

The noise from the TV filled the room and the moment stretched
into a dreary eternity, for Binta at least. Finally, she rose and threw
her veil over her head and slung one end over her left shoulder.
She made a move for the door. Reza hopped in front of her and
held his arms out by his sides uncertainly. They stood awkwardly
for a moment.

'Don't go.'

'Just get out of my way, Hassan.' She sounded resolute.

'I didn't mean to sound . . . you know, the way I did.'

'It doesn't matter.'

'Just . . . don't go.'

'You know, if you want to smoke your life away, there's hardly
anything I can do about it . . . especially since I'm not your mother.'
She walked past him and closed the door behind her.

She stood in the corridor and dabbed at her eyes with her veil.
A uniformed maid was walking towards her so she sighed and
hurried away.

Outside, under the sun-bleached parasol, Mallam Haruna sat on the bench looking out across the street. The music of the legendary Mamman Shata poured out amidst the static from the radio in his hand. Shata was at his impish best singing *Gagarabadau*, heaping assorted insults on a rival in love.

Allah ya tsine ma, tsohon mazinaci
Sai na badda ka, da kai da zuri'ar ka!

Mallam Balarabe had been standing over his wares, haggling with a buxom woman. They were laughing at a joke Mallam Haruna, preoccupied by other concerns, was too far gone to catch. He wasn't even listening to Shata's invective-laced lyrics. When he saw Binta emerge from the hotel, he stood up abruptly. He made as if to go after her but then halted.

'Is there a problem?' Mallam Balarabe turned to him, holding a hoop earring.

'No, nothing. Nothing.' But Mallam Haruna stepped off the kerb and stood by the side of the road. He watched Binta hail an okada and mount the pillion. The machine whisked her away, leaving in its wake a trail of white smoke that lingered in the air tenuously before dispersing.

Mallam Haruna went back to the bench and sat down. '*Lallai kam!*' he exclaimed for the umpteenth time. He threw one leg over the other and proceeded to shake his foot.

He had barely settled into this routine when he saw Reza emerge from the hotel. Mallam Haruna jumped to his feet yet again and hurried to the roadside as if he would rush across the street. Reza also hailed an okada and hopped on. When he, too, zoomed off, Mallam Haruna seriously contemplated slapping his cap on the ground and trampling on it. But he took off the cap with one hand, wiped the sweat off his razor-scraped scalp and put the cap back on. Then he turned and left, without even a word to his host, who was still engaged with the buxom woman.

PART TWO

The miseducation of Hassan 'Reza' Babale
(1986 - 2011 and beyond . . . perhaps)

19

*The playground of stallions is no place
for the crippled donkey*

San Siro shook off the lethargic cloud that had hovered over it for
a few days and, coaxed by the music of the itinerant Mamman
Kolo, became an agitated beast panting in the gathering dusk.

Reza heard the noise – music riding on the back of the evening
breeze into the ears of passers-by – from some distance. When
the chorus came, it was in the burnished voices of euphoric men
long given over to the lure of ganja and assorted dope, punctuated
by ecstatic whoops and delirious laughter.

Only Mamman Kolo with his old tambourine and the skills of
a snake charmer could stir San Siro, that slumbering beast, into
such a state of frenzy. Reza leaned by the entrance and, as he
expected, the place was packed with twenty or so men dancing
to Mamman Kolo's bawdy lyrics and the beats of his tambourine.
Reza luxuriated in air made thick and indolent by the aroma of
weed. He smiled as he took in the men puffing on joints as they
swayed to the music. In the corner, groups of boys were sucking
sholisho glue and cough syrup while passing on joints. Young
girls vending food or Zobo drinks stood with trays of wares deftly
balanced on their heads, watching the dance.

In the middle of the throng, Reza could see the fountainhead of
the revelry. Mamman Kolo never stopped smiling as he delivered

the solo and beat the tambourine on his bony hand, sometimes raising it high above his head. And when he saw Reza, his smile broadened and he skilfully wove him into his lyrics.

Reza, too, danced into the centre of the circle as Kolo sang his praises.

Kai bari dan uban mutum
Reza dodon kwalawa
Sara daya ya zub da goma

Reza raised his arm and symbolically sliced the air with it as if with a machete. A multitude of smoky voices rose in raucous acclamation. Reza stuck a fifty-naira note on Kolo's sweaty forehead, danced a few more steps and then pushed his way through the crowd.

Gattuso was standing by his door nodding to the tune. There was a frown on his face as he took money and handed out joints to two boys. They clamped their fists in their open palms in reverence as they walked past Reza, who nodded acknowledgement and patted Gattuso's bare shoulder, feeling his hand bounce off the taut, rubbery muscle.

'Reza, Reza!' Gattuso greeted. 'You are back. How is your old man?'

'The old man will live, I think.' Reza turned again to take in the crowded courtyard. 'I see Kolo is here.'

'Yes, you can see business is moving. I think he comes with djinns, the son of a whore.'

Mamman Kolo could strike up an impromptu party with a tap of his tambourine. And that was good business for San Siro. He was a peculiar fellow, Mamman Kolo. It was rumoured he came originally from Zaria. He would arrive when least expected, bringing along his trusted tambourine, a *joie de vivre* and anecdotes from far-flung places. He would talk about his adventures with itinerant showmen who roamed with reptiles and made children mount live hyenas to dissuade them from bed-wetting. He would talk about his sojourns with the ladies of easy virtue in Eko, the donkey-eating folks of Ezamgbo, the marabouts of Agadez, his escapades with the fishermen of Busa and his days in the illegal mines of Kebbi. But of his parents who left him an orphan, he would say nothing.

And just when he had sufficiently doused the place in his buccaneering romanticism, Mamman Kolo would up and leave unheralded in the night, so that the boys would wake up to his profound absence. For days afterwards, they would sit in the shades and, with languid eyes, talk about the days of flushed flowers Mamman Kolo had gifted them.

When Reza had left San Siro two days before to see his ailing father, the ambience had been suffused with an intangible melancholy, the sort that could linger if nothing dramatic happened. He now looked at the bubbly crowd and nodded. 'Yes, he comes with djinns.'

Gattuso cracked his knuckles. 'Your old man is better, you say.'

'Yes, he has been discharged. He will go for check-ups once in a while, you understand.' Reza turned and tried to enter Gattuso's room but the burly one was reluctant to make way.

'Come, let's talk about money.' Reza pretended not to notice the obstruction. When he pushed past Gattuso, he saw Rita, whom almost all the boys had had, sprawled on the rumpled sheets of the mattress. She scrambled into a sitting position and made a show of patting down her dishevelled hair. It was long and lustrous, and fake.

'Reza.' Her eyes avoided his.

Reza looked at the smoothness of her exposed thighs and surreptitiously grasped his crotch.

'Rita.' He stood uncertainly for a moment. He then turned and made for the door.

Incidentally, Dan Asabe, who had never had Rita, and seemed to harbour no desire to, was ambling just outside. He stood aside to let Reza pass. Dan Asabe bowed, inadvertently presenting his head, and the machete gash he had sustained from the rally.

It was this scar that interested Reza, who considered it skeptically. 'Your wound is healing.'

'Yes, it is.' Dan Asabe's bow deepened as Reza walked past him to his room, where Gattuso joined him.

The two men stood awkwardly for a minute. Outside, another ecstatic roar rolled on for a minute and died down to the sound of Mamman Kolo's tambourine and his soprano voice.

'You want to have—'

'No,' Reza barked. 'Let's talk about money.' He slumped onto his mattress.

Gattuso sauntered further into the room and sat down beside him. When they had finished balancing the accounts, Reza took the thick roll of money proffered and tucked it into his back pocket.

'I will travel tomorrow to get some new merchandise, you understand.'

Gattuso thought Reza seemed edgy and smiled. He drew closer, his smile taking on a dubious hue. 'Let me get you something.' His eyes gleamed. 'It's good stuff, *wallahi*.'

Reza looked at the new AC Milan poster glistening on the wall while he waited for Gattuso's return. He had put it up a couple of days before his trip. The old one had been taken down in a solemn ceremony witnessed only by Sani Scholar, who was given the honour of disposing of it. Being that Sani had no such reverence for the poster—he had no concept of empty spaces that needed to be occupied, bland spots that needed to be covered—he had shredded it and thrown the pieces into the garbage.

Gattuso came back with a wrap of nylon, still smiling. 'Just pour some of it in a bowl of fura. It will enhance your performance.'

Reza looked at him skeptically.

'Really, try it. If you like, I will ask Rita to come over so you can try it out.'

'No, no.' Reza threw the wrap on his mattress.

'So, who are you going to do it with?'

When Reza looked at him, Gattuso laughed and slapped him on the arm. The force of the blow made Reza recoil. Gattuso laughed some more and headed out to the girl waiting in his room.

Reza leaned on the doorjamb to watch the bustle outside. Kolo was tired, his voice was strained, but he kept going. The boys swayed languorously to the music like animated seaweed. Reza was thinking of breaking it up when he spotted Corporal Bako lurking by the entrance in a manner befitting a stray dog. One of the boys saw the policeman too and shouted; '*Wara, wara!*'

Some of the boys made to bolt, but Reza's voice rose above the din as he shouted for them to stop. The music ceased. The boys turned to the policeman and saw how unsure of himself he seemed. Reza stepped forward.

The policeman walked up to him and smiled coyly. 'Reza, the OC says you should keep the party down.'

There was a lull, in which a boy, dazed by dope, wobbled and slumped. The tambourine went up again and Mamman Kolo sang:

'OC, the mamafucker!

Sucks his father's cock.'

A thunderous cheer went up and the cowed officer withdrew under a blanket of jeers. After he had left, Reza asked for the party to break up.

Some of the boys left, swaying to the ganja fumes curling in their heads like the melodies of a snake charmer's flute. Others took refuge in the corners, puffing odorous fumes into the darkening skies.

Mamman Kolo came and sat with Reza on the bench in front of the rooms. Soon they were surrounded by other boys, who sat down on the floor when there was no more space on the bench.

Kolo proceeded to recount tales of his exploits in the Kebbi mines, where they dug gold for shifty Chinese contractors, whose pitch of voice Kolo found particularly amusing and made efforts to mimic, to the delight of the San Siro boys.

But perhaps because Reza already knew what was happening in the room behind them, he imagined he could hear, beneath the din of the enthralled boys, the passionate noises Gattuso and Rita were making.

Kolo held up a hand for silence. '*Wallahi*, I will pay anything to hear those people sing. I can imagine how awful it would sound.' He made screeching sounds and beat his tambourine to accompany the laughter that greeted his mimicry.

Reza rose, went to his room and dialled Binta's number on his phone. The phone rang almost interminably. He dialled again, and when he got no response, he hissed and shoved the phone back in his pocket.

He went out and sat with the boys as Kolo enthralled them until the glow of the setting sun spread across the sky like gold dust thrown from beyond the horizon.

It was at that time that Marufu came shuffling in. The click of his walking stick on the concrete filled the sudden silence. He winced each time he set down his heavily bandaged left leg. He looked at the space before him as he laboured forward. It was Dogo who first overcame his shock and rose to challenge the intruder.

'What do you want here, *barawo*?'

'What did he steal?' Kolo grinned.

'Condoms!'

'Shut it, Dogo,' Reza barked.

But Kolo cackled, his laughter lingering, drawing in the others who laughed with more restraint because of the scowl on Reza's face.

Marufu tried to stand straight. 'I want to speak to Reza.'

'Well, then, speak up.' Reza could barely contain himself. 'Whatever you have to say, you can say it in front of the boys, you understand.'

Marufu shuffled forward, sat down on the floor and proceeded to tender his apologies for jumping Hajiya Binta's fence. '*Wallahi*, I didn't know you had asked for that house to be left alone. You know me, I wouldn't have.'

Because Reza said nothing, Marufu had to repeat his excuse all over again, adding details he had left out the first time.

'Well, Reza,' Kolo cleared his throat, 'he has apologised. You know, we have all been caught in situations where we needed to jump fences occasionally. But since he has promised not to cross you anymore, please forgive him.'

The boys all chipped in a word for Marufu while he sat before Reza with his head bowed.

Reza sighed and cracked his knuckles. 'The way we do things, there has to be order, is that not so? We can't all be doing things anyhow, you understand?'

The boys nodded.

'When I say a house is off limits, there's a reason for it. We are not fools, you understand? But Marufu knew this and went to steal that woman's generator. There are consequences for things like this. Marufu could have been dead by now, but I said, well, this is Marufu, the footballer, our friend. We should just teach him a lesson.'

'He has learnt it,' Kolo offered, and the boys nodded.

'*Haba* Reza, I'm really sorry. It was the devil, I swear.' Marufu looked up with imploring eyes.

Reza shifted on the bench and looked at the expectant faces turned to him. He shrugged. 'Next time you fuck with the devil and cross me, you are dead-dead.'

Dogo jumped before Marufu, drew out his dagger and drew a line inches from his neck. Marufu flinched and the boys laughed.

'It's time for prayers.' Kolo stood up. 'After, I'll have some ganja.'

———

Later, while he sat in his room and allowed his senses to float off his fingertips to uncharted shores, listening to Mamman Kolo talk about the women of Cotonou, Reza thought about his mother.

He tried to remember her touch, her hands on his as she loosened his hold on her jilbab, but all he could remember with certainty was the exotic smell of her perfume. It was the only time he recalled touching his mother. And the last time he had seen her, three years back, it was that memory from fifteen years before that had decided the fate of their encounter.

His father had called him and asked him to come home, saying that there was an emergency. When Reza arrived, he found his mother cross-legged on the rug in his father's sitting room. He caught the gleam of gold in her teeth as she smiled at him. He turned and walked out, increasing his pace when he heard her calling after him, until he was sprinting through the dank alleyways.

Now he sat on his mattress, with Mamman Kolo's voice eddying in the background, and tried to reconstruct her face from that encounter. He tried to recall her shock when she saw him turning away from her but all he could remember was the dark line of kohl around her eyes, the slanting scarification on her cheek and the gleam in her teeth.

When his phone chimed, he picked it up, looked at the screen and raised a hand for silence.

'*Yallabai,*' he greeted. There were some noises on the other end and then the senator's voice.

'Reza, *yaya dai?*'

Reza greeted the senator again, unconsciously bowing his head in deference.

'Reza, where are you, is that noise I hear?'

'At home, sir, I am at home.'

'Oh, I thought you were with your girlfriend. You know, you young men of nowadays.' There was a laugh that resonated down the line. 'When I was your age, by this time you wouldn't have found me at home. I would have been out trying my charms on young girls. But now I am left to play squash with old men with sagging bellies. You play squash, don't you?'

Reza shook his head. 'No, sir, I don't.'

'Then what do you do with your life? Someday, I will bring you to the club so you can see me play. I am a pretty good player, *wallahi*.'

'I would like that.'

'But you must bring me your girlfriend, Reza. Bring her to greet me, *ko*?'

'Yes, sir. Perhaps someday.'

'Yes, we will arrange that, *ka ji ko*?'

'Yes, sir.'

'*Madalla! Madalla!* Well, my opponent is ready; let me go deal with him. But, Reza?'

'Yes, sir.'

'You remember what I said about the job you are going to do for us, *ko*? The last time you came to the house?'

'You haven't told me yet, sir.'

'Yes, yes, I know. Well, you remember Moses, my PA? I will give him the phone and you will talk, but whatever instructions he gives you, make sure you take it seriously, *ka ji ko*?'

'Yes, sir.'

'It is very important, Reza, so pay attention.'

Reza heard him asking Moses to take the phone while he went off to his game.

When Moses came on, he explained that it was important they discuss face-to-face and so they arranged to meet. Reza put down the phone with a smile and took a long drag on his joint.

20

An emaciated elephant is still better than ten frogs

There was, Hureira realised, something disturbing about the way Fa'iza bent studiously over her book. Perhaps it was the almost tangible determination with which she held the pen and the way her hand seemed to tremble. From her place on the mattress across the room, Hureira could not see what Fa'iza was writing, but she could see the bold, virile curlicues, the drawings that appeared indiscernible from where she was lying.

When Fa'iza raised her head, Hureira looked away. When she managed to look at the girl again, she saw her casting a haunted gaze at the wall.

Hureira crawled out of bed, avoiding Fa'iza's line of vision. She walked out of the room, stealing a look at the seated figure out of the corner of her eye and wondering if she should take her sleeping daughter away with her as well.

Hureira knocked on Binta's door and entered without being invited. She was momentarily taken aback by the sight of her mother seated at the dressing table, staring vacantly at her own reflection.

Their eyes met in the mirror, mother and daughter, and Hureira felt the disapproval refracting off the glass and reaching for her heart. But it passed quickly. Or was her mind playing tricks on her?

'Hajiya,' she whispered. 'Are you sure Fa'iza is all right?'

'What's wrong?'

The disinterest in her mother's voice brushed Hureira's face, wafted away through the parted curtains, through the window into the sunny courtyard. Hureira shook her head. 'She was having conversations in her dreams, and it went on all night. Now she is sitting in the room trying to bore a hole in the wall with her eyes. *Wallahi*, I think she is being possessed by djinns.'

This time, Binta turned and looked at Hureira. She hoped that the incredulity on her face would dissuade her daughter. 'Don't be silly, you are too old to be running around saying such nonsense, *kin ji ko?*'

Hureira stared back. 'That was how it happened to my neighbour's daughter, *wallahi.*'

'Hureira, stop this nonsense.'

'But Hajiya, I'm being serious.'

'Stop it, I said.' Binta stared her down this time. With Hureira's gaze directed at the open window, her countenance defined by her pouting lips and bland eyes, Binta added, 'I have had a bad night and I don't need you and your stupidity causing me more distress than you have already.'

'Bad night? What happened?'

Binta looked down at her palms. She had been surprised when she woke up and hadn't seen blood on her hands. 'Just a bad dream.' Her voice seemed to echo from another realm, one tottering between dreams and reality.

'Bad dream about what?' Hureira placed her hands on her hips.

Binta was still looking at her hands. Her dream had been of Yaro, of her holding his bloodied corpse in her arms and calling him by his given name. But she could not bring herself to tell Hureira that when she had woken up panting, certain she would see his blood on her hands, her first thought had been of Reza, of his face looming before her mind's eye.

'Nothing.' She spoke absently. 'Just a bad dream.'

Hureira shrugged. 'Well, I am certain Fa'iza is being plagued by djinns, *wallahi*. I suggest you call that ustaz of yours to look at her before it gets worse.'

'Ok, Hureira. Just go now and prepare breakfast, will you, before I starve to death?'

When Hureira got back to the room, Fa'iza was lying in the middle of the dark green rug, staring at the ceiling. Hureira stood by the door, hunched slightly forward while keeping half her body outside. When she called Fa'iza's name, the girl responded by moving her feet.

'Hajiya said you should go prepare breakfast.'

For some time nothing happened and then, finally, Fa'iza rolled onto her stomach and raised herself. She shuffled past Hureira, who leaned away from her, and went into the kitchen.

After breakfast, Ummi took the dishes to the kitchen and rushed back to sit beside Binta. She was enthralled by the wildlife documentary on TV, but covered her face with her hands each time a lion pounced on a gazelle or some other hapless prey. Binta herself sat staring at the screen, almost oblivious to the girl moulding her tiny frame into her side.

'Hajiya, why does the lion kill other animals?'

'I don't know, Ummi.'

Hureira, sitting on the rug, made to speak. She looked at Fa'iza, who sat with her hands on her lap staring straight ahead, and shut her mouth.

'Why are they so wicked? I hate lions.' Ummi's eyes were turned to her grandmother's face.

'Keep quiet and watch!' Binta glowered.

Ummi sat still, her eyes darting from Fa'iza's blank face to her mother's perplexed one. The noise from the TV filled the room but their own silence grew like cold fingers around their throats.

'I watched this documentary on TV the other day,' Hureira blurted. 'They talked about this stinking flower, the corpse flower. It blossoms only once in thirty years. Did you know about it, Fa'iza?'

Fa'iza looked at her blankly and shook her head.

'It stinks like a corpse, they said, and it's huge and ugly. But when it's blossoming, people travel to see it. You know how these white people are, going to see a flower that stinks like death.'

'I want to see it, Mommy.' Ummi sat up and turned an expectant face to her mother.

Hureira laughed. 'It's found in Indonesia and other such places.'

'I want to see it. Will you take me? I want to see it.'

'Yes, I will since that useless father of yours has bought me a private jet just so I can go globetrotting with you. *Aikin banza kawai.*'

Ummi now turned a bemused face from her mother to Binta, who had also cast a glance at Hureira, and then Fa'iza. Then she turned again to her mother, who was now scowling at the TV screen.

Fa'iza sighed absently and leaned back into the chair.

'But you know, I think that flower is special—'

'Oh, for God's sake, shut your mouth!' Binta eyed Hureira. 'You sit here talking about some useless flower in God-knows-where while your second marriage is crumbling. I wonder what kind of daughter you are. You are so hopeless your husband has not even come to take you back and you still sit here yapping about rubbish.'

This time, their silence was heavy, and they felt its immensity pressing down on their shoulders. Even the noise of the TV seemed to have been subdued, but not Ummi's spirit. She jumped up and said there was a phone ringing. She ran into Binta's bedroom.

'R is calling, Hajiya. Who is R?' Ummi returned with Binta's phone.

'Give me the phone, you!' Binta seized the phone from her. She scrambled to her feet and hurried into her room as she said hello into the speaker. The sound of her door slamming jolted Hureira, who got up and stamped to her room.

'Yes,' Binta cradled the phone.

'Hope you woke up well.' It was Reza on the other end.

'Yes.'

'I want to see you.'

She hesitated. 'Yes, so you could annoy me like you did last time, right?' She held her breath.

Finally, he laughed. 'No, no. I just want to be with you. No talking this time, just action, you understand.'

She smiled. 'You shameless boy, I am not one of your little girlfriends you should be saying such silly things to, you know.'

'Just action *zalla.*' And he laughed, a deep-throated laugh that rang in her ears and made her face flush.

———

She drifted, almost weightlessly, in the pungent smell of weed. It was only when she opened her eyes and saw him sitting shirtless by the window, puffing on the joint in his hand, that she realised where she was. Binta stretched and yawned. 'Hassan, stop smoking that thing in here, you could get arrested. Besides, it's giving me a headache.'

With his back turned to her, she could not see his face. She propped herself up on her elbows and remembered that she was naked under the sheet. Her clothes were on the chair across the room. She had taken them off one after the other and folded them carefully while he had waited on the bed.

'Just action.' She smiled at the now familiar tingling that thawed her insides as she did up the hook of her bra. 'You must have been on something.'

He turned to her and smiled and she saw how handsome he looked, how his glazed eyes seemed so peaceful and yet so far away, how young he really was.

'Action *zalla*.' He raised his joint at her before putting it back to his lips. He looked at her, then turned back to the window and watched the sprinklers watering the lawn.

'God, what am I doing?' Her voice was low because she was addressing herself.

'What?'

'I don't know. You are so young, Hassan. I don't know if this is right.'

'Why must it be right?' He spoke with a timbre in his voice that she had come to associate with what she had called his inner self: the dreamy-eyed philosopher awakened by ganja fumes. 'Why must anything be right or wrong? Why can't things be just as they are?'

She sighed. 'When you smoke this thing, I don't know what it does to you, you just talk rubbish sometimes.'

He smiled and put the joint to his lips. 'Maybe you should try it.'

'God forbid! I want you to quit. It's killing you.'

He shrugged. 'What doesn't? I will die when I die. We all will, you understand?'

Binta sighed again. 'My daughter was saying something earlier today, about some stupid flower that waits a lifetime to bloom.

'Thirty years, she said. And when it does, after all those years, it smells like a corpse.'

'Ha ha! What sort of flower is that?'

'I was just thinking how much like that flower I am. I have waited my whole life to feel . . . as I do when I'm with you, you know. I shouldn't be telling you such things but I just need to get it off my chest, you know. No one has ever made me feel this way. But like that flower, after all those years waiting, when I bloom, it doesn't feel right. I don't know if you understand me.'

He continued to puff on the joint, looking disturbingly peaceful. 'You mean it stinks.'

She surprised herself with her laughter. It rocked her. She laughed for a while, sniffling as she did. When she managed to stop, she wiped away the tears from the corners of her eyes. But they wouldn't stop, even after she no longer felt amused. That was when she knew she was actually crying.

Save the occasional movement of his hand to guide the joint to his lips, he kept still, as if reading the cipher in the curling fumes. It took him a while to speak. 'You know, when I was young, still a boy, there was this Eid day, and we were so excited with our new clothes. There was this cheap brocade our father bought for us, it was called Shonekan, it was kind of in vogue then, you understand.'

She knew it; she had bought it for her children, too, around '93. It had been a fallout from the political campaigns when the borders had been opened to cheap commodities that politicians had used to entice voters. All sorts of things had come in: salt, sugar, strange soaps with too much soda that scalded the hands and bleached clothes, cheap shiny fabrics that coloured the water they were to be washed in; petrol with blue, pink and green hues.

But the elections had been annulled when the military decided against handing over to the civilians. Instead Shonekan was put in charge until he was upended in a palace coup not long after. His name was given to all the strange commodities that traders had hoarded from the political campaigns and which flooded the markets as soon as politicking was over.

'Mine was white, sparkling and starched. We had just returned from the Eid and I was going to take it off so I wouldn't stain it while eating rice and stew, you understand? Then, Aminu, my little brother; my half-brother, accidentally spilled ink on it.'

He smoked his joint until she realised he had finished his story. When he turned to her and saw her perplexed face, he smiled with glazed eyes.

'We are like clothes, you understand. We get rumpled, and creased and torn, sometimes irreparably. Some of us are stitched up, patched up, others are discarded. Some clothes are fortunate. Others are not. They are born into misfortune and ink spills and whatnots, you understand?'

She rolled her eyes, chasing the meaning of what he said. 'Hassan Reza, you are high.'

He raised the stub in his hand in acknowledgement and took one long last drag.

'You really need to give these things up. Be a good man, for God's sake.'

'I am what I am.' He crushed the stub in the ashtray and turned to her.

'And what about that issue, about going back to school?'

He wagged a finger in front of his face. 'No talk, just action, you understand.'

'Seriously, Hassan.'

'Not now, please. I have an important assignment from my boss. Maybe after that.'

'What assignment?'

'Very important, you understand. Very important.'

———

He sat with his radio pressed to his ear, watching the entrance to the hotel across the street. He had seen her go in four hours before; had seen the boy go in before her. They were minutes apart. Fifteen minutes apart.

Mallam Haruna had even wandered into the hotel premises but unsure what he should be looking for or where, afraid of being harassed by hotel security, he had withdrawn and returned to his spot under his friend Mallam Balarabe's parasol.

He had noticed Balarabe's growing coldness since he took to spending most of the day under the old parasol staring grouchily across the street. They had run out of conversation, it would seem, especially as Mallam Haruna had not been forthcoming. Yet he would linger, long past Asr prayers.

But since he first saw her leaving the hotel five days earlier, he wanted to be sure. And then, today, when he saw Reza arrive ahead of her, he knew he was on to something.

It was twenty minutes past five when he saw her emerge through the gate. He stood up. And just as abruptly sat down again.

Balarabe turned to him. '*Lafiya*, Mallam Haruna?'

'Yes, I am fine.'

He watched Binta flag down a motorcycle taxi and climb onto the pillion. He watched the bike zoom away into the side street that led to her home.

He waited and some fifteen minutes later he saw Reza emerge and look up and down the street before he turned left and walked towards the market at the crowded junction.

21

If nothing touches the palm leaves, they do not rustle

Reza paced the wide living room, his footsteps echoing in the emptiness. It disturbed him, this emptiness. Gattuso, leaning on the window ledge cracking his knuckles, twisting his neck and punching his palm, could feel Reza's unease. And his anger.

Dogo and Joe came in and stood, one on each side of the door. They too sensed the anger; now swelling almost to a rage.

'What have you done with her?' Gattuso barked.

'Nothing, nothing,' Joe held up his arms by the side of his face. 'We just put her in the room.'

When Reza walked up to Joe and stared into his eyes – eyes glazed by inebriation – he could smell the gin on his breath, even though Joe had turned his face away.

Reza slapped the wall beside him. It trembled. Joe cringed.

'You useless drunk! You had to go fuck it up. You fucking let the guy go, mamafucker!'

'Reza, Dogo was supposed to cover the guy. You should ask him what happened.'

'Shut your dirty mouth!' Dogo bellowed.

'You shut your mouth!' Gattuso's voice resonated off the bare walls.

In the silence, Reza ground his teeth and finally, when he could bear it no longer, he punched Joe in the stomach and kicked him as he cowered. 'I should never have brought a useless drunk like you on this job. I will kill you and dump you in the gorge, I swear.'

When Reza reached for the gun in his jacket, Gattuso and Dogo jumped in and restrained him.

'Please, Reza,' Gattuso looked into his eyes.

Reza eyed their hands on his arms and slowly they let go of him. They remained standing close by, with pleading eyes. Joe sprawled on the terrazzo, looking up to see which way his fate would swing. It occurred to him then to say something. 'I will find him. I will get him.'

Contempt exploded in Reza's eyes. When he kicked Joe in the face, there was a crunching sound and he was sure he had knocked out a tooth. He felt pain rippling from his shin upwards.

He walked to the other window and stood staring out at the star-speckled heavens. It was supposed to be a simple mission – wait for the target, the one Moses had pointed out, in the car park of the garden, and then take him. When the young man had come out with a girl after an evening of revelry, and unlocked his car, they had jumped them, armed with chloroform-drenched hankies. The girl had been easy. Gattuso had held her and covered her nose until she grew numb in his arms. But Joe had been tipsy and couldn't hold down the target. The young man had struggled, pushed Joe aside and taken off. Reza had raised the gun, the one he had got from Moses – something the senator had contributed to the mission — but hesitated. He was not a man of guns but of steel, and a gunshot would have attracted unwanted attention. So he had watched their target bolt, watched their assignment crumble before it had even begun. And so they had bundled the girl into the waiting car and sped off.

He wished he could disappear into the shadows, into the night. But he had to explain what happened so he pulled out his phone and dialled. There was no answer. He dialled again and then finally shoved the phone back in his pocket. Two minutes later, his phone rang. He pulled it out, looked at the screen, then at the boys behind him. Joe was still sitting on the floor where Reza had left him, nursing his bruised jaw. Gattuso seemed to be contemplating the possibility of crushing his own skull with his thumbs and forefingers.

Reza put the phone to his ear. 'Hello, sir.'

'Yes.' Moses, the senator's PA, sounded crisp, business-like. 'Did you get him?'

Reza hesitated. 'No.'

'No?'

'No. He got away. But we got his girlfriend, you understand.'

'What girlfriend?'

'The one he was with.'

'Who gives a damn about her? Your instruction was to get the guy. What the hell happened?'

'It's a long story. He got away and we couldn't shoot him. But we got the girl. We can get him.'

'You have bungled this job big time. Oga will be very disappointed. Let the girl go. Nobody needs her. And get the hell out of the house. Bloody amateurs!' The line went dead.

Reza stood grinding his teeth. Finally, he walked across the room, and up the arching staircase.

The girl was in the last room on the balcony, the one in the corner, the one that might host guests when the house was eventually completed. There were three doors before that – all of them sturdy, ornate, with strips of plastic still clinging to them. The green of the doors stood out against the bare, unpainted walls. His footfall sounded off the terrazzo, echoing the emptiness of the large building. He unlocked the door and went in.

The drugged girl was lying on the red and blue plastic mat where she had been dumped, her decency saved by the jeans beneath her knee-length kaftan.

Reza stood a foot away from her and saw the darkened vein that ran diagonally across her forehead. It stood out on her smooth skin, as did the red sore on the back of her left hand where a mosquito had bitten her. She looked so fragile it would be easy to kill her. A bullet in the back of her head. A pillow over her face. Her neck might snap if he clamped his hands around her throat. He could even have her overdose on chloroform.

He marvelled at her hair, silky, unbraided, almost jet black. On her right hand, thrown carelessly beside her head, a ring gleamed. He knelt down beside her and the opulence of her perfume assailed him as he rolled the ring around her delicate finger. Real gold. He took a handful of her lustrous hair and ran his fingers through it, savouring its softness and the smell of luxuriant hair oil. He could not recall what Binta's hair smelt like but he was certain it did not smell this good.

Back in the living room, he saw the boys huddled over the girl's things scattered on the floor; her empty, expensive-looking purse lying close by. He checked to ensure that her Blackberry and iPhone were switched off. An elegant bottle of perfume caught Reza's eyes. *Caron Poivre*. It had to have been expensive. He could perceive it subtly exuding from the girl. There also were exotic hand and face creams in little tubes, a wallet with money, some naira and pounds sterling. In her wallet Reza also found her ATM cards, a student ID and a driver's licence from which he read her details: Leila Sarki, born March 16, 1988. He studied her face in the passport photograph. Even though she looked hassled in the photo, it was clear she was a very beautiful woman.

He threw the cards down amongst the scattered items on the floor. 'Put her things together. We are letting her go.'

Dogo looked up. 'What about the money?'

'Did I not give you your advance?' But then his eyes rested on the girl's wallet. 'Well, it doesn't look like we are going to get any balance from this, we might as well take what we can.'

Reza counted out some naira notes and handed them to Gattuso and then Dogo. He threw the rest carelessly over Joe's head. He shoved the pounds into his own pocket.

Gattuso knocked his knuckles together. 'So, we are just going to let her go like that?'

'Yes. The job has been bungled.'

'But—' He continued knocking his fists together until Reza prompted him. 'She looks like she is the daughter of someone important; we could pull a deal over her.'

Dogo clicked his thumb and forefinger. 'Yes! Thank you, brother; you just said what was on my mind. Ask her people to pay, or we kill her *kawai*!'

Reza thought for a while. 'Then we would have to move her to San Siro. The boss provided this place for his job. Since it would no longer be his job then we'd have to move her.'

Joe looked up at the baroque designs on the high POP ceiling; the blossom at the centre, with a couple of naked wires sticking out of it, fascinated him the most. He imagined a chandelier would dangle from it when the work was completed and he could almost see the thousand lights dancing in his eyes. 'What mamafucker built this house, mehn?'

'Fucking cool, right?' Dogo smiled and nodded. 'I want to be a don someday and own a house like this, man. Imagine dying in a grand place like this.'

'In your fucking dreams, man.' Joe's laughter was a staccato, guttural explosion. 'You will die in a goddam chicken coop.'

Dogo, too, laughed up to the ceiling and sat on the floor. He reached into his pocket for a cigarette and a lighter. 'Goddam chicken coop, man.' He lit up with unsteady hands and wiped his eyes with the back of his sleeve. 'Goddam chicken coop.'

Reza's phone chimed amidst the contrived laughter of Dogo and Joe that resonated off the unpainted walls. He held up his hand for silence.

'What have you done with the girl?' It was Moses.

'We let her go.'

'Goddamn it, you idiot.'

Reza smiled. He really hated this Moses. '*Wata rana zan ci ubanka, ka gane ko?*' And he knew he would enjoy plunging his dagger just beside that tie he always wore.

Moses chuckled mirthlessly. 'Well, go and bring her back. Your new instruction is to hold on to her.'

'Well, you asked me to let her go.'

'Find her.' The line went dead.

———

The cat with the white-tipped tail came late that night, long after Mallam Haruna had switched off his radio and finished his analysis of the day's news. It sat on the fence, between the loops of the razor wire and watched the couple; the woman with a bored countenance, the man more unsure of himself than he had ever been.

Binta had noted Mallam Haruna's unease right from when he offered to stand guard over her and wave away the midges tormenting her with the tail of his kaftan. He had backed down immediately when he saw the shocked expression on her face. Then he had spent five minutes trying to tell her how important it was for a man to protect the woman he loved from 'all enemies'.

That was how he got talking about scorpions and how he had been stung three times in the past. He punctuated his gory tale of feverish nights fighting off the venom with little nervous chortles.

Then he had attempted to mount his cap on her head, right on top of her hijab. It was so unheralded that she had wanted to flee.

'Is there something wrong with you this evening?'

'Oh no, not at all. Just wondering what you would look like with my cap on you.'

She gaped at him, as if she had somehow contrived to see through his skull and discovered that his cranium was packed full of semi-deflated balloons.

He seemed oblivious to her stare. 'You know I am the best cap washerman in this corner of the world, *wallahi*.'

He went into a fractured narrative about how he had learned how to wash caps in Maiduguri when he had been an almajiri and how he had married his first wife as *ladan noma*.

Binta's mind drifted. She wondered what she could do to get rid of Hureira since her husband had refused to come for her. She contemplated several possibilities, none of them practical, and concluded that other than escorting Hureira back to her own house, she had no choice but to accept that her daughter might end up permanently stationed in Fa'iza's room, while her matrimonial home in Jos collected the harmattan dust.

When her mind wandered back, Mallam Haruna was talking about his third or fourth son making a living driving a white man around Port Harcourt, and how he had been in an accident and now limped like a three-legged dog.

She felt his hand on her shoulder, a light slap at first and then the hand slid down just a bit.

'Mosquito,' he grinned.

The cat meowed, almost half-heartedly. It used its front paw to wipe its head, took several steps and then bounded off the fence, into Mama Efe's side of the wall.

Mallam Haruna launched into yet another disjointed narrative on how best to deal with the pestilence of mosquitoes using dried orange rinds sprinkled on embers. Then he reached out and slapped another mosquito on her back and yet again, his hand tarried.

She regarded him with a frown. 'Mallam Haruna, *yaya dai*?'

'Nothing, nothing,' he laughed, uneasily. 'Perhaps we could meet somewhere else.'

'What for?'

'Well,' he lowered his voice, 'well, we could just go somewhere else, you know, just get to know each other better.'

'What do you mean?'

He was unsettled by the bluntness of her tone. 'Well, you know, I was just saying we could go somewhere private, you know—'

'What for?'

He turned on his radio and fiddled with the knob, sweeping past stations.

She said nothing, only watched him search for a discernible voice in the sea of static. He switched the radio off just as suddenly as he had turned it on.

'So, what do you say?'

'To what?'

'You know, what I said, about going somewhere.'

'What do you have to say that you can't say here?'

'Well, we could go to Mr Biggs, or Mama Cass or La Crème, one of these fancy places, you know.'

'I am not hungry.'

'Well, I don't mean now, of course, silly. Perhaps tomorrow.'

'I have a kitchen and a store full of food. If I'm hungry, I know how to cook.'

He laughed, 'Binta *ke nan*. Why are you being difficult?' It came out as a statement.

'Mallam, I am not going anywhere with you. I am not a young girl to be gallivanting about.'

He lowered his head and sighed. He switched on the radio again and began fiddling with the knob.

'Switch it off, *dan Allah.*'

He put the radio by his side and then picked it up again. Then he removed his cap and scratched his scalp. Finally, he said he was leaving and they stood up.

She shook her hijab. '*Sai da safe.*'

'Binta,' he called as she made to leave. 'Perhaps, you know, we could go to a hotel, you and I—'

The crickets chirped, the midges buzzed. The night breathed. Finally, she hissed, a long, drawn-out sound of contempt. 'What the hell do you take me for?' She flapped her hijab as if to shake off his words and went into the house.

He stood alone, next to the bed of petunias Hadiza had planted, listening to the chaotic rhythm of his heart and the subtle, subtle breathing of the night.

———

Ustaz Nura, the teacher, polished the dirt off his sandals with a damp piece of cloth. He was diligent, scrubbing out the caked mud clinging to the clefts.

Behind him, his wife Murja bristled. 'So, which one of them is it going to be today?'

He shook his head. That action set his headache off again. It always happened when he had a bad night, as the one before. He had been looking forward to morning so he could escape his house and Murja's nagging.

As the years of their childless marriage lengthened, past the fifth and into the sixth, she had grown more insecure, more suspicious, eager to leap to incendiary conclusions. She was always plucking conspiracies of an impending invasion by a co-wife from Ustaz Nura's cheeky but innocent comments.

Her suspicions were not without reason. Her husband was often busy instructing the faithful, mostly women, on matters of deen, and also applied his services as a counsellor. He helped young women navigate the berged terrain of courtship and marriage. That was how she had fallen in love with him when she had been nineteen and he was a twenty-seven-year-old aalim with a dark, glistening beard, a kind voice garnished with a cultured Arab accent, and trousers that dangled inches above his ankles. He had impressed her with his informed discourse of Al Ghazali and Ibn Sina, of Freud and Dewey, for he had gone off to university and attained a diploma in psychology as well. But those days seemed so far gone, a distant memory dulled by years of aborted hopes.

And the previous night, when he had returned late from trying to exorcise a vexed djinn that had possessed Laminde, Alhaji Momoh's svelte daughter, and was obsessed with stripping her naked in the most public of places, Murja's restless mind brimmed with other notions.

When she asked him where he had been, tired and bleary-eyed, he had said, 'There was this girl who—'

That was as much she had let him say before she had unleashed her torrent. And the night that had already been stretched for him got longer.

That morning, as he was trying to extricate himself from the stifling cocoon of her jealousy, a boy came in to announce that the Ustaz was wanted outside.

'Who? Who wants to see him?' she glowered at the boy.

'It's Mallam Haruna.'

'Mhmmm.' She set herself on the settee, scowling at the wall.

Ustaz Nura put some money on the table and carried his *Qassasul Anbiya,* from which he would later regale his students with the miraculous deeds of the prophets. He took an uncertain glance at his wife before hurrying out.

Because of Mallam Haruna's reputation as a vibrant proponent of plural marriage, Murja was certain he had come to bring her husband news of some fresh divorcee or widow waiting to be proposed to. So she went out to the vestibule and leaned on the doorjamb, to listen in on the men seated on the *dakali.*

'I am telling you this, so you can preach to her, Ustaz,' Mallam Haruna was saying. 'She is your student, you need to preach to her, not so?'

Murja listened to her husband muttering *subhanallahi* as he learned of the impious rendezvous of the widow Hajiya Binta and the Lord of San Siro, that insufferable *dan iska* with short, spiky hair and lips darkened by ganja fumes.

22

*Only a wise man can make out
the greying hair on a sheep*

She lingered more and more in her tinted dreams and was astonished by the splash of red each time it came, leaving her gasping and panting in the night. Sometimes Fa'iza fled from the shadows in her dreams. Other times, she dared to chase them, quietly at first.

It was Hureira who first noticed, long before Fa'iza started screaming. She had woken up to see the zombified girl walking in the dark, arms stretched out before her, going back and forth across the room. Frightened, Hureira had readied to flee as soon as Fa'iza moved away from the door. Crossing the room, she had hoisted Ummi unto her shoulder, muttering a verse from the Qur'an, the one that she had heard as a child would scare evil djinns away: '*Innahu min Sulaimana, wa innahu bismilluhir ruhmanir rahim.*'

She had felt Fa'iza's hands on her and had frozen, right on the word *Sulaimana*. Quickly, she clamped her thighs together to prevent her bladder from disgorging and had felt how violent her heartbeat sounded. And all the time, Fa'iza's hands were tentatively running over her.

Eventually, the girl had reached for the ground and laid down on the rug, curling into a foetal position. She had snuffled, mumbled and then fallen silent, her breathing blending into the noises of the night.

Hureira had carried Ummi to her mattress and laid her down. Sitting beside her, she muttered whatever supplication she could pluck from the darkness, from her jumbled and inadequate memorisation, her whispered voice rivalling the desperate thuds of her heart.

The next morning, they took the bus to town, all four of them, to visit Munkaila in his Maitama apartment. Hureira complained about the heat and cursed the slow pace at which the long, seemingly endless lines of cars crawled forward.

Hajiya Binta turned to her. 'You could always go back to your husband, you know. The traffic isn't so bad in Jos.'

Hureira frowned.

Fa'iza had her face pressed into the window, looking out at the boys hawking chilled drinks and yoghurt, the girls with loaded trays of plantain chips, young men peddling wall clocks, mops, towel rails and just about everything else. She watched a boy, no more than thirteen, run after a bus, balancing a plastic bucket half-filled with sachet water on his head. She saw a bank note fly out of the window of the bus and the boy bend to pick it. Losing interest, she leaned back on the seat and closed her eyes. But Ummi kept pointing out things: two hawking girls racing each other to a customer in a sedan, a motorcycle narrowly missing a youth vending phone cards, a lovely dainty black dress with yellow trimming hanging outside a boutique. No one paid her any heed.

When they got to Bulet Junction, they took a cab to Maitama.

The courtyard, when they arrived, was strewn with the red blossoms of the lone flame tree, whose boughs stretched across the compound like probing fingers searching the sunlight. Under the tree, little Zahra was gathering the blossoms into a glass cup half filled with water, an unlit candle peeking over the top.

Munkaila was leaning against his car parked in front of the house, speaking into the phone. He shoved the phone in his pocket as he walked to meet them and stooped to greet his mother, the tail of his golden-brown kaftan splaying out around him. He put out two of his fingers on the ground to support his weight.

The exchange of greetings drew Zahra's attention and she came running with her glass of crimson blossoms. Binta wanted to hoist the girl in the air but Zahra was protective of her collection. She hugged her grandma's legs instead.

Hureira motioned to the cup. 'What's that?'

'My flowers,' Zahra looked up at her aunt.

'Zahra does this often,' Munkaila placed a hand on his daughter's head. 'When the flame tree is in bloom, she collects the blossoms in a glass and lights a candle.'

'Season of crimson blossoms.' There was something melancholic about the way Fa'iza said it. Her eyes were focused on the glass.

Zahra beamed proudly. 'I keep it in my room. All day. The candle goes off when it burns to the water level.'

'Blood.'

They all turned to look at Fa'iza. This time, she was staring into the distance that had opened up before her eyes, stretching beyond the foggy precipice of imaginings. She started when Binta mentioned her name and seemed baffled that they were all looking at her.

Inside, Zahra set down the glass on the coffee table in the middle of the living room, lit the candle and sat watching the flame and the blossoms floating in the glass. And because the news on TV was not as interesting as the cartoons she preferred, Ummi, too, joined her, sitting on the other side so that the glass table was between them and their eyes found each other's through the glass, over the top of the buoyant blossoms.

Binta's face glowed as she sat on the couch, holding the sleeping Khalida in her arms. Khalida was a pretty girl, unlike Zahra, and this prettiness – the dark eyes, the pointed nose, the demure smile – reminded Binta more of her dead son Yaro, than the child's mother Sadiya, who was busy in the kitchen making lunch.

Munkaila finished taking yet another call and put the phone on the footstool close to him. 'It's time for politics. All these politicians are busy collecting as much money as they can find *wallahi*.'

Hureira giggled. 'I thought that meant more money for you, so why are you complaining?'

'True, true. They are asking for dollars, and dollars have been scarce since yesterday.'

'How come?'

'It happens like that sometimes when the demand is too much.'

'And who are you for?' Binta held him with her eyes.

'Who am I for? Well, I don't know, Hajiya. I am not too keen on these elections.'

'Buhari will win, you will see.' There was an unnecessary passion in Binta's voice such that Munkaila only laughed. 'Hajiya *kenan*!'.

'What happened to this girl?' Hureira asked.

They turned to the TV where there was a headshot of a young woman dominating the screen.

'Oh, there was a kidnap last night,' Munkaila informed. 'They tried to kidnap the son of Alhaji Shehu Bakori but the boy got away and they made off with his cousin instead.'

Binta slapped her palms together. 'Oh, such a pretty girl. *Allah sarki!*'

Hureira shifted on her seat. 'Who is this Alhaji Bakori? His name sounds familiar?'

'Ah, ah, you don't know Alhaji Bakori, the tycoon? Anyway, you are not into politics so it is no surprise. He is a politician and businessman. The girl just came back from London where she has been schooling, I hear.'

Binta pinched her cheek with a thumb and forefinger. 'May Allah help them find her! I pray no harm comes to her! And may her abductors taste the wrath of Allah. *Tsinannu kawai!*'

They muttered their ameens and then fell silent.

'Let me help Aunty Sadiya in the kitchen.' Fa'iza rose.

Munkaila nodded. '*Toh, Allah ya bada sa'a.*'

But instead of making her way to the kitchen, Fa'iza stooped over the glass and stared at the flower. The longer she stared, the more scrunched up her face became. Eventually she shivered, threw her hijab on one of the empty seats and made her way to the kitchen.

When she left, Munkaila turned to his mother. 'What's wrong with that girl?'

'Djinns,' Hureira sounded certain.

Binta eyed her. 'Oh, shut up for God's sake, who asked you?'

'But Hajiya, *wallahi*, I know.' Hureira looked in the direction of the kitchen and lowered her voice. 'You should see what she does at night. I've told you, that was how it started with our neighbour's daughter. She needs exorcism, I swear.'

Munkaila gaped. 'Exorcism, *kuma*? Hureira, you can truly run your mouth.'

'*Haba*! Imagine what she might do when she is possessed. I am afraid for my daughter, *wallahi*.'

Binta hissed. 'Then maybe you should go back to your husband.'

'*Gaskiya*, Hajiya, I don't like the way you keep shoving this thing in my face each time I say something.'

'Oh, shut your mouth and don't be talking rubbish.'

'Oh no, I won't. Each time I say anything you bring up this issue of . . . of—'

'Of what, *mara kunya*? Of what?'

'That is enough, both of you,' Munkaila's voice filled the room, bearing a steely but quiet authority.

After Sadiya and Fa'iza had set the table, Binta asked for her lunch to be served on the rug. She was not used to eating at the table, she said. And so, out of deference, they all joined her on the floor. All but Munkaila, who set his plate on the footstool and drew it close to him, between his legs.

Binta watched with fascination and mild disdain as Sadiya's wrist flicked and her bangles jingled as she served the sauce. She watched her sit down, smile demurely and start eating with what Binta reluctantly admitted was commendable grace.

Hureira, having satisfied herself that the djinns that had taken possession of Fa'iza were easily agitated by blood or its likes, watched guardedly as the girl spooned some tomato sauce onto her rice and retreated to a corner.

Later, while Fa'iza was doing the dishes, Sadiya came in and stood behind her. Fa'iza turned to her and smiled. It was brief, nervous, betraying perhaps a deeper unease, like a mirror cracked from within. Whatever it was, Sadiya did not miss it.

'You have been quiet, Fa'iza.'

'Me? Quiet?'

'Yes, Fa'iza.'

Fa'iza shrugged. 'I just don't feel like talking much.'

'And why is that, if I may ask?'

'Why? I don't know, *wallahi*.'

Sadiya sighed. 'Have you been ill lately? You look listless.'

'Ill? No. I am fine.'

Sadiya moved closer and started rinsing the dishes. They worked in a silence punctuated by the squeaks of clean, wet dishes, by the splash of water in the sink, by the clink of utensils.

'Do you want to talk about your problems, Fa'iza?'

'Problems? What problems?'

'About what happened, back in Jos. About your father and brother?'

The dish in Fa'iza's hand slipped back into the sink, spilling water onto the worktop and the floor. She moved to get the mop but Sadiya held her arm.

'Don't worry about that. We will clean it up when we are done.'

Fa'iza turned her face away and deftly wiped her eyes with the back of her arm. Sadiya noticed. She waited. But then she felt a shield crawling up over Fa'iza, she felt the moment slipping away from her. She didn't know how to deal with these things, but she knew someone who did.

When the dishes were done and neatly stacked on the draining board, Sadiya clapped her hands together. 'Listen, Fa'iza. I am thinking you might want to go into therapy—'

'Therapy? What's that?'

Sadiya chuckled. 'My uncle, he is a doctor, a psychologist. He helps people like you, people with emotional . . . issues, you know. Perhaps, we could go see him someday, if you feel like it.'

Fa'iza looked at Sadiya with evident incredulity. Her laugh, when it came, after a long interval, was hollow and ringed with sadness. It made Sadiya want to cry.

'Aunty Sadiya, I'm fine, *wallahi*.'

'It's just to talk, I promise. Nothing more.'

Fa'iza again contemplated the proposal.

'You don't have to say anything now. Perhaps you could think about it. I will take care of everything when you are ready.'

From the living room, Hureira's euphoric cackling, riding above everyone else's laughter, floated into the kitchen and made them turn towards the noise. After a brief moment, Fa'iza turned back and looked at the neatly stacked dishes and shrugged. 'I am going back to the living room.'

Sadiya nodded.

The relic of laughter was still evident on Binta's face when Fa'iza rejoined them, for she was still grinning and shaking her head. They were watching *The World's Funniest Animals*. Fa'iza wondered what was it in the grainy videos of animals doing stupid things that had triggered such an explosion of wild hilarity.

Binta was wiping the tears from the corner of her eyes and was still giggling when her phone chimed. When she looked at the screen and saw who was calling, she looked up to find everyone looking in her direction. She went into the dining area and turned into the corner so they would not see her. But they heard her voice clearly asking the person on the other end of the line to call her back.

———

The girl with silky, tousled hair, sat on the mat, still looking groggy. The vein on her forehead remained prominent, dark against her skin. Her eyes were heavy as she raised them to the two masked men, one short, the other tall, standing across the bare room, not far from the locked door.

'You've been kidnapped,' Gattuso announced from behind his mask. 'If you don't cooperate, we kill you dead. If your people don't cooperate, we kill you dead. They don't pay money, we kill you dead. You play pranks with us, we kill you dead-dead. Understand?' He tormented the sudden silence with the rattle of his cracking knuckles.

The girl held her head in her hands.

It was the chloroform, Reza knew. 'The headache will pass. You will be all right.'

'Who are you? What do you want with me?' There was a hint of an exotic accent to her Hausa.

'The boy you were with, was he your boyfriend?'

She looked up at Reza. 'He's my cousin, *God damn it.*' She said the last words in English.

The two men looked at each other.

'Your cousin, right? How are you related exactly?'

'He got away, didn't he?'

Gattuso punched his palm. 'You will answer the question. How are you related?'

'Please, just let me go. Whatever your problem is, I know nothing about it.'

'Answer the goddam question!'

She started crying.

Reza noticed Gattuso's increased restlessness, noticed his eyes jumping around, looking for something to smash. He guided him out and locked the door behind them.

They strode back to the living room where Dogo and Joe were playing Whot. Reza sat down and mulled over this new information. He understood now why Moses had called to ask them to hold on to her. Inadvertently, their mission, whatever it was, was still on course.

When her screams, muffled by the folds of emptiness, and the sounds of her fists on the door reverberated around the wide expanse of the house, he went back up, with Gattuso on his heels. She tried to rush past him when he opened the door. It was easy to grab her arm and fling her back onto the mat. Despite the fire that raged and leapt in her eyes each time she reached for his throat, she was weak and still unsteady from the drug. He parried her assault with relative ease but she kept striking wildly. She fell when he slapped her. There was a profundity to the silence ushered in by the sound of him striking her. It was the sort of silence that reminded him of the desolation in his heart.

She sat still, holding her breath, looking into his face as he held her upper arms. He saw a shade of dread crawl up into her eyes and felt her go limp. He enjoyed watching the fear he struck in her eating away her resistance.

'You will give us the name and contacts of your people.'

She gave them a name to look for in her phone: her uncle, the tycoon.

'He'd better pay up.' Gattuso thumped the door.

The girl looked at him briefly, over Reza's shoulder, and then turned her eyes back to the taller man. Reza stood up and said they would send up food.

'Wait, please.'

Reza halted, still facing the door. When the silence lengthened, he turned and saw her lower her head. 'What?'

'I'm having my monthlies.'

His eyes widened. 'Well, I wasn't planning on touching you, you understand.'

She shook her head. 'I need pads.'

'Oh! Ok. Pads. Indeed. Right, then. Pads.'

He went out and Gattuso locked the door from outside.

———

Gattuso, who had gone up with the food and a pack of pads, returned to announce that the girl had asked for Reza. Since his return from the pharmacy, Reza had sat beneath the window, legs stretched out before him, looking up at the floral patterns on the ceiling. He had gone out to get the pads, and to explore this largely isolated part of Jabi, where their operation base was, so he could get some air and clear his head. He had felt embarrassed asking for sanitary pads and had been relieved when the attendant did not seem to find his request particularly odd.

On the long trek back, he was comforted by the large expanse of uninhabited buildings lining the streets, some finished but empty, others uncompleted. It was a rich neighbourhood, he could see from the layout and the size of the houses. He had been reassured, as he had been the first time he came to look at the place, that there would be no one within earshot no matter how loudly she screamed.

He looked at Gattuso standing at the foot of the staircase, one hand resting on the railing, eyes expectant.

'What the hell for?'

'I don't know. She just said I should get the tall one.'

'Tell her I am not here.'

But he saw how all three of them looked at him, eyes full of questions they wouldn't ask. He got up and dusted off his trousers, put on his mask and brushed past Gattuso on his way up.

The girl was standing by the window, which had been sealed from the outside with roofing sheets, her delicate fingers resting on the burglarproof bars.

He asked what she wanted.

'I just wanted to thank you, for the pads, you know.' She turned to face him now.

He wondered why women had to be particular about the most inconsequential of things.

'I need water, to wash.'

He turned to leave.

'Why are you doing this?'

There was something appealing and natural about her accent when she spoke English, unlike the contrived nasal accents of the university girls who spoke and gesticulated flamboyantly when they came with their boyfriends to buy weed. He paused, wanting her to say more but still not wanting to answer the question.

'I just want to understand what's happening . . . please.'

How much of what was happening did he really understand himself? 'You just keep your mouth shut and you won't get killed.'

'You've killed people before, *yeah? I saw it in your eyes.'*

Now he thought he saw her disappearing, melding into the blackness, into the night that grew as the walls fell away. That night, six years before, when Mike Two Guns had towered over him, demanding his money.

At thirty-five, Two Guns had dwarfed all the boys with his height, his bristling muscles and the legend of the two pistols he carried beneath his omnipresent jacket, the faded brown one he never washed. He had been the local go-to guy for all sorts of drugs, running his business through the boys, stocking them up with illicit goods they had to pay for in advance of retail, even if it meant from their own pockets. Most times, he slurred and swayed, high on coke or Tramol. Reza had chanced upon him stoned, sprawling beneath the Atili tree in the football field.

Two Guns had woken up to find Reza keeping watch over him and had leaned on the young man's shoulder as he staggered home. He had never allowed any of the boys to know where he lived. He had always drifted in the background, sometimes springing from behind the trees and walls to deliver a line before jumping back into the shadows. The import of that did not escape Reza.

He had been pleased when Two Guns started sending him to his weed suppliers to restock, or to shake up some of the other boys who were defaulting on payment. The boys had to be milked whenever Two Guns needed money, which was often. He was constantly in debt. No one knew exactly to whom or to what extent.

But then Two Guns started making crazy demands, even on Reza. And when Reza could not pay up, Two Guns prodded him on the chest and blew smoke in his face. 'Look, Reza, or whatever the fuck your name is, if you need to sell your bitch of a mama, sell her and get me my money. Otherwise, I'll waste you, you hear?'

Reza knew something had to give.

On a moonlit night when Mike Two Guns was high on Tramol and alcohol, staggering home and singing to himself, Reza followed him. In the football field where he had first earned Two Guns' trust, Reza snuck up on him and grabbed him from behind. The first three stabs were quick and Two Guns seemed astonished to see blood gushing from his stomach.

Reza stood panting, surprised by how easy it was to stab someone. He had been in knife fights where people had been cut before, he was not called Reza for nothing, but he had never actually stabbed anyone. He thought Two Guns would slump and die, as he had seen in movies, but the man staggered forward, grabbing Reza's shirt. Reza gasped. Suppressing the fear that came over him, he tried to loosen the grip on his shirt but Two Guns held on tightly, even though he was too weak to do anything else. Beyond the gleam of tears highlighted by the moonlight, Reza could see the questions floating in the wounded man's eyes. He had to finish it, end the tyranny that had subdued the boys and would certainly swallow him if he let it. He tightened his grip on the handle of the knife and plunged it in once more.

'Please, just die.' Tears streamed down Reza's face. 'Just die.'

When Two Guns, grunting, had pulled him closer, Reza stabbed him again. And again. He continued to stab until Two Guns' grip slackened and the man fell, first to his knees and then to the dust, wheezing, choking on his own blood.

Reza had felt powerful as he looked at the dying man as he lay in the dust. He had felt a kind of freedom he had never imagined possible.

He never bragged about it or even mentioned it but the next morning when the corpse was discovered in the field, the boys looked in Reza's eyes and knew he was the one who had liberated them from the oppression of Two Guns. There was a new overlord, and he resided at San Siro. One after the other they had come to offer him the *'yan daba* greeting – tapping their right fists into their left palms and bowing their heads in reverence.

He took over the weed market but avoided coke and the cocktails; they made a man weak, like Two Guns. He wanted to be different, to run his business differently. He would not live in dread of the police, so he made an arrangement with them. It was these little decisions that set him apart.

Sometimes he saw the life dying out in Two Guns' eyes and the shock of betrayal after he had stabbed him the first few times. Sometimes he remembered how, at that point, he loathed Two Guns for his weakness. He remembered the exhilaration he had felt, something he had experienced each time he stuck a knife into someone he thought deserved it. And there had been the tear-jerking gratification he had felt seeing Two Guns lying in the dust and listening to his wheezing breath fading into the long, long night.

'*Yeah?*' The girl's voice intruded into his reverie. She was looking at him, expectantly.

He looked at her hair, at her modest breasts, her gracious hips. 'There's nothing beautiful about killing people.'

When she looked up, their eyes met, briefly, before she looked down.

He turned and went out of the room. Locking the door behind him, he reached into his pocket for his phone.

23

The sight of dark clouds should not make one throw away the water in the pitcher

The gold necklace stood out against Binta's skin and dazzled her as the lights shimmered off the accents of its chain. She smiled sadly into the mirror, reached out and caressed the pendant between her thumb and forefinger.

'Hassan, I really can't accept this.'

Reza put his arms around her, pressing himself into her back. 'You don't like it?'

'No, no, Hassan. I do. But I just can't . . . take it.'

'I want you to have it, in place of the ones I took from you the first time.'

'Oh, I see. Is this some kind of payback then?'

'Yes, if you like.'

'But it's more expensive than mine.'

He crushed her against him so that she raised her head and laughed. He lifted her to the bed, undid her wrapper and cast it aside, running his hands over her hips. When he ran his hand over her cornrows, he was disappointed her hair wasn't silky, like Leila's. He rolled off her but she climbed on top of him, kissing him awkwardly.

She noticed he wasn't responding as passionately as he usually did, so she sat astride his lean body and cast an enquiring gaze at him. He lowered his eyes to her sagging breasts and for the first time wondered what he was doing with her.

When he looked up and saw disappointment clouding her face, he turned her over on her back, but her probing look bothered him. So he turned her over again and positioned her on all fours. Eager to get it over with, he slid into her from behind, thrusting lethargically at first. But the noises she made, moaning with fervour, awakened his desire and he thrust with more gusto, his crotch slapping against her rear. It took him forever to come.

After he had emptied himself into her, grunting like a desperate animal, she lay beside him and played with the little anthills on his head. 'You made me miss the madrasa today.'

'Sorry about that.'

She thanked him for the necklace and he laughed and ran a finger down her body to her navel and back up. 'I wanted to see you yesterday.' He circled her nipple with his finger.

'I know. I went to see my son. He lives with his family in Maitama.'

'Oh. Is he the one I'm supposed to see to ask for your hand?' he laughed.

Binta laughed too, a laughter that rolled and eventually petered into hollowness. Before then, it had never occurred to her that he would have such notions, and when she looked at his eyes and saw he was joking, she felt relieved. She slapped him lightly on the shoulder. 'He will shoot you the moment he sees this hair of yours.'

Reza ran his hand over his hair and laughed some more. She thought there was some strain in his laughter this time.

'Have you ever been in love before?' The question came out of her suddenly and she wondered why she was asking.

'Love? Ha ha!'

'You must have loved. You young ones have that luxury.'

He thought for a while. 'There was a girl, once. I was young, you understand. Back in secondary school. We used to walk home together. She was cute, a little plump, you understand.'

'What happened to her?'

'I don't know. Some rich dude came and her parents married her off. The next time I saw her, she was carrying this hideous baby and she said, "Reza, see the ugly child I have. If it had been yours, it would have been cute."'

Binta laughed, slapping his chest.

He sat up and reached for the backpack he had placed at the foot of the bed when he came in. From inside, he produced two takeaway packs of rice and chicken and a carton of juice. He set them on the little table in the middle of the room and pulled the table closer to the bed.

'Have some chicken.'

Binta sat up. 'Were you heartbroken? When the girl got married, I mean.'

'I suppose I was. I wanted to leave town.' He started eating.

'Was that why you left home?' She knew she was reaching deep into him, into the dark chambers where he hid his most private memories.

'No, no,' He filled his mouth with food and she had to wait for him to swallow.

'What happened?'

He stared into the mist of reminiscence. 'I was seventeen or so, I don't really remember, you understand.' His voice sounded distant. 'I was lying in my room; I had been stoned the night before so I was in all morning with the hangover. And these women, my father's wives, they started talking about her . . . that woman. She had just come from Saudi and left. And they started talking about what she had been doing in Saudi and stuff, you understand, calling her all sorts of names and saying how useless I was and stuff. I just got up and went out.'

He paused and took a sip. 'They saw me and their mouths hung open like this.' He let his jaw drop for a while. 'I just walked out.'

When the silence grew longer, she asked him what had happened next.

'Nothing. I just left. I wasn't doing anything there anyway, you understand? Just saw a car heading this way and I got in. Had no idea what I would do. I just left.'

She patted him on the back and leaned against him. She had often wondered, in her many moments of doubt, what it would feel like to just open the door and go, like a bird escaping from a cage. There had been times she had felt like walking but had lacked the mettle. She felt that way as she rested her head on his back, contemplating, even if frivolously, the possibility of walking away, with him, to places where they could live and love, unencumbered by communal shackles and familial expectations. But she knew it was impossible. He had his whole life ahead of him and she had to prepare herself for the inevitability of loss, of his tiring of her. She sighed and lay back on the bed.

Reza tore a chunk of meat. 'Come on, it's all good now. Come, let's eat.'

She smiled sadly and sat up again to join him.

He did not notice that she only picked at the food and, when he was done eating, he reached into his bag once more and brought out several bundles of notes. He slapped them on the table one after the other while she gaped at him with a half-eaten piece of chicken in her hand.

'Where did you get all this?'

Reza seemed delighted by the look on her face and when he laughed, the room resonated with a rich self-satisfaction she had formerly only associated with Munkaila.

'I need you to keep this for me.'

'Where did you get all this money? Did you steal it?'

'Hey, relax. I told you I was going to be handling some business for my boss. This is just the advance.'

'Advance! What sort of business is this?' She put down the meat. She could see rebellion crawling into his eyes. But she too was feeling confrontational.

'You are not my mother, you know.' His voice was calm but resolute.

'Oh, what are you trying to say now?'

'Nothing. Nothing.' He started shoving the money back in the bag. 'I won't have you judge me.'

'I am not judging you. I am just asking questions.'

He sprang to his feet. 'Why must you ask questions? Why?!'

She could see his taut muscles rippling with restrained anger so she started gathering her things. As she stood before the mirror, tying her wrapper, adjusting her dress, the gleam of gold around her neck caught her eyes. She unclasped the necklace and placed it on the table. She felt him grab her and spin her around, his arm raised, ready to strike her.

The moment congealed into a haunting image: him standing over her, arms poised, frozen, one motion away from striking, eyes angry and daring, facial muscles quavering; her looking up to him in consternation, terrified even.

When he put his arm down and turned away from her, Binta put her hand on the cheek he almost struck, imagining the pain he would have inflicted on her, imagining the dent it would have made to her pride. Above the wild thumps of her heart, she felt the ripple of the sheer menace that had just rocked the nest they had built together and cushioned with desire and other sentiments they refused to name.

———

Hureira could not understand Fa'iza's agitation as she drew furious lines in her secret book. Upon her return from school and without even taking off her uniform, Fa'iza had pulled out her secret book and started drawing, her brow furrowed and her fingers clamped hard on the pen. But Hureira knew the manifestation of an imminent djinn possession, she knew the signs. Not inclined to take the risk of her body appealling to some dark, ethereal entities, she removed herself from Fa'iza's presence and went to sit out on the veranda, next to Hadiza's petunias, and began clipping her nails.

She was still sitting there when the Short Ones entered in long, floral dresses – Abida in gold, Kareema in sunset orange. Their veils trailed behind them as they swung their hips, almost to a rhythm.

'Aunty Hureira.' Even that seemed chorused.

Hureira smiled, collected the novellas Abida was holding, skimmed over the covers and flipped through the pages. She kept one beside her. 'I'm going to read this.'

The girls looked at one another. The consent came eventually, after some hesitation, in the form of a nod. And when Hureira told them Fai'za was acting crazy inside, they excused themselves and went in.

They found Fa'iza attempting to hide away the book she had been drawing in and trying, at the same time, to wipe away tears. It was Abida who enquired what had happened.

Fa'iza sat down against the wall with a bland expression. She looked up at the girls. 'So which books have you brought for me?'

She collected them and looked through unenthusiastically. Her apathy deepened when she learnt that Hureira had taken the one she had been looking forward to reading the most. She shrugged but said nothing.

Abida patted her on the knees. 'Don't worry, you will like these ones.'

'Sure, sure.' Kareema walked to the mirror and patted her cheeks. 'And where is your aunt?'

'My aunt? I don't know. She went out, I guess.'

'Mhmmm.'

'What?'

'Oh, nothing.' Abida's laughter sounded contrived, even she knew. 'Nothing, really.'

'What are you not telling me?'

The Short Ones noted yet again Fa'iza's increasing indifference to the little things that used to animate her.

Abida took hold of her hand. 'Amin, what's wrong with you?'

'Me? Nothing.'

Kareema scoffed, 'Sure, there is. You are acting funny.'

'Sure, sure.'

'Acting funny? I don't know—' but as she said it, her voice quaked and she started snivelling. Abida put her arm around her shoulders and Fa'iza leaned onto her. When Ummi, back from playing at the neighbours', barged in with her stuffed doll, she was astounded by the sight of a teary-eyed Fa'iza, with the Short Ones sitting on either side of her looking morose.

'Why are you beating my sister?'

The Short Ones laughed. Fa'iza smiled through her tears. 'They are not beating me, silly.'

But Ummi was already flying out of the room to report the incident to her mother. Hureira rushed in and found the girls laughing.

She turned to her daughter. 'Stupid girl, is that how they beat someone?' She hissed and went back to the veranda.

Kareema stretched on the bed and started humming. It was obvious there was something she was itching to say. Abida knew. She, too, was worried.

'So, what's with Hajiya and Reza?' Kareema asked at last.

'Karee-ma!' Abida clapped her hands.

'Hajiya? Reza? What do you mean?'

'What's she doing with him?'

'With him? I don't know.' Fa'iza waved away the mental image of the man's shoes she had seen the other day at the front door, and then on Reza's feet.

'Well, people have been saying things, you know.' Abida leaned away from Fa'iza.

'Things? What things?'

'Sure, sure. Things about the way Hajiya is running around with Reza.' Kareema spat out his name as if it stung her tongue.

'Karee-ma!'

'Oh, shut up, Abida. Have you not heard what the women from the madrasa have been saying about how she was seen going into Shagali Hotel with Reza.'

Fa'iza put her hand over her mouth. '*Oh, la ilaha ilallahu!* Kareema, how could you say such a thing?'

'Abida, tell her.'

Abida looked away.

'Tell her, I said.'

'How can I say what I don't know?'

'Well, tell her about San Siro. You were there. You saw that.'

'Saw what? Abida, what did you see?'

'Well, I don't know. We saw Hajiya at San Siro. Very early in the morning.'

'Sure, sure.'

'But we didn't know what she went there to do.'

'Oh, stop being ridiculous, Abida. Did you not see her with Reza?'

'So?'

'She has been going to San Siro and now all the women are talking about her going to Shagali to have a tryst with that *dan iska*.'

Fa'iza sat motionless as the Short Ones argued. Kareema got up and went to the mirror to inspect her face. She reached for Hureira's make-up kit and took a lipstick. She didn't particularly like the shade but she applied it nonetheless. She reapplied her eye pencil and stood arms akimbo. 'Well, come on, let's go.'

Abida patted Fa'iza on the shoulder and said they would return later. They walked past Hureira, still sitting on the veranda, who watched them go, swinging their hips as they went.

Before they reached the gate, Hajiya Binta, returning from her escapade, pushed it open from the outside and stepped in. They saw how she turned her eyes away from them, feigning interest in the yellow-headed lizard on the wall.

'*Sannu*, Hajiya,' Kareema snorted.

Binta caught the unmistakable inflection of disdain in the greeting. She turned to catch the expression on the girl's face. Kareema's shoulder brushed her, ever so lightly, as she walked past her. Abida stooped briefly, coyly, as she walked past the gaping woman.

'*Lallai*! These children,' Binta closed the door and hurried past Hureira, whose greetings she acknowledged only with a nod. In her room, she yanked the veil off her shoulders and threw it down along with her handbag and collapsed on the bed.

Reza's face kept looping in her mind. She had never looked rage in the face like that and the menace she had seen had stunned her. If he had struck her, she knew it would have broken not just her face and her pride, but her heart as well.

She waved away his pleading face as he knelt on the floor, his voice so close to her ears, his arms around her, strong, protective, as he swore to kill himself first before ever hitting her, as he threatened to kill himself if she did not forgive him.

She put her palm on her left cheek, where he would have struck her if he had not restrained himself, where he had kissed her as she was leaving the room, and suddenly felt tired. Tired from being strong, from daring him and telling him off even though her heart had been trembling all the time. She lay down on the bed and allowed her tears to seep into the bed covers.

She dreamt, fitfully, of fireflies kissing her face with their glowing lamps and sending tingling pulses through to her heart.

They crawled in through a tear in the mosquito netting on the window, one at a time, until they were all over her, touching her everywhere. She became a luminous mass and started to levitate, hanging just a foot from the ceiling. But then they descended on her bag and when it ruptured into flames, she saw the money. She reached out for it, and crashed to the floor.

Sitting up panting, she grabbed the bag and pulled out the money, all five wads, and piled them on the bed. A quarter of a million. She thumbed the necklace around her throat. He was just a desperate young man who needed her guidance. But she would find ways to hurt him, if he ever again attempted to hit her. Now she thought of ways to convince him to open that bank account. She would never feel safe being his vault, where he deposited his things. All sorts of things.

24

Only a stupid blind man picks a quarrel with his guide

Reza locked the door and turned to the girl curled up in a foetal position on the mat. Before her were an untouched bowl of noodles, a loaf of bread and a mug of tea that had gone cold. He looked at her eyes, which betrayed the gnawing hunger she felt, which she refused to raise to his masked face, and at her lustrous hair.

'They tell me you haven't been eating.'

Her eyes moved slowly to the level of his boots.

'Do you want to kill yourself, Leila?'

She raised her eyes briefly when she heard mention of her name.

'I know your name. Leila.' He pulled out a pack of cigarettes from his pocket and slid down against the door. Sitting on the floor, he lit up and inhaled. 'I have seen your licence and student ID. I've always thought Leila was spelt with an 'a', but yours is with an 'e'. I would have been curious, if I were the curious type, you understand?'

Her eyes, ringed by day-old kohl, flicked up to meet his.

He had spent the night at San Siro listening to Mamman Kolo interspersing his anecdotes, peopled by iniquitous djinns and cheaply-perfumed prostitutes, with his tambourine. He had realised how much he missed San Siro in the few days since their mission began. After he had collected money for the sales made by Sani Scholar, he rewarded him with a handful of dirty weed. It was, in their kind of business, essential to reward loyalty. And Scholar, who had no use for weed since he did not smoke it, would know how to dispense of it and earn himself respect among the boys.

On his way back, in a rather crowded bus heading to Wuse, he had seen the man with a child in a bag. He could not erase the image from his mind. And when he returned to the mansion, he had sat down quietly, away from the others playing cards on the living room floor, contemplating the atrociousness that a hunger for riches induces in men.

He blew a stream of smoke ceiling-wards and sighed. 'The world is pretty fucked, you understand?'

The girl waved away a mosquito that had been preying on her foot, her kaftan rustling softly.

He took another drag. 'I guess it has always been that way.'

He relished the cigarette for some time, pausing to consider the stick in his hand as if to determine how much weight it had lost since his last drag. 'Some people are trying to find new cures, others are creating new weapons. And then there are those who are trying to kill themselves. Pretty fucked, you understand.'

She looked up at his eyes and looked away.

'I saw this man today. I never wanted to kill someone as much as I wanted to stick this man.'

He watched the ribbons of smoke curling up to the ceiling, remembering the enduring image his mind had grasped from the encounter.

'He had this bag, a big travelling bag, you understand? Black. And he got onto the bus with it. The conductor wanted to collect the bag and put it in the boot but the man refused. And he was holding onto the bag tightly as he sat right next to me.' He paused to take a drag. 'But the conductor, he had felt something in the bag. And he sat down and kept looking at this shifty man, you understand? So when the man wanted to get off, the conductor offered to help him with the bag but he refused again.'

Leila sat up weakly, but Reza paid her no heed. He continued staring at the ceiling.

'So he hailed a policeman and asked him to look into the man's bag. There was . . . a child, in the bag. Three years old. Dead. Suffocated. She was the cutest little girl I've ever seen. I can still see her now, her face, the coloured beads at the ends of her braids—'

He measured the weight of his cigarette again as he watched the horror come into Leila's face. Then he leaned his head back against the door and put the cigarette to his lips. 'He said she was his brother's daughter.'

'But why?' Her voice, long unused, sounded rusty. She cleared her throat, with a grace that suggested good breeding.

Reza crushed the butt of the cigarette on the floor and lit another one. 'Rituals, you understand. He wanted to use her head and body parts for charms and stuff, to get rich. Kai! I wanted to kill him *wallahi.*'

'He was arrested, wasn't he?'

'Unfortunately, yes.'

'Unfortunately?'

'Yes. Never wanted to stick anyone so bad in my life, you understand? Never. I will look for him someday and kill him, I swear.'

For an instant, she glimpsed the hardness in his eyes. But in a moment he blinked it away. When her body, weakened already from hunger, was racked by a mild shiver, she pulled her limbs closer to her and put her arms around her shins.

'The world is pretty fucked, you see.' Reza rose and slapped the dust from his jeans. 'Anyway, eat your food. That's all I came to tell you. Eat your food.'

He turned and hurried out, but she had caught a glimpse of the tears forming in his eyes.

———

Reza set down the LED lamp in the middle of the room, away from the girl on the mat who watched him from the half-shadow as he turned to leave. But he hesitated, looking at the lamp casting its white light on the wall.

'Wait.'

He watched her mouth trying to form words she seemed unsure about.

She stopped and tried to compose herself. She drew her legs close to her body. 'I've been sad about the little girl, you know.'

He sighed.

'I'm so sorry.'

'What are you sorry about?'

The words now tumbled out of her. 'I'm sorry she died, I'm sorry he killed her. I'm sorry you didn't get to kill him.'

When she started crying, he remembered what the man in that Bollywood flick had done, how he had drawn the girl to his chest and rocked her shoulders and patted her thick, lustrous hair. He looked at Leila's bowed head, at her hair that was beginning to lose its gloss and its scent. He wanted to sweep away the rebellious strands that had fallen out of line. But she was not his girl. She was the girl he would have to, if the need arose, put down and dispatch. Probably in the gully – where she would rot before she was discovered. He imagined what she would look like as she decayed: how her eyes would putrefy and her hair would fall off her shrinking cranium, how worms would crawl between her fine, little lips and eat her tongue. He shook his head and then felt a certain provocation because he could not find a kinder euphemism for kill (murder, exterminate, terminate, slay, execute). Something more . . . humane, perhaps. Even 'put down', if considered carefully, had a quality one could only associate with brutality. Like something the Americans, with their crazy infatuation with animals, would do to a tired, broken pet. As that murderer had done to that little girl in a bag.

'I know you're going to kill me, you are just going to kill me, and I don't want to die. Please, please.'

He listened to her crying, a strange sound that made him restless. 'I will not kill you.' And he meant it. He sat down on the floor, on the blind side of the lamp so his masked face was shadowed, and from his pocket pulled out a joint Gattuso had rolled earlier. But realising that the pungent smoke would choke the room, he put it away and waited for her to calm down.

'Why are you holding me?' she sniffled.

He sighed and reached again for the joint, which he lit before he changed his mind again. He took a drag. 'It is necessary. That's all you need to know, you understand?'

'Is it money you want? Have you called my uncle? What did he say?'

The pungent smoke filled the already clammy room. When she pulled her scarf and held it to her nose, he put the joint out and unlocked the door. With his foot, he kept it from opening all the way.

'Can I go out, for a while? For some air, I mean?'

He cleared his throat. 'What course are you studying?'

'What?'

'Your ID card. It says you are a student at some university in London. What course?'

'Oh. Palaeontology.'

He had never heard of it. And when she explained that she studied fossils in relation to the history of life, he laughed so loud that Gattuso called out from downstairs. Reza said he was fine.

'You are as stupid as all the rich people I know.'

'What?'

'Rich people. They are all stupid, you understand.'

'How so?'

'See, we here, people go to school, they study medicine and things so they can cure sick people from useless diseases caused by poverty, you understand. You rich brats, you go to schools in London and America. UCLA – you must have heard of it – you go there and study stupid courses no one gives a shit about, playing around with bones of long dead animals when people are dying and there are no doctors to treat them—'

'Well—'

'Well what?'

She was silent and he could see the hurt in her eyes. But he imagined she would, someday, if she survived this, dig up his bones and put them in an exhibition in a British museum. Or his father's, who was at that time, no more than a fossil clothed in weary tissues. A relic of times gone by, of an unrequited love for a woman of malevolent temperament. And when he looked at Leila's hurt eyes, it reminded him of the expression on his mother's face when she saw him turning away from her in disgust.

He walked out and locked the door behind him.

25

If we had not known the origins of the vulture, it would have claimed to have come from Medina

Fa'iza, who seemed to have lost her faculties completely, started screaming without making a sound. It was a strange occurrence that only Hureira, now fully convinced of the presence of malicious djinns in Fa'iza, could have anticipated.

It would have been a totally unremarkable day but for the incident. Hajiya Binta had woken up and complained about how brightly the sun shone so early in the morning. Her foul mood had intensified because of the campaign rally that had stormed the neighbourhood in the early hours. A bus mounted with a public address system crawled along the streets, blaring some campaign song that was too loud for the lyrics to be discerned.

Grumbling, Binta had thrown off the bed covers and yanked aside her curtains. 'What accursed bastards torment us this morning, eh?'

Over the loops of the razor wire she saw the sky blue banners of the CPC and heard chants of 'Sai Buhari!' from a multitude, beneath the hostile blare of the PA. Though she shared their passion for Buhari, she did not approve of this boisterousness, especially not at this hour of the day.

Being a Friday when classes at the madrasa were not held, she sat at home enshrouded in a sullen haze that Hureira managed to avoid by keeping out of sight. And then the phone call had come, from Reza. He was at the hotel already.

'Again?'

'Yeah, I don't know what's happening. Just need you to come, you understand, please.'

'Yeah, so you can threaten me again, right?'

'No, no, please. Listen, you understand, I am feeling bad about this. Really bad, *wallahi*. I want to make it up to you.'

And even though she stalled and made him plead some more, she knew, as he uttered those words, that she was going to put on her perfume and go.

She left a little later, having painted her face with subdued make-up. And Hureira, much relieved, wondered at the cause of this girlish exuberance.

A little after Zuhr prayers when the sun was still bright and burning intensely in the middle of the sky, Fa'iza pushed open the gate and stomped in, dragging her school bag on the ground and awakening a trail of dust that stalked her homeward progress. Little Ummi ran to keep up but by the time she reached the gate, Fa'iza was already at the front door.

Hureira, stretched out like a cat on the couch, luxuriating in the breeze from the ceiling fan, looked up and saw Fa'iza's bleary eyes. And when the girl, rather uncharacteristically, did not even offer a greeting and hurried to her room, Hureira concluded that it was yet another manifestation of the djinns' presence. She was paralysed by fear and indecision. When Ummi eventually came in and made for their room, she called her daughter and sat her down next to her. She did not want Ummi anywhere near a person whose sanity was so evidently suspect.

Hureira considered what form Fa'iza's demons would take, whether they would strip her naked and have her walk out to the market, baring her virginal endowments to the eyes of the traders, or have her turn violent, shredding people's clothes and yanking their hair. She had heard how strong the possessed could be, how they could wrestle down four grown men and snap their bones like dry twigs.

Eventually, after the minute hand had crawled and covered a quarter of the clock, Hureira got up and went to check on Fa'iza, muttering under her breath the verse she believed would shield her from iniquitous djinns.

'*Inna hu min Sulaymana wa innnahu bismillahir rahmanirrahim.*'

Tentatively, she prodded the bedroom door, which squeaked on its hinges as it swung open. Fa'iza was crouching on the floor, violently crumpling a piece of paper into a ball, which she threw against the wall. Then she picked up her pen and bent down over her book. Her brow arched in furious concentration as she pressed down hard on the paper, whimpering all the time. Hureira watched her, mesmerized by this Fa'iza who was not Fa'iza, this entity sitting in their house, spurting violence onto paper.

She ran to her phone on the couch and dialled Hajiya Binta's number. The phone rang unanswered. When she heard Fa'iza groaning like an angry imp, she pulled Ummi by the hand and led her out of the house.

At the gate, she met the Short Ones who, having noted Fa'iza's strange frame of mind at school, had decided to check on her as soon as they had changed out of their uniforms.

Hureira let out her breath. 'Fa'iza's djinns are raving.'

'Djinns? What djinns?'

'Yes, she is shredding things already.'

Kareema burst the bubble gum she had been chewing and cocked her head to consider Hureira's face. 'Fa'iza is not afflicted by djinns.' The condescending note in her voice did not register with Hureira, whose mind was already preoccupied with other notions.

'Oh, just shut it and go get the ustaz. She needs exorcism. Quick. Quick. My cousin is being driven mad by these blasted beings.'

The sisters looked at each other but the sheer hysteria evident on Hureira's face alarmed them. They shrugged and left, Hureira urging them to hurry along. She remained at the gate, holding on to her daughter.

Ummi squatted and picked up a rock with which she scrawled meaningless patterns on the floor. Hureira chewed her nails, turning every now and then to look at the house, and then outside, in the direction the Short Ones had gone.

A brown bulbul perched on the razor wire and seemed to consider the troubled woman with optimistic eyes. It hopped twice from one loop to another and tweeted into the glaring afternoon sun. Hureira looked at the bird, and unimpressed by its colouring, and distressed by her cousin's state of mind, she chewed more of her nails and spat the bits towards the bird.

———

Ustaz Nura stood in the living room and caressed his beard as he listened to Hureira's hysterical account of Fa'iza's apparent descent into insanity. Not grasping much from Hureira's discordant narrative, he asked to be taken to the troubled girl.

Fa'iza was huddled against the wall, still in her school uniform, but with her hijab thrown aside, lying on the mattress like a great tent flattened by a storm. When she saw Ustaz Nura standing at the door, she reached for her headscarf and put it on. She hid her face between her knees and wiped her tears.

She responded to his salaam, but not to his cautious calling of her name. He wanted to know if he was speaking to Fa'iza, or, as Hureira had suggested, some malevolent entity occupying her form. It was something he was practised in, by the constant exposure his vocation provided. He had been punched by a possessed girl and could have sworn it was a full-grown man who had struck him.

So from a safe distance, well beyond the reach of her arm, he prodded Fa'iza. The only symptom of possession she had manifested thus far had been shielding her face, which hardly confirmed anything in itself. So when she said she was certainly Fa'iza, not some supernatural creature possessing her body, he asked her to look at him. She raised her head, but kept her eyes away from his. It was a good sign. Troublesome djinns were prone to dare, to look one in the eyes and goad.

'Why are you crying, Fa'iza? What upsets you?'

'I am forgetting—' she sobbed.

'Forgetting? What are you forgetting?'

But she wouldn't say anything more. She choked on her tears each time she tried to speak.

He turned to Hureira, who had been standing at the door, along with the Short Ones and little Ummi, and asked what Fa'iza had been writing. Hureira pointed to the crumpled paper Fa'iza had discarded. Ustaz Nura went and picked it up and returned to his place.

'Fa'iza, is it ok for me to look at what you've been writing? Can I unfold the paper?'

She looked at the balled paper in his hand and looked away again.

He unfolded the paper, pausing every now and again to ensure that she had no objection. The drawing was a rough sketch of a face; angry, urgent lines, thick eyebrows, a nondescript nose. He looked up at Fa'iza. She had stopped crying but her face was still turned away from him.

'Who is this, Fa'iza?'

She sniffled. 'I have forgotten what Jamilu's face looked like. How can I forget what he looked like? How can I? He was my brother and they killed him. They killed him, right in front of me.'

She was overtaken by tears yet again.

And the man, precipitously invited to confront otherworldly rascals, suddenly found before him a devastated girl, possessed only by trauma and an immense sense of loss.

———

While Ustaz Nura was having a private conversation with Fa'iza, the Short Ones sat in the living room and listened to Hureira recount, in rather dramatic fashion and complemented with elaborate gesticulations, the one case of exorcism she had witnessed back in Jos.

With Ummi nestled on her lap, Hureira told them how the victim, a profligate girl who went about with uncovered hair and tight-fitting dresses at just about the time mean-spirited apparitions stalked the nights, was possessed by a pair of black djinns who claimed her as a wife and, through supernatural means, disposed of any man who dared to challenge them. Hureira narrated how the girl wrestled down half a dozen men in their prime and broke the wrist of one as he tried to restrain her from tearing off her clothes and running naked to the street.

'She was incredibly strong, *wallahi*. You should have seen how she was flinging these hefty men against the wall and breaking their bones as if they were broomsticks.'

'Ha!' Kareema gaped. 'I thought you said she broke only one man's wrist.'

'Sure.'

'One man? Every one of them had a bone broken.'

Kareema's eyes widened further. 'How can a wimpy girl break the bones of six grown men?'

'*Lallai kam*! This girl! You are underestimating the power of these demons, *wallahi kuwa*.'

'Aunty Hureira, you are adding salt to this story *wallahi*. *Haba!*'

For once, Abida hesitated to say sure, sure.

'*Ke*! Kareema, don't be impertinent. I am not your mate, *kin ji ko?*'

Kareema made a clucking sound and turned her face away.

Abida sighed. 'It must be a terrible thing to forget your brother's face like that.'

'Sure, sure.'

They were silent for a while and then Abida started fanning herself with the novella she had been holding. 'I can't imagine how that could happen.'

'It must be the djinns. They are eating away her memories.'

The sisters looked at each other and said nothing. The silence distended and filled the room. It was at that point that Hureira's phone chimed. Ummi got off her mother's lap and fetched the device from the coffee table.

Hureira looked at the screen and hissed when she saw that it was her husband. '*Dan iska!*'

Abida thought Hureira was being particularly odd. 'Aunty Hureira, won't you take the call?'

She leaned back on the couch with a smirk on her face, not unlike Munkaila's, watching the phone ring, shaking her thighs with unstated rage.

And when the phone started chiming again, the girls looked at her furious face, and just when they thought she wouldn't take it, she snapped it up.

'So you remember I still exist?'

'Hureira.'

'What? What do you want?'

There was hesitation at the other end. 'You didn't even greet me. You are such a lousy woman, you know.'

'Yes, I know. Tell me something new.'

'Ok. I'm taking a second wife.'

Her immediate inclination had been to chuckle, to laugh it off as a bluff. But it dawned on her that he was using his honest-to-God tone, the one he reserved for those moments when he made threats he intended to see through. But she wanted to be sure.

'Well, then, go ahead.'

'Ok. I just thought you should hear it from me.'

She hesitated. *'Allah ya bada sa'a.'*

'Ameen.'

'You are not kidding, are you?'

'Well, you wait and see.' With that he cut the call.

Hureira felt beaten by the determination in his voice, by the stinging indifference. She called him back and when he did not answer, she was certain he hadn't been bluffing.

She threw the phone beside her. *'Kutuman buran uba!'*

The girls were astonished, first by the expletive, and then by the manifestation of rage on Hureira's face, more comprehensive than anything they had seen her demonstrate previously. And when she suddenly burst into tears, crying inconsolably, they did not understand that she was being eaten, from the inside out, by the vicious jaws of jealousy.

————

'Gattuso, she's dying!' Dogo stood at the top of the staircase, gripping the banister. He turned and ran back to the room where the girl was being held, leaving his voice ringing in the emptiness of the mansion.

Gattuso went up the stairs, two at a time, abandoning his meal of bread and Coca-Cola, which he had been enjoying shirtless, sitting astride the wooden scaffold that served them as a bench. When he got to the room, Dogo was bent over the girl, who was clutching her stomach and writhing on the floor, far from her mat in the corner of the room. She had knocked over the plate of food purchased from a restaurant close to the park, which Dogo had brought up minutes before, and had made her already dirty kaftan dirtier. There were tears trickling out of the sides of her closed eyes.

'What the hell did you do to her?'

'Me? Nothing. Nothing. I just brought the food and found her like this.'

She lay still now, whimpering, lips parted, turning from side to side. Gattuso looked her over but couldn't find any visible injury.

'What's wrong with her?' Dogo was peering over Gattuso's shoulder.

'I don't know. She's faking it.' Gattuso straightened, not convinced by his own verdict. He considered Dogo, who also turned an expression of enquiry back on him. It then occurred to Gattuso that, in his hurry, he had neglected to put on his mask. But the girl's eyes had been closed since he entered the room. He retreated, and when Dogo went out after him, he locked the door.

At the edge of the balcony, from where they had an expansive view of the living room below, Dogo spoke in a whisper.

'You really think she's faking it?'

Gattuso ground his teeth, as if chewing the question. 'What the fuck do I know? Where the hell is Joe?'

'Not back from his break. You think we should call Reza? Where did he go anyway?'

'Said he had some business to take care of.'

'Business?'

'That's what he said.'

'You really think there is something going on with him and that Hajiya?'

Gattuso punched his fist and turned his head until he heard the little cracking sounds of his spine snapping into place. He leaned on the banister.

'So, you think we should call him?' Dogo asked again.

After some contemplation, in which his palm was familiarly brutalised by his fist, and a crude racket squeezed out of his knuckles, Gattuso shook his head. He fished in his pocket and, to his disappointment, discovered not joints but a cigarette. He lit it and they took turns smoking, in a portentous silence.

And just when peace, in little instalments, was returning to their minds, and to the house, the troubled girl started knocking on the door. Weakly. Then urgently. They looked at each other. Gattuso turned away and continued to smoke, but he was visibly agitated by her repetitive pounding. He threw down the stub and watched it fall all the way down to the living room.

They opened the door and found Leila on the floor, one hand clutching her abdomen, the other on her head, tugging at her hair. If she was faking it – and Gattuso suspected she wouldn't have such acting talent – she was doing so convincingly. He knelt by her to hear what she was saying.

'Do we take her to the hospital?' Dogo leaned in, his hands on his knees.

'Are you out of your mind?'

'Then where the fuck is Reza?'

26

A snail will never claim to have horns
where rams are gathered

'Your phone is ringing.'

Binta looked at her phone, lying next to her on the armrest of the chair, and then at Reza who was sitting on the bed with a disappointed expression on his face. 'I know.'

He chuckled, 'Who is it?'

'My daughter.'

'Oh. When is she leaving?'

'I really don't know. I just want her gone. It's bad for a woman to leave her husband's house like that.' Binta adjusted the salmon-pink veil around her neck with a casual elegance.

Reza found the movement titillating. And he liked her veil, the translucence and the flushed hue that, to him, was suggestive of a newly-wed. Of bridehood. The particular reason for that connotation did not interest him for the time being but he loved it. He loved that the veil made her look younger. That she was sitting down with him in that hotel room, even if she had refused to let him touch her.

'Perhaps, if you take the veil off you will be more comfortable, you understand.'

'No. Thank you.'

'Here, let me help you.'

'Don't come near me.' Her voice was curt, but she was not sorry. She wanted to punish him. 'You are not laying a hand on me, ever again.'

He cleared his throat. 'Even lovingly?'

Binta hissed.

He sidled up to her and drew the footstool closer so that when he sat on it, he was barely a foot away from her. He attempted to take her hand. She slapped his away.

'What do I have to do to win back your trust?'

'Look, we need to get some things straight.'

'What things?'

'If ever there's going to be anything between us again, then you need to be more responsible.'

'How?'

'First, if you ever raise your hand against me—'

'I won't, ever. I promise.'

'Well, if you do, I will have my son beat you up and have you thrown in jail. I'm not kidding.'

'Ok. Agreed.'

She sighed. 'And you need to open an account. I am not comfortable keeping your money.'

'Will you help me open it, please?'

'No.'

'Please.'

'I said no.'

'*Haba*, Hajiya.'

'Look, Hassan. I'm serious here. We can't go on like this.'

'Ok, ok. I will. I will. Is that all?'

She resisted the urge to smile. 'You have to take that exam and go back to school.'

'Oh, mehn!' He threw back his head. 'Not that, please.'

'Well, in that case, I suppose we are done then.'

'Look, I can't be doing that now, you understand. I've got commitments. Maybe later.'

'Perhaps, when you make up your mind to do that, then we can see what happens, assuming you haven't found a younger girl to occupy your interest.'

He reached in his pocket and found a joint. He searched for his lighter.

'You won't smoke that here.'

'Come on, cut me some slack, *saboda Allah mana*.'

She stood up. 'Well, you can have your weed, while I head home.'

'You are making things a bit tight for me. I need to cool off somehow, you understand.'

'No weed.' Her face indicated that her resolve was absolute.

Groaning, Reza slumped on the bed. He was tempted to leave but he knew he would be haunted by the image of her terrified face as he had raised his hand to strike her. It was the image that had lingered in his heart since the incident, each time thoughts of her occurred to him. And such thoughts had been sequential, a conveyor belt of guilt, haunting his conscience. He never again wanted to see her eyes, hitherto always filled with adoration, inundated with fear of him.

'Hassan, I am trying to help you. I care for you and I want you to get your life on track.'

'My life is on track, you understand. My life is on track.'

'It's not and you know it.'

She sat down beside him and, as she would her own son, talked to him about the importance of education. Again. He got up, sat by the window, fetched a cigarette from his pocket and, without deigning to look at her, lit it.

'I don't understand why you insist on this going to school business.'

When his phone rang, he pulled it out of his pocket and looked at the screen for a moment, then shoved it back in his jeans.

'Answer your call.'

'Don't worry, it's just Gattuso. My brother. My friend.'

'Gattuso?' Binta chuckled. 'Where do you guys get your names from?'

Reza, smoking pensively, went and sat on the chair Binta had vacated not long before, where the depression her weight had made in the cheap foam still tarried. He sat down, one leg thrown over the armrest. 'Why do you keep pushing and pushing and making demands like this? I am who I am, you understand? This is who I want to be.'

Binta fiddled with her fingers. 'My husband, God rest his soul, was killed by some Christian boys he employed. They were people he called by their birth names and did business with. My sister's husband and her son were hacked to death by their Christian neighbours because a woman urged them to. But my sister and her daughters were saved from being raped and murdered by a Christian woman whose husband had been killed by some Muslim youths.'

She dabbed her eyes with the corner of her veil, adding a damp patch, splotched with the blackness of her kohl, to the ruddy fabric.

Reza paused with his cigarette held inches from his ear. 'Why are you telling me all this?'

She looked up from her fingers into his eyes. 'Because I want you to understand why I have not given up on humanity, and why I won't give up on you.'

———

Binta climbed off the bike, having been intercepted at the turn to her house by Mallama Umma, who stood and flagged her down. Binta paid the bike man and he zoomed away, making a dramatic turn as he went, his knees almost grazing the ground and his rear tyre firing up a storm of dust. The move upset the women, who turned their faces away and covered their noses, Umma with her hijab, Binta with her veil.

'*Dan iska kawai,*' Mallama Umma coughed.

They waved away the dust and exchanged pleasantries in the fashion of elderly women. They enquired after each other's health and grandchildren and Mallama Umma, regarding with disapproval Hajiya Binta's girlish veil, commented that her friend was ageing with grace. Binta observed prudently that Umma's new hijab was both regal and quite appropriate.

Umma wondered, and this, she explained, was her reason for flagging her down, if Binta would be interested in visiting Laraba, a much younger classmate at the madrasa who had just put to bed. Her fifth, Umma said, and fortunately without complications. So, although unprepared, Binta found herself walking along with Mallama Umma to a *barka* visit.

As they walked, two women in the afternoon sun, past the houses and power poles defaced by campaign posters, Umma attempted to channel the conversation they were having about the health merits of moringa leaves to a subject that had been causing her some irritation of late.

Binta had forgotten, and it did not really matter to her then, how the conversation had started, but she found it engaging. Perhaps because Mallama Umma was such an easy person to talk to.

'Oh, I do take zogale juice, at least once every Friday. And I have introduced my son, Munkaila, to it. He takes it every time he comes.'

'That's very good, Hajiya. It will serve him well, and his children too.'

'Yes, I always serve them kwadon zogale each time they visit. They love it, the little ones.'

'Yes, and you know how all these educated children have been saying we are old-fashioned and eat useless leaves. Now they are the ones researching and discovering that our parents who raised us on these things weren't entirely clueless.'

'*Wallahi kuwa*, Mallama Umma.'

'Hajiya Binta, there is something I've been meaning to ask you.'

Binta noted the weightiness with which Umma ushered in this aspect of the conversation and she felt a deep sense of foreboding.

'Yes?'

'Well, not that I believe all these things, but I feel it is only fair to ask you concerning what has been said and is being said. All these . . . rumours.'

'Rumours? What rumours?'

But as they made the turn to Laraba's house, they spotted Kandiya walking towards them from the other end of the lane in the artless manner peculiar to her. They watched her flip-flops rouse small plumes of dust, her arms swinging.

Kandiya greeted them, Mallama Umma more reverently, Binta observed. But then again, Umma was older, more learned in the deen and perhaps more deserving of veneration from the younger Kandiya, whose manners had always been questionable anyway. Binta imagined that she caught a gleam of disdain in Kandiya's eyes and in her tone of voice when she addressed her.

Together, they went into Laraba's house and from the door Kandiya announced: 'Salamu alaikum, we've come for *barka!*'

'*Wa alaikumus salaam*, your felicitations are welcomed. Come on in.'

In Laraba's tiny room, warmed by the embers in the *kasko* placed in the middle, they found Murja, Ustaz Nura's wife, occupying one of the seats in the room, cradling the newborn. Laraba sat on the bed, all puffy-faced with a tired smile on her lips.

'You are welcome.'

The women took turns holding the baby, a boy Binta felt squirmed like a clay animation and yowled like a young goat. They made observations about his sallow eyes.

When Binta prayed for the child's good health and prosperity, Murja chortled.

'See how people turn into saints overnight. They don't realise you need to come to God with a pure heart before He answers your prayers. *Qulbun saleem*. That's what the Qur'an says.'

The sarcasm did not register with Binta and she handed the baby to Mallama Umma unperturbed. An uncomfortable silence followed, until the baby started crying again.

Umma unfurled the shawl and examined the baby's pallid, sagging skin. 'This boy is afflicted by jaundice. He needs medication.'

'*Haba!*' Laraba sat up. 'I mentioned to his father last night that there was something wrong with this boy. He said we should take him to the hospital.'

'Yes, take him to the hospital, but herbs will cure him better.' Umma tugged at his skin. It felt as if it would peel off. 'It's definitely jaundice.'

Murja seemed impressed. 'How do you know such things merely by looking?'

Umma only chuckled smugly.

Binta stretched her neck to observe the child. 'No wonder he has been shrieking like a demon. That's why it's always important to have babies checked out in the hospitals first.'

Kandiya's laughter was shocking, not only for its spontaneity but also for its supercilious tone. 'Hajiya Binta *shagali!*'

Binta looked at her, baffled.

Laraba was uncomfortable. 'Mallama Umma, what herbs should I get for him? I have never experienced this with my four other births.'

'Oh, you will do well to take him to the hospital first.'

Murja sighed as she considered Binta. 'I think the world is coming to an end.'

Kandiya turned to face Murja. 'Truly?'

'Of course. The sin of some people is enough to provoke Allah's wrath and He will smite the earth overnight.'

'*Wallahi kuwa.*'

'Imagine all these shameless sugar mommies running after young boys, taking them to hotels and doing *iskanci* with them.'

'*Allah ya kyauta,*' Laraba squirmed. She wanted the conversation steered in a different direction. 'One never gets used to labour pains.' She chuckled uneasily. 'I thank Allah for His blessings though.'

Kandiya waved away Laraba's comments. 'Murja, you speak as if these things don't happen among us when some of our women are now doing such things. Running around with all these bloody junkies.'

Binta bowed her head. She placed a hand over her chest, feeling her pulse race. She closed her eyes and hoped when she opened them again, she would discover it had all been a dream, a really bad one. When she opened her eyes, the challenge became how to walk out of the room as the women looked at her and saw her for what she was – a fornicator.

She felt her breaths coming in spurts, so she sprang to her feet. '*Toh*! I will be leaving now, Laraba.'

Avoiding their eyes, she put some bank notes on the baby's shawl.

'*Haba*, Hajiya Binta, all this money for what?' Laraba's nervous grin could not effectively conceal her discomfort with the turn the conversation had taken, and the fact that it was happening in her room when Binta, sinner or otherwise, had come to felicitate with her and pray for her newborn.

'Buy some baby soap. *Allah ya raya.*' Binta raised the curtain and walked out into the sun. The walk home, though not long, seemed interminable. Her eyes were blurred with tears and the task of putting one foot in front of the other proved daunting.

The only thing she was certain about was her earnest desire not to run into anyone she knew, so she kept her head down, dabbing her tears with her rose-coloured veil.

———

Binta had little time to contemplate what had happened for she returned home to major upheaval. Fa'iza's state of mind, calm now, had been overshadowed in the interval by Hureira's hysterics.

The fact that her husband had decided, in her prolonged absence, to take a second wife had set off a tempest within her. At first, she had only sat down and shaken her legs, but the more she thought about it, the more enraged she became. Eventually, the gale drove her to smash her phone against the wall and watch it splinter to the floor, after her husband, yet again, refused to take her call.

'Kutuman buran ubannan!' She cursed as she took a pair of scissors to a wax print fabric he had bought for her for the previous Eid. She felt triumphant after she had shredded it and the jagged pieces lay around her, like the aftermath of a confetti shower.

Binta returned home to find Hureira throwing her things into a suitcase, determined to stomp back to Jos and knock some sense into her husband in her own peculiar fashion.

'Hajiya, sai na ci ubanshi, wallahi!' Hureira promised as she threw clothes into the suitcase and hurled her toothbrush against the wall, somewhat disappointed that it was not breakable, and that the sound of something being destroyed had not eased her rage.

Binta leaned on the doorjamb. She had been unable to lock eyes with anyone since her return and there was nothing she wanted more than to bury herself in a cave and die. But there was a greater chaos in her home than her state of shame.

'Your quarrel is with your husband, Hureira. Not his dead father. And I won't permit the use of such language in my house, in front of the children.'

Much as she wanted Hureira gone, Binta knew that in that state of mind, fuelled by the fury which drives women and men to crimes of passion, no good would come out of Hureira's departure. And it was late in the day already to be travelling to Jos. So she prevailed on her daughter to put off her return until the next morning, by which time she hoped her abominable temper would have simmered to a tolerable degree, and the roads would be safer.

Binta had heard only in passing what had transpired in her absence with regards to Fa'iza. But then Hureira's antics had not allowed her time to process the information and act on it. And for the half hour Fa'iza had been sitting in the living room, curled up on the seat by the corner watching TV, it did not seem to Binta like the right time to discuss the circumstances of the girl's mind.

So Binta retreated to her room wondering what she would do with herself, how she could bear to be seen in public. And when Ummi announced that Mallam Haruna was waiting to see her, outside, Binta said she was not available.

Ummi returned minutes later. 'He said he would not leave until you see him.'

Outside, in the tangy breeze of the mild harmattan, Mallam Haruna sat on the veranda. He lifted his gleaming cap, scratched his head and replaced it. He stood up and paced for a short while before deciding instead to occupy his period of waiting by listening to his transistor radio. The BBC Hausa Service was talking about yet another attack by 'unknown gunmen' who had shot several men at a drinking place in Maiduguri.

When Binta, smelling of lavender and wearing a lavish hijab, came out finally, the speech he had memorised dissipated into the night, leaving him grasping for words. He was oblivious to Binta's distracted air and assumed, from her hunched shoulders and occasional grunts, that she was as unimpressed by his small talk as he himself was. He fell silent, restraining his hand from reaching for his radio's power button.

In the intervening silence, the cat with the white-tipped tail emerged from the night. It walked regally through the loops of the razor wires and paused only briefly to cast a somewhat bemused look at the elderly couple, as if gauging Mallam Haruna's unease and Binta's preoccupation with her thoughts. It arched its back and sauntered off, leaving the couple to their affairs.

Mallam Haruna cleared his throat. 'You see these people are growing bolder by the day.'

Binta mumbled. Could he not see that she was covered in shame, or was his nose impervious to her smell of sin?

'These Boko Haram people. Now they are hurling grenades and gunning down people out relaxing. It is in the news. They just killed six people. Just like that.'

'*Allah ya kyauta.*'

'Ameen,' he smiled broadly. 'You see, that's why I like you. When you hear such disturbing news, you always say a good prayer. It is a great thing.'

She looked at him, and perhaps for the first time that night, noticed that he was indeed uncomfortable. The fact that he had tucked his hands between his thighs, which were pressed together, had seemed inconsequential to her. 'Thank you.'

'Hahaha! Oh, no need to thank me, it is the truth *ai*.' But then, he seemed to have run out of things to say. In his head, he struggled to piece together that speech he had prepared for her. 'Prayer is important, yes.'

Binta grunted.

'Oh, it is, you must agree. When you have some mystery men running around and shooting down people or throwing grenades at them, sometimes you want them to just focus on the politicians and leave the masses to their poverty, but no. They kill the politicians and kill the poor folks. Anyway, when you have a situation like this, you just pray to God. *Shikenan.*'

Binta chuckled. 'So you expect them to kill the politicians—'

'The corrupt ones, the bad ones.'

'You want them to kill the bad politicians and spare the others?'

'*Kwarai kuwa.*' He emphasised his assent with vigorous nodding.

'Have you forgotten that when trouble comes, it affects all, not just the bad ones?'

'How can I forget when Allah himself said so?' When he said that, it occurred to him that the conversation was heading in a totally different direction from that which he had intended. This talk of God and His pronouncements would not help his cause in the least. He took some time pondering over what to say next.

Binta shifted and cleared her throat. 'Well, I should be going in now. It is getting late.'

'Well, I wouldn't object to that, if I were not so enamoured with your company. You know, I was thinking, why shouldn't we go out for a proper date someday.'

'How?'

'Well, you know, just go out, me and you, to somewhere romantic, just the two of us.'

She only grunted.

'*Haba*! Binta, why not give me a chance? I am a match for any young man, *wallahi,* more than a match even. I am virile and I have experience.'

Binta gaped at him.

He was stunned by her reaction, by her glaring eyes. But he was on a roll; he might as well say what was on his mind. 'Hajiya Binta, by the God who made me, I am desperate to . . . well, to taste of your sweetness.'

She contemplated his words and wondered exactly what he meant by this *tasting of her sweetness.* Was it possible he knew, or was he just being his usual thoughtless self? But who could prove anything? Who had seen her actually sleeping with Reza? Or was it not said that the mat of shame is rolled up with belligerence. 'Mallam Haruna, are you high on drugs?'

'Binta—' He placed a hand on her thigh and squeezed. He savoured the tenderness of her flesh before she slapped his hand away and jumped to her feet.

'Mallam Haruna! My God! What impropriety is this?'

He stood up and looked down at his sandalled feet with the innocence of a child being scolded, a child who knew with certainty that the reprimand was a great injustice being done to him.

'Leave my house, and never set foot here again. I am a widow; it doesn't make me a loose woman. *Dan iska kawai.*' She stormed up to her door.

He felt guilty, at first, and then insulted that she had called him depraved, to his face, this woman he loved, this woman he wanted to marry, this woman whose sweetness he was desperate to taste of, this *depraved* woman garbed in the paraphernalia of virtue.

'How dare you?'

'Mallam Haruna—'

'How dare you? When my two eyes are witnesses to your depravity, when I have seen you leaving the hotel with that insufferable bastard Reza?'

The night weighed down on her shoulders, shrouded her faculties in folds of darkness and pressed down her tongue, for some time. 'Thank you for spying on me.' She turned and shuffled away. She did not look back, even when he called her name with a voice laden with regrets, and a hint of unfulfilled desires.

27

It is impractical to eat danwake with a spear

It was interesting, Reza thought, watching the daybreak in Leila's prison. There was no sunlight streaking through the window. There was merely a sensation of lightness that could only come with the dissipation of darkness. He watched the outline of Leila's body stretched out on the mat, shades of contours standing out against the shadows, her breathing even, almost soothing.

When she began to stir, he reached out and turned on the LED lamp and flooded the room with white light. Leila scrambled up and retreated against the wall. She gathered her clothes about her and, certain there had not been any noticeable attempt to violate her, looked relieved. But her frightened eyes searched the chamber, her breathing rapid.

'I'm not going to touch you, *kin gane ko?*' His husky voice filled the room.

She mumbled. 'What are you doing here? What do you want?'

'Heard you were sick yesterday.'

She drew herself together, trying to moderate her breath with her hands placed over her heart.

'Is it some kind of disease you have or something?'

'Please, let me go. Just let me go.'

'Leila. You know I can't do that.'

'I am ill; I need to see the doctor. *I'm going to die here.*'

'Could it be menstrual cramps? I mean, I hear women have such . . . issues. Not that I know much about it, you understand?'

She peered through the darkness at his masked face and started gnawing at the cuff of her kaftan. Then she startled the awakening day with the sounds of her crying. He stood up, dusted the seat of his trousers and unlocked the door.

———

He came back an hour later with her breakfast and some pills in a blister pack, which he placed gingerly at the edge of the mat. The sun was fully up now and the room was brighter but the lamp was still on. He removed a book from under his arm and put it beside the food.

'I found this on my way back yesterday at a second-hand bookseller's. I thought you could do with something to read. Keep you company, you understand?'

She leaned forward and looked at the book cover, then leaned back again.

'What? You've read this before?'

'Everyone has read *Life of Pi*.'

He chuckled. 'Not me. I have little patience for reading novels.'

'*That's obvious, isn't it?*' She spoke in English.

'Is he famous, this writer? Never heard of him.'

'*I don't expect you would have.*'

His eyebrows arched when he noted the curtness in her tone. Disregarding her attitude, which he concluded was not without cause since women in the red zone were given to such eccentricities, he smiled and shook his head. 'So, is it an interesting story? What is it about?'

She took time arranging herself into a dignified pose, shaking her head to flick her hair away from her face.

'Can you tell me about the ransom negotiations, *please?*'

Reza cleared his throat. 'The negotiations, yes. Still . . . ongoing, you understand?'

'What did my uncle say? Is he paying?'

Reza turned and headed to the door. When he unlocked it, he paused, 'The drugs are for your cramps. I got them from a pharmacy.'

He turned and left, locking the door behind him.

———

He sat down with Gattuso and Joe on the balcony, smoking pot and looking at their feet dangling off the balustrade. Dogo was sleeping on the floor of the living room, having quenched the fire of his lust for a hawking girl – who had caught his fancy at Jabi Park when he had gone for lunch – with the heady fumes of ganja.

They smoked the first rolls in silence, revelling in the miasma, in the tenuous peace it bred in them, in the journeys on which the wavering smoke took their tormented minds. By the time they were into their second rolls, Joe waved his hand before his face, as if suddenly irritated by the languid bands of smoke that lingered before him. 'Reza, what exactly is happening to payday?'

Reza looked away.

'Look, man, I want to know what's happening. I thought her father agreed to pay.'

'Her uncle, not her father,' Gattuso corrected.

'Yeah, whatever. Ten mills, man. That was three days ago.'

'Four.' Gattuso cracked his knuckles. 'Four days.'

'Whatever, man. That's like forever ago, you know.'

'What's going on, Reza?'

'We get paid, when the time is right, you understand?'

Joe pulled out a bottle of gin from his pocket, took a swig and wiped his mouth with his arm. 'You know, man, let's arrange the drop. Ten mills, man. Ten mills!'

'Joe, we get paid when the time is right.'

Joe jumped off the balustrade. He puffed on his joint and blew the smoke out with an impatient gesture. 'This girl is going to die on us, man.' He looked Reza in the face. 'And then we get nothing. Nothing!'

He stormed away, leaving a vague, foreboding cloud in his wake.

They smoked in silence, the two men left. But from the way Gattuso smoked, pausing every now and then to torment any bone in his body that would make a cracking sound with unusual brusqueness, Reza knew that he, too, was suppressing some concerns itching to be voiced.

'You have something to say?'

'Reza, this girl almost died yesterday. She almost fucking died.'

'Well, we will all die someday.'

'She was rolling on the ground and we almost took her to the hospital where they would have arrested us promptly. If this deal isn't going to work out, let's cut our losses and get the hell out of here.'

'Meaning?'

'Get rid of the girl and go. I am missing San Siro. Sitting here in this shitty place listening to this rich girl screaming like a dying witch is not my kind of thing, you know.'

Reza smoked on in silence, nodding his head.

'What's stopping this deal from going through? I thought the uncle agreed to pay.'

'This is not about the money.'

'What the fuck is it about then?'

Reza looked at him and pondered the question. It occurred to him then that he could not, with certainty, provide an answer.

'Have you even thought about it, Reza? About what this is all about?'

'Oh, Gattuso, get the hell out of my face. Don't be asking me stupid questions.'

'Stupid questions? What is happening to you? You were not like this before. You took care of everything. Now your shit is falling apart and you don't even give a damn.'

'What is falling apart, Gattuso? What are you trying to say?'

Gattuso, emboldened by the excitement of the moment, drew near and looked Reza in the eyes. 'Look, man, this shit, this thing going down here, we don't know what it is. We are sitting ducks here. We have an opportunity to make some money and get out but we are holding out. For what?'

'We were hired to do a job, Gattuso.'

'And what is that job exactly?'

'Hold on to the girl. That's what we are being paid to do.'

'Yeah, hold on to her? For what? We don't know shit about what we are doing and we are the ones holding on to this girl because you are never here. You are so into that mamarish Hajiya woman, you've got your head so far up her arse, you need to open your eyes—'

Gattuso suddenly found himself on the floor, trying to clear the sparkling little lights blurring his vision and the whistling sound filling his ear. The numbness grew on his jaw and he realised he had been hit.

Reza was standing over him, struggling to contain the rage that had overtaken him. Finally, he walked away.

Gattuso felt his jaw, trying to figure out what damage it had suffered. He worked the bone with his fingers and concluded he would be all right. He looked around and saw the remnant of his joint on the floor. He picked it up and put it to his lips.

———

'Yeah?'

'I need to speak to the senator.'

'He is in a meeting now. What's going on?'

'I need to speak to him now.'

'Reza, is everything ok? You sound agitated. The senator is in a meeting and you know he can't talk to you while this thing is on. What's the problem?'

Reza gripped the phone harder. He could imagine Moses' face on the other end and felt once more an irrepressible urge to smash a fist into that face. 'What's going on? We are in the dark here.'

'No, you are not. You have your instructions. Keep to them.'

'We reached an agreement with her uncle days ago for the ransom—'

'Hold on to the girl until you are told otherwise, that is your instruction.'

'What if she dies?'

'Well, you make sure she doesn't. God! You guys are really amateurs. I wonder why he insisted you should handle this,' And he ended the call with a hiss, a long drawn-out sound that stung Reza's ego like the tail of a horsewhip.

———

Moses slipped the phone into his pocket and placed the file on the table in front of the senator. The senator, who had been reading a document, looked up at the young assistant over the rim of his glasses.

'Yes, Moses?'

'It's those boys, sir. They are getting restless about the job.'

'Is that so?'

'Yes, sir. I was wondering myself, sir, why hold on to the girl when there is nothing to be gained from her?'

Senator Maikudi sat back in his chair and removed his glasses. He rubbed his face and smiled. 'Do you play chess, Moses?'

'No, sir.'

'So you won't necessarily understand. Politics is like chess, you see. You move your pieces randomly sometimes. Other times you use your pawns to hold down aspects of play. Sometimes you sacrifice the pawns. But you always keep your eye on the big picture. There is a bigger picture here.'

'Exactly, sir.'

'Make sure they remain in position until I instruct otherwise.'

'Yes, sir.'

'Good. Now I need to have some tea.'

———

She was standing by the window when Reza unlocked the door. His immediate thought was that she was trying to prise open the window and attempt an escape, but he saw that she was looking at him expectantly and that the window behind her had suffered no damage from her delicate fingers.

'Some clothes, for you, you understand.'

She looked down at her dirty clothes and then at the new ones he had laid down on the mat. They were the sort sold by rambling roadside traders pushing ware-laden carts. Cheap things. But neat. She remained by the window waiting for him to leave.

'How are you feeling now?'

'I'm not dead yet.'

He laughed and stood awkwardly, uncertain how best to position his arms, looking at her as she flattened her hair with her palm and as much grace as her circumstance would allow.

'So, this course you are studying, this . . .' he searched for the word.

'Palaeontology.'

'Yes, that. What made you want to study that?'

'I thought you said it was a stupid course. Why are you asking now?'

Reza caught a glimmer of what he feared she had lost when she first looked into his eyes. Spirit. Passion.

'Well then, never mind. I was just trying to make small talk. It is not important, you understand.'

She sat down on the mat, and he could see the passion ebbing from her eyes as she brushed back her hair with her hands and sniffled. But she was not crying. 'You don't know why you are keeping me here, do you?'

'What?'

'It's not for the ransom, is it? Because my uncle would have paid days ago, I'm sure.'

'Well, there are some complications, you understand.'

'What complications?'

'Just complications.'

For the first time since that first night, she looked into his eyes framed by the mask and saw a glimmer of uncertainty.

'It's politics, isn't it?' And she proceeded, with the most minimal of gestures, to elaborate her theory of how her uncle's political adversaries must be behind the kidnap. Not for the ransom, but for some political purpose, to keep her incorrigible uncle focused on her plight, distracting him from some political endgame they were trying to achieve.

She paused and thought of the plausibility of her own theory, not now looking at Reza, who, behind his mask, was gaping.

'I wasn't even the target. My cousin was. It all makes sense now.' And this she muttered, more to herself than to him.

'Haha! You have your brain pumped full of nonsense.' His laughter sounded contrived, even to himself.

'Not nonsense. Can't you see? You and I are like . . . let's say I am your prisoner and you are my jailer and we are on a ship at sea. Let's say the ship capsizes and we are adrift, clinging on to a log or something. Would you then want to handcuff me to secure me?'

Reza contemplated the scenario she had portrayed and since in his mind, the sea had always been a body of blue-green water travelling to distant shores, lapping them tenderly, he laughed. 'Whatever. No one escapes me.'

Leila smiled. *'There is the sea to think about. There is the frigging sea to think about.'*

He lit a cigarette and the enthusiastic sound the lighter unleashed in the silence was almost startling. He turned his back to her and puffed for some time. 'You smoke?'

She shook her head.

'You must be used to people smoking around you. In England, people smoke a lot, not so?'

'I had a boyfriend who smoked.'

'Oh, I see. And you are going to marry this . . . boyfriend?'

She smiled wryly. 'I don't think my mum would have liked that idea. Anyway, I don't like him enough. Actually we are no longer together.'

'Ah, the mother.'

'Yes. The mother.'

Thoughts of his mother, the great whore of Arabia, whose musky fragrance still eddied in his memory, wafted before his mind like the cigarette smoke.

'And your father? What would he say if you brought this *bature* boyfriend home?'

'My father died when I was six.' She hugged herself. 'I hardly knew him.'

'Allah ya jikan shi.'

'Ameen.' She leaned back against the wall and stretched her legs before her. 'What would your mother say if she knew you kidnapped someone?'

'Ha!' He restrained himself from declaring her a whore. 'She won't know.' He got up and headed to the door.

'I would like to see my mother again.' There were tears, not in her eyes but in her voice, and it made Reza stop and look back at her. 'I hope you will find it in your heart to let me go so I can see her again and tell her I love her.'

He stood by the door wondering about the bond between mothers and their children, something he knew he would never fully understand.

'Mallam Audu.'

'Who? That's not my name.'

'So what's your name then?'

'Nothing. I don't have a name.'

'I have to call you something and since you won't tell me, Mallam Audu it is.'

He looked at her with his hand still resting on the ornate doorknob. 'What do you want?'

She sighed. 'My mother told me something. She often said, *Leila, even if you know the world would end tomorrow, plant a tree.*'

Reza contemplated what she said and shrugged. When he spoke, it was in English. '*And what fucking use will that be?*'

He opened the door and as he turned the key to lock it from the outside, he heard her voice through the door shouting; '*Remember the sea, Mallam Audu! Remember the sea.*'

28

Honour is milk that once spilt cannot be recovered

After Subhi prayers, Hureira waited for the first light of dawn and then, with her face set in a warlike mien, donned her hijab, picked up her suitcase and went out into the awakening sun. The space she left in the house, previously filled by a nebulous brooding and the pungent smell of belligerence, was replaced by a sense of relief akin to the coming of rain to tortured flora after an interminable dry season.

Having seen off her daughter, admonishing her against setting aflame her matrimonial home, Binta watched Hureira go and then turned back to the house with a heart floating giddily on the morning breeze. She went to the kitchen and prepared herself and the young ones a sumptuous breakfast with fried potatoes and omelettes dressed with fresh tomatoes and onions sliced into neat rings. She made some kidney sauce and finished with a dumame in miyan taushe. Then she sat down to eat.

But still, there were shadows in the house. The first was little Ummi, who, despite her not so cordial relations with her intemperate mother, was sad to see her go. And there was Fa'iza, who had seemed uninterested in the affairs around her and had sat down calmly to try to sketch her brother's forgotten face in a notebook. She had gone to the mirror and seen how hollow her eyes were, how like a stranger's they seemed to her. And then her eyes fell on Ali Nuhu's face stuck in the corner of the mirror. She spent some time regarding it as if seeing it there for the first time. Without any ceremony or provocation, she proceeded to peel the sticker off the mirror and crumpled it in her palm. Then she devoted some time to taking down all the images of the film star in the room. She ripped them off the walls, off the wardrobe, the door panel and the covers of her notebooks. Where they stubbornly refused to come off, she tore off the covers. It was this hunt that led her to her easel that had lain forgotten at the foot of the wardrobe ever since she passed her fine arts class. She peeled off the film star's face and rested the easel against the wall.

By the time she was done, she had a heap of crumpled stickers in the middle of the room. She gathered the pile into her hands and went out to the back where she dumped it all into the garbage bin.

Fa'iza sat down on the couch in the living room, her back board-straight, her legs folded into the lotus position like a Sufi mystic. She turned her face to the blank TV screen and, with the devotion of a spiritualist, proceeded to summon her brother's face with the sheer will of her mind.

When Binta emerged from her room and saw the girl shrouded in a disturbing aura of calm, a serenity that made her uneasy and afraid to distract her, she packed her things and went off to the madrasa, careful not to disturb the girl on her way out. With Hureira gone, she imagined what it would be like to have Reza visit the house again. The only trouble would be getting rid of Ummi and Fa'iza since it was Saturday and they would not be going to school. But she would find a way.

Following the incident at Laraba's, thoughts of entirely forfeiting her studies at the madrasa had crossed her mind overnight. But realising that her silence would have encouraged these rumours, burying her in shame, Binta decided to face her accusers and, before it grew any worse, put an end to their malice.

She was still thinking of the shari'ah's ruling on falsely accusing decent women of depravity when she reached the madrasa and found two groups of women. One was huddled around Mariya while she tried to interest them in wares from the huge bag beneath her desk; make-up kits, perfumes from Arabia, henna from India, bottled honey and the usual variety of sex boosters and creams.

Another group had formed at the back, clustered around Mallama Umma, going over previous lessons under the guidance of the matron. Ustaz Nura was not in class, neither was his wife, Murja.

Binta was enthralled by some of the wares on Mariya's desk and reached for a jar of pure honey. When she asked if it was definitely pure, Mariya scowled at her.

'Well, it isn't adulterated, if that's what you mean.'

The other women turned to her. Binta felt cowed by the attention. 'Well, you know sometimes people do add sugar—'

'Binta, keep my thing if you are not buying. Who are you to come here with accusations? Imagine the hyena calling the dog a savage,' Mariya hissed.

That wasn't how Binta had imagined the scenario would play out and before she could marshal her thoughts, Ladidi, the skinny woman famed for her half-dozen divorces and her children fathered by as many men, waved her hand before her nose and cleared her throat. 'What is that God awful smell?'

The women sniffed the air and having failed to perceive it, they turned to Ladidi. After an appropriate interval, in which Ladidi savoured the attention, she made a declaration that stunned the entire class, including Mallama Umma's earnest group devoted to the study of hadith at the rear.

'It's the smell of zina, wallahi. I could perceive it from anywhere! There is a fornicator in this class.' And she spat and turned her back to the slimy mucus that slid sordidly down the wall.

'Who are you calling a fornicator, Ladidi? Are you making false accusations against me? Can you prove anything?'

Ladidi chuckled. 'Who mentioned your name?' she hissed. 'But did they not say that a guilty person would sweat even in the rain? Aikin banza.'

Binta put down the bottle of honey on the table and, in the heavy silence that followed, walked to her seat in the middle of the class. She sat down and bowed her head. But then Shafa'atu, the young bride, who was stationed just behind Binta, and was queasy already with the burgeoning seed inside her, got up abruptly and knocked over her bag in the process. She gathered her books from the floor and holding her hand over her mouth, hurried out of the class.

Ladidi adjusted her hijab, spat on the floor, cast a sidelong glance at Binta whose head was still bowed, and walked out of the class. Two other women followed her.

And then Mallama Umma resumed her tutorials with a voice made unnecessarily loud as to take in the entire class and with a fervour that was driven by restrained fury.

Binta could hear her, but she was not listening. The words cascaded off her consciousness and registered only in the background of her thoughts. Her mind was numbed by the recollection of the silence that had accompanied her to her seat. Her vision was blurred by the film of tears that lingered in her eyes because she would not let them run down her cheeks. She had no idea how long she sat like that: head bowed, tears imprisoned in her eyes and a whistling silence in her mind. When she stood up, she became conscious of the abrupt silence around her. She picked up her bag and walked out with as much dignity as she could muster, her pace measured, her shoulders held straight, defiant even. But inside, she could feel the weight of her heart. And it felt so much heavier than she ever remembered.

———

Gattuso was in the living room, hefting the improvised weights he had found in the store where the masons left some of their work tools: a pair of paint containers, one on each end of a metal pipe filled with concrete. Feeling the weak pipe bending in his hand as he lifted reminded him of the weights at San Siro, the ones that helped him build muscles like a great, brawny zebu. His intermittent grunts jabbed the emptiness of the room and when he looked up and saw Reza leaning on the banister looking down at him, his anger bloated. He put down the weights and sat up on the scaffold, panting.

Reza descended the rest of the stairs, crossed the room and sat on the bench next to Gattuso, who had picked up his shirt and was wiping away his sweat.

'You made me hit you, Gattuso.'

Gattuso ground his teeth and hunched forward.

If Reza noticed his agitation, he did not acknowledge it. For a while, he tapped his foot on the terrazzo to a rhythm in his head.

'We are holding Leila for the senator not because he wants the ransom, but because her uncle, Alhaji Bakori, is his rival for the control of the party in this zone. The longer we hold the girl, the more he distracts his rival and takes control of the party ahead of the elections.'

Gattuso's face, like that of a great bovine, betrayed no excitement. Until, finally, the words percolated and his face transformed and bore witness to the escalated rage he felt inside. He punched his palm. The smacking sound irritated Reza.

'So after the elections, we let the girl go? Do we take the ransom?'

Reza scratched his head. It was in that moment that, for some inexplicable reason, he thought of the little girl in the black bag. He saw, in his mind, her dead face and the brightly coloured plastic beads at the tips of her braids. Blue, red, yellow and green. He saw the face of the man who had put her there. His desire to shove a knife into the heart of that murderer resurfaced with an urgency that astounded him. The thought of his cold metal entering that man's warm heart excited him so much that he could feel a stir in his crotch.

He wondered why he was thinking of that girl when Gattuso was waiting for him to answer his question. He got up and left, leaving Gattuso as clueless as he had been before. Before he went far, his phone chimed and, seeing that it was his brother Bulama, he knew at once that it had something to do with his father.

———

That evening as he walked towards San Siro, he realised how much he had missed the place. The narrow crowded streets that bustled with vendors sitting by the roadside sharing pilfered gossip, desperate housewives engaged in frenzied shopping for the evening meal, and zealous motorcycle taxis that dove into the riotous dirt roads, terrifying bargain hunters and traders with their reckless driving and blaring horns. The sounds blended – the boisterous horns, the chattering, the wails of beckoning traders and the occasional ruckus of belligerent junkies – to create a noise storm. Reza had missed all that.

He saw Sani Scholar's mother, Jummalo, prodding the firewood in her tripod as she set up for the evening sales. There were bowls of bean paste and sliced yam sprinkled with salt, which she would shortly torment in a pan of vegetable oil. When she saw Reza, she abandoned her task and straightened, placing one wiry arm on her narrow waist whilst she threw her worn, green veil over her shoulder with the other. It made Reza think of Hajiya's Binta's bridehood veil, the one she had worn with so much grace.

Without any preamble, Jummalo launched into her habitual lament about her son's inconsequential bulk and his stagnant ambition, about how she was trying to make his life and that of his siblings better and how, in order to prepare for her business, she went to sleep way past midnight and woke up long before the first cockcrow.

Reza's eyes wandered. Across the street, outside the dreary little police post next to San Siro, he saw ASP Dauda Baleri sitting on a bench, flanked by his lieutenants. In the evening light, and even from that distance, Reza could see how much darker the policeman had become, how much less refined he seemed than when he had first arrived, and thought how much he and the office he lorded over had become an excellent study in decrepitude.

His mind drifted to his old father suffering the desolation of age, a malady that had defied all known remedies and would surely put his heartbroken father in the damp earth in a short while.

'*Wallahi* I haven't seen Sani in two days. Two days, Reza! And all I want is for him to make something out of his life.'

Reza noticed that the end of her veil kept slipping off her shoulder as she embellished her lament about life's inequities with dramatic gesticulations. He looked at the arms that she waved before her like the branches of a juvenile tree. He remembered then Leila's peculiar logic of planting trees when the world was ending.

'Let me get to San Siro and see if he is there. I will ask him to come see you.' And with that he walked away from her. When he crossed the street, the policemen flanking Baleri waved at him timidly. Baleri himself sat in their midst, stony-faced; his bleary eyes locked with Reza's, who walked past without even an acknowledging nod.

From the silence that oozed from San Siro, Reza knew that Mamman Kolo had left. He had packed up his tales of dubious djinns and bleached whores along with the rattles of his tambourine and, as was his practice, disappeared into the night. Some boys were in the courtyard smoking pot with familiar indolence. They hailed Reza as he walked in. Sani Scholar, who had been in one of the rooms leafing through the pages of an old sports magazine, hurried out, beaming.

They shook hands and Sani rushed back to fetch his notebook, in which he had diligently kept records of his transactions.

In his room at last, Reza sat down on his mattress reacquainting himself with the smells of his private space. He rolled on the mattress childishly and put his legs up on the wall, looking at the rain-stained ceiling. He reached for his phone and dialled Binta's number.

'Hassan.'

'What's wrong?'

'Nothing.'

'Well, your voice, it sounds—'

'I'm ok.'

'Your voice sounds distressed. What happened?'

There was some hesitation. 'We need to talk, Hassan.'

'Want to go to the hotel?'

'No.'

'I just got a call that my father is not doing too well and I need to go take him to the hospital but I could spare some time to see you.'

'No, go take care of your father. When you get back then we see, ka ji?'

'Are you pregnant?' he laughed. Binta did not. When he noticed this, he stopped. 'Sorry, I shouldn't have said that.'

She said nothing.

'I will be back tomorrow. Can we meet at the hotel?'

'No. Come to the house. Hureira is gone.'

'But the girls—'

'I will send them off, maybe to Munkaila's. But call before you come.'

'OK.'

He put down the phone beside him just as Sani Scholar came in. And because of the rants he had been subjected to by Jummalo, Reza found himself examining Sani to see if he really was as pathetic as his mother seemed to think. Sani was small-framed but there was a steely disposition in his eyes that had given Reza the confidence to leave San Siro in his care while he and his right-hand men were away.

Scholar sat down and presented the money from the sales he had made. He had everything written down. The details of the transactions did not interest Reza, but he indulged his acolyte. And when Sani presented the money to him, he shoved it in his pocket without counting. He had resolved, at that moment, not to restock until he settled the affair with Leila, which he hoped to do in the next couple of days.

They talked about Mamman Kolo's departure, which had taken place two days before.

As Sani recounted Kolo's last day at San Siro, he noticed the distraction that had characterised Reza since he returned. It did not surprise him when Reza rose and said he was leaving to see his father who was fighting against old age.

Reza watched him close up his book and rise to his feet, he watched him walk to the door. 'Scholar.'

When Sani turned back, Reza wondered if he should proceed with what he intended to say. 'You wanted to become a doctor, not so?'

Sani laughed. But it was hollow and Reza recognised it as the sound of defeat. 'Yeah?'

'I need to retake my WAEC.'

Reza got off the mattress and walked out of the room. He locked the door and turned to Sani, who was standing beside him, his eyes gleaming with expectation. Reza counted out some notes and handed them to him. 'Here, take this. Go and register for the exam, you understand. You will be more useful to your mother that way.'

Sani's eyes widened and in them Reza saw emotions passing like the phases of the moon, graduating from one level of intensity to the next. Reza realised then that he loved the boy like a brother. Almost.

All that talk of the sea and planting trees and the certainty of his father's demise, which he felt was closer than ever, was tampering with his constitution. And he did not like it. Not one bit.

He put his hand on Sani's shoulder. 'Scholar, don't be like me. Go to school. Make something of your life. Don't let someone else mess with your head, you understand? Now get out of here.'

29

The chicken is never declared in the court of the hawks

Hajiya Binta sat on the prayer rug shrouded in a sullen mist, long after she was done saying the Maghrib prayer. She could not keep track of the tasbih as her thoughts drifted between the divine and the worldly, where the words of the perpetual divorcée Ladidi and the accusatory glare of the madrasa women haunted her. She manipulated the prayer beads absently, the constant click of the plastic beads providing some rhythm to her despondence.

The thought of relocating to Jos, where she had lost everything, appealed to her now. She felt stifled by the events of the last few days and she needed to get away, away from the women of the madrasa and their judgements, away from Reza and his unintended allure.

The sound of the gate opening and the voice of a boy salaaming from without seemed to reach her from a dream. She hesitated until she was certain the persistent boy was real. Since Fa'iza had gone off along with Ummi to visit the Short Ones, Binta went to the door where the boy announced that there was a man outside asking permission to see her. She was shocked, upon enquiry, to discover that the man was Ustaz Nura himself. She was overtaken by panic. How would he view her now? Never had the thought of sudden death appealed to her more. People are more likely to mitigate the severity of their judgements on the dead.

She went back inside and sprayed herself with perfume, then regretted it immediately. It would give the impression she was trying to seduce the good man of God and worse, Ustaz Nura had taught them not too long ago how women who tempt men with their perfumes are no different from fornicators. It was a hadith. And yet, the abominable smell of fornication, for which she had been taunted by that waif-like Ladidi, was, at that moment, more pronounced in her mind than ever.

She lighted incense and tucked the sticks in the corners of the rooms so that the entire house was soon suffused by wispy white smoke unleashing a rich fragrance. When she went out, she found Ustaz Nura standing just inside the gate, caressing his beard. She waited for him by the bed of Hadiza's petunias and watched him walk towards her, the hem of his pants blown about his shins by the passing breeze.

He graciously declined her invitation to enter the living room and asked her not to bother when she offered to fetch the mat so they could sit on the veranda. His business was brief, he assured her.

When he commenced his speech with the pious preamble, 'Innal hamda lillah . . .' she knew for certain he was there on matters pertaining to her sins. She listened to him praise Allah and his Noble Prophet and appeal for refuge from the accursed Shaytan, whose obnoxious handiwork seemed to be manifesting in her garden like a plague of weevils. She bowed her head while it lasted. Then she fiddled with her fingers beneath her hijab as he launched into a discourse of his encounter with Fa'iza the previous day. About how the symptoms of trauma were unlike those of demonic possession, and how only a brash woman of Hureira's ilk would mistake the two.

'She is not possessed, Hajiya Binta, she is traumatised. I am surprised you didn't notice how much she is suffering.'

Binta bowed her head further.

'From my little understanding of psychology, *masha Allah*, Fa'iza is in need of prayers and support. She needs someone she can talk to. That's all. In other climes, she would have gone for what they call *professional help*, seen a psychiatrist and all that.'

'But Ustaz, these things happened two years ago. Why is she . . . acting up now?'

'Well, I think her mind shut that bit of memory somewhere, buried it. But now it's resurfacing and she is finding it hard to process. Haven't you noticed all these things she's been going through?'

Binta was shocked when he eventually told her that Fa'iza had forgotten her brother's face. She did not know that such a loss, the worst sort imaginable since it went without notice, was possible. For the loss of a loved one, tragic as it is, does not, in any way, compare to the loss of the memory of who they were.

'*Masha Allah*, there is some other thing I have been meaning to discuss with you.'

Binta's heart skipped. And when he launched, as delicately as he could manage, into talks of rumours about her rendezvous, Binta wished the earth would grow a mouth wide enough to swallow her in one great gulp. He assured her that he believed nothing of those 'filthy rumours' because the Prophet, peace be upon him, had encouraged one to think only good of the faithful. But regardless, he would rather she did not put herself in such positions as to compromise her integrity as a good Muslim woman, a mother of decent children who were all older and more refined than that 'sleazy hemp dealer'.

'But Ustaz, *wallahi*, these rumours are untrue. I am . . . erm—' Binta covered her face with her hijab.

'The rumours are not without cause, Hajiya. If, for instance, on my way here, I saw Reza sneaking out of this house, or see you talking with such a famed *dan iska*, *subhanallah*, that would arouse some suspicions in me, don't you think? If someone else had seen him, he could say, oh! I saw him and her doing this and that, *subhanallah*. That would do great injustice to your dignity, you see.'

Binta wiped the tears from her eyes.

Ustaz Nura, experienced in handling such matters of sin and remorse, allowed the moment to linger, allowed her to feel the full weight of her turpitude upon her heart, which the honey-coated lance of Shaytan had pierced. '*Masha Allah*, Hajiya Binta, I hope these tears are cleansing your heart. Whatever you have done, or not done, you will find Allah most forgiving and most merciful. Repent and you will find His arms open to receive you.'

Feeling very sorry for her, and with a certainty that she had indeed been swayed by her lonely heart into the path of mortal sin, Ustaz Nura took his leave as the muezzin's call for the last prayer of the day rent the nascent night.

———

After Ustaz Nura left, Binta said her Isha prayers and remained on the rug, sitting much as she had done before he came. The mist of sadness that had shrouded her earlier had grown in shades and was now scented with remorse. She dwelled in this stupor, teary-eyed and sniffling, contemplating her failings, until Fa'iza and Ummi returned from their visit. With her back turned to them, she mumbled a response to their greetings. After the girls left, she summoned the strength to do what she had to do.

She reached into the depths of her chest of drawers and pulled out her photo albums, two of them, bulging with memories. Her search for one particular photograph led her through the hazy labyrinths of reminiscence. She flipped from page to page, making infrequent sorties into a faded past: Hadiza's haunting eyes on her first day at school staring back from the photograph; an image of Zubairu, much younger than when he had died, decked out in an elaborately embroided kaftan with palazzo pants, his zanna cap planted at a jaunty angle atop his thick afro. She remembered the little patch of prosperity he had traversed before the ravages of loss set in and his afro gave way to a more modest cut and a beard that eventually grew wild. And in that fashion, she wandered from the black and white photos to the ones whose colours had suffered the devastation of time, smiling in some instances and fighting back tears at others. She was surprised to see how young Hureira had seemed at her first wedding and how empty her expression had been in another photo as she held little Ummi in a fluffy shawl, her eyes bereft of that maternal glow. She chuckled at the sight of Munkaila's scrawny neck sticking out of the top of the famous spandex shirt that characterised his undergraduate days, holding up the V-sign. She could not, at that moment, reconcile the balding, pudgy man he had become with the scrawny youth who looked every inch his father's son. She smiled when she came upon a picture of herself in Medina, dressed in a pilgrim's white garb and the Prophet's Mosque behind her in the background while hundreds of devotees milled around. She prayed she would have another opportunity to go there and seek Allah's forgiveness, before her eventual passing. She was delighted by the joy she saw in Hadiza's eyes as she leaned on her then fiancé's shoulder, a joy she was happy she could still see in her daughter's face even after years of marriage.

And then she came upon that photo of her children lined up against the wall like bandits facing a firing squad. Her beloved Yaro, looking like a reluctant passer-by coerced into a family photo. She ran her thumb repeatedly over his face, which, as always, reminded her of her mother's. Finally, she pulled the picture out of the plastic sheath and pressed it to her bosom, which was rocked with sobs and the chill of long-suppressed remorse. She fell back on the bed, called him by his birth name and told him she was sorry while she wept. That she wished she had told him she loved him even once. That she wished she could have just one more minute so she could tell him that and keep him close to her bosom where no bullet would find him.

Some time later, she found the picture that had set her off on that journey into the fields of wilting flowers in the first instance. She wiped her eyes clean and went to look for Fa'iza in her room.

She found her niece mixing paints on a palette sitting before a canvas mounted on her little easel. Her immediate reaction was shock. Was this another manifestation of the insanity that trauma had induced? Binta looked into the girl's enquiring eyes, which exuded tranquility. It was a calm that Binta found as comforting as it was disquieting. There is nothing quite like fighting against loss and, despite one's best efforts, losing all the same. She stood by the door and felt there was, beyond Fa'iza herself, some change in the room. Something she could not identify immediately. Shutting the door behind her, she saw Fa'iza's eyes widen as she walked towards her and round the easel.

'What are you doing, Fa'iza?'

'Me? I am going to paint.' She resumed mixing the colours that would best depict the tones of sepia that dominated her dreamscape.

'Paint? Paint what?'

Fa'iza rolled her eyes. 'What will I paint? You will see, Hajiya, when I'm done.'

Binta would have been worried but for the serenity Fa'iza was oozing. She wondered if she was misreading the signs. She stood uncertainly and Fa'iza, perplexed by her aunt's presence in her room, stopped what she was doing and sat down on the mattress. Binta sat down next to her and put an arm around her shoulders.

'I am sorry, Fa'iza, I didn't realise what you have been going through.'

Fa'iza lowered her eyes and fidgeted with her fingers. 'I'm fine now, *wallahi kuwa*.'

With words having fled her, Binta offered Fa'iza the picture she had found. 'I remembered that I had this picture from when you were younger. It may help.'

Fa'iza looked at the picture taken during a distant Eid and the aroma of fried meat filled her nostrils. Her parents were seated on the couch and she and Jamilu sat between them. He was nine then, and she could see the face she had struggled to recollect. She saw that his eyes were set determinedly like a man's, hooded by his brow cast in a half-scowl. And then she remembered how he used to smile, how the light would come on in his eyes and how the left corner of his lips went up first. Then she started crying, pressing the photo to her bosom.

Binta pulled the girl to her and put her arms around her.

———

Reza sat by his father's bed listening to the old man wheezing as his ribs rose and fell. He was distressed by the sight of the man's bony face, the lips hanging open and, worse, by the smell of sickness he emitted. The smell, mixed with the waft of disinfectant that filled the air, had a nauseating effect on Reza, who wanted to be elsewhere. And when one of the patients at the far end of the ward started coughing as if determined to spew out his innards, Reza patted his father's hand and walked out into the night. He stood under the veranda, in the night breeze. He looked at the figures of women seated there, eating, chatting as they prepared for another night tending to sick relatives. He looked around for a quiet corner where he could enjoy a cigarette.

'Reza.'

He recognised the voice of his stepmother Talatu, who had first given him this name. She beckoned to him and they sat on the edge of the veranda, braving the midges that assaulted them.

Talatu cleared her throat. 'Your brother Bulama left to take his wife home.'

Reza regarded her worried face lined with crow's feet and the wrinkles on her forehead. Time and worry would do that to anyone. He knew the only thing that bonded them was the old man inside. If he died, Reza doubted he would ever see this woman again, or worry about her son Bulama and his pregnant wife, who had served them half-cooked rice and stew that tasted like wet paper.

'That's ok. There is nothing for them to do here.'

'It was a nice thing your mother Maimuna did today, calling to wish your father a quick recovery.'

Reza grunted.

'It has been ages since we heard from her.'

He looked around and saw two women in the courtyard lawn setting up a camp stove; he marvelled at how sickness bonded people.

'We didn't always get along well, your mother and us. This co-wives thing.' She chuckled. 'We were young and stupid really.'

Reza looked away, first to his right, then to his left. 'I will be heading back tomorrow.'

'Oh, you have done well. May Allah reward you. The doctor said your father will be fine. Old age, you know, and hypertension.'

He nodded at her. 'Yes, he will be all right.'

In the subsequent silence, he thought about Leila and her talk of the sea and planting trees. His mind drifted to San Siro and then to Hajiya Binta.

'You know, Reza, I was thinking you could take your brother Aminu with you. Teach him some trade. He could help you with your business. He is a smart boy.'

Reza gaped at her, at her pleading eyes tinged with desperation, and only after a while did he realise that his jaw had dropped. 'Look, Talatu, I have to go, you understand. I have to go.'

As he got up, his phone rang. It was Moses.

Reza walked away from his stepmother, who looked at him in evident shock, as he put the phone to his ear. 'Yes?'

'Where are you?'

'What do you want?'

'Where is the girl?'

'Where she should be.'

'Move her.'

'What?'

'Move her. The police have been tipped off about your location. They will be there in the next thirty minutes. She mustn't be found. Move her. Don't leave any evidence. Move her now. Then await further instructions.'

Reza stood for a full minute contemplating the best course of action in the circumstances. He was so far away there was hardly anything he could do but to trust his lieutenants. He dialled a number and put the phone to his ear.

'Gattuso. *Wara wara.*'

'And the girl?' Gattuso sounded alert.

'Drug her. Move her to San Siro. I will make arrangements for her to be moved elsewhere before I arrive. Don't leave any evidence behind. Move now, Gattuso, move now, you understand?'

30

If the hyena roams and the guinea fowl roams, someday there will be an encounter

That Sunday morning, with sunlight streaming through her curtain and warming her heart still chilled by the misery of the night before, Binta sat on her bed trying to convince herself that what assailed her was not the smell of giant cockroaches. Having concluded that she would never find them, no matter how many hours she invested in the hunt, she got out of bed and lit Indian incense. Then she said a special prayer to God to avert whatever catastrophe lurked in the shadows. She went out to water the blue petunias, and sat on the veranda. That was where Ummi and Fa'iza came to join her. They sat watching the finches hopping in the yard, their chirping filling the morning. Two brown doves perched on the power cable watching the little birds pecking at the grains in the sand with avuncular condescension.

Ummi sidled up to Binta and whispered in her ear, 'You know what Fa'iza did last night?'

Binta shook her head. She stole a glance at Fa'iza touching the delicate flowers, her face bright, and calm.

Ummi cupped her mouth around Binta's ear. 'She was busy all night playing with paints.'

'*Yar gulma,*' Fa'iza's voice was without malice or anger. She did not even turn to look at Ummi.

Ummi's eyes widened a fraction. 'Hajiya, I am not a gossip, am I?'

'Of course not.' Binta patted the girl on the head. 'Fa'iza, how is your painting coming along?'

Fa'iza smiled. 'My painting? Oh, you'll see. When I'm done.'

'Being mysterious, are we?'

Fa'iza beamed again and said nothing.

'*Yauwa*! Hajiya, you said yesterday we would be going to see Khalida and Zahra. Are we still going?' Ummi took hold of her grandmother's hand and looked into her eyes.

'Of course, yes. You and Fa'iza will go. Munkaila should be home today.'

'And you? What will you do when we are gone?'

Binta sighed. 'I will have time to rest, dear.'

Fa'iza looked at Binta, and in the brief moment their eyes locked, Binta saw the knowing look in the girl's eyes. She was convinced that Fa'iza knew what she would be up to. She looked down at her hands and fidgeted. How long had Fa'iza known?

Fa'iza rose. 'I'm going in to paint before we leave.'

Binta kept her eyes averted.

'Let me go and watch,' Ummi rose and went in after her.

Binta remained by the petunias feeling the weight of her heart pulling her body towards the damp earth, like the slender green stalk of a flower overwhelmed by its blossom. She wanted Reza, of that there was no doubt. She craved what they had. It mattered to her that at the twilight of her sexual life, her desires had finally been unleashed. She was inching closer to his redemption – her redemption, to making him a better person. And all these people, including her niece, who had no inkling of the lifetime of deprivation she had endured, now looked at her with eyes that gleamed with accusations. It was getting to the time when she would have to make a choice between who she was and who she wanted to be. That she had to confront these choices so late in her life was lamentable. But, in the final analysis, there was really only one option – an end to the affair, a new beginning for her, elsewhere, far away.

But once Reza called her, not long after Subhi, to announce his imminent arrival, she knew she did not have the strength to go through with her decision.

A little blue butterfly had settled on the petunias, its yellow-speckled wings flapping. It took off and flew away, past the power cables and up into the grey skies. The pigeons had left and only a couple of finches remained on the fence, chirping intermittently.

After salaaming loudly at the gate, Mallam Haruna pushed open the side door and seemed surprised to find Binta in the yard. She stood up when she saw him and waited with a scowl on her face as he approached, smiling expansively.

'Hajiya Binta—'

'*Kai* Mallam Haruna!' There was fire in her voice. 'What do you want here?'

'*Haba* Binta! I just came to—'

'Oh, you came to see the great whore, is that not so?'

'Why are you talking like this?'

'I know all the things you've been going round saying about me. Have you come to laugh in my face now, eh? Look, I don't want to have anything to do with you. Just allow me to whore myself to whomever I please. Leave my house and never come back. *Munafiki kawai.*'

She turned and walked away. When she reached the door and turned to look at him, he was gaping, shoulders slouched, his eyes full of hurt. And surprise. She went in and slammed the door so hard that the noise rattled him out of his shock.

———

In the living room, Zahra and Ummi struggled to keep Khalida away from the glass of crimson blossoms they had set up on the coffee table. Khalida shrieked and kicked each time they prevented her from tampering with the glass, which had also caught Fa'iza's fancy. She sat on the couch and looked at it, contemplating how best she could capture its essence in her paintings.

Munkaila, who was listening to the news about the kidnapped niece of Alhaji Bakori, was irritated by the shrieks of his little daughter.

'For God's sake, shut that girl up and let me listen to the news.'

Sadiya pulled the child onto her lap and soothed her. '*Allah sarki!* So this girl has finally been found.'

'This kidnapping business is becoming too much.' Munkaila's eyes tarried on the beautiful girl on the screen. It was the picture of Leila Sarki that the TV stations had been using since her kidnap. He turned away when he noticed that Sadiya was eyeing him with habitual jealousy. 'Imagine that it took them this long to find her.'

He listened, with a smirk on his face, as the police spokesman came on air to explain how their raid on a mansion had forced the kidnappers out of hiding and how their security blanket had compelled them to drop the kidnapped girl outside a hospital where his vigilant men found her.

Sadiya shook her head. '*Alhamdulillah*, they have found the girl alive.'

Munkaila's phone rang. It was Hadiza. When she asked how work on the new house was progressing, he talked about the challenges of having his furniture, lampshades and chandeliers shipped in from Paris and his rugs from Turkey. He asked her what colours he should paint Hajiya Binta's quarters, especially her bedroom. But Hadiza sounded distracted.

'It's Hureira, she explained. Her husband called to say she's been making trouble for him since her return.'

'That stupid girl.'

Hureira had told her husband she would rather drink a gallon of poison and set herself ablaze than have him take a second wife. But he had already completed the matrimonial arrangements and was not inclined to alter them. His integrity was at stake. Besides, Hureira was incapable of providing the peaceful ambience a family needed.

Munkaila thought these threats perfectly within Hureira's capabilities, considering her propensity for irrational undertakings. He remembered how, when they were young, she had set his jeans ablaze when he ventured to predict that she would not find a man stupid enough to marry her. He resolved to call her and talk some sense into her. 'Have you told Hajiya, yet?'

'I can't reach her on the phone.'

'Ok, keep trying, I will call Hureira and talk to her.'

He dialled Hureira's number but she did not take the call, so he sat there grinding his teeth.

Sadiya, familiar with her husband's temper, fetched him a glass of water and hoped he would not end up hurling it against the wall, as he had done several times in the past. He was not that enraged yet, but in this state, she knew it wouldn't take much to tip him over the edge.

The intercom buzzed and a voice announced that there was a certain Mallam Haruna at the gate demanding to see Alhaji Munkaila.

Sadiya and Fa'iza took the children upstairs and Munkaila rose to receive his guest.

Mallam Haruna smiled shyly and stooped to shake Munkaila's hand. Munkaila was used to men older than his father showing him deference because he was of good fortune. He noticed Mallam Haruna's starched kaftan and gleaming cap and knew the man was out to make an impression. When he asked how Mallam Haruna managed to get his zanna cap in such excellent state, the man beamed.

'So you didn't know that that is what I do for a living. I wash caps for the senators and honourable members, all these top politicians, *wallahi kuwa*.'

Munkaila smiled indulgently. 'That is very interesting. I have given my caps to be washed and they have been brought back in such an unwholesome state that I have felt discouraged. I shall have you wash my caps instead.'

Mallam Haruna, in the fashion of one who luxuriated in the company of moneyed men, sat down and talked at length about the skills of caring for caps and the calibre of people who appreciated the services he rendered.

But Munkaila was not disposed to banter. Especially not coming from a man harbouring the incongruous notion of wanting to marry his mother. 'Mallam Haruna, is there something in particular you want to discuss?'

Mallam Haruna assesed the smirk on the younger man's face and cleared his throat. 'Oh yes, yes. I can understand that, since I am a serious-minded businessman myself. But as you know, the tale of the spider is always about his wife, Koki. I am here to discuss issues that concern your mother, and her reputation.'

———

Upstairs, in her room littered with mementoes of Munkaila's many foreign trips, Sadiya sat down with Fa'iza and enquired after her health. She wondered what could be responsible for the calm Fa'iza exuded. She wasn't certain if it was something they should worry about as she knew insanity was often garbed in the robes of enlightenment.

'Me? I am fine, *wallahi*,' Fa'iza smiled.

'Have you given some thoughts to what we discussed last time, about seeing my uncle?'

'Your uncle? Oh no. I don't think that will be necessary.' Fa'iza got off the bed and went to look at an ornamental blue orb with intricate gold designs placed on the bedside drawer. 'This is beautiful. Does it have a use?'

Sadiya smiled. 'No. It's just decorative. Your cousin bought it from a Syrian in Paris.'

'Paris? I hear that's a lovely place. I would like to go there someday.'

'You will *insha Allah*.'

Fa'iza sat down and patted Khalida, who was sleeping on the bed. 'Aunty Sadiya, how long do you think before Alhaji finishes the new house?'

Sadiya smiled again. 'You want to come live with us, in the new house?'

Fa'iza sighed. There was nothing she wanted more than for Hajiya to move away from that house, from the temptation that assailed her there. 'In the new house? Yes. I want us to leave that place.'

'Well, I am sure in the next month or so the house will be completed. Your cousin is really anxious to move in. He's got work going on there every day.'

'Really?'

'Yes. And you know, the house is going to have a fountain in the courtyard. It's going to be lovely, you need to see it. He is importing the furniture from Paris and the rugs from Istanbul.'

'Istanbul? That's Turkey, right?'

'Yes—'

Munkaila burst into the room. Sadiya recoiled, for his face had that expression of menace he assumed when he was in the frame of mind to smash her glasses against the wall. But he turned to Fa'iza, who cowered when he unleashed the thunder in his throat. 'What am I hearing about this *dan iska* called Reza?'

———

Binta rested her head on his chest as he leaned his back on the headrest. She sighed. And Reza sighed too. Their lovemaking had been awkward; their kisses were perfunctory, lacking passion, as if they were strangers to each other's bodies.

He caressed her shoulder absently with his fingers and stared at the wall. Memories of his first time in the house, when he had pricked her with his dagger, assailed him. He searched for the scar on her neck in vain.

'I am sorry.' The words tumbled out so fast they surprised him. He put his arm around her and squeezed her to his chest.

'Sorry? For what?'

'For the first time I came into this room. For what I did to you.'

Her silence stretched into the fields of reminiscence. She thought of her life before the day he had first scaled her fence, how different it had been since then; how, in equal measure, she had been happy and despondent; and how she had to bring an end to this affair that was, of late, causing her more distress than happiness. She sighed, 'Things happen for a reason.'

Reza held her tighter and buried his face in her greying hair. Thoughts of his sick father came to him, how badly he smelt from his illness. He wondered if he himself would repulse his grandchildren if he ever grew to be that old.

She played with the curly strands of hair on his chest, picking at one after the other and stretching them to their full length. She basked in the comfort of his being there, of the masculine scent he exuded. But this sensation passed when the shadow of her recent encounters crept into her mind. And the cause of all this opprobrium was the man on whose chest her head rested. She sighed again. 'Were there people outside when you came in?'

'Just some kids playing. There were some men talking, you understand—'

'They saw you?'

'No. I walked past twice. The third time, they were gone. I was careful. It was easier climbing the fence though.'

She sighed. 'Yes. But now the wires are there. We have to be careful, Hassan.'

'We have been careful—'

'We need to be more careful. People have been saying things.'

Reza grunted. 'Have you ever seen the sea?'

She raised her head and looked at his face, her eyes wide with bewilderment.

He was looking away into the distance, beyond her walls. When he spoke, it was in the distracted fashion of one given over to baffling reveries. 'I have been thinking of the sea. All that water; sometimes patient, sometimes raging. All that water, you understand. Can you imagine what it could do?'

'I saw the sea only once, Hassan. From the little window of a plane on my way to the hajj.'

'Is it far, Mecca?'

'Not so much now. Just a little under five hours.'

He sighed and for a while he was silent. 'She called last night . . . that woman. She wants me to join her in Jeddah. Imagine. She said she would book my flight and make all the arrangements.' He chortled. 'She even spoke to my father and wished him well.'

'That was nice of her. And what did you say to her?'

His face darkened. For a long while he ground his teeth. 'You know, I think she is getting lonely, you understand? I told her she would die alone and they would dump her corpse somewhere because no one would grieve over her.'

Binta sat up. 'That was not a good thing to say, Hassan. She was trying to make amends. You shouldn't have said that. You should give her a chance.'

But she could see from his face that he was already shutting the door to that conversation, as if he had discovered a draft coming in through a half-opened window, rattling his heart, which had been fossilized by the callousness of fate. She tried to say something that would keep that window open for a little longer but he pulled her to him.

'I want to see the sea someday.' He stroked her head absently. And as far gone as his mind was in the blue-green of the sea, he imagined for a moment what it would be like to have Leila lying on his chest. He imagined his hand stroking her silky, scented hair and the colour of the sea reflected in her eyes. He remembered that first girl he had fallen in love with when he was a teenager, the one who had gone on to have that hideous baby. He remembered what being in love felt like, how his heart used to flutter when he saw her smile at him in the coy fashion of a lovestruck teenager. But beneath the waves of sadness, there was a tinge of anger and regret. Anger at Gattuso and Joe and Dogo who, because they feared they would be caught, had abandoned Leila outside a hospital at midnight. And regret that he did not, in his own way, say goodbye to her.

Binta gripped his hand, perhaps with some unintended force. He looked at her and saw the tint of fire in her eyes; the sort only jealousy could ignite.

'There is another woman, isn't there, Hassan?'

'What?'

She moved away from him. 'There is another woman.'

'What are you talking about?'

'You are seeing another woman.'

'Me? What woman?'

She eyed him with such intensity that it made his comportment thaw. 'There is another woman.' This time she was certain. 'The way you touched me just now, it wasn't me on your mind, it was her. The other woman.' She got out of the bed and started putting on her clothes. 'I should have known. The way you've been making love to me recently, I should have known. In your mind it was her. *Iskancin banza!*'

He got out of the bed and calmly collected his clothes piled on the side of the bed, grinding his teeth as he did so. When he was done dressing, he turned to her. 'I have a lot of things to deal with, you understand. I've got these runs, some crazy business I don't fully understand yet and it's giving me sleepless nights. Now the job is bungled and I have some explaining to do and I don't know where to start, you understand? My father is lying in a hospital and I am here, with you. He was the only one who ever gave a damn about me, you understand? And I am here, with you, you understand? I need to be at San Siro now to ask the boys how they messed things up. I turn my back one fucking minute and they mess things up. I need to ask them, you understand? But no! I am here, with you. And look what you are doing.'

Her heart whirled with that tortuous sensation that drives lovers to passion-induced savagery. She wanted to hurl something at him, to make him bleed. But when she looked into his eyes and saw the vortex of emotions, she thought of her son Yaro, to whom she never gave the chance to tell her how confused he must have felt. She went round the bed and tried to hug him but Reza resisted. She persisted until he allowed her to press him to her heart. How could the world not understand what he was going through, how he needed her, how she needed to save him as she had failed to do with her own son? How could they judge her?

It was the first time their troubled hearts truly embraced, melting into each other. It was the first time his heart touched hers. It was, despite their shared ardour and litany of memories, the closest he ever came to feeling love for her. 'God, I am sorry.'

And she was certain she heard the hint of tears in his voice.

He did not want her to see his heart, naked as it was then, or the tears in his eyes. 'I have to go now. I have to go, you understand?'

He pushed her aside and hurried out of the room. She ran after him, calling his name, the one no one else remembered but her. When he crossed the living room and opened the door, she dashed after him. He was halfway to the gate when it was pushed open and Ummi rushed in. She did not acknowledge him and sped past him to her grandmother who was frozen by the door. But Fa'iza, who was at the gate, recognised him immediately and her heart stopped. Reza marched on until a man appeared behind Fa'iza. He rightly assumed him to be Binta's rich son. They regarded each other, Reza in bewilderment, Munkaila in sheer rage, the sort the younger man knew inspired men to murderous deeds.

Beyond Reza, Munkaila saw his mother, whose guilt was evident on her face and in her hastily flung-on dress that left her shoulder bare and exposed the straps of a black bra. He latched the door behind him.

And that was precisely when Binta remembered that she had woken up that Sunday morning to the unmistakable smell of giant cockroaches.

31

The sweetness of ululation will not render it to loss

Again Binta Zubairu found herself ensnared in a lingering daymare. Her mournful curtains, which bordered this dream, took on a deeper shade of grief and blurred the boundaries so that she had no idea when she was dreaming and when she was not. Surrounded by faces she only saw as a blur, of pensive friends and wailing kin, she sat on her bed chanting at intervals the mantra of her grief: 'Innalillahi wa inna ilaihi raji'un.'

The offers of condolences passed into a haze and she was certain she would wake up to find Munkaila sitting on her couch, jingling his car keys around his chubby finger. And when she thought of that finger and his plump cheeks and the potbelly he was rather fond of caressing being eaten away by the hosts of the earth, tears streamed out of her eyes. Her Munkaila shrouded only in white muslin thrust into the belly of the earth. Her Munkaila who resented even the ants that ran wild on his Italian shoes.

In the days that followed, the defining moment looped in her head with cinematic precision. The expressions on Munkaila's face played out so vividly, the wild chaotic chase, the sight of Reza speeding away, his footfalls now echoing in the labyrinth of reminiscences, her chaotic screams for them to stop. And the last word her son had uttered, the way in which he had addressed her: a half growl that had conveyed all the contempt he felt for her.

While Binta was lost in these dreams that lingered too long, it was left to her sister Asabe and her daughter Hadiza to accept condolences and see to the administration of the house of grief. They had arrived, with their husbands, as soon as the news had reached them. Hureira, too, had made an impromptu return, also accompanied by her husband, who had spent only a night and had since returned to Jos. But Hureira had been wailing so much she had promptly constituted herself a nuisance.

Sadiya, who had come to see Munkaila one last time before he was buried the day he died, stationed herself in a corner of Binta's room surrounded by her relatives and friends. In their midst, she sat, swaying between anger and bafflement.

It was her disgusted relatives, who had barely waited for the completion of the third day prayers, who ushered the widow and her children into a waiting car and drove her back to her parents' house, far from where her husband died trying to save his mother's honour.

The men sat under the canopies set up in the yard, bowing their heads, sighing and clicking at the backs of their throats. The women remained indoors, falling on each other and wailing occasionally. Sometimes they talked, in the tents and indoors, about the tragedy, so that in the end several versions emerged. Some of them suggested Reza strangled Munkaila with his bare hands. Others had it that Munkaila had chanced upon his mother and that insufferable rogue going at it butt naked.

But Binta knew, as did Fa'iza, who had sealed herself in a cocoon of silence, exactly what had happened. And in their silence, conjectures and speculations blossomed. So she sat in her grief contemplating the boundaries between lingering nightmares and tenuous reality. On the third night, she got up, picked her way through the sleeping figures in the living room and went out into the night. The yard was doused in moonlight and a pale breeze played with her hijab as she wandered in the yard. When she found herself at the spot, she had no idea how long she stood there until Hadiza and Asabe, alarmed by her absence, rushed out to look for her.

'Yaya, come in now. It's ok.' Asabe put her arms around her sister. They had never been close because there had always been

a chasm of reverence between them. Asabe was six years younger
and at the time they should have forged closer ties, Binta had
married and Asabe was left to play big sister to their siblings. But
grief had always brought them together. The devastation of the
interminable Jos riots that had forever altered the landscape of
their lives drew them closer, when Binta lost her husband, and
then Asabe's own spouse and son were taken from her.

'It was here,' Binta gestured. Her face glistened with tears. 'He
was lying right here.'

'Hajiya, it's ok. Let's go in now.' Hadiza gently pushed her
mother's hands down, away from the spot where Munkaila had
fallen. She put her arms around her mother's shoulder and tried
to guide her away. Binta fell to her knees and the women knelt
by her, imploring her to rise.

'He didn't want to fight him. He didn't want to but Munkaila,
he chased him. He chased him and they went round the house
and he tried to unlock the gate but Munkaila, he chased him.'

'Shush. Yaya, it's ok. It was destined to happen.'

'I was screaming for them to stop, I was saying Munkaila stop,
Munkaila stop. But he wouldn't listen. Fa'iza was screaming. So
much screaming . . .' Her voice trailed off. She sniffled and covered
her face with her hijab.

Hadiza tried to rouse her, but Asabe urged her to leave her alone.

'They went round the house again. And then Munkaila didn't
come out. And Hass . . . Reza ran out and unlocked the gate and
we came round and he was lying right there, right there. And
the wood was there, beside him. He had struck him on the back
of the head. And he was panting like this . . . like this . . .' She
inhaled deeply then froze.

She remembered the sound of Munkaila falling, a sound befitting
a man of his bulk. She could not, however, bring herself to describe
how he had looked at her as she and Fa'iza tried to help him up.
How he had growled, 'Mother' with such contempt that she still
felt the sting. How his last conscious movement had been to push
her hands away from him. She had never seen anyone die with so
much anger. She knew her family was afflicted by the incurable
curse of incendiary rage and it was that rage, that legacy of her
late husband Zubairu, that had killed Munkaila, more than the

blow to the head. And she wept, there in the silvered night, right where her son had died.

———

Gattuso looked at Reza sitting by the little window, looking out at the herd of cows grazing in the field of wilted grass, being shepherded by a boy no more than fourteen. The stench of an unwashed body reached him. But it was the look on Reza's face that distressed him the most.

'Reza, I have been here five minutes and you haven't said anything.'

Reza sighed. 'Sorry, brother. I've been preoccupied. I never meant to kill him, you understand. I wanted to get away but he kept coming after me. I just struck him so I could get away. She must be very sad now, Hajiya. Have you seen her since it happened?'

Gattuso cracked his knuckles.

Reza sensed there was something wrong. He turned and regarded Gattuso, who bowed his head and shook it intermittently. When Gattuso looked up, he saw that his eyes were bleary, his face swarthy. But it was the sense of loss in his eyes that troubled Reza. He left the window and crossed the little hut to sit with his friend on the narrow bamboo bed.

'Gattuso, what's wrong?'

Gattuso heaved and leaned back against the mud wall. 'You are so lost in this woman, you don't even realise what you have put us through, we the boys who have stood by you all these years, Reza?'

Reza sighed and scratched the five-day stubble that had been irritating him. 'I'm sorry, man. I'm sorry. How are the boys?'

Gattuso punched his fist in his open palm. 'They raided San Siro as soon as they got news that that man had died. You know the new OC, that mamafucker. Most of us heard that you had been involved in a murder and took off immediately. They raided San Siro and got Joe.'

Gattuso sniffled. It made Reza sit up.

'What happened?'

'He was so angry we didn't collect the ransom he went and got himself drunk. When they came he was too sozzled to run. They took him into custody and hours later they shot him, in the cell. They said he wanted to escape. The mamafuckers. They shot him in cold blood.'

'They shot Joe?'

Gattuso wiped his eyes. He stood up and went to the window, where Reza had been moments before. In the distance, the sun was setting, casting a reddish glow on the plains spread out before him. The herd had moved on and only a flock of egrets ambled along in the pale grass. The silence in the little mud room irritated him and he wondered what it must have been like for Reza, who had spent days in the shack, the temporary hideout in the plains of Gwandara. He looked around and saw the familiar squiggle he had made on the walls with a nail. Patterns without meaning or ideas behind them. In the two nights Gattuso had spent hidden away in that room, it was the only thing he could do to get things out of his mind. It had been a little over a year before, when he had got into a fight and broken a young man's limb. When he learned that the boy's father was an army captain, he knew he had to go underground. Reza had shoved a key in his hand and told him how to find the shack. He had stayed there, etching inane patterns into the wall for two days that tested the limits of his sanity. On the third day, he saw Reza approaching from the distance, smiling, and he knew the matter had been settled with the captain. Gattuso never knew how, and never asked. But he remained grateful to Reza.

And when news reached San Siro that the man Reza had whacked in the head had died, and Reza had slunk away and had not been seen or heard from for days, Gattuso knew he would be at the little shack in the plains, tormenting himself with solitude.

He turned and saw Reza sitting on the bamboo bed that had gathered a season-long shower of dust, head bowed as he wept.

'The sun is setting.' Gattuso cracked his knuckles.

Reza wiped away the tears from his eyes.

Gattuso reached into his pocket and fetched a packet of cigarettes. 'Let's have a smoke, for Joe.'

They sat down on the dirty floor, their backs against the walls, and puffed their grief into the bare *azara* rafters. In silence gilded with ribbons of smoke, they honoured the memory of Joe.

After two sticks, Gattuso stretched his legs. 'That man was an important man. The police have been all over this one. They have been hunting down people. Too much heat, Reza. This is just the excuse that fucking policeman needed to ruin us.'

Reza shook his head absently. 'I just want her to know that I never meant for it to happen this way, you understand. The bastard wouldn't get off my case. I just whacked him so I could get away. It wasn't even a serious blow but the fucker just keeled over and died. Fucking rich, spoilt bastard.'

'So what do we do now?'

'I don't know if we can fix this, Gattuso. But I will talk to the senator and see what he can do.'

Reza reached out for another stick and Gattuso lit it for him. He had endured five days of empty spaces but had found the gaps in his mind occupied by circuitous thoughts.

'Reza.'

'Mhm.'

'Any news about your father?'

'He has been discharged. Two days ago.'

'You went to see him?'

'No. You know they will be looking for me there. I called.'

A cricket started chirping. It was jarring at first but the familiar rhythm grew on Reza. It was therapeutic. And a strange bird in the night cawed, a lyrical and haunting sound that rent the night and disrupted the rhythm of the cricket. After a while the insect resumed its solo from the crevice.

'Gattuso.'

'Mhm.'

'Have you heard anything about Hajiya?'

Gattuso hesitated. 'No, man. I'm sorry. We have all been underground. Don't even know where some of the guys are.'

'I just want to tell her I didn't mean for this to happen.'

Again, the bird in the night cawed. It repeated the haunting sound and then took off in a flurried flapping of wings.

The ends of their cigarettes glowed eerily in the dark of the night. In the darkness of their grieving hearts, there was only silence.

———

From his couch, Senator Buba Maikudi observed Dauda Baleri sitting across from him and concluded he did not like the policeman. But he smiled and shook his hand.

'So you are the man.'

'I am, sir.' Baleri was awed by the little man with boyish eyes. He had been stunned when he had first got the call from the senator four days before. He had immediately thought it was a scam, until he had been asked for his account number and had got confirmation of his account being credited.

'Well, you must understand we are in the middle of campaigns. We have the primary elections tomorrow and all these people won't let us rest, you see.'

'I can see that, sir. I have been waiting to be let in for almost two and half hours, sir.'

'Oh, really, officer? I am so sorry to hear that. You know how these things are.' Senator Maikudi wondered if he had made a mistake reaching out to this man, but it was an act of desperation. Now he had to find a way to get rid of him. To get ahead in politics required the ability to make such instinctive decisions and he knew Baleri was not a keeper. He didn't know why and was not inclined to bother figuring it out at that moment. He did not feel it necessary to invite Musa to serve tea to this policeman.

'Like I said the first time we spoke on phone, there are no permanent friends in politics but permanent interests. I can see you are an ambitious man. You remind me of myself when I was your age.' He leaned forward. 'So let's work together and see how we can be of benefit to each other. What do you say?'

'I am very honoured, sir. Very honoured—'

'Now, you know, I have asked you to do something. Perhaps I should explain the expediency involved in this matter. I want these boys found. I don't want them interrogated. Never. I suppose you know what to do.'

Baleri smiled. 'I've already got one, sir. The others I will find.'

'Yes. So I have been informed. Good job.'

'Even . . .'

'Yes?'

'Even Reza, sir? Considering you have a special relationship with him.'

The senator leaned forward and held up one finger before his face. He froze in that pose for so long that Baleri wondered if he was having a heart attack.

'He is the priority. He must never be allowed to talk. If you can ensure that never happens, I will make sure you are set up for good.'

'I understand, sir.' A smile spread on Baleri's face.

The senator simultaneously appreciated and resented the greed in that smile. He reached for the briefcase by the side of his couch and opened it. He counted out a wad of notes and put them on the coffee table between him and the policeman. He summoned his assistant Moses with a buzzer.

'Moses, fetch us an envelope, will you?'

'Right away, sir.' Moses adjusted his tie and went out.

The policeman eyed the bundle of money on the table as discreetly as he could. He wondered exactly how much was there. He needed that new car and with this, and whatever he would earn from getting Reza, he was sure to get a decent vehicle that he could drive to Christy and show her the incalculable folly in turning him down. He would show her he could be a success.

Moses returned with the envelope but went round to whisper in the senator's ear. The senator nodded and cleared his throat and smiled at Baleri. 'I'm afraid there has been a development, officer.'

———

The senator thought Reza looked very much like the fugitive he had become. Fortunately, he had asked for him to be let in through the rear. He didn't, under any circumstance, want his association with Reza to be known. 'You look terrible, my friend.'

Reza caressed his haggard beard. 'That is the least of my worries, sir.'

'Indeed. Indeed.'

Musa came in with the tea tray and put it down on the rug just in front of the senator. He knelt down and poured two cups. When asked, Reza said yes, he would like some milk. The notion of having tea without milk was incomprehensible to him. In that particular instance, he wasn't opposed to the idea of tea at a quarter to midnight. It would be the first decent thing he had put in his mouth in five days.

The senator watched Reza savour the beverage and felt a tinge of remorse. Reza had been loyal, and would continue to be, he knew. But he had become a liability.

'Reza, I am not happy with you, you know.'

'My apologies, sir.'

'A simple task like this, you and your people messed it up. You got the wrong person. And then you lost the wrong person.'

'My apologies, sir.'

'I am not happy with you at all.' He sipped his tea and reclined on his leather cushion.

'I will make it up to you, Alhaji. I promise.'

'And how will you do that?'

'We could get her back.'

The senator laughed. 'As if she was any use to me in the first place.'

'Then I shall do anything you desire, sir. Anything. Just give me another chance.'

The senator mulled the offer, whose sincerity he did not doubt. Someone with Reza's skill was an asset. He could get in the gutters and do the dirty jobs. He sat up and took another sip.

'You see, Reza, these things we do, the struggle and agitation and call for justice, is it not for you, the masses?'

'Indeed, sir.'

'If this country improves, is it not you and your generation that will enjoy it? I am old now, what more do I want from this world, eh?'

Reza nodded.

'I make these agitations and fight this dirty war and the people I am fighting for insult me and insult my father, that poor, hardworking man. May Allah have mercy on his soul.'

'Ameen.'

'They insult us and we still fight for them. You know why?'

Reza shook his head.

'Because they don't understand what we are doing for them. It's like a sheep, you see, when it's raining and you try to get it under shelter, it might think you have bad intentions towards it. But is it not a kind thing you are doing for it?'

'Indeed, sir.'

'You see.' He posed dramatically, arms outstretched, mouth agape, beady eyes bright, holding an expression of hurt as if just realising that he had been under-appreciated for many years. 'But we will continue to fight for them because they are our people and the future we fight for is for our children, not so?'

'Indeed, sir.'

He raised his cup again and paused with it halfway to his lips. 'Drink your tea Reza, drink your tea, *ka ji ko?*'

Reza drank, savouring the richness of the milk. When his cup was empty, he cursed the person who first thought that tea was best served in tiny cups. 'Sir, there is a problem I was wondering if you could help me with.'

'Yes, I heard about it. I have been informed that you were the one who got into a fight with Alhaji Munkaila and killed him.'

'You know him, sir?'

'Ah! Of course. He has done some business for me. He was a good man, Munkaila. May Allah illuminate his grave.'

'Ameen. Ameen.'

'*Kai!* Reza, you did not do well killing a good man like that.'

'It was not intentional. I never meant for it to happen—'

'I hear you were having a thing with his old woman, *ko? Kai!* Reza, you are a proper *dan iska* like this and I never knew.' He threw his head back and laughed. 'And I was asking you to introduce your girlfriend to me. I should have said womanfriend.'

Reza was at first stunned by the laughter, considering his emotional stake in the whole tragic affair. But the senator was laughing about it. There could be some chance he might help.

He stopped laughing and became serious. 'You are in a bad situation, my friend. A very bad situation, *gaskiya*.'

'I know, sir. And I know you can help me.'

The senator was quiet for a while and Reza's anxiety grew. 'You see, the trouble is that the man you killed, he has friends in important places. And they have an interest in getting you. But I have an interest in you too. You are my man, not so?'

Reza nodded eagerly.

'I have spoken to my friend, the Assistant Inspector General. He said there is something he can arrange. They can get someone else in your place, you know, a scapegoat, but they have to pin this on someone. But he will need to see you first. Don't worry about anything, I have arranged for my men to take you and bring you back. When you go, tell him what you just told me, tell him it was an accident. You know how to cry *ai*? Cry and tell him how remorseful you are. He likes to hear such things. He will arrange to get someone else in your place, perhaps one of those condemned criminals or armed robbers.'

'Thank you, sir. Thank you very much.'

'Reza, all these favours I am calling in for your sake, they are costing me *fa*. And yet I said do this one job for me and you messed it up, eh?'

'I apologise, sir.'

'Go, Moses will take you to see the man. Cooperate with him, ok? And whatever happens, call me and let me know.'

'Yes, sir.'

He asked Reza to summon Moses and wait for him outside. When Reza reached the door, the senator called his name.

'Make sure, after this mess is cleared up, that you go back to school. Make something better of your future.'

'I will. I will. *Nagode sosai.*'

The senator nodded in acknowledgement and waved Reza away.

Moses entered and closed the door. 'Sir?'

'Is Baleri in position?'

'Yes. He is ready.'

'When it's done, give him his money. I don't want to see him. I don't think I like him.'

'No problem, sir.'

The senator nodded. And Moses nodded.

Reza, who had always wanted to punch Moses, admired how neat he looked even at midnight, with his shirt tucked in and his tie looking freshly pressed. Moses led him out through the rear door to the car park and to a car where three men in dark suits were waiting.

'The senator says you should take him to the AIG. Thereafter, take him to where he needs to go. It is an emergency.'

'You are lucky, the senator likes you.' One of the men put his arm around Reza and opened the rear door of the car.

By the time, the car started moving Reza realised he was flanked by two men. He looked back through the rear windscreen and saw Moses standing where they had left him, watching the car drive away. He suddenly noticed that the two men had their hands under their suits and realised, all too belatedly, that there was something very wrong.

32

When surrounded by vultures, try not to die

Abida sat before her mirror applying a subdued tone of lipstick and puckering her lips to even out the pigment while Kareema, sitting on the bed behind her, flipped through some of the *soyayya* novellas scattered on the bed.

'Abida, we are not going for a wedding you know.'

Abida put down the lipstick and picked up an eye pencil. 'This is the sixth day. At least we can wear some make-up. It's not like we are the chief mourners anyway.' Abida paused, pencil in hand, thinking of how Fa'iza had seemed calm throughout the period of grief and wondered if it were possible for one to become inured to seeing loved ones being killed. She put down the eye pencil, wiped off the lipstick with a piece of cloth and sat staring at her reflection in the mirror.

Kareema adjusted the veil over her shoulder, picked up the TV remote on the bed and turned it on. The small 14-inch TV their father had bought for them came alive with some enthusiastic kalangu dance. She flipped the channel. 'Abida, we are never going to get to the *ta'aziya* if you keep staring at your face in the mirror like that.'

They had spent the first three days of mourning with Fa'iza, sharing her grief and her mattress, being her voice as she kept silent for days, and wondering where her strength stemmed from.

In subsequent days, after they had resumed school, they would change out of their uniforms upon their return and go over to Fa'iza's, staying until nightfall, receiving condolences as Fa'iza sat staring into space.

'Can you imagine what it would be like to have all your loved ones killed right before your eyes?' Abida's voice echoed from the field of imaginings.

Kareema sighed. 'Amin is stronger than you think. It is Munkaila's wife I am worried about. She seemed shocked, as if she would just keel over and die. Good thing she left after the third day. I mean, I would have if I were her. How could I stay under the same roof as a mother-in-law who had brought not only shame but death to her family?'

She flipped the channel once more and an image on the screen caught her attention. A young man, shirtless, was lying on the ground, obviously dead. Kareema turned on the volume.

'. . . the suspect simply identified as Reza, a notorious criminal, was shot dead by the police while resisting arrest in connection with the murder of businessman Alhaji Munkaila Zubairu. The police spokesman said . . .'

The remote fell out of Kareema's hand and clattered on the floor.

Abida turned to her sister and saw the beginning of tears in her eyes.

———

Binta wandered into Fa'iza's room but discovered she could not remember why she was there once she looked into her niece's eyes. She found Fa'iza setting up her easel, which she had put aside to accommodate the mourners. The death had not quelled her desire to daub the canvas with the colours of her dreams. Binta looked aimlessly about, her eyes avoiding Fa'iza's, as the girl paused to see what her aunt needed.

When Binta's eyes fell on the finished painting resting against the wall, she knelt by it. The canvas was dominated by shades of reddish-brown and, in the middle, a shocking violent splash of red, the colour that had often startled Fa'iza out of her nightmares.

'What is this?'

'This? It's a painting I did.'

'Oh.'

Binta inclined her head to one side and looked at the painting. Despite careful consideration, she was more confounded than enlightened.

Fa'iza regarded her aunt, the subdued slant of her shoulders, the defeated tilt of her head. 'It's abstract. Those used to be the colours of my dreams. I still dream like that sometimes, but it doesn't scare me as much anymore.'

Binta sat down on the rug and studied the painting, the mix of reddish-brown pushed around in the background and that startling red splashed in the middle. Blood and sepia. Her fingers touched the edge of the canvas tentatively. 'I was wrong.' Her voice echoed from a realm her mind had wandered to.

'Wrong? About what?'

'About you. I thought you were fighting against loss and losing.'

'Me?'

Binta had never been an art enthusiast and had never possessed the necessary awareness to decipher it, especially abstract paintings, which had always contrived to baffle her. The cheap poster of some blossoming flowers that had hung on the wall in the living room served merely decorative purposes and had been taken down in the days of mourning. Not being sufficiently informed as to judge the aesthetics of Fa'iza's work, she was however astonished by how the girl had taken her fears and nightmares and made them into something beautiful.

'It is me.' Binta's voice still reverberated with the timbre of introspection. 'I was the one fighting against loss all the while.'

Fa'iza was bemused. She was familiar with grief-induced insanity and wondered if that was what was afflicting her aunt. She reached out as if to touch Binta but put her hand down beside her.

Binta chuckled. 'You know, someone said life is like a dress. Some are made fortunate, others not so. So when it gets torn or stained, all you can do is wash it, mend it or cut it up and make something new out of it.'

She turned and saw Fa'iza's baffled face, one eyebrow raised higher than the other, lips set at an angle, one corner slanting upwards. Binta wiped the tears from her face and patted the girl on the shoulder. 'You won't understand, I think. Not right away.'

Binta shuffled back to her room, where she searched through the camphor-scented clothes in her suitcase. There was the bundle of cloth Reza had bought for her. It brought back memories she was wasn't ready to confront. It was easy to decide to get rid of it. But there were also all those wads of notes he had brought, still sitting at the bottom of her box.

Picking up the reading glasses by her bedside, she went out to the living room, past Hadiza and Asabe, who had Ummi sitting between her legs, her head resting between her thighs as she plaited her hair. Binta went to the alcove where her sewing machine remained, forgotten in the days of mourning. She sat on the stool and proceeded to oil the machine.

Hadiza and Asabe observed what she was doing and averted their eyes each time they thought she was going to look up. But Binta was oblivious and carried on with her task. She slapped down the feed dogs with mild irritation and the thunk jarred the other women. From the old TV carton, she fished out an old, blue dress. She cut it up and returned to the sewing machine, put on her glasses and put her foot down on the treadle. She pedalled away and the ferocity with which she went about the task made Asabe abandon Ummi's hair, half-braided, and focus her attention on Binta.

Ummi felt the unbraided part of her head and patted the hair that was standing on end. When she saw where the women's eyes were focused, she looked at Binta. 'Hajiya, what are you doing?'

'I am mending a dress.' Conscious of the eyes turned on her, Binta looked from one face to another. Hadiza's eyes gleamed with tears and Asabe's with anxiety. And in Ummi's eyes was curiosity. Binta bent her head and carefully lined the edges of the dress.

That was when she noticed the motifs on the printed fabric, of pretty, little, yellow butterflies captured in different phases of flight. She traced one with her finger. Carefully. It occurred to her then that in the final analysis, dreams can be dainty and beautiful, like butterflies, and just as fragile.

ACKNOWLEDGEMENTS

In the long, windy night it took to write this book, I have garnered an almost endless stream of support from amazing friends and loved ones.

I am grateful to my publishers, both at Parresia and Cassava Republic, for their incredible faith and commitment. Azafi Omoluabi-Ogosi, Richard Ali, Bibi Bakare-Yusuf and Emma Shercliff. Thank you for believing in this work and for making it the best it could be. May the butterfly endure and soar. May the splayed leaf remain evergreen.

To the wonderful and elegant Ellah Allfrey, thank you for rekindling faith and sustaining it. And for the diligence and assurances.

To Ranka Primorac, for the push. The amazing Zoe Wicomb, thank you for your incredible magnanimity. I can't thank you enough.

For insisting on grappling with the unwieldy beast that was the very first draft of this book, I am grateful to Nicola Baloch. *Danke*. And for always enduring any of my first drafts and somehow finding the kindest and most encouraging things to say, I say thank you to Uche Peter Umez. A writer could never wish for a better friend. *Daalu*.

For standing by me through my arid patch, I am indebted to my late uncle, Ibrahim Gambo (IBB), may your long night be illuminated by divine incandescence. Rest on, *Nengba*. The teacher who became a friend and remains a mentor, Ahmed Garba, for prodding me on, *jazakallahu khaira*. And to Yoila Jatau and his wonderful, wonderful family, for the support, the friendship and the warmth. I shall never forget. *Nagode sosai*.

My bosses, colleagues and friends at Media Trust, thanks for the support and encouragement, especially my most understanding boss Theophilus Abbah. You are a good man. And The Distinguished, Abdulkareem Baba Aminu, for the nods, prods, headshakes and *tsokana*. *Nagode kwarai*.

And to the fellows who know a little of my secrets: Rufai, Abdul, Salma, Yahya, Naja. I love you guys to bits. And remember I know ALL your secrets.

And to the Special Ones: Maryam, Faris and Suhaila for the happy troubles. All this for you. Love you lots.

My parents, the ageing ones who will never age in my eyes, in my mind, may the walk be a long and enjoyable one. May the evening sun be fair and kind to you. Thanks mom and dad, for a storied life.

Soprattutto EEP. Grazie di tutto. Sei la migliore.

Thank you all.

Weird Fact!!!

After devouring another animal, a crocodile usually feels like taking a nap. It crawls onto a riverbank, stretches out in the sun, and drifts off to sleep with its mouth wide open. Small birds—plovers—take care of its teeth. The plovers dash in and out of the croc's open mouth, picking morsels of left-over meat from between the reptile's sharp, pointed teeth. This way, the croc avoids dental problems and the plovers get a free lunch.

Within this book are more than 80 other truly **Weird Facts to Blow Your Mind** – not to mention the minds of your friends, teachers and, of course, parents!

Don't miss the other titles in this mind-blowing series:

Gross Facts to Blow Your Mind
Awesome Facts to Blow Your Mind
Scary Facts to Blow Your Mind

Cartoonist **Skip Morrow**'s previous books include *The Official I Hate Cats Book* and *The Second Official I Hate Cats Book*, both of which were bestsellers.

Judith Freeman Clark is a freelance writer. Her previous books include *The Almanac of American Women* and *The Gilded Age*.

Stephen Long is a produced playwright and tends a flock of bla⟨ sheep at his home in Vermont.

ISBN 0-8431-3579-4

$4.9⟨
$6.99 Cana⟨

0 78814 03579 2

PRICE STERN SLOA⟨
L o s   A n g e l e s

P9-ECF-295